Bloodsucking Fiends

Bloodsucking Fiends

A LOVE STORY

CHRISTOPHER MOORE

Perennial

An Imprint of HarperCollins*Publishers*

A hardcover edition of this book was published in 1995 by Simon & Schuster, Inc. It is here reprinted by arrangement with Simon & Schuster, Inc.

HarperCollins books may be purchased for educational, business, or sales promotional use. For information please write: Special Markets Department, HarperCollins Publishers Inc., 10 East 53rd Street, New York, NY 10022.

First Spike edition published 1999.

Reprinted in Perennial 2002.

Library of Congress Cataloging-in-Publication Data is available.

ISBN 0-380-72813-3

03 04 05 06 FOLIO/RRD 10

ACKNOWLEDGMENTS

The author gratefully acknowledges those people who helped in the research and writing of *Bloodsucking Fiends:*

Mark Joseph and Mark Anderson for help with research in the Bay Area. Rachelle Stambal, Jean Brody, Liz Ziemska, and Dee Dee Leichtfuss for their careful reads and thoughtful suggestions. My editors, Michael Korda and Chuck Adams, for their clean hands and composure. And my agent, Nick Ellison, for his patience, guidance, friendship, and hard work.

In memory of my father:
JACK DAVIS MOORE

PART I
Fledgling

CHAPTER 1
Death

Sundown painted purple across the great Pyramid while the Emperor enjoyed a steaming whiz against a dumpster in the alley below. A low fog worked its way up from the bay, snaked around columns and over concrete lions to wash against the towers where the West's money was moved. The financial district: an hour ago it ran with rivers of men in gray wool and women in heels; now the streets, built on sunken ships and gold-rush garbage, were deserted—quiet except for a foghorn that lowed across the bay like a lonesome cow.

The Emperor shook his scepter to clear the last few drops, shivered, then zipped up and turned to the royal hounds who waited at his heels. "The foghorn sounds especially sad this evening, don't you think?"

The smaller of the dogs, a Boston terrier, dipped his head and licked his chops.

"Bummer, you are so simple. My city is decaying before your eyes. The air is thick with poison, the children are shooting each other in the street, and now this plague, this horrible plague is killing my people by the thousands, and all you think about is food."

The Emperor nodded to the larger dog, a golden retriever.

"Lazarus knows the weight of our responsibility. Does one have to die to find dignity? I wonder."

Lazarus lowered his ears and growled.

"Have I offended you, my friend?"

Bummer began growling and backing away from the dumpster. The Emperor turned to see the lid of the dumpster being slowly lifted by a pale hand. Bummer barked a warning. A figure stood up in the dumpster, his hair dark and wild and speckled with trash, skin white as bone. He vaulted out of the dumpster and hissed at the little dog, showing long white fangs. Bummer yelped and cowered behind the Emperor's leg.

"That will be quite enough of that," the Emperor commanded, puffing himself up and tucking his thumbs under the lapels of his worn overcoat.

The vampire brushed a bit of rotted lettuce from his black shirt and grinned. "I'll let you live," he said, his voice like a file on ancient rusted metal. "That's your punishment."

The Emperor's eyes went wide with terror, but he held his ground. The vampire laughed, then turned and walked away.

The Emperor felt a chill run up his neck as the vampire disappeared into the fog. He hung his head and thought, Not this. My city is dying of poison and plague and now this—this creature— stalks the streets. The responsibility is suffocating. Emperor or not, I am only a man. I am weak as water: an entire empire to save and right now I would sell my soul for a bucket of the Colonel's crispy-fried chicken. Ah, but I must be strong for the troops. It could be worse, I suppose. I could be the Emperor of Oakland.

"Chins up, boys," the Emperor said to his hounds. "If we are to battle this monster, we will need our strength. There is a bakery in North Beach that will presently be dumping the day-old. Let's be off." He shuffled away thinking, Nero fiddled while his empire went to ashes; I shall eat leathery pastries.

As the Emperor trudged up California Street, trying to balance the impotence of power with the promise of a powdered-sugar doughnut, Jody was leaving the Pyramid. She was twenty-six and pretty in a way that made men want to tuck her into flannel sheets and kiss her on the forehead before leaving the room; cute but not beautiful.

As she passed under the Pyramid's massive concrete buttresses she caught herself limping from a panty-hose injury. It didn't hurt, exactly, the run that striped the back of her leg from heel to knee, the result of a surly metal file drawer (Claims, X-Y-Z) that had leaped out and snagged her ankle; but she was limping nonetheless, from the psychological damage. She thought, My closet is starting to look like an ostrich hatchery. I've either got to start throwing out L'eggs eggs or get a tan on my legs and quit wearing nylons.

She'd never had a tan, couldn't get one, really. She was a milk-white, green-eyed redhead who burned and freckled with sun.

When she was half a block from her bus stop, the wind-driven fog won and Jody experienced total hair-spray failure. Neat waist-length waves frizzed to a wild red cape of curl and tangle. Great, she thought, once again I'll get home looking like Death eating a cracker. Kurt will be so pleased.

She pulled her jacket closer around her shoulders against the chill, tucked her briefcase under her breasts like a schoolgirl carrying books, and limped on. Ahead of her on the sidewalk she saw someone standing by the glass door of a brokerage office. Green light from the CRTs inside silhouetted him in the fog. She thought about crossing the street to avoid him, but she'd have to cross back again in a few feet to catch her bus.

She thought, I'm done working late. It's not worth it. No eye contact, that's the plan.

As she passed the man, she looked down at her running shoes (her heels were in her briefcase). That's it. Just a couple more steps . . .

A hand caught in her hair and jerked her off her feet, her briefcase went skittering across the sidewalk and she started to scream. Another hand clamped over her mouth and she was dragged off the street into an alley. She kicked and flailed, but he was too strong, immovable. The smell of rotten meat filled her nostrils and she gagged even while trying to scream. Her attacker spun her around and yanked on her hair, pulling her head back until she thought her neck would snap. Then she felt a sharp pain on the side of her throat and the strength to fight seemed to evaporate.

Across the alley she could see a soda can and an old *Wall Street Journal,* a wad of bubble gum stuck to the bricks, a "No Parking" sign: details, strangely slowed down and significant. Her vision began to tunnel dark, like an iris closing, and she thought, These will be the last things I see. The voice in her head was calm, resolved.

As everything went dark, her attacker slapped her across the face and she opened her eyes and saw the thin white face before her. He was speaking to her. "Drink," he said.

Something warm and wet was shoved into her mouth. She tasted warm iron and salt and gagged again. It's his arm. He's shoved his arm in my mouth and my teeth have broken. I'm tasting blood.

"Drink!"

A hand clamped over her nose. She struggled, tried to breathe, tried to pull his arm out of her mouth to get air, sucked for air and nearly choked on blood. Suddenly she found herself sucking, drinking hungrily. When he tried to pull his arm away she clutched at it. He tore it from her mouth, twisted her around and bit her throat again. After a moment, she felt herself fall. The attacker was tearing at her clothes, but she had nothing left to fight with. She felt a roughness against the skin of her breasts and belly, then he was off her.

"You'll need that," he said, and his voice echoed in her head as if he had shouted down a canyon. "Now you can die."

Jody felt a remote sense of gratitude. With his permission, she gave up. Her heart slowed, lugged, and stopped.

CHAPTER 2
Death Warmed Over

She heard insects scurrying above her in the darkness, smelled burned flesh, and felt a heavy weight pressing down on her back. Oh my God, he's buried me alive.

Her face was pressed against something hard and cold—stone, she thought until she smelled the oil in the asphalt. Panic seized her and she struggled to get her hands under her. Her left hand lit up with pain as she pushed. There was a rattle and a deafening clang and she was standing. The dumpster that had been on her back lay overturned, spilling trash across the alley. She looked at it in disbelief. It must have weighed a ton.

Fear and adrenaline, she thought.

Then she looked at her left hand and screamed. It was horribly burned, the top layer of skin black and cracked. She ran out of the alley looking for help, but the street was empty. I've got to get to a hospital, call the police.

She spotted a pay phone; a red chimney of heat rose from the lamp above it. She looked up and down the empty street. Above each streetlight she could see heat rising in red waves. She could hear the buzzing of the electric bus wires above her, the steady stream of the sewers running under the street. She could smell dead fish and diesel fuel in the fog, the decay of the Oakland mudflats across the bay, old French fries, cigarette butts, bread crusts and fetid pastrami from a nearby trash can, and the residual odor of Aramis wafting under the doors of the brokerage houses and banks. She could hear wisps of fog brushing against the buildings like wet velvet. It was as if her senses, like her strength, had been turned up by adrenaline.

She shook off the spectrum of sounds and smells and ran to the phone, holding her damaged hand by the wrist. As she moved, she felt a roughness inside her blouse against her skin. With her right hand she pulled at the silk, yanking it out of her skirt. Stacks of money fell out of her blouse to the sidewalk. She stopped and stared at the bound blocks of hundred-dollar bills lying at her feet.

She thought, There must be a hundred thousand dollars here. A man attacked me, choked me, bit my neck, burned my hand, then stuffed my shirt full of money and put a dumpster on me and now I can see heat and hear fog. I've won Satan's lottery.

She ran back to the alley, leaving the money on the sidewalk. With her good hand she riffled through the trash spilled from the dumpster until she found a paper bag. Then she returned to the sidewalk and loaded the money into the bag.

At the pay phone she had to do some juggling to get the phone off the hook and dialed without putting down the money and without using her injured hand. She pressed 911 and while she waited for it to ring she looked at the burn. Really, it looked worse than it felt. She tried to flex the hand and black skin cracked. Boy, that should hurt. It should gross me out too, she thought, but it doesn't. In fact, I don't really feel that bad, considering. I've been more sore after a game of racquetball with Kurt. Strange.

The receiver clicked and a woman's voice came on the line. "Hello, you've reached the number for San Francisco emergency services. If you are currently in danger, press one; if the danger has passed and you still need help, press two."

Jody pressed two.

"If you have been robbed, press one. If you've been in an accident, press two. If you've been assaulted, press three. If you are calling to report a fire, press four. If you've—"

Jody ran the choices through her head and pressed three.

"If you've been shot, press one. Stabbed, press two. Raped, press three. All other assaults, press four. If you'd like to hear these choices again, press five."

Jody meant to press four, but hit five instead. There was a series of clicks and the recorded voice came back on.

"Hello, you've reached the number for San Francisco emergency services. If you are currently in danger—"

Jody slammed the receiver down and it shattered in her hand, nearly knocking the phone off the pole. She jumped back and looked at the damage. Adrenaline, she thought.

I'll call Kurt. He can come get me and take me to the hospital. She looked around for another pay phone. There was one by her bus stop. When she reached it she realized that she didn't have any change. Her purse had been in her briefcase and her briefcase was gone. She tried to remember her calling card number, but she and Kurt had only moved in together a month ago and she hadn't memorized it yet. She picked up and dialed the operator. "I'd like to make a collect call from Jody." She gave the operator the number and waited while it rang. The machine picked up.

"It looks like no one is home," the operator said.

"He's screening his calls," Jody insisted. "Just tell him—"

"I'm sorry, we aren't allowed to leave messages."

Hanging up, Jody destroyed the phone; this time, on purpose. She thought, Pounds of hundred-dollar bills and I can't make a damn phone call. And Kurt's screening his calls—I must be very late; you'd think he could pick up. If I wasn't so pissed off, I'd cry.

Her hand had stopped aching completely now, and when she looked at it again it seemed to have healed a bit. I'm getting loopy, she thought. Post-traumatic loopiness. And I'm hungry. I need medical attention, I need a good meal, I need a sympathetic cop, a glass of wine, a hot bath, a hug, my auto-teller card so I can deposit this cash. I need . . .

The 42 bus rounded the corner and Jody instinctively felt in her jacket pocket for her bus pass. It was still there. The bus stopped and the door opened. She flashed her pass at the driver as she boarded. He grunted. She sat in the first seat, facing three other passengers.

Jody had been riding the buses for five years, and occasionally, because of work or a late movie, she had to ride them at night. But tonight, with her hair frizzing wild and full of dirt, her nylons ripped, her suit wrinkled and stained—disheveled, disoriented, and desperate—she felt that she fit in for the first time. The psychos lit up at the sight of her.

"Parking space!" a woman in the back blurted out. Jody looked up.

"Parking space!" The woman wore a flowered housecoat and Mickey Mouse ears. She pointed out the window and shouted, "Parking space!"

Jody looked away, embarrassed. She understood, though. She owned a car, a fast little Honda hatchback, and since she had found a parking space outside her apartment a month ago, she had only moved it on Tuesday nights, when the street sweeper went by—and moved it back as soon as the sweeper had passed. Claim-jumping was a tradition in the City; you had to guard a space with your life. Jody had heard that there were parking spaces in Chinatown that had been in families for generations, watched over like the graves of honored ancestors, and protected by no little palm-greasing to the Chinese street gangs.

"Parking space!" the woman shouted.

Jody glanced across the aisle and committed eye contact with a scruffy bearded man in an overcoat. He grinned shyly, then slowly pulled aside the flap of his overcoat to reveal an impressive erection peeking out the port of his khakis.

Jody returned the grin and pulled her burned, blackened hand out of her jacket and held it up for him. Bested, he closed his overcoat, slouched in his seat and sulked. Jody was amazed that she'd done it.

Next to the bearded man sat a young woman who was furiously un-knitting a sweater into a yarn bag, as if she would go until she got to the end of the yarn, then reknit the sweater. An old man in a tweed suit and a wool deerstalker sat next to the knitting woman, holding a walking stick between his knees. Every few seconds he let loose with a rattling coughing fit, then fought to get his breath back while he wiped his eyes with a silk handkerchief. He saw Jody looking at him and smiled apologetically.

"Just a cold," he said.

No, it's much worse than a cold, Jody thought. You're dying. How do I know that? I don't know how I know, but I know. She smiled at the old man, then turned to look out the window.

The bus was passing through North Beach now and the streets were full of sailors, punks, and tourists. Around each she could see a faint red aura and heat trails in the air as they moved. She shook her head to clear her vision, then looked at the people inside the bus. Yes, each of them had the aura, some brighter than others. Around the old man in tweeds there was a dark ring as well as the red heat aura. Jody rubbed her eyes and thought, I must have hit my head. I'm going to need a CAT scan and an EEG. It's going to cost a fortune. The company will hate it. Maybe I can process my own claim and push it through. Well, I'm definitely calling in sick for the rest of the week. And there's serious shopping to be done once I get finished at the hospital and the police station. Serious shopping. Besides, I won't be able to type for a while anyway.

She looked at her burned hand and thought again that it might have healed a bit. I'm still taking the week off, she thought.

The bus stopped at Fisherman's Wharf and Ghirardelli Square and groups of tourists in Day-Glo nylon shorts and Alcatraz sweatshirts boarded, chattering in French and German while tracing lines on street maps of the City. Jody could smell sweat and soap, the sea, boiled crab, chocolate and liquor, fried fish, onions, sourdough bread, hamburgers and car exhaust coming off the tourists. As hungry as she was, the odor of food nauseated her.

Feel free to shower during your visit to San Francisco, she thought.

The bus headed up Van Ness and Jody got up and pushed through the tourists to the exit door. A few blocks later the bus stopped at Chestnut Street and she looked over her shoulder before getting off. The woman in the Mickey Mouse ears was staring peacefully out the window. "Wow," Jody said. "Look at all those parking spaces."

As she stepped off the bus, Jody could hear the woman shouting, "Parking space! Parking space!"

Jody smiled. Now why did I do that?

CHAPTER 3
Oh Liquid Love

Snapshots at midnight: an obese woman with a stun gun curbing a poodle, an older gay couple power-walking in designer sweats, a college girl pedaling a mountain bike—trailing tresses of perm-fried hair and a blur of red heat; televisions buzzing inside hotels and homes, sounds of water heaters and washing machines, wind rattling sycamore leaves and whistling through fir trees, a rat leaving his nest in a palm tree—claws skittering down the trunk. Smells: fear sweat from the poodle woman, rose water, ocean, tree sap, ozone, oil, exhaust, and blood—hot and sweet like sugared iron.

It was only a three-block walk from the bus stop to the four-story building where she shared an apartment with Kurt, but to Jody it seemed like miles. It wasn't fatigue but fear that lengthened the distance. She thought she had lost her fear of the City long ago, but here it was again: over-the-shoulder glances between spun determination to look ahead and keep walking and not break into a run.

She crossed the street onto her block and saw Kurt's Jeep parked in front of the building. She looked for her Honda, but it was gone. Maybe Kurt had taken it, but why? She'd left him the key as a courtesy. He wasn't really supposed to use it. She didn't know him that well.

She looked at the building. The lights were on in her apartment. She concentrated on the bay window and could hear the sound of Louis Rukeyser punning his way through a week on Wall Street. Kurt liked to watch tapes of "Wall Street Week" before he went to bed at night. He said they relaxed him, but Jody suspected that he got some latent sexual thrill out of listening to balding money managers talking about moving millions. Oh well, if a rise in the Dow put a pup tent in his jammies, it was okay with her. The last guy she'd lived with had wanted her to pee on him.

As she started up the steps she caught some movement out of the corner of her eye. Someone had ducked behind a tree. She could see an elbow and the tip of a shoe behind the tree, even in the darkness, but something else frightened her. There was no heat aura. Not seeing it now was as disturbing as seeing it had been a few minutes ago: she'd come to expect it. Whoever was behind the tree was as cold as the tree itself.

She ran up the steps, pushed the buzzer, and waited forever for Kurt to answer.

"Yes," the intercom crackled.

"Kurt, it's me. I don't have my key. Buzz me in."

The lock buzzed and she was in. She looked back through the glass. The street was empty. The figure behind the tree was gone.

She ran up the four flights of steps to where Kurt was waiting at their apartment door. He was in jeans and an Oxford cloth shirt—an athletic, blond, thirty-year-old could-be model, who wanted, more than anything, to be a player on Wall Street. He took orders at a discount brokerage for salary and spent his days at a keyboard wearing a headset and suits he couldn't afford, watching other people's money pass him by. He was holding his hands behind his back to hide the Velcro wrist wraps he wore at night to minimize the pain from carpal tunnel syndrome. He wouldn't wear the wraps at work; carpal tunnel was just too blue-collar. At night he hid his hands like a kid with braces who is afraid to smile.

"Where have you been?" he asked, more angry than concerned.

Jody wanted smiles and sympathy, not recrimination. Tears

welled in her eyes. "I was attacked tonight. Someone beat me up and stuffed me under a dumpster." She held her arms out for a hug. "They burned my hand," she wailed.

Kurt turned his back on her and walked back into the apartment. "And where were you last night? Where were you today? Your office called a dozen times today."

Jody followed him in. "Last night? What are you talking about?"

"They towed your car, you know. I couldn't find the key when the street sweeper came. You're going to have to pay to get it out of impound."

"Kurt, I don't know what you're talking about. I'm hungry and I'm scared and I need to go to the hospital. Someone attacked me, dammit!"

Kurt pretended to be organizing his videotapes. "If you didn't want a commitment, you shouldn't have agreed to move in with me. It's not like I don't get opportunities with women every day."

Her mother had told her: Never get involved with a man who's prettier than you are. "Kurt, look at this." Jody held up her burned hand. "Look!"

Kurt turned slowly and looked at her; the acid in his expression fizzled into horror. "How did you do that?"

"I don't know, I was knocked out. I think I have a head injury. My vision is . . . Everything looks weird. Now will you please help me?"

Kurt started walking in a tight circle around the coffee table, shaking his head. "I don't know what to do. I don't know what to do." He sat on the couch and began rocking.

Jody thought, This is the man who called the fire department when the toilet backed up, and I'm asking him for help. What was I thinking? Why am I attracted to weak men? What's wrong with me? Why doesn't my hand hurt? Should I eat something or go to the emergency room?

Kurt said, "This is horrible, I've got to get up early. I have a meeting at five." Now that he was in the familiar territory of self-interest, he stopped rocking and looked up. "You still haven't told me where you were last night!"

• • •

Near the door where Jody stood there was an antique oak hall tree. On the hall tree there was a black raku pot where lived a struggling philodendron, home for a colony of spider mites. As Jody snatched up the pot, she could hear the spider mites shifting in their tiny webs. As she drew back to throw, she saw Kurt blink, his eyelids moving slowly, like an electric garage door. She saw the pulse in his neck start to rise with a heartbeat as she let fly. The pot described a beeline across the room, trailing the plant behind it like a comet tail. Confused spider mites found themselves airborne. The bottom of the pot connected with Kurt's forehead, and Jody could see the pot bulge, then collapse in on itself. Pottery and potting soil showered the room; the plant folded against Kurt's head and Jody could hear each of the stems snapping. Kurt didn't have time to change expressions. He fell back on the couch, unconscious. The whole thing had taken a tenth of a second.

Jody moved to the couch and brushed potting soil out of Kurt's hair. There was a half-moon-shaped dent in his forehead that was filling with blood as she watched. Her stomach lurched and cramped so violently that she fell to her knees with the pain. She thought, My insides are caving in on themselves.

She heard Kurt's heart beating and the slow rasp of his breathing. At least I haven't killed him.

The smell of blood was thick in her nostrils, suffocatingly sweet. Another cramp doubled her over. She touched the wound on his forehead, then pulled back, her fingers dripping with blood. I'm not going to do this. I can't.

She licked her fingers and every muscle in her body sang with the rush. There was an intense pressure on the roof of her mouth, then a crackling noise inside her head, as if someone were ripping out the roots of her eyeteeth. She ran her tongue over the roof of her mouth and felt needlelike points pushing through the skin behind her canines: new teeth, growing.

I'm not doing this, she thought, as she climbed on top of Kurt and licked the blood from his forehead. The new teeth lengthened. A wave of electric pleasure rocketed through her and her mind went white with exhilaration.

In the back of her mind a small voice shouted "No!" over and over again as she bit into Kurt's throat and drank. She heard herself moaning with each beat of Kurt's heart. It was a machinegun orgasm, dark chocolate, spring water in the desert, a hallelujah chorus and the cavalry coming to the rescue all at once. And all the while the little voice screamed NO!

Finally she pulled herself away and rolled off onto the floor. She sat with her back to the couch, arms around her legs, her face pressed against her knees, ticking and twitching with tiny convulsions of pleasure. A dark warmth moved through her body, tingling as if she had just climbed out of a snowbank into a hot bath.

Slowly the warmth ran away, replaced by a heart-wrenching sadness—a feeling of loss so permanent and profound that she felt numbed by the weight of it.

I know this feeling, she thought. I've felt this before.

She turned and looked at Kurt and felt little relief to see that he was still breathing. There were no marks on his neck where she had bitten him. The wound on his forehead was clotting and scabbing over. The smell of blood was still strong but now it repulsed her, like the odor of empty wine bottles on a hangover morning.

She stood and walked to the bathroom, stripping her clothes off as she went. She turned on the shower, and while it ran worked down the remnants of her panty hose, noticing, without much surprise, that her burned hand had healed completely. She thought, I've changed. I will never be the same. The world has shifted. And with that thought the sadness returned. *I've felt this before.*

She stepped into the shower and let the scalding water run over her, not noting its feel, or sound, or the color of the heat and steam swirling in the dark bathroom. The first sob wrenched its way up from her chest, shaking her, opening the grief trail. She slid down the shower wall, sat on the water-warmed tiles and cried until the water ran cold. And she remembered: another shower in the dark when the world had changed.

She had been fifteen and not in love, but in love with the excitement of touching tongues and the rough feel of the boy's hand on her breast; in love with the idea of passion and too full of too-sweet wine, shoplifted by the boy from a 7-Eleven. His name was Steve Rizzoli (which didn't matter, except that she would always remember it) and he was two years older—a bit of a bad boy with his hash pipe and surfer smoothness. On a blanket in the Carmel dunes he coaxed her out of her jeans and did it to her. To her, not with her: she could have been dead, for her involvement. It was fast and awkward and empty except for the pain, which lingered and grew even after she walked home, cried in the shower, and lay in her room, wet hair spread over the pillow as she stared at the ceiling and grieved until dawn.

As she stepped out of the shower and began mechanically toweling off, she thought, I felt this before when I grieved for my virginity. What do I grieve for tonight? My humanity? That's it: I'm not human anymore, and I never will be again.

With that realization, events fell into place. She'd been gone two nights, not one. Her attacker had shoved her under the dumpster to protect her from the sun, but somehow her hand had been exposed and burned. She had slept through the day, and when she awoke the next evening, she was no longer human.

Vampire.

She didn't believe in vampires.

She looked at her feet on the bath mat. Her toes were straight as a baby's, as if they had never been bent and bunched by wearing shoes. The scars on her knees and elbows from childhood accidents were gone. She looked in the mirror and saw that the tiny lines beside her eyes were gone, as were her freckles. But her eyes were black, not a millimeter of iris showing. She shuddered, then realized that she was seeing all of this in total darkness, and flipped on the bathroom light. Her pupils contracted and her eyes were the same striking green that they had always been. She grabbed a handful of her hair and inspected the ends. None were split, none broken. She was—as far as she could allow herself to believe—perfect. A newborn at twenty-six.

I am a vampire. She allowed the thought to repeat and settle in her mind as she went to the bedroom and dressed in jeans and a sweatshirt.

A vampire. A monster. But I don't feel like a monster.

As she walked back from the bedroom to the bathroom to dry her hair, she spotted Kurt lying on the couch. He was breathing rhythmically and a healthy aura of heat rose off his body. Jody felt a twinge of guilt, then pushed it aside.

Fuck him, I never really liked him anyway. Maybe I am a monster.

She turned on the curling iron that she used every morning to straighten her hair, then turned it off and threw it back on the vanity. Fuck that, too. Fuck curling irons and blow dryers and high heels and mascara and control-top panty hose. Fuck those human things.

She shook out her hair, grabbed her toothbrush and went back to the bedroom, where she packed a shoulder bag full of jeans and sweatshirts. She dug through Kurt's jewelry box until she found the spare keys to her Honda.

The clock radio by the bed read five o'clock in the morning. I don't have much time. I've got to find a place to stay, fast.

On her way out she paused by the couch and kissed Kurt on the forehead. "You're going to be late for your meeting," she said to him. He didn't move.

She grabbed the bag of money from the floor and stuffed it into her shoulder bag, then walked out. Outside, she looked up and down the street, then cursed. The Honda had been towed. She'd have to get it out of impound. But you could only do that during the day. Shit. It would be light soon. She thought of what the sun had done to her hand. I've got to find darkness.

She jogged down the street, feeling lighter on her feet than she ever had. At Van Ness she ran into a motel office and pounded on the bell until a sleepy-eyed clerk appeared behind the bulletproof window. She paid cash for two nights, then gave the clerk a hundred-dollar bill to ensure that she would not, under any circumstances, be disturbed.

Once in the room she locked the door, then braced a chair against it and got into bed.

Weariness came on her suddenly as first light broke pink over the City. She thought, I've got to get my car back. I've got to find a safe place to stay. Then I need to find out who did this to me. I have to know why. Why me? Why the money? Why? And I'm going to need help. I'm going to need someone who can move around in the day.

When the sun peeked over the horizon in the east, she fell into the sleep of the dead.

CHAPTER 4

Blooms and the City of Burned Clutches

C. Thomas Flood (Tommy to his friends) was just reaching redline in a wet dream, when he was awakened by the scurry and chatter of the five Wongs. Geishas in garters scampered off to dreamland, unsatisfied, leaving him staring at the slats of the bunk above.

The room was little bigger than a walk-in closet. Bunks were stacked three high on either side of a narrow aisle where the five Wongs were competing for enough space to pull on their pants. Wong Two bent over Tommy's bunk, grinned apologetically, and said something in Cantonese.

"No problem," Tommy said. He rolled over on his side, careful not to scuff his morning erection on the wall, and pulled the blankets over his head.

He thought, Privacy is a wonderful thing. Like love, privacy is most manifest in its absence. I should write a story about that—and work in lots of geisha girls in garters and red pumps. *The Crowded Tea House of Almond-Eyed Tramps*, by *C. Thomas Flood*. I'll write that today, after I rent a post-office box and look for a job. Or maybe I should just stay here today and see who's leaving the flowers . . .

Tommy had found fresh flowers on his bed for four days running and they were beginning to bother him. It wasn't the flowers themselves that bothered him: gladiolas, red roses, and two mixed bouquets with big pink ribbons. He sort of liked flowers, in a masculine and totally non-sissy way, of course. And it didn't bother him that he didn't own a vase, or a table to set it on. He'd just trotted down the hall to the communal bathroom, removed the lid of the toilet tank, and plopped the flowers in. The added color provided a pleasant counterpoint to the bathroom's filth— until rats ate the blossoms. But that didn't bother him either. What bothered him was that he had been in the City for less than a week and didn't know anyone. So who had sent the flowers?

The five Wongs let loose with a barrage of bye-byes as they left the room. Wong Five pulled the door shut behind him.

Tommy thought, I've got to speak to Wong One about the accommodations.

Wong One wasn't one of the five Wongs with whom Tommy shared the room. Wong One was the landlord: older, wiser, and more sophisticated than Wongs Two through Six. Wong One spoke English, wore a threadbare suit thirty years out of style, and carried a cane with a brass dragon head. Tommy had met him on Columbus Avenue just after midnight, over the burning corpse of Rosinante, Tommy's '74 Volvo sedan.

"I killed her," Tommy said, watching black smoke roll out from under the hood.

"Too bad," Wong One said sympathetically, before continuing on his way.

"Excuse me," Tommy called after Wong. Tommy had just arrived from Indiana and had never been to a large city, so he did not recognize that Wong One had already stepped over the accepted metropolitan limit of involvement with a stranger.

Wong turned and leaned on his dragon-headed cane.

"Excuse me," Tommy repeated, "but I'm new in town—would you know where I can find a place to stay around here?"

Wong raised an eyebrow. "You have money?"

"A little."

Wong looked at Tommy, standing there next to his burning car with a suitcase and a typewriter case. He looked at Tommy's open, hopeful smile, his thin face and mop of dark hair, and the English word "victim" rose in his mind in twenty-point type— part of an item on page 3 of *The Chronicle*: "Victim Found in Tenderloin, Beaten to Death With Typewriter." Wong sighed heavily. He liked reading *The Chronicle* each day, and he didn't want to skip page 3 until the tragedy had passed.

"You come with me," he said.

Wong walked up Columbus into Chinatown. Tommy stumbled along behind, looking over his shoulder from time to time at the burning Volvo. "I really liked that car. I got five speeding tickets in that car. They're still in it."

"Too bad." Wong stopped at a battered metal door between a grocery store and a fish market. "You have fifty bucks?"

Tommy nodded and dug into the pocket of his jeans.

"Fifty bucks, one week," Wong said. "Two hundred fifty, one month."

"One week will be fine," Tommy said, peeling two twenties and a ten off a thinning roll of bills.

Wong opened the door and started up a narrow unlit staircase. Tommy bumped up the stairs behind him, nearly falling a couple of times. "My name is C. Thomas Flood. Well, actually that's the name I write under. People call me Tommy."

"Good," Wong said.

"And you are?" Tommy stopped at the top of the stairs and offered his hand to shake.

Wong looked at Tommy's hand. "Wong," he said.

Tommy bowed. Wong watched him, wondering what in the hell he was doing. Fifty bucks is fifty bucks, he thought.

"Bathroom down hall," Wong said, throwing open a door and throwing a light switch. Five sleepy Chinese men looked up from their bunks. "Tommy," Wong said, pointing to Tommy.

"Tommy," the Chinese men repeated in unison.

"This Wong," Wong said, pointing to the man on the bottom left bunk.

Tommy nodded. "Wong."

"This Wong. That Wong. Wong. Wong. Wong," Wong said, ticking off each man as if he were flipping beads on an abacus, which, mentally, he was: fifty bucks, fifty bucks, fifty bucks. He pointed to the empty bunk on the bottom right. "You sleep there. Bye-bye."

"Bye-bye," said the five Wongs.

Tommy said, "Excuse me, Mr. Wong . . ."

Wong turned.

"When is rent due? I'm going job hunting tomorrow, but I don't have a lot of cash."

"Tuesday and Sunday," Wong said. "Fifty bucks."

"But you said it was fifty dollars a week."

"Two fifty a month or fifty a week, due Tuesday and Sunday."

Wong walked away. Tommy stashed his duffel bag and typewriter under the bunk and crawled in. Before he could work up a good worry about his burning car, he was asleep. He had pushed the Volvo straight through from Incontinence, Indiana, to San Francisco, stopping only for fuel and bathroom breaks. He had watched the sun rise and set three times from behind the wheel— exhaustion finally caught him at the coast.

Tommy was descended from two generations of line workers at the Incontinence Forklift Company. When he announced at fourteen that he was going to be a writer, his father, Thomas Flood, Sr., accepted the news with the tolerant incredulity a parent usually reserved for monsters under the bed and imaginary friends. When Tommy took a job in a grocery store instead of the factory, his father breathed a small sigh of relief—at least it was a union shop, the boy would have benefits and retirement. It was only when Tommy bought the old Volvo, and rumors that he was a budding Communist began circulating through town, that Tom senior began to worry. Father Flood's paternal angst continued to grow with each night that he spent listening to his only son tapping the nights away on the Olivetti portable, until one Wednesday night he tied one on at the Starlight Lanes and spilled his guts to his bowling buddies.

"I found a copy of *The New Yorker* under the boy's mattress," he slurred through a five-pitcher Budweiser haze. "I've got to face it; my son's a pansy."

The rest of the Bill's Radiator Bowling Team members bowed their heads in sympathy, all secretly thanking God that the bullet had hit the next soldier in line and that their sons were all safely obsessed with small block Chevys and big tits. Harley Businsky, who had recently been promoted to minor godhood by bowling a three hundred, threw a bearlike arm around Tom's shoulders. "Maybe he's just a little mixed up," Harley offered. "Let's go talk to the boy."

When two triple-extra-large, electric-blue, embroidered bowling shirts burst into his room, full of two triple-extra-large, beer-oiled bowlers, Tommy went over backward in his chair.

"Hi, Dad," Tommy said from the floor.

"Son, we need to talk."

Over the next half hour the two men ran Tommy through the fatherly version of good-cop-bad-cop, or perhaps Joe McCarthy versus Santa Claus. Their interrogation determined that: Yes, Tommy did like girls and cars. No, he was not, nor had he ever been, a member of the Communist party. And yes, he was going to pursue a career as a writer, regardless of the lack of AFL-CIO affiliation.

Tommy tried to plead the case for a life in letters, but found his arguments ineffective (due in no small part to the fact that both his inquisitors thought that *Hamlet* was a small pork portion served with eggs). He was breaking a sweat and beginning to accept defeat when he fired a desperation shot.

"You know, somebody wrote *Rambo*?"

Thomas Flood, Sr., and Harley Businsky exchanged a look of horrified realization. They were rocked, shaken, crumbling.

Tommy pushed on. "And *Patton*—someone wrote *Patton*."

Tommy waited. The two men sat next to each other on his single bed, coughing and fidgeting and trying not to make eye contact with the boy. Everywhere they looked there were quotes carefully written in magic marker tacked on the walls; there were books, pens, and typing paper; there were poster-sized photos of authors. Ernest Hemingway stared down at them with a gleaming gaze that seemed to say, "You fuckers should have gone fishing."

Finally Harley said, "Well, if you're going to be a writer, you can't stay here."

"Pardon?" Tommy said.

"You got to go to a city and starve. I don't know a Kafka from a nuance, but I know that if you're going to be a writer, you got to starve. You won't be any damn good if you don't starve."

"I don't know, Harley," Tom Senior said, not sure that he liked the idea of his skinny son starving.

"Who bowled a three hundred last Wednesday, Tom?"

"You did."

"And I say the boy's got to go to the city and starve."

Tom Flood looked at Tommy as if the boy were standing on the trapdoor of the gallows. "You sure about this writer thing, son?"

Tommy nodded.

"Can I make you a sandwich?"

If not for a particularly seedy television docudrama about the bombing of the World Trade Center, Tommy might, indeed, have starved in New York, but Tom senior was not going to allow his son to be "blowed up by a bunch of towel-headed terrorists." And Tommy might have starved in Paris, if a cursory inspection of the Volvo had not revealed that it would not survive the dampness of the drive. So he ended up in San Francisco, and although he could use some breakfast, he was more worried about flowers than about food.

He thought, I should just stick around and see who's leaving the flowers. Catch them in the act.

But he had been unemployed for more than a week, and his midwestern work ethic forced him out of his bunk.

He wore his sneakers in the shower so his feet wouldn't have to come in contact with the floor, then dressed in his best shirt and job-hunting jeans, grabbed a notebook, and sloshed down the steps into Chinatown.

The sidewalk was awash with Asians—men and women moving doggedly past open markets selling live fish, barbecued meat, and thousands of vegetables that Tommy could put no name to. He passed one market where live snapping turtles, two feet across, were struggling to get out of plastic milk crates. In the next window, trays of duck feet and bills were arranged around smoked pig heads, while whole naked pheasants hung ripening above.

The air was heavy with the smells of pressed humanity, soy sauce, sesame oil, licorice, and car exhaust—always car exhaust. Tommy walked up Grant and crossed Broadway into North Beach, where the crush of people thinned out and the smells changed to a miasma of baking bread, garlic, oregano, and more exhaust. No matter where he went in the City, there was an odoriferous mix of food and vehicles, like the alchemic concoctions of some mad gourmet mechanic: Kung Pao Saab Turbo, Buick Skylark Carbonara, Sweet-and-Sour Metro Bus, Honda Bolognese with Burning Clutch Sauce.

Tommy was startled out of his olfactory reverie by a screeching war whoop. He looked up to see a Rollerblader in fluorescent pads and helmet closing on him at breakneck speed. An old man, who was sitting on the sidewalk ahead feeding croissants to his two dogs, looked up momentarily and threw a croissant across the sidewalk. The dogs shot after the treat, pulling their cottonrope leashes tight. Tommy cringed. The Rollerblader hit the rope and went airborne, describing a ten-foot arc in the air before crashing in a violent tangle of padded limbs and wheels at Tommy's feet.

"Are you okay?"

Tommy offered a hand to the skater, who waved it away. "I'm fine." Blood was dripping from a scrape on his chin, his Day-Glo wraparound sunglasses were twisted on his face.

"Perhaps you should slow down on the sidewalks," the old man called.

The skater sat up and turned to the old man. "Oh, Your Majesty, I didn't know. I'm sorry."

"Safety first, son," the old man said with a smile.

"Yes, sir," the skater said. "I'll be more careful." He climbed to his feet and nodded to Tommy. "Sorry." He straightened his shades and skated slowly away.

Tommy stood staring at the old man, who had resumed feeding his dogs. "Your Majesty?"

"Or Your Imperial Highness," the Emperor said. "You're new to the City."

"Yes, but . . ."

A young woman in fishnet stockings and red satin hot pants, who was swinging by, paused by the Emperor and bowed slightly. "Morning, Highness," she said.

"Safety first, my child," the Emperor said.

She smiled and walked on. Tommy watched her until she turned the corner, then turned back to the old man.

"Welcome to my city," the Emperor said. "How are you doing so far?"

"I'm . . . I'm . . ." Tommy was confused. "Who are you?"

"Emperor of San Francisco, Protector of Mexico, at your service. Croissant?" The Emperor held open a white paper bag to Tommy, who shook his head.

"This impetuous fellow," the Emperor said, pointing to his Boston terrier, "is Bummer. A bit of a rascal, he, but the best bug-eyed rat dog in the City."

The little dog growled.

"And this," the Emperor continued, "is Lazarus, found dead on Geary Street after an unfortunate encounter with a French tour bus and snatched back from the brink by the mystical curative scent of a slightly used beef jerky."

The golden retriever offered his paw. Feeling stupid, Tommy took it and shook. "Pleased to meet you."

"And you are?" the Emperor asked.

"C. Thomas Flood."

"And the 'C' stands for?"

"Well, it doesn't really stand for anything. I'm a writer. I just added the 'C' to my pen name."

"And a fine affectation it is." The Emperor paused to gnaw the end of a croissant. "So, C, how is the City treating you so far?"

Tommy thought that he might have just been insulted, but he

found he was enjoying talking to the old man. He hadn't had a conversation of more than a few words since he arrived in the City. "I like the City, but I'm having some problems."

He told the Emperor about the destruction of his car, about his subsequent meeting of Wong One, of his cramped, filthy quarters, and ended his story with the mystery of the flowers on his bed.

The Emperor sighed sympathetically and scratched his scruffy graying beard. "I'm afraid that I am unable to assist you with your accommodation problem; the men and I are fortunate enough to count the entire City as our home. But I may have a lead on a job for you, and perhaps a clue to the conundrum of the flowers."

The Emperor paused and motioned for Tommy to move closer. Tommy crouched down and cocked an ear to the Emperor. "Yes?"

"I've seen him," the Emperor whispered. "It's a vampire."

Tommy recoiled as if he'd been spit on. "A vampire florist?"

"Well, once you accept the vampire part, the florist part is a pretty easy leap, don't you think?"

CHAPTER 5
Undead and Somewhat Slightly Dazed

French people were fucking in the room next door; Jody could hear every groan, giggle, and bed spring squeak. In the room above, a television spewed game-show prattle: "I'll take Bestiality for five hundred, Alex."

Jody pulled a pillow over her head.

It wasn't exactly like waking up. There was no slow skate from dreamland to reality, no pleasant dawning of consciousness in the cozy twilight of sleepiness. No, it was as if someone had just switched on the world, full volume, like a clock radio playing reality's top forty irritating hits.

"Criminal Presidents for a hundred, Alex."

Jody flipped onto her back and stared at the ceiling. I always thought that sex and game shows ended at death, she thought. They always say "Rest in peace," don't they?

"Vas-y plus fort, mon petit cochon d'amour!"*

She wanted to complain to someone, anyone. She hated waking up alone—and going to sleep alone, for that matter. She had

---

* *"Do it harder, my little love pig!"*

lived with ten different men in five years. Serial monogamy. It was a problem she had been getting around to working on before she died.

She crawled out of bed and opened the rubber-lined motel draperies. Light from streetlights and neon signs filled the room. Now what?

Normally she would go to the bathroom. But she didn't feel the need to.

I haven't peed in two days. I may never pee again.

She went into the bathroom and sat on the stool to test her theory. Nothing. She unwrapped one of the plastic glasses, filled it with water and gulped it down. Her stomach lurched and she vomited the water in a stream against the mirror.

Okay, no water. A shower? Change clothes and go out on the town? To do what? Hunt?

She recoiled at the thought.

Am I going to have to kill people? Oh my God, Kurt. What if he changes? What if he already has?

She dressed quickly in her clothes from the night before, grabbed her flight bag and the room key and left the room. She waved to the night clerk as she passed the motel office and he winked and waved back. A hundred bucks had made them friends.

She walked around the corner and up Chestnut, resisting the urge to break into a run. Outside her building she paused and focused on the apartment window. The lights were on, and with concentration she could hear Kurt talking on the phone.

"Yeah, the crazy bitch knocked me out with a potted plant. No, threw it at me. I was two hours late for work. I don't know, she said something about being attacked. She hasn't been to work for a couple of days. No, she doesn't have a key; I had to buzz her in . . ."

So I didn't kill him. He didn't change or he wouldn't have been able to go to work at all in the daylight. He sounds fine. Pissed, but fine. I wonder if I just apologize and explain what happened . . .

"No," Kurt said into the phone. "I took her name off the mailbox. I don't really care, she didn't fit the image I'm trying to build anyway. I was thinking about asking out Susan Badistone: Stanford, family money, Republican. I know, but that's why God made implants . . .''

Jody turned and walked back to the motel. She stopped in the office and paid the clerk for two more days, then went to her room, sat down on the bed and tried to cry. No tears would come.

In another time she would have called a girlfriend and spent the evening on the phone being comforted. She would have eaten a half gallon of ice cream and stayed up all night thinking about what she was going to do with her life. In the morning she would have called in sick to work, then called her mother in Carmel to borrow enough money for a deposit on a new apartment. But that was another time, when she had still been a person.

The little confidence that she had felt the night before was gone. Now she was just confused and afraid. She tried to remember everything she had ever seen or heard about vampires. It wasn't much. She didn't like scary books or movies. Much of what she could remember didn't seem true. She didn't have to sleep in a coffin, that was obvious. But it was also obvious that she couldn't go out in the daylight. She didn't have to kill every night, and if she did bite someone, he or she didn't necessarily have to turn into a vampire—an asshole, maybe, but not a vampire. But then again, Kurt had been an asshole before, so how could you tell? Why had she turned? She was going to have to get to a library.

She thought, I've got to get my car back. And I need a new apartment. It's just a matter of time before a maid comes in during the day and burns me to a crisp. I need someone who can move around during the day. I need a friend.

She had lost her address book with her purse, but it didn't really matter. All of her friends were currently in relationships, and although any of them would offer sympathy about her breakup with Kurt, they were too self-involved to be of any real help. She and her friends were only close when they were single.

I need a man.

The thought depressed her.

Why does it always come to that? I'm a modern woman, I can open jars and kill spiders on my own. I can balance a checkbook and check the oil in my car. I can support myself. Then again, maybe not. How *am* I going to support myself?

She threw her flight bag on the bed and pulled out the white bakery bag full of money and emptied it on the bed. She counted the bills in one stack, then counted the stacks. There were thirty-five stacks of twenty one-hundred dollar bills. Minus the five hundred she had spent on the hotel: almost seventy thousand dollars. She felt a sudden and deep-seated urge to go shopping.

Whoever had attacked her had known she would need money. It hadn't been an accident that she had turned. And it probably hadn't been an accident that he had left her hand in the sunlight to burn. How else would she have known to go to ground before sunup? But if he wanted to help her, wanted her to survive, why didn't he just tell her what she was supposed to do?

She gathered up the money and was stuffing it back in the flight bag when the phone rang. She looked at it, watched the orange light strobing in rhythm to the bell. No one knew where she was. It must be the front desk. After four rings she picked up.

Before she could say hello, a gravelly calm male voice said, "By the way, you're not immortal. You can still be killed."

There was a click and Jody hung up the phone.

He said, *be killed*, not *you can still die. Be killed.*

She grabbed her bag and ran out into the night.

CHAPTER 6
The Animals

The daytime people called them the Animals. The store manager had come into work one morning to find one of them hanging, half-naked, from the giant red S of the Safeway sign and the rest of them drunk on the roof, pelting him with Campfire marshmallows. The manager yelled at them and called them Animals. They cheered and toasted him by spraying beer on each other.

There were seven of them now that their leader was gone. They wandered into the store around eleven and the manager informed them that they were getting a new crew chief: "This guy will whip you into shape—he's done it all, his application was four pages long."

Midnight found the Animals sitting on the registers at the front of the store, sharing worries over a case of Reddi Wip.

"Screw this hotshot from back East," said Simon McQueen, the oldest. "I'll throw my fifty cases an hour like always, and if he wants more, he can do it himself." Simon sucked a hit of nitrous oxide from the whipped cream can and croaked, "He won't last longer'n a fart on a hot skillet."

Simon was twenty-seven, muscular and as wiry-tense as a banjo string. He was pockmarked and sharp-featured, with a great mane of brown hair that he kept out of his face with a bandanna and a black Stetson, and he fancied himself a cowboy and a poet. He had never been within six-gun range of a horse or a book.

Jeff Murray, a has-been high school basketball star, pulled a can of whipped cream from the open case and said, "Why didn't they just promote one of us when Eddie left?"

"Because they don't know their ass from a hot rock," Simon said. "Can up," he added quickly.

"They probably did what they thought best," said Clint, a myopic, first trimester born-again Christian, who, having recently been forgiven for ten years of drug abuse, was eager to forgive others.

"Can up," Simon repeated to Jeff, who had upended the whipped cream can and was pushing the nozzle. Jeff inhaled a powerful stream of whipped cream that filled his mouth and throat, shot from his nostrils, and sent him into a blue-faced choking fit.

Drew, the crew's pot supplier and therefore medical officer, dealt Jeff a vicious blow in the solar plexus, causing the ex–power forward to expel a glob of whipped cream approximately the size of a small child. Jeff fell to the floor gasping. The glob landed safely on register 6.

"Works as good as the Heimlich maneuver"—Drew grinned—"without the unwanted intimacy."

"I told him to hold the can up," Simon said.

There was a tap on the glass at the front of the store and they all turned to see a skinny dark-haired kid in jeans and flannel waiting by the locked door. He wore a price gun low on his right hip.

"That would be our hotshot."

Simon went to unlock the door. Clint grabbed the case of whipped cream and shoved it under a register. The others ditched their cans where they could and stood by the registers as if awaiting inspection. They were sensing the end of an era; the Animals would be no more.

"Tom Flood," the new guy said, offering his hand to Simon.

Simon did not take his hand, but stared at it until the new guy withdrew it, embarrassed.

"I'm Sime; this is Drew." Simon waved the new guy in and

locked the door behind him. "We'll get you a time card."

The new guy followed Simon to the office, pausing to look at the glob of whipped cream on register 6, then at Jeff, still gasping on the floor.

"Can up," the new guy said to Jeff.

Simon raised an eyebrow to the rest of the crew and led the new guy into the office. While he was digging in the drawers for a fresh time card, the new guy said, "So, Sime, do you bowl?"

Simon looked up and studied the new guy's face. This could be a trap. He stepped back and squared off like a gunfighter at high noon. "Yeah, I bowl."

"What do you use?"

"I like a twelve-pound Butterball."

"Net or no net?"

"No net," Simon said.

"Yeah, nets are for grannies. I like a fourteen-pound self-basting, myself." Tommy grinned at Simon.

Simon grinned back and offered his hand to shake. "Welcome aboard." He handed a time card to Tommy and led him out the office. Outside, the crew waited. "Dudes," Simon announced. "This is Tom Flood."

The crew fidgeted and eyed Tommy.

"He's a bowler."

The crew let out a collective sigh of relief. Simon introduced them each, tagging them each with what they did. "That's Jeff on the floor, cake-mix aisle, plays basketball. Drew, frozen food and budmaster. Troy Lee, glass aisle, kung-fu fighter." Troy Lee, short, muscular, wearing a black satin jacket, bowed slightly.

"Clint," Simon continued, "cereal and juices; he's buddies with God." Clint was tall and thin with curly black hair, thick horn-rims, and a goofy, if beatific, smile.

Simon pointed to a stout Mexican in a flannel shirt. "Gustavo does the floors and has forty kids."

"Cinco niños," Gustavo corrected.

"Excuse the fuck out of me," Simon said. "Five kids." He moved down the line to a short, balding guy in corduroys. "Barry does soap and dog food. His hair fell out when he started scuba diving."

"Fuck you, Sime."

"Save your money, Barry." Simon moved on. "This dark-skinned fellow is Lash, dairy and non-foods. He says he's studying business at Frisco State, but he's really a gunrunner for the Bloods."

"And Simon wants to be Grand Dragon for the Klan," Lash said.

"Be good or I won't help you with your master's feces."

"Thesis," Lash corrected.

"Whatever."

"What do you do, Sime?" Tommy asked.

"I am on a quest for the perfect big-haired blonde. She must be a beautician and she must be named Arlene, Karlene, or Darlene. She must have a bust measurement exactly half that of her IQ and she must have seen Elvis sometime since his death. Have you seen her?"

"No, that's a pretty tall order."

Simon stepped up, nose to nose with Tommy. "Don't hold back, I'm offering a cash reward and videotape of her trying to drown me in body lotion."

"No, really, I can't help you."

"In that case, I work the can aisle."

"When's the truck due?"

"Half an hour: twelve-thirty."

"Then we've got time for a few frames."

There are no official rules for the sport of turkey bowling. Turkey bowling is not recognized by the NCAA or the Olympic Committee. There are no professional tournaments sponsored by the Poultry Farmers of America, and footwear companies do not manufacture turkey bowling shoes. Even the world's best turkey bowlers have not appeared on a Wheaties box or the "Tonight" show. In fact, until ESPN became desperate to fill in the late-night time slots between professional lawn darts and reruns of Australian-rules football, turkey bowling was a completely clandestine sport, relegated to the dark athletic basement of mailbox baseball and cow tipping. Despite this lack of official recognition, the fine and noble tradition of "skidding the buzzard" is practiced nightly by supermarket night crews all over the nation.

Clint was the official pinsetter for the Animals. Since there was always wagering, Clint's religion forbade his playing, but his participation, in some part, was required to ensure that he would not squeal to the management. He set ten-quart bottles of Ivory liquid in a triangle pattern at the end of the produce aisle. The meat case would act as a backstop.

The rest of the crew, having chosen their birds from the freezer case, were lined up at the far end of the aisle.

"You're up, Tom," Simon said. "Let's see what you got."

Tommy stepped forward and weighed the frozen turkey in his right hand—felt its frigid power singing against skin.

Strangely, the theme from *Chariots of Fire* began playing in his head.

He squinted and picked his target, then took his steps and sent the bird sliding down the aisle. A collective gasp rose from the crew as the fourteen-pound, self-basting, fresh-frozen projectile of wholesome savory goodness plowed into the soap bottles like a freight train into a chorus line of drunken grandmothers.

"Strike!" Clint shouted.

Simon winced.

Troy Lee said, "Nobody's that good. Nobody."

"Luck," Simon said.

Tommy suppressed a smile and stepped back from the line. "Who's up?"

Simon stepped up and stared down the aisle, watching Clint set up the pins. A nervous tick jittered under his left eye.

Strangely, the theme from *The Good, the Bad, and the Ugly* began playing in his head.

The turkey was heavy in his hand. He could almost feel the giblets pulsing with tension—the Butterball version of the Tell-Tale Heart. He strode to the line, swinging the turkey back in a wide arc, then forward with an explosive yell. The turkey rocketed, airborne, three quarters of the way down the aisle before touching down and slamming through the soap bottles and into the base of the meat case, smashing metal and severing wires in a shower of sparks and smoke.

The store lights flickered and went out. The huge compressors that ran the store's refrigeration wound down like dying airliners. The smell of ozone and burned insulation filled the air. A moment of dark silence—the Animals stood motionless, sweating, as if waiting for the deadly sound of an approaching U-boat. Battery back-up modules switched on safety lights at the end of each aisle. The crew looked from Simon, who stood at the line with his mouth hanging open, to the turkey, sticking, blackened and burned, in the side of the meat case like an unexploded artillery shell.

They checked their watches: exactly six hours and forty-eight minutes to exact repairs and stock the shelves before the manager came in to open the store.

"Break time!" Tommy announced.

They sat on a row of grocery carts outside the store, their backs against the wall, smoking, eating, and, in the case of Simon, telling lies.

"This is nothing," Simon said. "When I was working a store in Idaho, we ran a forklift through the dairy case. Two hundred gallons of milk on the floor. Sucked it up in the Shop-Vac and had it back in the cartons ten minutes before opening and no one knew the difference."

Tommy was sitting next to Troy Lee, trying to get up the courage to ask a favor. For the first time since arriving in San Francisco, he felt as if he fit in somewhere and he didn't want to push his luck. Still, this was his crew now, even if he had padded his application a bit to get the job.

Tommy decided to dive in. "Troy, no offense, but do you speak Chinese?"

"Two dialects," Troy said around a mouthful of corn chips. "Why?"

"Well, I'm living in Chinatown. I kinda share a place with these five Chinese guys. No offense."

Troy clamped a hand over his mouth, as if appalled with Tommy's audacity. Then he jumped to his feet into a kung-fu stance, made a Bruce Lee chicken noise, and said, "Five Chinese guys living with you? A pasty-faced, round-eyed, barbarian pig dog?" Troy grinned and dug in the bag for another handful of chips. "No offense."

Tommy's face heated with embarrassment. "Sorry. I just wondered if—I mean, I need an interpreter. There's some weird shit going on at my place."

Troy vaulted back to his seat on the carts. "No problem, man. We'll go there in the morning when we get off—*if* we don't get fired."

"We won't get fired," Tommy said with confidence he didn't feel. "The union—"

"Jesus," Troy interrupted and grabbed Tommy's shoulder. "Check this out." He nodded toward Fort Mason at the edge of the parking lot. A woman was walking toward them. "She's out a little late," Troy said; then, to Simon, he shouted, "Sime, skirt alert."

"Bullshit," Simon said, checking his watch. Then he looked in the direction where Troy was pointing. A woman was, indeed, walking across the parking lot toward them. From what he could tell at that distance, she had a nice shape.

Simon climbed down from the carts and adjusted his black Stetson. "Stand back, boys, that redhead is down here for a reason, and I'm packing that reason right here." He patted his crotch and fell into an affected bow-legged gait toward the woman.

"Evening, darlin', you lost or just in search of excellence?"

Jeff, who was sitting beside Tommy opposite Troy, bent over and said, "Simon is the master. That guy gets more pussy than all of the Forty-Niners put together."

Tommy said, "Doesn't look like he's doing that well tonight."

They couldn't hear what Simon was saying to the woman, but it was obvious she didn't want to hear it. She tried to walk away from him, and Simon stepped in front of her. She moved in another direction and he cut her off, smiling and chattering the whole time.

"Leave me alone!" the girl shouted.

Tommy leaped off the carts and ran toward them. "Hey, Simon, lighten up."

Simon turned and the woman started away. "We're just getting acquainted," Simon said.

Tommy stopped and put his hand on Simon's shoulder. He lowered his voice as if sharing a secret. "Look, man, we've got a lot to do. I can't afford to lose you all night while you show this babe the meaning of life. I need your help, dude."

Simon looked at Tommy as if he'd just exposed himself. "Really?"

"Please."

Simon slapped Tommy on the back. "I'm on it." He turned back toward the store. "Break's over, dudes. We've got some wrenching to do."

Tommy watched him go, then broke into a run after the woman. "Excuse me!"

She turned and eyed him suspiciously, but waited for him to catch up to her. He slowed to a walk. As he approached her he was surprised at just how pretty she was. She looked a little like Maureen O'Hara in those old pirate movies. His writer's mind kicked in and he thought, This woman could break my heart. I could crash and burn on this woman. I could lose this woman, drink heavily, write profound poems, and die in the gutter of tuberculosis over this woman.

This was not an unusual reaction for Tommy. He had it often, mostly with girls who worked the drive-through windows at fast-food places. He would drive off with the smell of fries in his car and the bitter taste of unrequited love on his tongue. It was usually good for at least one short story.

He was a little breathless when he reached her. "I just wanted to apologize for Simon. He's—he's—"

"An asshole," she said.

"Well, yes. But—"

"It's okay," she said. "Thanks for coming to the rescue." She turned to walk away.

Tommy swallowed hard. This was why he had come to the City, wasn't it? To take a few risks? To live on the edge. Yes. "Excuse me," he said. She turned again. "You're really beautiful. I know that sounds like a line. It is a line. But—but it's true in your case. Thanks. 'Bye."

She was smiling now. "What's your name?"

"C. Thomas Flood."

"Do you work here every night?"

"I just started. But yes, I will be. Five nights a week. Graveyard shift."

"So you have your days free?"

"Yes, pretty much. Except when I'm writing."

"Do you have a girlfriend, C. Thomas Flood?"

Tommy swallowed hard again. "Uh, no."

"Do you know where Enrico's is on Broadway?"

"I can find it." He hoped he could find it.

"I'll meet you there tomorrow night, a half hour after sunset, okay?"

"Sure, I guess. I mean, sure. I mean, what time is that?"

"I don't know; I have to get an almanac."

"Okay then. Tomorrow evening then. Look, I've got to get back to work. We're sort of in the middle of a crisis."

She nodded and smiled.

He shuffled awkwardly, then walked away toward the store. Halfway across the parking lot he stopped. "Hey, I don't know your name."

"It's Jody."

"Nice meeting you, Jody."

"See you tomorrow, C. Thomas," she called.

Tommy waved. When he turned around again, the Animals were all staring at him, slowly shaking their heads. Simon glared, then turned abruptly and stormed into the store.

CHAPTER 7
Suitors

After enduring a reasonable amount of bitterness from the crew over using his position to make a move on the girl in the parking lot, Tommy was able to persuade them to get back to work. Simon, Drew, and Jeff performed some mechanical magic on the meat case with a hammer, some jumper cables, and a can of Bondo, and by morning everything was running as if greased by the gods. Tommy met the manager at the front door with a smile and a report that his first night had gone great. The best crew he had ever seen, he said.

He rode to Chinatown with Troy Lee. They found a parking place a few blocks from Tommy's room and walked the rest of the way. The sun was up only an hour, but already the merchants were open and the sidewalks crowded. Delivery trucks blocked the streets as they dropped off their loads of fresh fish, meat, and vegetables.

Walking through Chinatown with Troy Lee at his side, Tommy felt as if he were carrying a secret weapon.

"What's that stuff?" Tommy asked, pointing to a stack of celerylike stuff on a produce table.

"Bok choy—Chinese cabbage."

"And that?"

"Ginseng root. They say it's good for the wood."

Tommy stopped and pointed in the window of a herbalist. "That looks like hunks of deer antler."

"It is," Troy said. "It's used to make medicine."

As they passed the fish market Tommy pointed to the huge spiny turtles trying to escape their milk crates. "Do people eat those?"

"Sure, people who can afford them."

"This is like a foreign country."

"It is," Troy said. "Chinatown is a very closed community. I can't believe you live here. I'm Chinese and I've never even lived here."

"This is it," Tommy said, stopping at the door.

"So you want me to ask them about the flowers, and what else?"

"Well, about vampires."

"Give me a break."

"No, this guy I met, the Emperor, he said it could be vampires." Tommy led the way up the steps.

"He's bullshitting you, Tommy."

"He was the one that told me about the job at your store, and that turned out to be true."

Tommy opened the door and the five Wongs looked up from their bunks. "Bye-bye," they said.

"Bye-bye," Tommy said.

"Nice place," Troy said. "I'll bet the rent is a killer."

"Fifty bucks a week," Tommy said.

"Fifty bucks," the five Wongs said.

Troy motioned Tommy out of the room. "Give me a minute here."

Troy closed the door. Tommy waited in the hall, listening to the nasal, banjo sounds of the conversation between Troy and the five Wongs. After a few minutes Troy emerged from the room and motioned for Tommy to follow him back down to the street.

"What goes?" Tommy asked when they reached the sidewalk.

Troy turned to him; he seemed as if he was trying to keep from laughing. "These guys are just off the boat, man. It was kind of hard to understand them, they speak some regional dialect."

"So?"

"So, they're here illegally, smuggled over by pirates. They owe the pirates like thirty grand for the trip, and if they get caught and sent back to China, they still owe the money. That's like twenty years' wages in the provinces."

"So?" Tommy asked. "What's that got to do with the flowers?"

Troy snickered. "I'm getting to that. You see, they want to be citizens. If they become citizens, they can get better jobs and pay off the pirates faster. And they can't be sent back."

"And the flowers?"

"The Wongs are leaving the flowers. They're courting you."

"What!"

"They heard somewhere that in San Francisco men marry men. They figure that if they can get you to marry them, then they can be citizens and stay here. You've got secret admirers, dude."

Tommy was indignant. "They think I'm gay?"

"They don't know. I really don't think they care. They asked me to ask you for your hand in marriage." Troy finally lost control and started laughing.

"What did you tell them?"

"I told them I'd ask."

"You fucker."

"Well, I didn't want to tell them no without asking you. They said that they'd take good care of you."

"Go tell them I said no."

"You got something against Asians? Too good for us?"

"No, it's not that. I—"

"I'll tell them that you'll think about it. Look, I've got to get home and get some sleep. I'll see you at work tonight." Troy walked away.

"You're cleaning garbage cans tonight, Troy. I'm in charge, you know? You better not tell Simon and the guys."

"Whatever you say, Fearless Leader," Troy called over his shoulder.

Tommy stood on the sidewalk trying to think of a better threat.

A half block away Troy turned and yelled, "Hey, Tommy!"

"What?"

"You'll make a lovely bride."

Tommy, murder in his eyes, broke into a run after Troy Lee.

Sunset. Consciousness hit Jody like a bucket of cold water.

She thought, I miss waking up groggy and waiting for the coffee to brew. Waking up with your worries already in full stride just sucks.

What was I thinking? Giving myself only a half hour to get ready for a date? I have nothing to wear. I can't show up in a sweatshirt and jeans and ask this guy to move in with me. I don't even know anything about him. What if he's a drunk, or a woman beater, or a psycho killer? Don't those guys always work nights in grocery stores? The neighbors always say that: "He worked nights and kept to himself. Who would have thought that he stir-fried the paperboy?" He did say I was beautiful, though, and everybody has their faults. Who am I to judge? I'm a . . .

She didn't want to think about what she was.

Jody had thrown on her jeans and was furiously trying to put on what little make-up she had with her.

She thought, I can read small print in the dark, I can see heat coming off a hiding rat from a hundred yards, and I still can't put on mascara without poking myself in the eye.

She stepped back from the mirror and tried to fight the self-criticism—tried to look at herself objectively.

I look like a late-night TV plea for the fashion-impaired, she thought. This won't work.

She broke away from the mirror, then took one last look and primped her hair, then started out the door, then took one last look, then started out the door, then paused for a last look . . .

"No!" she said aloud. She ran out the door, down the steps, and to the bus stop on the corner, where she bounced from foot to foot as if waiting for the bathroom at a beer-drinking contest.

• • •

Tommy had spent the day trying to avoid the five Wongs. He watched the room until he was sure they had all left, then he sneaked in and grabbed some clean clothes, showered, dressed, and sneaked out. He took a bus to Levis Plaza, where he napped on a park bench while pigeons and seagulls scavenged around him. Late afternoon brought a cold wind off the bay that chilled him awake.

He walked up Sansome toward North Beach, trying to rub the crease out of the back of his head left by the bench slats. As he passed a group of teenagers who were posturing and panhandling at the curb, one pudgy boy shouted, "Sir, can you spare a quarter for some eyeliner?"

Tommy dug in the pocket of his jeans and handed the kid all of his change. No one had ever called him "sir" before.

"Oh, thank you, sir!" the kid gushed in a high feminine voice. He held the fistful of change up to the others as if he had just been handed the cure for cancer.

Tommy smiled and walked on. He figured that panhandlers had cost him about ten dollars a day since he had come to the City—ten dollars that he really couldn't afford. He didn't seem to be able to look away and walk on like everyone else. Maybe it was something you developed after a while. Maybe the constant assault of despair callused your compassion. A plea for money for food always made his stomach growl, and a quarter was a small price to pay to quiet it. The plea for eyeliner appealed to the writer part of him, the part that believed that creative thought was worth something.

Yesterday he had heard a tourist tell a homeless man to get a job.

"Pushing a shopping cart up and down these hills *is* a fucking job," the homeless guy had said. Tommy gave him a buck.

It was still light when Tommy reached Enrico's on Broadway. He paused momentarily and looked over the few customers who were eating on the patio by the street. Jody wasn't there. He stopped at the host's station and reserved a table outside for a half hour later.

"Is there a bookstore around here?" he asked.

The host, a thin, bearded man in his forties, with perfect an-chorman-gray hair, raised an eyebrow, and with that small gesture made Tommy feel like scum. "City Lights is one block up on the corner of Columbus," the host said.

"Oh, that's right," Tommy said, batting himself on the forehead as if he'd just remembered. "I'll be back."

"We are giddy with anticipation," the host said. He spun curtly on one heel and walked away.

Tommy turned and started up Broadway until he was accosted by a barker outside a strip joint, a man in a red tailcoat with a top hat.

"Tits, slits, and clits. Come on in, sir. The show starts in five minutes."

"No, thanks. I have a dinner date in a few minutes."

"Bring the little lady back with you. This show can turn a maybe into a sure thing, son. We'll have her sitting in a puddle before you leave."

Tommy squirmed. "Maybe," he said. He hurried along until the barker two doors up, this one a buxom woman wearing leather and a ring in her nose, stopped him.

"The most beautiful girls in town, sir. All nude. All hot. Come on in."

"No, thanks. I have a dinner date in a few minutes."

"Bring her—"

"Maybe," Tommy said, walking on.

He was stopped three more times before he reached the end of the block, and each time he declined politely. He noticed that he was the only one who stopped. The other pedestrians just walked on, ignoring the barkers.

Back home, he thought, it's impolite to ignore someone who is speaking to you, especially if they call you "sir." I guess I'm going to have to learn City manners.

She had fifteen minutes before she was supposed to meet Tommy at Enrico's. Allowing for another bus ride and a short walk, she had about seven minutes to find an outfit. She walked into the Gap on the corner of Van Ness and Vallejo with a stack of hundred-dollar bills in her hand and announced, "I need help. Now!"

Ten salespeople, all young, all dressed in generic cotton casual, looked up from their conversations, spotted the money in her hand, and simultaneously stopped breathing—their brains shutting down bodily functions and rerouting the needed energy to calculate the projected commissions contained in Jody's cash. One by one they resumed breathing and marched toward her, a look of dazed hunger in their eyes: a pack of zombies from the perky, youthful version of *The Night of the Living Dead*.

"I wear a size four and I've got a date in fifteen minutes," Jody said. "Dress me."

They descended on her like an evil khaki wave.

Tommy sat at a patio table with only a low brick planter box between him and the sidewalk. To avoid the titty bar barkers, he had crossed the street eight times in the half block from City Lights Bookstore to Enrico's and he was a little jangled from dodging traffic. He ordered a cappuccino from a waiter who fawned over him like a mother hen, then stared in amazement when the waiter returned with a cup the size of a large soup bowl and a plate of brown crystalline cubes.

"These are raw sugar cubes, honey. So much better for you than that white poison."

Tommy picked up the soup spoon and reached for a sugar cube.

"No, no, no," the waiter scolded. "We use our demitasse spoon for our cappuccino." He pointed to a tiny spoon that rested in the saucer.

"Demitasse," Tommy repeated, feeling reckless. In Indiana the use of the word "demitasse" was tantamount to leaping out of the closet in scandalous flames. San Francisco was a great city! A great place to be a writer! And gay guys seemed like pretty nice people, once you got past their seeming obsession with Barbra Streisand music. Tommy smiled at the waiter. "Thanks, I may need a little help with the forks."

"Is she special?" the waiter asked.

"I think she's going to break my heart."

"How exciting!" the waiter gushed. "Then we'll make you look marvelous. Just remember, use from the outside first on the forks. The big spoon is for winding pasta. Is this your first date?"

Tommy nodded.

"Then order the raviolis—bite-size—no muss, no fuss. You'll look good eating them. And order for her, the rosemary chicken with roasted bell peppers and wild mushrooms in cream sauce— a beautiful dish. Tastes horrid, but on a first date she won't eat it anyway. You don't have time to run home and change, do you?"

The waiter looked at Tommy's flannel shirt as if it were a foul, dead animal.

"No, this is all I have clean."

"Oh well, it does have a certain Mr. Green Jeans charm, I guess."

Tommy caught a flash of red hair out of the corner of his eye and looked up to see Jody walking into the café. The waiter followed his gaze.

"Is that her?"

"Yes," Tommy said, waving to catch her attention. She spotted him, smiled, and approached the table.

Jody was dressed in a khaki skirt, a light-blue chambray blouse, light-blue leggings, and tan suede flats. She wore a woven leather belt, a green tartan scarf tied around her shoulders, silver earrings, bracelet, and necklace, and carried a suede backpack in place of her airline flight bag.

The waiter, keeping his gaze fixed on Jody, bent and whispered in Tommy's ear, "The flannel is fine, honey. I haven't seen anyone that over-accessorized since Batman." He stood and pulled the chair out for Jody. "Hi, we've been waiting for you."

Jody sat.

"My name is Frederick," the waiter said with a slight bow. "I'll be serving you this evening." He pinched the fabric of Jody's scarf. "Lovely tartan, dear. Sets off your eyes. I'll be back with some menus."

"Hi," Jody said to Tommy. "Have you been waiting long?"

"A little while, I wasn't sure of the time. I brought you something." He reached under the table and pulled a book out of a City Lights bag. "It's an almanac. You said you needed one."

"That's very sweet."

Tommy looked down and mimed an "Aw, shucks, it was nothing."

"So, do you live around here?" Jody asked.

"I'm sort of looking for a place."

"Really? Have you been in town long?"

"Less than a week. I came here to write. The grocery store is just a . . . just a . . ."

"Job," Jody finished for him.

"Right, just a job. What do you do?"

"I used to be a claims clerk at Transamerica. I'm looking for something else, now."

Frederick appeared at the table and opened two menus in front of them. "If you don't mind me saying," he said, "you two are just darling together. There's a Raggedy-Ann-and-Andy energy going between you two that is simply electric."

Frederick walked away.

Jody eyed Tommy over the menu. "Have we just been insulted?"

"I hear the rosemary chicken breast is wonderful," Tommy said.

CHAPTER 8
Dinner with the Vampire

"Is there something wrong with your food?"
"No, I'm just not very hungry."
"You're going to break my heart, aren't you?"

CHAPTER 9

He Knows If You've Been Bad or Good, So You'd Better . . .

For the few days he had been in San Francisco, because of the newness of it all, because of the mystery of the flowers and the worries of finding a job, Tommy had completely forgotten that he was horny. He had always been horny, and had accepted that he always would be horny. So when Jody sat down across from him and the tsunami of hormones washed over him, he was quite shocked that he had ever forgotten.

Through dinner he missed most of her small talk and bought all the polite lies she told about her eating habits because his mind was busy with a single obsessive thought: She must move that scarf so I can see her breasts.

When Tommy finished eating, Frederick came to the table. "Was there something wrong with your food?" he asked Jody.

"No, I'm just not very hungry."

Frederick winked at Tommy and took their plates. Jody sat back, unwrapped her scarf and threw it over the back of her chair. "What a nice night," she said.

Tommy ripped his gaze from the front of her blouse and pretended to look out over the street. "Yep," he said.

"You know, I've never asked a man out before."

"Me either," Tommy said.

He had decided that he would throw himself at her feet and beg. Please, please, please, take me home and have sex with me. You have no idea how badly I need it. I've only done it twice in my life and both times I was so drunk that I had to be told about it the next day. Please, for the love of God, end this suffering, fuck me now or kill me!

"Would you like a cappuccino?" he asked.

She shook her head. "Tommy, can I trust you? Can I be honest with you?"

"Sure."

"Look, I don't want to be too forward, but I think I have to be . . ."

"I knew it." He fell forward until his head hit the table, rattling the silverware. He spoke into the tablecloth. "You just broke up with a guy, and this date seemed like a good idea at the time, but you think that you're still in love with him. And I'm a really nice guy and you'll always be my friend. Right?"

"No. I wasn't going to say that."

"Oh, then you've just gotten out of a bad relationship and you're not ready to get into another one. You need to be alone for a while and find out what you really want. Right?"

"No . . ."

"Right," Tommy said into the tablecloth. "But things are moving a little too fast and maybe we should see other people for a while. I knew it. I knew you would break my—"

Jody whacked him on the back of the head with a soup spoon. "Ouch!" Tommy sat up, rubbing the rising lump. "Hey, that hurt."

"Are you okay?" she asked, holding the soup spoon at ready.

"That really hurt."

"Good." She put the spoon down. "I was going to say that I don't want to be too forward, but you and I both need a place to live, and I need some help with some things, and I like you, and I was wondering if you wanted to get a place together?"

Tommy stopped rubbing his head. "Now?"

"If you don't have other plans."

"But we haven't even, you know . . ."

"We can just be roommates if you'd like. And if you need to think it over, I'll understand, but I really need your help."

Tommy was stunned. No woman had ever said anything like that to him before. In just these few minutes she had come to trust him enough to lay herself open to total rejection. Women didn't do that, did they? Maybe she was nuts. Well, that would be okay; she could be Zelda to his F. Scott. Still, he felt as if he owed her some sort of confession that would leave him equally vulnerable.

"Five Chinese guys asked me to marry them today," he said.

Jody didn't know what to say, so she said, "Congratulations."

"I didn't accept."

"Thinking it over?"

"No, I wouldn't two-time you."

"That's sweet, but technically you'd be six-timing me."

Tommy smiled. "I like you, I really do."

"Then let's move in together."

Frederick appeared at the table. "Well, I can see things are going along just swimmingly between you two."

"Check, please," Jody said.

"Right away." Frederick headed back into the café in a bit of a snit.

Tommy said, "You're going to break my heart, aren't you?"

"Irreparably. Would you like to go for a walk?"

"Sure, I guess."

Frederick returned to the table with the check wallet. Jody pulled a wad of cash out of her backpack and handed him a hundred-dollar bill. As Tommy started to protest, standing to dig money out of his jeans pocket, Jody picked up her soup spoon and brandished it threateningly. "I'll get this." Tommy sat back down. To Frederick, Jody said, "Keep the change."

"Oh, you are too generous," Frederick gushed. He started backing away from the table in a half-bow.

"And, Frederick," Jody added, "Batman is far more over-accessorized than I am."

"I'm sorry you heard that," Frederick said. "An overdeveloped sense of fashion will be my downfall." He looked at Tommy. "You're right, she's going to break your heart."

"Have you seen Coit Tower?" she asked as they walked.

"From a distance."

"Let's go there. It's all lit up at night."

They walked for a while without talking. Jody walked on the inside and dealt with the barkers with a shake of her head and a wave of dismissal. To one barker she said, "Thanks, but we're going to put on our own show."

Tommy coughed and tripped over a crack in the sidewalk. He looked at her as if she'd just announced the Second Coming.

"I have to go to work at midnight," he said.

"You'll have to keep an eye on the time, then."

"Right. I will."

I can't believe I'm being this aggressive, Jody thought. I hear myself say these things and it's as if they're coming out of someone else's mouth. And he just agrees. I'd have become a tramp a long time ago if I'd known what a great sense of control it gives you.

They passed two tall women with enormous breasts and impossibly narrow hips unloading wigs, wads of sequins, and a boa constrictor from the back of a rusted-out Toyota. Shift change at the strip joints, Jody thought.

Tommy was riveted. Jody watched the heat rise in his face, just as it had when she caught him staring at her own breasts.

He's so open, like a little kid, Jody thought. A cute little neurotic kid. I was lucky to find him. Lucky, considering everything that has happened.

They turned on Kearny and Jody said, "So what do you think about my offer?"

"It sounds okay, if you're sure. But I won't get my first paycheck for a couple of weeks."

"Money isn't a problem. I'll pay."

"No, I couldn't . . ."

"Look Tommy, I meant it when I said I need your help. I'm

busy all day. You will have to find the place and rent it. And I have a lot of other things that you'll have to do. For one, my car is in impound and someone has to get it out during the day. If it would make you feel better, I can pay you so you'll have the money."

"Is that why you asked me if I had my days free in the parking lot last night?"

"Yes."

"So it could have been anyone who worked the right hours?"

"Your buddy works the right hours, and I didn't ask him. No, I thought you were cute."

"I can't deal with that."

He walked along looking straight ahead, saying nothing. They had passed into a neighborhood of apartment houses with security bars on the windows and electric locks on the doors. Ahead, Jody saw waves of red heat signatures coming out of one dark doorway. They were too hot for one person and too cool to be a lightbulb. She focused and could hear men whispering. She suddenly remembered the phone call: *"You're not immortal. You can still be killed."*

"Let's cross the street, Tommy."

"Why?"

"Just come on." She grabbed his jacket and yanked him into the street. When they were on the opposite sidewalk, Tommy stopped and looked at her as if she had just hit him on the head with a spoon.

"What was that all about?"

She waved for him to be quiet. "Listen."

Someone behind them was laughing. Laughing loudly enough to be heard without Jody's acute hearing. They both turned and looked back. A thin man dressed in black was standing under a street lamp a block away.

"What's so funny?" Tommy asked.

Jody didn't answer. She was staring at something that wasn't there. There was no heat signature coming off the man in black.

"Let's go," Jody said, hurrying Tommy up the street. As they passed the doorway across the street, Jody looked over and flipped a middle finger to the three toughs that had been waiting to ambush them. You guys are nothing, she thought. Laughter from the man in black still rang in her ears.

It had been a long time since the vampire had heard the sound of his own laughter, and hearing it made him laugh all the louder. So the fledgling had found herself a minion. It had been a good idea to leave her hand partially exposed to the daylight. She had learned that lesson quickly. So many of them just wandered until daylight and burned to death, and he couldn't even enjoy the show unless he wanted to join them in perdition. This one was interesting: so reluctant to give herself to the blood.

They only seemed to have two instincts, the hunger and the hiding. And this one had controlled the hunger on her first feeding. She was almost too good. So many of them, if they lasted the first night, went mad trying to live with their new senses. One night and he had to send them to hell with a snap of the neck and a fare-thee-well. But not this one. She had made him laugh; afraid of a few mortals whom she could crush like insects.

Perhaps she was protecting her new servant. Perhaps he should kill the boy, just to watch her reaction. Perhaps, but not yet. Some other fly in her ointment then. Just to keep the game going.

It felt so good to laugh after so long.

CHAPTER 10
Walking, Talking, and Bumping in the Night

Coit Tower jutted out of Telegraph Hill like a giant phallus. Impressive as it was, all lit up and overlooking the City, it made Tommy feel nervous, inferior, and pressured to perform. She had as much as admitted that she was going to take him to bed—had even offered to solve the problem of the Wongs. She was a dream come true. It scared the hell out of him.

She took his hand and looked out over the City. "It's pretty, isn't it. We're lucky it's a clear night."

"Your hand is freezing," he said. He put his arm around her and pulled her close. God, I'm smooth, he thought, a complete stud. I'm making a move on an older woman—an older woman with money. Now what? My arm is lying on her shoulder like a dead fish. I'm a geek. If I could just turn my mind off until it's all over. Just get shit-faced and do it. No, not that. Not again.

Jody stiffened. She thought: I'm not cold. I haven't been cold since I changed, nor warm, for that matter. Kurt used to say I was always cold. How strange. I can see the heat around Tommy but there's none around me.

"Feel my forehead," she said to Tommy.

Tommy said, "Jody, we don't have to do this if you're not ready. I mean, maybe, like you said, we should just be roommates. I don't want to pressure you."

"No, feel my forehead and see if I have a fever."

"Oh." He put his hand on her forehead. "You're as cold as ice. Do you feel okay?"

Oh my God! How could I have been so stupid? She tore away from him and began pacing. The guy outside her apartment, the laughing man on Kearny Street, he had been cold. And so was she. How many vampires were out there that she hadn't seen?

"What's the matter?" Tommy asked. "Did I say something wrong?"

I've got to tell him, she thought. He's not going to trust me if I keep it from him.

She took his hand again. "Tommy, I think you ought to know. I'm not exactly what I seem to be."

He stepped back. "You're a guy, aren't you? I knew it. My dad warned me that this could happen here."

Maybe not, she thought.

"No, I'm not a guy."

"Are you sure?"

"Are you?"

"There's no need to get nasty."

"Well, how would you feel if I asked you if you were a girl?"

Tommy hung his head. "You're right. Sorry. But how would you feel if five Chinese women asked you to marry them? Things like that don't happen in Indiana. I can't even go back to my room."

"I can't either," she said.

"Why not?"

"Give me a minute to think, okay?"

She didn't want to go back to the motel on Van Ness again. The vampire knew she had been there. But he'd probably know even if she moved.

"Tommy, we need to get you a motel room."

"Jody, I'm getting mixed messages here."

"No, don't take it wrong. I don't want to send you back to that room with the Wongs. I think we should get you a room."

"I told you, I don't get paid—"

"My treat. It'll be an advance on your new job as my assistant."

Tommy sat down on the sidewalk and stared up at the lighted shaft of Coit Tower. He thought, I have no idea what I am supposed to be or what I'm supposed to do. First she wants me for my body, then she wants me as an employee, then she doesn't want me at all. I don't know whether I'm supposed to kiss her or fill out an application. I feel like one of those nervous little dogs from an electroshock test. Here's a bone, Spot. Zap! You didn't really want that, did you?

He said, "Whatever you want me to do, I'll do."

"Okay," Jody said. "Thanks." She bent and kissed him on the forehead.

I have no idea what I'm supposed to do, she thought. If we go to a motel and go to bed together, then he'll have to go to work, and when he comes back in the morning he'll come back to the room, open the door, and the sunlight will hit me. Bursting into flames is no way to impress someone on the first date. Separate rooms is the only way to go. He's going to get fed up and leave me like all the rest.

"Tommy, can you go get your stuff tomorrow?"

"Whatever you say."

"I can't explain now, but I might be in a little trouble and I have a lot of things to do. I need you to do a lot of things for me tomorrow. Can you do that after working all night?"

"Whatever you say," he said.

"I'm going to get you a room at my motel. I won't be around until tomorrow night. I'll meet you at the motel office at sunset. When you come back to the room in the morning, the papers for my car will be on the bed, okay?"

"Whatever you say." Tommy looked dazed. He stared into his lap.

"I'll give you money for an apartment. Try to find a place that's furnished. And no windows in the bedroom. Try to keep it under two thousand a month."

Tommy didn't look up. "Whatever you say."

I've taken over his mind, she thought. It's just like in the movies, when the vampire can control people's actions. I don't want that. I don't want to force him with my will. It's not fair. He was helpless enough, but now I've turned him into a zombie. I want help, but I don't want this. I wonder if there's enough of his mind left even to function, or if I've ruined him.

"Tommy," she said sternly, "I want you to climb to the top of the tower and jump off."

He looked up. "Are you out of your mind?"

She threw her arms around him, kissed him, and said, "Oh, I'm so glad I didn't turn you into a vegetable."

"I'll give you time," he said.

Jody stood outside the four-story apartment building on Chestnut, watching and listening. There were no lights on in Kurt's apartment. Already it had become Kurt's apartment, not hers, not theirs. The moment she asked Tommy out, she had transferred whatever dreams and delusions she attached to being a couple to Tommy. It was always that way for her. She didn't like to be alone.

She and Tommy had walked Telegraph Park talking about their past lives and avoiding the subject of a singular, future life until it was time for Tommy to go to work. Jody had called a cab from a pay phone and dropped Tommy off at the store with a kiss and a promise. "I'll see you tomorrow night."

It was only when she got out of the cab at the motel that she realized that the registration and pink slip for her car were still at Kurt's.

Why didn't I take a damn key when I left?

She toyed with the idea of ringing the bell, but the thought of looking Kurt in the eye after what she had done to him . . . No, she'd have to get in on her own. Going through the two fire doors and the security bolts wasn't an option.

The building was a pseudo-Victorian, the facade decorated with prefabricated bolt-on gingerbread. Jody tried to imagine herself climbing the front of the building and shuddered. To her relief, the side panels on the fourth-floor bay window were closed. No way in there.

There was a five-foot-wide alley between Kurt's building and the one next to it. The bedroom window was on that side. No gingerbread for handholds there.

She went to the alley and looked up. The bedroom window was open and the wall was as smooth as polished stone. She eyed the space between the two buildings. With her hands against one side and her feet against the other, she could spider her way up the wall. She'd seen guys climbing chimney crevices at Yosemite that way. Experienced climbers, with equipment. Not secretaries who avoided escalators for fear of breaking a heel.

She focused on the open window and listened. The sound of someone breathing deeply, sleeping. No, it was the sound of two people sleeping.

"You bastard."

She leaped into the air and caught herself between the two buildings, six feet off the ground, her feet against one, hands against the other. She was amazed that she could do it, but it wasn't that hard. It wasn't hard at all. She tested her weight against the tension in her limbs and it felt solid. She held herself with one hand while she pulled her skirt up over her hips with the other, then she tried a tentative step up.

Hand, foot, hand, foot. When she paused to look down she was right under Kurt's window, forty feet off the ground, with only a garbage can and a stray cat to break her fall. She tried to catch her breath, then realized that she wasn't out of breath. She felt as if she could hold herself there for hours if she needed to. But the fear of falling pushed her on. *You're not immortal. You can still be killed.*

She pushed the screen loose from the window with her left hand, got a grip on the windowsill, then loosed the tension in her legs and swung down against Kurt's building. Hanging by one hand, she removed the screen with the other and lowered it to the floor inside, then pulled herself up to the windowsill, where she crouched and looked around the room.

Two people were in the bed. She could see their heat signatures rising through the covers and being dissipated by the cold breeze coming through the window. No wonder I complained about the cold. She stepped into the room and waited to see if the sleepers stirred. Nothing.

She moved to the side of the bed and looked at the woman with almost scientific detachment. It was Susan Badistone. Jody had met her at Kurt's office picnic and had disliked her immediately. Her straight blond hair was spread over the pillow. Jody twisted a lock of her own curly red hair around her finger. So this is what he wanted. And that's an after-market nose if I've ever seen one. But it's all about appearances, isn't it, Kurt?

Jody grabbed the covers and lifted them far enough to look under. She's got the body of a twelve-year-old boy. Oh Kurt, you should have let her finish the surgery schedule before you brought her home.

She let the covers fall and Susan stirred. Jody backed away from the bed slowly. She had kept all of her papers in an expandable file under the sink in the bathroom. She went to the bathroom and palmed the cabinet open. The file was still there. She grabbed it and headed for the window.

"Who's there?" Kurt said. He sat up in bed and stared into the dark.

Jody ducked below the light coming in the window and watched him.

"I said, who's there?"

"What's a matter?" a groggy Susan said.

"I heard something."

"It's nothing, honey. You're just jumpy after what that horrible woman did to you."

I could snap her scrawny blond neck, Jody thought. Then, in thinking it, in knowing that she could actually do it, she was no longer angry. I'm not "that horrible woman," she thought. I'm a vampire, and no amount of plastic surgery, or breeding, or money will ever make you my equal. I am a god.

For the first time since the transformation Jody felt calm, comfortable in her own skin. She waited there in the dark until they fell asleep again, then she climbed out the window and replaced the screen. She stood on the window ledge and threw the expandable file on the roof, then leaped up, grabbed the gutter, and pulled herself onto the roof.

At the back of the building she found a steel ladder that went all the way to the ground. The climb between the two buildings had been completely unnecessary.

Okay, not a particularly smart god, but at least a god who has her original nose.

CHAPTER 11
Lather, Rinse, Repent

The Animals were humming the wedding march when Tommy walked in the store. Tommy was rattled from the cab ride from Telegraph Hill. Evidently the cabdriver, who had a nervous tic and the habit of screaming, "The fuckers!" at indeterminate intervals and for no particular reason, felt that if you weren't going to top a hill without all four wheels leaving the ground and land in a shower of sparks, you might as well not top it at all, and, in fact, should avoid it by taking a corner on two wheels and crushing your passengers against the doors. Tommy was sweat-soaked and a little nauseated.

"Here comes the bride," Troy Lee said.

"Fearless Leader," Simon said, "you look like you just left a three-toweler." Simon measured the success of any social event by the number of towels it took to clean up afterward. "Was a time in my life," Simon would say, "when I only owned one towel and I never had any fun."

"You're not still pissed at me?" Tommy asked.

"Hell, no," Simon said. "I had me a three-toweler myself tonight. Took two choir girls from Our Lady of Perpetual Guilt out in the truck and taught them the fine art of slurping tadpoles."

"That's disgusting."

"No, it ain't. I didn't kiss 'em afterward."

Tommy shook his head. "Is the truck in?"

"Only fourteen hundred cases," Drew said. "You'll have plenty of time to plan the wedding." He held out a stack of bride magazines to Tommy.

"No, thanks," Tommy said.

Drew chucked the magazines behind him and held out a can of whipped cream with his other hand. "Take the edge off?"

"No, thanks. Can you guys stack the truck? I've got some stuff I want to do."

"Sure enough," Simon said. "Let's go do it."

The crew headed to the stockroom. Clint stayed behind.

"Hey, Tommy," he said, his head down, looking embarrassed.

"Yeah?"

"A pallet of kosher food came in tonight. You know, getting ready for Hanukkah and everything. And it's supposed to be blessed by a rabbi."

"Yeah. So?"

"Well, I was wondering if I could say a few words over it. I mean, they're not washed in the Blood or anything, but Christ was Jewish. So . . ."

"Knock yourself out, Clint."

"Thanks," Clint said. Taken with the Spirit, he scurried off to the stockroom.

Tommy went to the news racks by the registers and gathered up an armload of women's magazines. Then, glancing over his shoulder to make sure that none of the Animals was watching, he took them into the office, locked the door, then sat down at the desk and began his research.

He was about to move in with a woman for the first time, and he didn't know a thing about women. Maybe Jody wasn't crazy. Maybe they were all that way and he was just ignorant. He flipped quickly through the tables of contents to get an overview of the female mind.

There was a pattern here. Cellulite, PMS, and men who don't commit were the enemies. Delightfully light desserts, marriage, and multiple orgasms were the allies.

Tommy felt like a spy, as if he should be microfilming the pages under a gooseneck lamp in some back room of a Bavarian castle stronghold, and any minute some woman in SS gear would burst in on him and tell him that she had ways of making him talk. Actually, that last part wouldn't be too bad.

Women seemed to have some collective plan, and most of it seemed to involve getting men to do stuff that they didn't want to do. He skimmed an article entitled: "Tan Lines: Sexy Contrast or Panda Bear Shame?—A Psychologist's View," then flipped to one entitled: "Men's Love for Sports Analogies: How to Use Vince Lombardi to Make Him Put the Seat Down." ("When one player falls in, the whole team gets a wet butt.") He read on: "When it's fourth and ten and Joe Montana decides to go for it, would his linemen tell him that they won't go to the store to get him tampons? I don't think so." And: "Of course Richard Petty doesn't want to wear a helmet, but he can't drive without protection either." By the time Tommy got to the warnings about never using Wilt Chamberlain or Martina Navratilova as examples, he was completely disenchanted. How could you deal with a creature as devious as woman?

He turned the page and his heart sank even further. "Can You Tell Him He's a Lousy Lay?: A Quiz."

Tommy thought, This is exactly the kind of thing that made me stay a virgin until I was eighteen.

1. **It's the third date and you're about to have an intimate moment, but when he drops his shorts you notice he's less blessed than you expected. Do you:**

    A: Point and laugh.
    B: Say, "Wow! A real man at last." Then turn and snicker to yourself.
    C: Say, "Is that what they mean by microbiology?"
    D: Just go ahead with it. He might be shamed into making a commitment. And what do you care if all your sons are nicknamed Peewee?

2. You decide to do the dread deed, and just as things are starting to get hot he comes, rolls over, and asks, "Was it good for you?" You:

   A: Say, "God, yes! That was the best seventeen seconds of my life!"
   B: Say, "Sure, as good as it gets for me with a man."
   C: Put a Certs in your navel and say, "That's for you, Mr. Bunnyman. You can have it on your way back up, after the job is finished."
   D: Smile and throw his car keys out the window.

3. After fumbling in the dark, he thinks he's found the spot. When you tell him that's not it, he forges ahead anyway. You:

   A: Grab the lamp off the nightstand and beat him with it until he gets off you.
   B: Grab the lamp off the nightstand and beat him to death with it.
   C: Grab the lamp off the nightstand, turn it on, and say, "Would you look where you're at?"
   D: Wait patiently until he finishes, wishing the whole time that you had a lamp on your nightstand.

The phone in the office rang. Tommy closed the magazine.

"Marina Safeway."

"Tommy, is that you?" Jody asked.

"Yeah, I have on my phone voice."

"Look, you're registered into room two-twelve at the Van Ness Motel—the corner of Chestnut and Van Ness. There's a key waiting for you in the office. The papers and keys for my car are on the bed. I left some papers for you to take to Transamerica and some money too. I'll meet you at the motel office a little after sunset."

"What room are you in?"

"I don't think I should say."

"Why? I'm not going to come in and jump you or anything."

"It's not that. I just want things to be right."

He took a deep breath. "Jody?"

"Yes."

"Is there a lamp on the nightstand in your room?"

"Sure, it's bolted down. Why?"

"No reason," Tommy said.

Suddenly, from the back of the store, the Stones belted out "Satisfaction" from a boom box cranked to distorted fuzz level. Tommy could hear the Animals chanting, "Kill the pig!" in the background.

"I've got to go," he said. "I'll see you tomorrow night."

"Okay. Tommy, I had a nice time tonight."

"Me too," he said. He hung up and thought: She's evil. Evil, evil, evil. I want to see her naked.

Jeff, the failed power forward, burst into the office. "The truck is stacked, dude. The ski boat is charged! We're talking luau in the produce aisle."

The Clark 250, self-propelled, professional floor-maintenance machine, is a miracle of janitorial design. Approximately the size of a small desk, the Clark 250 sports two rotating scrub disks at the front of the machine, as well as an onboard reservoir that distributes soap and water, and a squeegeed vacuum that sucks it up. It is propelled by two overpowered electric motors that will drive its gum-rubber tires over any flat surface, wet or dry. A single operator, walking behind the Clark 250, can, in less than an hour, scrub four thousand square feet of floor, and buff it to a shine in which he can see his soul, or so the brochure claims. What the brochure neglects to mention is that if the squeegee is retracted and the vacuum turned off, a single operator can slide along behind the Clark 250 on a river of soapy froth.

The Animals called the machine the ski boat.

• • •

When Tommy came around the corner of aisle 14, he saw Simon, shirtless, wearing his cowboy hat, cooking weenies over thirty cans of Sterno on a stainless-steel rack that normally was used to display potato chips.

"I love the smell of napalm in the morning," Simon said, waving a barbecue fork. "It smells like victory."

"Cowabunga!" Drew screamed. He was sliding through two inches of soapsuds behind the ski boat, towing Lash toward a makeshift ramp by a length of clothesline. Lash hit the ramp, went airborne, and flipped in the air with a battle cry of "Workman's Comp!"

Tommy stepped aside as Lash landed on his chest and plowed a drift of suds with his face. Drew powered down the boat.

"Eight-two," Barry shouted.

"Nine-one," said Clint.

"Nine-six," said Drew.

"Quatro-uno," said Gustavo.

"A four-one from the Mexican judge," Simon said into his barbecue-fork microphone. "That's got to hurt his chances for getting into the finals, Bob."

Lash spit out a mouthful of soap and coughed. "The Mexican judges are always tough," he said. He wore a beard of suds that made him look like a thin, wet version of Uncle Remus.

Tommy helped Lash to his feet. "Are you okay?"

"He's fine," Simon said. "His personal trainer is here." Simon grabbed a coconut off the shelf and lopped the top off with a huge knife from the meat department. "Dr. Drew," he said, holding the coconut out to Drew, who took a pint of rum from his hip pocket and splashed some in the shell.

"Down this," Simon said, handing the coconut to Lash. "Kill the pig, partner."

The Animals chanted "Kill the pig" until Lash had downed the whole drink, coconut milk and rum washing streams though his beard of suds at the corners of his mouth. He stopped to breathe and threw up.

"Nine-two!" Barry shouted.

"Nine-four," Drew said.

"Six-one," Simon drawled. "Penalty points for chunks."

"Fuego," Gustavo said.

Simon jumped in Gustavo's face. "Fuego? What fucking number is Fuego? You can be disqualified as a judge, you know?"

"Fuego," Gustavo said, pointing over Simon's shoulder to the chip rack, where three dozen weenies had burst into flames and were spewing black smoke.

The smoke alarm went off with a Klaxon scream, drowning out the Rolling Stones.

"It rings into the fire department," Drew shouted in Tommy's ear. "They'll be at the door in a minute. It's your job to head them off, Fearless Leader."

"Me? Why me?"

"That's why you make the big bucks."

"Kill that stereo and put out the fire," Tommy yelled. He turned and was heading for the front door just as Clint came out of the stockroom.

"The kosher stuff is all blessed, and I prayed over some of the gentile food for good measure. You know, Tom, the guys said that you might be getting married, and I'm getting my minister card in the mail soon, so if you need—"

"Clint," Tommy interrupted, "clean-up in the produce aisle." He went to the front door, unlocked it, and went outside to wait for the fire department. The bay was socked in with fog and the beam from the lighthouse on Alcatraz cut a swath across Fort Mason and the Safeway parking lot. Tommy thought he could make out the figure of someone standing under one of the mercury lights. Someone thin, dressed in dark clothing.

A fire truck pulled into the parking lot, siren off, its flashing red lights cutting the fog. As the fire truck's headlights swept across the lot, the dark figure dodged and ran, staying just ahead of the lights. Tommy had never seen anyone run that fast. The thin guy seemed to cover a hundred yards in only a few seconds. A trick of the fog, Tommy thought.

CHAPTER 12
Fashionably Doomed

There were five police cars parked at the Van Ness Motel when Tommy got off the bus across the street. He thought: They've come to get me for turning in a false alarm to the fire department. Then he realized that only Jody knew that he was coming to the motel. Pity, he thought, I would have gotten a lot of writing done in prison.

He crossed the street and was met at the office door by a uniformed police woman.

"Crime scene, sir. Move along unless registered."

"Am registered. Need shower," Tommy said. He'd learned his lesson about saying too much when he had talked to the angry fireman at the store. They didn't want to hear why it happened, they just wanted to be sure that it didn't happen again.

"Name?" the cop said.

"C. Thomas Flood."

"ID?"

Tommy handed her his Indiana driver's license.

"Says 'Thomas Flood, Junior.' No 'C.'"

"'C' is pen name. Thomas is writer," Tommy said.

The cop adjusted her baton. "Are you trying to give me a hard time?"

"No, I just thought you wanted to talk that way. What's going on?" Tommy looked over the cop's shoulder at the motel manager, a tall, balding guy in his forties who was wiping fingerprints off his bulletproof window with a towel, looking as if he was going to start crying any minute.

"Were you in the motel last night, Mr. Flood?"

"No, I just got off work at the Marina Safeway. I'm night-crew leader there."

"You live in the City then?" The cop raised an eyebrow.

"I've just been here a few days. I'm still looking for a place."

"Where can we reach you if the detectives need to talk to you?"

"At the store from midnight to eight. But I'm off tonight. I guess I'll be here. What's going on?"

The cop turned to the motel manager. "You have a C. Thomas Flood registered?"

The manager nodded and held up a key. "Room two-twelve," he said.

The cop gave Tommy back his license. "Get that changed if you're going to stay in the City. You can go to your room, but don't cross any of the yellow tape."

The cop walked out of the office. Tommy turned to the manager. "What's going on here?"

The manager motioned for Tommy to come closer to the window. The manager bent over and whispered through his talk hole: "The maids found a woman's body in the dumpster this morning—a woman from the neighborhood, not a guest."

"Murdered?" Tommy whispered.

"Her and her poodle. This looks horrible for the motel. The police are talking to all of the guests as they check out. They knocked on your friend's door, but she didn't answer." The manager passed Tommy's key through the slot, along with a business card.

"They want her to call the detective at that number when she gets in. Would you give it to her?"

"Sure," Tommy said. He took the key and stood there trying to think of something to say to relieve the manager's anxiety. "Uh, sorry about your dumpster," he said.

It didn't work. The manager burst into tears. "That poor little dog," he sobbed.

On the bed were a stack of official-looking papers, a map of San Francisco, and a thick envelope filled with cash. There was a note clipped to the papers. It said:

Dear Tommy,

Here's the stuff to get my Honda out of impound. Use some of this cash to pay the fines. I don't know where the impound lot is, but you can ask any policeman.

You will have to go to the Transamerica Building to get my last check. (I marked it on the map.) I've left a message on the personnel department's voice mail that you are coming.

Good luck finding an apartment. I forgot to mention that you want to avoid getting a place in the Tenderloin (also on map).

Sorry I'm being so mysterious. I'll explain everything tonight.

Love,
Jody

Why in the hell *was* she being so mysterious? He opened the envelope and took out a stack of hundred-dollar bills, counted them, then put them back in the envelope. Four thousand dollars. He had never seen that much money in one place. Where did she get that kind of money? Certainly not filling out claims at an insurance company. Maybe she was a drug dealer. A smuggler. Maybe she embezzled it. Maybe it was all a trap. Maybe when he got to the impound lot to pick up her car, the police would arrest him. She had a lot of nerve signing her note "Love." What would the next one say? *"Sorry you have to do hard time in the big house for me. Love, Jody."* But she *did* sign it that way: *"Love."* What did that mean? Did she mean it, or was it habit? She probably signed all of her letters with "Love."

Dear Insured, We are sorry but your policy will not pay for your barium enema as it was done for recreational purposes. Love, Jody. Claims Dept. . . ."

Maybe not.

Maybe she did love him. She must trust him, she had given him four grand.

He shoved the money in his back pocket, picked up the papers, and left the room. He ran down the steps to the ground level and tripped over a large black plastic bag full of dead woman. A coroner's deputy caught him by the arm before he fell.

"Easy there, fella," the deputy said. He was a big, hairy guy in his thirties.

"I'm sorry."

"It's okay, kid. She's sealed for freshness. My partner went to get the gurney."

Tommy stared at the black bag. He'd only seen one dead person in his life, his grandfather. He hadn't liked it.

"How did it . . . I mean, was it murder?"

"I'm betting creative suicide. She broke her own neck, drained out her blood, then killed the dog and jumped into the dumpster. The ME's betting murder, though. You pick."

Tommy was horrified. "Her blood was drained?"

"Are you a reporter?"

"Nope."

"Yeah, she was about a gallon low, and no visible wounds. The ME had to go into the heart for a blood sample. He was not pleased. He likes things simple—decapitation by cable car, massive gunshot trauma—you know."

Tommy shuddered. "I'm from Indiana. Stuff like this doesn't happen there."

"Stuff like this doesn't happen here either, kid."

A tall, thin guy in coroner blues came around the corner pushing a gurney with a small, gray, dead dog on it. He picked up the dog by a rhinestone leash. "What do I do with this?" he asked the big hairy guy. The dog spun slowly at the end of the leash like a fuzzy Christmas ornament.

"Bag and tag it?" said Big Hairy.

"A dog? That's a new one on me."

"I don't give a shit. Do what you want."

"Well," Tommy interrupted, "you guys have a good day." He hurried away to the bus stop. As the bus pulled up he looked back and saw the two coroners tucking the little dog into the woman's body bag.

Tommy got off the bus at a coffeehouse near Chinatown where he had seen guys in berets scribbling in notebooks and smoking French cigarettes. If you were looking for a place to sit and stare into the abyss for a while, always look for guys in berets smoking French cigarettes. They were like road signs: "Existential Crisis, Next Right." And the incident with the body bag had put Tommy in the mood to contemplate the meaninglessness of life for a few minutes before he started hunting for an apartment. They had treated that poor woman like a piece of meat. People should have been crying and fainting and fighting over her will. It must be some sort of protection mechanism, more of that ability that city people had for ignoring suffering.

He ordered a double mocha at the counter. A girl with magenta hair and three nose rings frothed it up while Tommy searched though a stack of used newspapers on the counter, separating the classified sections. When he paid the girl she caught him staring at her nose rings and smiled. "Thought is death," she said, handing him the mocha.

"Have a nice day," Tommy said.

He sat down and began flipping though the classifieds. As he read through the apartments for rent, the money in his pocket seemed to shrink. Here was the reason why people seemed so distracted. They were all worrying about making rent.

An ad for a furnished loft caught his eye. He was a loft kind of guy. He imagined himself saying, "No, I can't hang around, I've got to get back to the loft and write." And, "Sorry, I left my wallet in the loft." And writing, "Dear Mom, I've moved into a spacious loft in fashionable SOMA."

Tommy put the paper down and turned to a beret guy at the next table who was reading a volume of Baudelaire and building up a drift of Disc Bleu butts in the ashtray. "Excuse me," Tommy said, "but I'm new in town. Where would I find fashionable SOMA?"

The beret guy looked irritated. "South of Market," he said. Then he picked up his book and cigarettes and walked out of the café.

"Sorry," Tommy called after him. Maybe if I had asked him in French . . .

Tommy unfolded the map Jody had left him and found Market Street, then a neighborhood marked "SOMA." It wasn't far from where Jody had marked the Transamerica Pyramid. He folded up the map and tore the loft ad out of the classifieds. This was going to be easy.

As he prepared to leave, he looked up to see an enormously fat man in a purple velvet robe enter the café carrying a leather sample case decorated with silver moons and stars. He sat at a table near Tommy, his bulk spilling over either side of the cane chair, and began removing things from the sample case. Tommy was captivated.

The fat man's head was shaved and there was a pentagram tattooed on his scalp. He covered his table with a piece of black satin, then placed a crystal ball on a pedestal of brass dragons in the center. Next he unwrapped a deck of tarot cards from a purple silk scarf and placed them by the crystal ball. Last he removed a sign from the sample case and set it up on the table. It read: "Madame Natasha. Palmistry, Tarot, Divination. Psychic Readings $5.00. All proceeds go to AIDS research."

Madame Natasha was sitting with his back to Tommy. As Tommy stared at the pentagram tattoo, Madame Natasha turned to him. Tommy looked away quickly.

"I think you need a reading, young man," Madame Natasha said, his voice high and feminine.

Tommy cleared his throat. "I don't believe in that stuff. Thanks, though."

Madame Natasha closed his eyes as if he were listening to a particularly moving passage of music. When he opened them again he said, "You're new to the City. A little confused and a little scared. You're an artist of some kind, but you don't make your living that way. And you've recently turned down a proposal of marriage. Am I right?"

Tommy dug into his pocket, "Five dollars?"

"Have a seat," Madame Natasha said, waving him to a seat at his table.

Tommy moved to the seat across from Madame and handed him a five-dollar bill. Madame Natasha picked up his tarot cards and began shuffling. His hands were tiny and delicate; his nails painted black. "What shall we ask the cards today?" Madame said.

"I've met this girl. I want to know more about her."

Madame Natasha nodded solemnly and began laying the cards out on the table. "I don't see a woman in your near future."

"Really?"

Madame pointed to a card on the right of the pattern he had laid out. "No. You see the position of this card? This card rules your relationships."

"It says 'Death.'"

"That does not necessarily mean physical death. The Death card can be a card of renewal, signifying a change. I would say that you recently broke up with someone."

"Nope," Tommy said. He stared at the stylized picture of the skeleton with the scythe. It seemed to be laughing at him.

"Let's try again," Madame Natasha said. He gathered the cards, shuffled them, and began laying them out again.

Tommy watched the spot where his relationship card would fall. Madame paused, then turned the card. Death.

"Well, well, what a co-in-kee-dink," Madame Natasha said.

"Try again," Tommy said.

Again Madame shuffled, and again, when he laid down the relationship card, it was Death.

"What does it mean?" Tommy asked.

"It could mean a lot of things, depending on your other suits." Madame waved to the other cards in the pattern.

"Then what does it mean with the other cards?"

"Honestly?"

"Of course. I want to know."

"You're fucked."

"What?"

"As far as relationships?"

"Yes."

"You're fucked."

"What about my writing career?"

Madame Natasha consulted the cards again, then, without looking up, said, "Fucked."

"I am not. I'm not fucked."

"Yep. Fucked. It's in the cards. Sorry."

"I don't believe in this stuff," Tommy said.

"Nevertheless," Madame Natasha said.

Tommy stood up. "I have to go find an apartment."

"Do you want to consult the cards about your new home?"

"No. I don't believe the cards."

"I could read your palm."

"Will it cost extra?"

"No, it's included."

"Okay." Tommy held out his hand and Madame Natasha cradled it delicately. Tommy looked around to see if anyone was looking, tapped his foot as if he was in a hurry.

"Goodness, you masturbate a lot, don't you?"

A guy at a nearby table spit coffee all over his paperback Sartre and looked over.

Tommy pulled his hand away. "No!"

"Now, now, don't lie. Madame Natasha knows."

"What's that got to do with an apartment?"

"Just checking my accuracy. It's like zeroing out a polygraph."

"Not a lot," Tommy said.

"Then I'll have to adjust my reading. I would have rated you a wankmaster of the first degree. It's nothing to be ashamed of. Considering your relationship card, I'd say it's your only option."

"Well, you're wrong."

"As you wish. Let me see your palm again."

Tommy surrendered his palm reluctantly.

"Oh, good news at last," Madame Natasha said. "You will find an apartment."

"Good," Tommy said, pulling his hand back again. "I've got to go."

"Don't you want to know about the rats?"

"No." Tommy turned and headed toward the door. As he reached it he turned and said, "I'm not fucked."

The Sartre reader looked up from his book and said, "We all are. We all are."

CHAPTER 13
To-Do List of the Fashionably Doomed

When you know the future is grim, there is no need for speed. Tommy decided to walk to the financial district. He shuffled along with the hang-dog look of the cosmically fucked.

He walked through Chinatown, spotted three of the Wongs buying lottery tickets at a liquor store, and headed up to the room to get his typewriter and clothes before they returned. His spirits lifted a little when he climbed down the narrow stairway for the last time, but Madame Natasha's words came back to dump on him again: *"I don't see a woman in your near future."*

It had been one of the reasons he had come to San Francisco—to find a girlfriend. Someone who would see him as an artist. Not like the girls back home, who saw him as a bookish freak. It was all part of the plan: live in the City, write stories, look at the bridge, ride cable cars, eat Rice-A-Roni, and have a girlfriend—someone he could tell his thoughts to, preferably after hours of godlike sex. He wasn't looking for perfection, just someone who made him feel secure enough to be insecure around. But not now. Now he was doomed.

He looked up at the skyline and realized that he had navigated wrong, arriving in the financial district, several blocks from the Pyramid. He zigzagged from block to block, avoiding eye contact with the men and women in business suits, who avoided eye contact in turn by checking their watches every few steps. Sure, he thought, they can check their watches. They have a future.

He arrived at the foot of the Pyramid a little breathless, his arms aching from carrying his belongings. He sat on a concrete bench at the edge of a fountain and watched people for a while.

They were all so determined. They had places to go, people to see. Their hair was perfect. They smelled good. They wore nice shoes. He looked at his own worn leather sneakers. *Fucked.*

Someone sat down next to him on the bench and he avoided looking up, thinking that it would just be another person who would make him feel inferior. He was staring at a spot on the concrete by his feet when a Boston terrier appeared on the spot and blew a jet stream of dog snot on his pant leg.

"Bummer, that's rude," the Emperor said. "Can't you see that our friend is sulking?"

Tommy looked up into the face of the Emperor. "Your Highness. Hello." The man had the wildest eyebrows Tommy had ever seen, as if two gray porcupines were perched on his brow.

The Emperor tipped his crown, a fedora made of panels cut from beer cans and laced together with yellow yarn. "Did you get the job?"

"Yes, they hired me that day. Thanks for the tip."

"It's honest work," the Emperor said. "There's a certain grace in that. Not like this tragedy."

"What tragedy?"

"These poor souls. These poor pathetic souls." The Emperor gestured toward the passersby.

"I don't understand," Tommy said.

"Their time has passed and they don't know what to do. They were told what they wanted and they believed it. They can only keep their dream alive by being with others like themselves who will mirror their illusions."

"They have really nice shoes," Tommy said.

"They have to look right or their peers will turn on them

like starving dogs. They are the fallen gods. The new gods are producers, creators, doers. The new gods are the chinless techno-children who would rather eat white sugar and watch science-fiction films than worry about what shoes they wear. And these poor souls desperately push papers around hoping that a mystical message will appear to save them from the new, awkward, brilliant gods and their silicon-chip reality. Some of them will survive, of course, but most will fall. Uncreative thinking is done better by machines. Poor souls, you can almost hear them sweating."

Tommy looked at the well-dressed stream of business people, then at the Emperor's tattered overcoat, then at his own sneakers, then at the Emperor again. For some reason, he felt better than he had a few minutes before. "You really worry about these people, don't you?"

"It is my lot."

An attractive woman in a gray suit and heels approached the Emperor and handed him a five-dollar bill. She wore a silk camisole under her jacket and Tommy could make out the top of her lace bra when she bent over. He was mesmerized.

"Your Highness," she said, "there's a Chinese chicken salad on special at the Café Suisse today. I think Bummer and Lazarus would love it."

Lazarus wagged his tail. Bummer yapped at the mention of his name.

"Very thoughtful of you, my child. The men will enjoy it."

"Have a good day," she said, and walked away. Tommy watched her calves as she went.

Two men who were passing by, embroiled in an argument about prices and earnings, stopped their conversation and nodded to the Emperor.

"Go with God," the Emperor said. He turned back to Tommy. "Are you still looking for a domicile, or just a woman now?"

"I don't understand."

"You wear your loneliness like a badge."

Tommy felt as if his ego had just taken a right to the jaw. "Actually, I met a girl and I'm going to rent us a place this afternoon."

"My mistake," the Emperor said. "I misread you."

"No, you didn't. I'm fucked."

"Pardon?"

"A fortune-teller told me that there was no woman in my future."

"Madame Natasha?"

"How did you know?"

"You mustn't give too much credence to Madame Natasha's predictions. He's dying and it darkens his vision. The plague."

"I'm sorry," Tommy said. In fact, he felt relieved, then guilty for the reason behind it. He had no right to feel sorry for himself. The Emperor had nothing except his dogs, yet his sympathy was all directed toward his fellowman. I'm scum, Tommy thought. He said, "Your Highness, I have a little money now, if you need . . ."

The Emperor held up the bill the woman had given him. "We have all that we need, my son." He stood and tugged on the ropes that held Bummer and Lazarus. "And I should be off before the men revolt from hunger."

"Me, too, I guess." Tommy stood and made as if to shake hands, then bowed instead. "Thanks for the company."

The Emperor winked, spun on one heel, and started to lead his troops away, then stopped and turned back. "And, son, don't touch anything with an edge while you're in the building? Scissors, letter openers, anything."

"Why?" Tommy asked.

"It's the shape of the building, a pyramid. They'd rather people not know about it, but they have a full-time employee who just goes around dulling the letter openers."

"You're kidding."

"Safety first," the Emperor said.

"Thanks."

Tommy took a deep breath and steeled himself for his assault on the Pyramid. As he walked out of the sun and under the massive concrete buttresses, he could feel a chill through his flannel shirt, as if the concrete had stored the damp cold of the night fog and was radiating it like a refrigerator coil. He was shivering by the time he reached the information desk. A guard eyed him suspiciously.

"Can I help you?"

"I'm looking for the Transamerica personnel department."

The guard made a face as if Tommy had been dipped in sewage. "Do you have an appointment?"

"Yes." Tommy waved Jody's papers under the guard's nose.

The guard picked up a phone and was punching numbers when a second guard came up behind him and took the receiver. "He's fine," the second guard said. "Send him up."

"But—"

"He's a friend of the Emperor."

The first guard hung up the phone and said, "Twenty-first floor, sir." He pointed to the elevators.

Tommy took an elevator to the twenty-first floor, then followed the signs until he found the right department. An officious-looking older woman told him to have a seat in the reception room, she would be right with him. Then she took great pains to act as if he had been sucked off the planet.

Tommy sat on a black leather sofa that sighed with his weight, chose a magazine from the black stone coffee table, and waited. During the next hour he read a household-hints column ("Coffee grounds in that cat box will fill your house with the delightful aroma of brewing espresso every time kitty heeds the call"); an article on computer junkies ("Bruce has been off the mouse for six months now, but he says he takes life one byte at a time"); and a review of the new musical *Jonestown!* ("Andrew Lloyd Webber's version of the Kool-Aid jingle is at once chilling and evocative. Donny Osmond is brilliant as Jim Jones.") He borrowed some whiteout from the officious-looking woman and touched up the finish on his sneakers, then dried them under a halogen reading light that looked like a robot's arm holding the sun. When he started pulling cologne sample cards out of *GQ* and rubbing them on his socks, the woman told him he could go on in.

He picked up his shoes and walked into the office in his stocking feet. Another officious-looking woman, who looked remarkably like the first officious-looking woman, down to the little chain on her reading glasses, had him sit down across from her while she looked at Jody's papers and ignored him.

She consulted a computer screen, tapped on a few keys, then waited while the computer did something. Tommy put his shoes on and waited.

She didn't look up.

He cleared his throat. She tapped on the keys.

He reached down, opened his suitcase, and took out his portable typewriter. She didn't look up.

She tapped and looked at the screen.

He opened the typewriter case, rolled a piece of paper in the machine, and tapped on a few keys.

She looked up. He tapped a few more keys.

"What are you doing?" she asked.

Tommy tapped. He didn't look up.

The woman raised her voice. "I said, what are you doing?"

Tommy kept typing and looked up. "Pardon me, I was ignoring you. What did you say?"

"What are you doing?" She repeated.

"It's a note. Let me read it for you. 'Couldn't anyone else see that they were all slaves of Satan? I had to cleanse the world of their evil. I am the hand of God. Why else would security have let me into the building with an assault rifle in my suitcase? I am a divine instrument.'" Tommy paused and looked up. "That's all I have so far, but I'll guess I end it with an apology to my mom. What do you think?"

She smiled as if hiding gas pains and handed him an envelope. "This is Jody's final paycheck. Give her our best. And you have a nice day now, young man."

"You too," Tommy said. He gathered up his stuff and left the office whistling.

• • •

Fashionable SOMA looked to Tommy an awful lot like a light in-dustrial area: two- and three-story buildings with steel roll-up doors and steel-framed windows. The bottom floors housed eth-nic restaurants, underground dance clubs, auto-repair shops, and the occasional foundry. Tommy paused outside of one to watch two long-haired men pouring bronze into a mold.

Artists, Tommy thought. He had never seen a real artist, and although these guys looked more like bikers, he wanted to talk to them. He took a tentative step through the doorway.

"Hi," he said.

The men were wrestling with a huge ladle, the two of them gripping the long metal handle with asbestos gloves. One looked up. "Out!" he said.

Tommy said, "Okay, I can see you guys are busy. 'Bye." He stood on the sidewalk and checked his map. He was supposed to meet the rental agent somewhere around here. He looked up and down the street. Except for a guy passed out on the corner, the street was empty. Tommy was thinking about waking the guy up and asking him if this was, indeed, the fashionable part of SOMA, when a green Jeep pulled up beside him and skidded to a stop. The driver, a woman in her forties with wild gray hair, rolled down the window. "Mr. Flood?" She said.

Tommy nodded.

"I'm Alicia DeVries. Let me park and I'll show you the loft."

She backed the Jeep into a spot that seemed too short for it by six inches, running the wheels up over the curb, then she jumped out, dragging after her a purse roughly the size of Tommy's suit-case. She wore sandals, a dashiki, and multicolored Guatemalan cotton pants. There were chopsticks stuck here and there in her hair, as if she were prepared at any minute to deal with an emer-gency stir-fry.

She looked at Tommy's suitcase. "You look like you're ready to move in today. This way."

She breezed by Tommy to a fire door beside the foundry. Tommy could smell the patchouli in her wake.

She said, "This area is just like Soho was twenty years ago. You're lucky to have a shot at one of these lofts now, before they go co-op and start selling for a million dollars."

She unlocked the door and started up the steps. "This place has incredible energy," she said, without looking back. "I'd love to live here myself, except the market's down right now and I'd have to sell my place in the Heights."

Tommy dragged his suitcase up the steps after her.

"Do you paint, Mr. Flood?"

"I'm a writer."

"Oh, a writer! I do a little writing myself. I'd like to write a book myself some weekend, if I can find the time. Something about female circumcision, I think. Maybe something about marriage. But what's the difference, right?" She stopped at a landing at the top of the stairs and unlocked another fire door.

"Here it is." She threw the door open and gestured for Tommy to enter. "A nice work area and a bedroom in the back. There are two sculptors that work downstairs and a painter next door. A writer would really round the building out. What's your take on female circumcision, Mr. Flood?"

Tommy was still about three topics behind her, so he stood on the landing while his brain caught up. People like Alicia were the reason God made decaf. "I think everyone should have a hobby," he said, taking a shot in the dark.

Alicia jammed like an overheated machine gun. She seemed to look at him for the first time, and did not seem to like what she saw. "You *are* aware that we'll need a significant security deposit, *if* your application is accepted?"

"Okay," Tommy said. He entered the loft, leaving her standing on the landing.

The loft was roughly the size of a handball court. It had an island kitchen in the middle, and windows ran along one wall from floor to ceiling. There was an old rug, a futon, and a low plastic coffee table in the open area near the kitchen. The back wall was lined with empty bookshelves, broken only by a single door to the bedroom.

The bookshelves did it. Tommy wanted to live here. He could

see the shelves filled with Kerouac, and Kesey, and Hammett, and Ginsberg, and Twain, and London, and Bierce, and every other writer who had lived and written in the City. One shelf would be for the books he was going to write: hardbacks in thirty languages. There would be a bust of Beethoven on that shelf. He didn't really like Beethoven, but he thought he should have a bust of him.

He resisted the urge to shout, "I'll take it!" It was Jody's money. He had to check the bedroom for windows. He opened the door and went in. The room was as dark as a cave. He flipped the light switch and track lighting along one wall came on. There was an old mattress and box springs on the floor. The walls were bare brick. No windows.

Through another door was a bathroom with a freestanding sink and a huge claw-foot tub that was stained with rust and paint. No windows. He was so excited, he thought he would wet himself.

He ran out into the main living area where Alicia was standing with her hand on her hip, mentally shoving him into the pigeon-hole of abusive barbarism she had made for him.

"I'll take it," Tommy said.

"You'll have to fill out an—"

"I'll give you four thousand dollars in cash, right now." He pulled the wad of bills out of his jeans.

"How many keys will you need?"

CHAPTER 14
Two Losts Do Not Make a Found

Consciousness went off like a flashbulb of pain: a dull ache in her head, sharp daggers in her knees and her chin. Jody was slumped in the shower. The water was still running—had been running on her all day. She crawled out of the shower stall on her hands and knees and pulled towels out of the rack.

She sat on the bathroom floor and dried herself, blotting away the water with rough terry cloth. Her skin felt tender, almost raw. The towels were damp from fourteen hours of steam. The ceiling dripped and the walls ran with condensation. She braced herself against the sink and climbed to her feet, then opened the door and stumbled through the room to the bed.

Be careful what you ask for, she thought. All the regret about waking up a little too alert, coming out of sleep like a gunshot, came back on her. She hadn't thought about falling asleep in the same way. She must have been in the shower at sunup, dropped to the shower floor, and stayed there throughout the day.

She sat up on the bed and gently touched her chin. Pain shot up her jaw. She must have hit it on the soap dish when she went out. Her knees were bruised as well.

Bruised? Something was wrong. She jumped to her feet and went to the dresser. She turned on the light and leaned into the mirror, then yelped. Her chin was bruised blue, with a corona of yellow. Her hair was hopelessly tangled and she now had a small bald spot where the water had worn away at her scalp.

She backed away and sat back on the bed, stunned. Something was wrong, seriously wrong, beyond her injuries. It was the light. Why had she turned on the light? The night before she would have been able to see herself in the mirror by the light filtering in under the bathroom door. But it was more than that. It was a tightness in her mouth, pressure, like when she had first gotten braces as a child.

She ran her tongue over her teeth and felt the points breaking through the roof of her mouth just behind her eyeteeth.

She thought, I'm breaking down from lack of . . . She couldn't even make herself think it. This will get worse. Much worse.

Now she could feel the hunger, not in her stomach, but in her entire body, as if her veins were going to collapse on themselves. And there was a tension in her muscles, as if piano strings were tightening inside her body, sharpening her movements, making her feel as if she would jump through a window any second.

I've got to calm down. Calm down. Calm down. Calm down.

She repeated the mantra to herself as she got up and walked to the phone. It seemed to take an incredible effort to push the zero button and wait for the desk clerk to come on.

"Hi, this is room two-ten. Is there a guy in the lobby waiting? Yes, that's him. Would you tell him I'll be down in a few minutes?"

She put down the phone and went to the bathroom, where she turned off the shower and wiped down the mirror. She looked at herself in the mirror and fought the urge to burst into tears.

This is a project, she thought. She turned her head and looked at her bald spot. It was small enough that she could cover it with a new part held by a couple of hairpins. Her bruised chin might require some explaining.

She started to run her fingers though her hair to facilitate the preliminary untangle, fighting the tension in her arms that seemed to be increasing every second. A large moth buzzed into the bathroom and went for the light above the mirror. Before she knew what had happened, she snatched it out of the air and ate it.

She stared at her reflection and was horrified by the red-haired stranger who had just eaten a moth. Even so, a warmth ran though her like good brandy. The bruise on her chin faded as she watched.

The first thing she saw when she turned the corner at the lobby was Tommy's grin.

"Good," he said. "You're dressed for moving. I like your hair pinned up like that."

Jody smiled, and stood awkwardly in front of him, thinking she should greet him with a hug, but afraid to get too close to him. She could smell him and he smelled like food. "You found a place?"

"An incredible loft, south of Market. It's even furnished." He seemed as if he would burst with excitement. "I used all the money; I hope that's okay."

"Fine," Jody said. She just wanted to get him alone.

"Get your stuff," he said. "I want to show it to you."

Jody nodded. "I'll be just a minute. Have the desk clerk call a cab."

She turned to leave. Tommy caught her by the arm. "Hey, are you okay?"

She motioned for him to move within whisper range. "I want you so badly I can hardly stand it."

She pulled away and ran up the steps to her room. Inside she gathered what few belongings she had and checked herself in the mirror one last time. She was wearing jeans and the chambray blouse from the night before. She unbuttoned her blouse and did a straitjacket escape from her bra, then buttoned the blouse halfway up. She stuffed the bra into her day pack and locked the room for the last time.

When she returned to the lobby, Tommy was waiting outside by a blue DeSoto cab. He opened the door for her, climbed in, and gave the driver the address.

"You're going to love it," he said. "I know you are."

She moved closer to him and held his arm tightly between her breasts. "I can't wait," she said. A tiny voice in her head asked,

What are you doing? What are you going to do to him? It was so faint and foreign that it might have come from someone outside on the street.

Tommy pulled away from her and dug into his jeans pocket, coming out with an envelope. "Your check's in here. I didn't open it."

She took it and put it in her day pack, then moved on him again.

He scooted to the door and nodded toward the driver, who was watching them in the rearview mirror. "Forget him," Jody whispered. She licked Tommy neck and shuddered with the taste and warmth of his flesh.

"I couldn't get your car out of impound. It has to be the owner."

"Doesn't matter," she said, nuzzling into the space under his jaw.

The cab stopped and the driver turned to them. "Six-ten," he said.

Jody threw a twenty over the seat, reached over Tommy and opened the door, dived out and dragged him out of the cab after her. "Where is it?"

Tommy just had time to point to the door before she pushed him at it. She climbed on his back as he unlocked the door, then bolted past him and dragged him up the steps.

"You're really excited about this, aren't you?" he asked.

"It's great." She stopped at the fire door at the top of the stairs. "Open it," she commanded.

Tommy unlocked the door and threw it open. "This is it!"

She went through, catching the front of his shirt and pulling him in.

"Look at all these bookshelves," he said.

She ripped his shirt off and kissed him hard.

He pulled up for air and said, "The bedroom doesn't have any windows, just like you wanted."

"Where?" she demanded.

He pointed to the open door and she pushed him through it. He fell face down on the bare mattress. She flipped him over, hooked her hands into the waist of his jeans and ripped them off him.

"So you like it?" he asked.

She ripped her shirt open and held him to the bed, one hand on his chest while she took off her own jeans. She climbed on him and muffled his next question with a kiss.

He finally got the message and returned her kiss and tried to match her urgency, then didn't have to try at all. She pulled away from the kiss as her fangs unsheathed, then guided him into her as he moaned. Jody growled deep in her chest, pushed his head to the side and bit him on the neck.

"Ouch!" Tommy shouted. She held him down and snarled into his neck.

Dust from the old mattress filled the air and was stirred by the movement of their bodies.

"Oh jeez!" Tommy shouted, digging his fingers into her bottom. Jody answered him with a catlike scream as she came, then fell on his chest and licked the blood that dribbled from the punctures on his neck.

She twitched and shuddered while he repeated, "Oh jeez," over and over again between gasps. After a few minutes she rolled off him and lay on the bed feeling the warm nourishment running though her.

Tommy rubbed his neck. "That was great," he said. "That was incredible. You are—"

Jody rolled over. "Tommy, I have to tell you something."

"You're beautiful," he said.

Jody smiled at him. The urgency was gone now and she was feeling guilty. I could have killed him, she thought.

Tommy reached over and touched her lips. "What's that on your teeth? Did you hurt yourself?"

"It's blood, Tommy. It's your blood."

He felt his neck again, which was completely healed. "My blood?"

"Tommy, I've never done anything like that before. I've never been that way before."

"Me either. It was great!"

"I'm a vampire."

"That's okay," Tommy said. "I knew this girl in high school

who gave me a hickey that covered the whole side of my neck."

"No, Tommy. I'm really a vampire." She looked him in the eye and did not smile or look away. She waited.

He said, "Don't goof on me, okay?"

"Tommy, have you ever seen anyone tear a pair of jeans like that before?"

"That was my animal attraction, right?"

Jody got out of bed, went to the bedroom door and closed it, shutting out the light from the living area. "Can you see anything?"

"No," he said.

"Hold up a number of fingers. Don't tell me how many."

He did.

"Three," Jody said. "Try again."

He did.

"Seven."

"Jeez," he said. "Are you psychic?"

She opened the door. Light spilled in.

"You have an incredible body," Tommy said.

"Thanks. I need to lose five pounds."

"Let's do it again, without our shoes on this time."

"Tommy, you have to listen to me. This is important. I'm not kidding you. I am a vampire."

"C'mon, Jody, come over here. I'll take your shoes off for you."

Jody looked up at the ceiling. There were open steel beams twenty feet above. "Watch." She jumped up and grabbed on to a beam and hung. "See?"

"Jeez," Tommy said.

"Do you have a book here?"

"In my suitcase."

"Go get it."

"Be careful. You could fall."

"Get the book, Tommy."

Tommy went into the living area, looking up at her as he walked under. He returned with a volume of Kerouac.

"Now what? Come down from there. You're making me nervous."

"Close the door and open the book."

He closed the door and the room went dark again. Jody read a half page aloud before he opened the door again.

"Jeez," he said.

She let go of the beam and dropped to the floor. Tommy backed away from her to the bed and sat down.

"If you want to leave, I'll understand," she said.

"When we were making love . . . you were cold inside."

"Look, I didn't mean to hurt you."

Tommy's eyes were wide. "You really are a vampire, aren't you?"

"I'm sorry. I needed help. I needed someone."

"You really are a vampire." It was a statement this time.

"Yes, Tommy. I am."

He paused for a second to think, then said, "That's the coolest thing I've ever heard. Let's do it with our shoes off."

PART II
Nesting

CHAPTER 15
Learning the Licks

They took their shoes off and did it again. The second time was less urgent and they tried to impress each other with their respective repertoires of mattress tricks. Jody was careful not to appear too experienced and Tommy pulled on everything he had ever read, from *Penthouse* to *National Geographic,* trying not to appear too naive, while fighting the urge to shout "Gee whiz" with her every move. There was entirely too much thinking involved on both their parts and they finished thinking, Well, that was pretty okay. Jody's fangs stayed safely sheathed behind her canines.

She said, "What was that you shouted at the end?"

"It was a Bantu love cry. I think it translates, 'Oh baby, polish my lip saucer.'"

"Interesting," Jody said.

They lay there for a while, not talking, feeling uncomfortable and a little embarrassed. Whatever intimacy they shared physically was not echoed emotionally. They were strangers.

Tommy felt that he should confess something personal, something to match the outrageous trust she had put in him by telling him her secret. At the same time he was curious, and a little bit afraid. It wasn't as if she had shown him a hidden tattoo. She was a vampire. How do you match that? How do you file that? Under "Adventure," he thought. I wanted adventure, and here it is.

"Tommy," she said, not looking at him, talking more or less to the ceiling, "I'll understand if you don't want to stay, but I'd like you to."

"I've never lived with anyone before. This is all new to me. I mean, you probably have a lot more experience than I do at this."

"Well, not exactly like this. I've lived with a few guys."

"A few?"

"Ten, I think. But not under these circumstances."

"Ten? You must be ancient. No offense. I mean, I knew that you were older, but I thought it was just a few years. Not centuries."

She rolled over and looked him in the eye. "I'm twenty-six."

"Sure, you look twenty-six. But you've probably looked this way for years. You probably have pictures of yourself with Abraham Lincoln and stuff, right?"

"No, I'm twenty-six. I've been twenty-six for about six months."

"But how long . . . I mean . . . Were you born like . . ."

"I've been a vampire for four days."

"So you're twenty-six."

"That's what I've been telling you."

"And you've lived with ten guys?"

She got out of bed and started gathering her clothes. "Look, I don't use the best judgment when it comes to relationships. Okay?"

He turned away from her. "Well, thanks a lot."

"I didn't mean you. I meant in the past."

He sat on the edge of the bed and hung his head. "I feel so used."

"Used?" She leaped over the bed and stood in front of him. "Used?" She put her finger under his chin and lifted it until he was looking at her. "I've trusted you with the biggest secret I have. I've offered to share my life with you."

"Oh, like that's an exclusive privilege." He pulled away from her and resumed pouting.

Jody snatched a shoe off the floor and prepared to whack him with it, then remembered what she had done to Kurt and dropped it. "Why are you being such an asshole?"

"You drank my blood!"

"Yeah, well, I'm sorry about that."

"You didn't even ask."

"And you didn't protest, either."

"I thought it was a sex thing."

"It was."

"It was?" He stopped pouting and looked up at her. "Does that turn you on?"

Jody thought, Why are men never prepared for the toxic radiation of afterglow? Why can't they ride it through without becoming detached whiners or aggressive jerks? They don't get it, that cuddling afterward has nothing to do with warm, fuzzy feelings; it's just the most intelligent way to ride the wave of postcoital depression.

"Tommy, I came so hard, my toes curled. No man has ever made me feel like that before." How many times have I said that? she thought.

"Yeah?"

She nodded.

He smiled, feeling proud of himself. "Let's do it again."

"No, we need to talk."

"Okay. But then . . ."

"Put on your clothes."

Tommy scampered naked out of the bedroom to get a fresh pair of jeans from his suitcase. As he dressed, the infinite possibilities of life swam through his head. Only a week ago he had been staring down the barrel of a life spent in a factory town—of a union job, of a series of financed Fords, a mortgage, too many kids, and a wife who'd go to fat. Sure, there was a certain nobility in being responsible and raising a family—seeing that they never did without. But when his father told him on his eighteenth birthday that he needed to start planning his retirement, he felt his future tighten on him like an anaconda. His father had made it clear that the money for college wasn't there—so after he went to the City and starved, he could come home and get a job down at the factory and get down to the business of being an adult. But not now. He was a City guy now, part of the world; he was involved with a vampire, and the danger of living a normal, boring life had passed completely. He knew he should be afraid, but he was too elated to think about it.

He slid into his jeans and ran back to the bedroom, where Jody was getting dressed. "I'm hungry," he said. "Let's go out and get something to eat."

"I can't eat," she said.

"Not at all?"

"Not as far as I know. I can't even keep a glass of water down."

"Wow. Do you have to have blood every day?"

"I don't think so."

"Does it have to be—I mean, can you use animals, or does it have to be people?"

Jody thought about the moth she had eaten and felt as if she'd just downed a cocktail mixed of two parts shame and five parts disgust, with a twist of nausea. "I don't know, Tommy. I didn't exactly get an instruction book."

He was bouncing around the room like a hyperactive child. "How did it happen? Did you sell your soul to Satan? Am I going to turn into a vampire? Are you in a coven or something?"

She wheeled on him. "Look, I don't know. I don't know anything. Let me get dressed and we'll go get something for you to eat. I'll explain then, okay?"

"Well, you don't have to bite my head off."

"Maybe I do," she snarled, surprised at the acid in her voice.

Tommy backed away from her, his eyes wide with fear. She felt horrible. Why did I say that? This was happening too often, this loss of control—showing her burned hand to the bum on the bus, knocking Kurt out, eating the moth, and now threatening Tommy; none of it seemed to be by choice. It was as if vampirism carried with it a crampless case of rattlesnake PMS.

"I'm sorry, Tommy. This has been hard."

"It's okay." He picked up the jeans she had destroyed and began emptying the pockets. "I guess these are done for." He pulled out the business card that the motel manager had given him. "Hey, I forgot to tell you. This cop wants to talk to you."

Jody stopped in the middle of tying her shoes. "Cop?"

"Yeah, an old lady was killed at the motel last night. There were a zillion cops around when I got there this morning. They wanted to talk to everyone that was staying in the motel."

"How was she killed, Tommy? Do you know?"

"Somebody broke her neck and . . ." He stopped and stared at her, backing away again toward the bathroom.

"What?" she demanded. "Her neck was broken and what?"

"She'd lost a lot of blood," he whispered. "But there weren't any wounds." He bolted into the bathroom and shut the door.

Jody could hear him throw the lock. "I didn't kill her, Tommy."

"That's fine," he said.

"Open the door. Please."

"I can't, I'm peeing." He turned on the water.

"Tommy, come out, I'm not going to hurt you. Let's go get you something to eat and I'll explain."

"You go ahead," he said. "I'll catch up to you. Wow, I really had to go. Must have been all that coffee I drank today."

"Tommy, I swear I didn't know anything about this until you told me."

"Look at this," he said through the door, "I found that crucifix I lost last week. And what's this? My lucky vial of holy water."

"Tommy, stop it. I'm not going to hurt you. I don't want to hurt anybody."

"Oh, my garlic wreath. I wondered where I'd put that."

Jody grabbed the door knob and yanked. The doorjamb splintered and the door came away in her hand. Tommy dived into the tub and peeked over the edge at her.

She said, "Let's go get you something to eat. We need to talk."

He pulled himself up slowly, ready to dive down the drain if she made a move. She backed away.

He looked at the ruined doorjamb. "We're going to lose our deposit now; you know that, right?"

Jody threw the door aside and offered her hand to help him

out of the tub. "Can I buy you some fries? I'd really like to watch you eat some French fries."

"That's weird, Jody."

"Compared to what?"

They walked to Market Street where, even at ten o'clock, the sidewalks were crowded with bums and hustlers and teams of podiatrists who had escaped the Moscone Convention Center to seek out burgers, pizzas, and beer in the heart of the City. Jody watched the heat ghosts trailing the street people while Tommy handed out coins like a meter-maid angel trying to atone for a lifetime of giving chickenshit tickets.

He dropped a quarter into the palm of a half-fingered glove worn by a woman who was pretending to be a robot, but who looked more like a golem newly shaped from gutter filth. Jody noticed a black aura around the woman, as she had seen around the old man on the bus; she could smell disease and the rawness of open lesions and she almost pulled Tommy away.

A few steps away she said, "You don't have to give them all money just because they ask, you know."

"I know, but if I give them money I don't see their faces when I'm about to fall asleep."

"It doesn't really help. She'll just spend it on booze or drugs."

"If I was her, so would I."

"Good point," Jody said. She took his arm and led him into a burger joint named No Guilt: orange Formica tables over industrial-gray carpet, giant backlit transparencies of food glistening with grease, and families gleefully clogging their arteries together. "Is this okay?"

"Perfect," Tommy said.

They took a table by the window and Jody trembled while Tommy ordered a brace of burgers and a basket of fries.

She said, "Tell me about the woman who was killed."

"She had a dog, a little gray dog. They found them both in the dumpster at the motel. She was old. Now she'll always be old."

"Pardon?"

"People always stay the age that they died at. My big brother died of leukemia when I was six. He was eight. Now when I think of him, he's always eight, and he's still my big brother. He never changes, and the part of me that remembers him never changes. See. What about you?"

"I don't have any brothers or sisters."

"No, I mean, are you going to stay the same? Will you always look like this now?"

"I haven't thought about it. I guess it could be true. I know I heal really fast since it happened."

The waitress brought Tommy's food. He squirted ketchup on the fries and attacked. "Tell me," he said around a mouthful of burger.

Jody started slowly as she watched his every bite with envy, telling him first about her life before the attack, of growing up in Monterey and dropping out of community college when her life didn't seem to be moving fast enough. Then of moving to San Francisco, of her jobs and her loves and the few life lessons she had learned. She told him about that night of the attack in too much detail, and in the telling she realized how little she understood about what had happened to her. She told him about waking up, and of how her strength and senses had changed, and it was here that words began to fail her—there were no words to describe some of the things she had seen and felt. She told him about the call at the motel and about being followed by the other vampire. When she had finished she felt more confused than when she had started.

Tommy said, "So you're not immortal. He said that you could be killed."

"I guess; I don't seem to change. All my childhood scars are gone, the lines on my face. My body seems to have lifted a little."

Tommy grinned. "You do have a great body."

"I could lose five pounds," Jody said. She inhaled sharply and her eyes went wide, as if she'd just remembered some explosives she'd left in the oven. "Oh my God!"

"What?" Tommy looked around, thinking she had seen something frightening, something dangerous.

"This is horrible."

"What is it?" Tommy insisted.

"I just realized—I'm always going to be a pudgette. I have jeans I'll never get into. I'm always going to need to lose five pounds. "

"So what, every woman I've ever known thought she needed to lose five pounds."

"But they have a chance, they have hope. I'm doomed."

"You could go on a liquid diet," Tommy said.

"Very funny." She pinched her hip to confirm her observation. "Five pounds. If he'd only waited another week to attack. I was on the yogurt-and-grapefruit diet. I would have made it. I'd be thin forever." She realized that she was obsessing and turned her attention to Tommy. "How's your neck, by the way?"

He rubbed the spot where she had bitten him. "It's fine. I can't even feel a mark."

"You don't feel weak?"

"No more than usual."

Jody smiled. "I don't know how much I . . . I mean, I don't have any way of measuring or anything."

"No, I'm fine. It was kind of sexy. I just wonder how I healed so fast."

"It seems to work that way."

"Let's try something." He held his hand by her face. "Lick my finger."

She pushed his hand away. "Tommy, just finish eating and we can go home and do this."

"No, it's an experiment. My cuticles get split from cutting boxes at the store. I want to see if you can heal them." He touched her lower lip. "Go ahead, lick."

She snaked out a tentative tongue and licked the tip of his finger, then took his finger in her mouth and ran her tongue around it.

"Wow," Tommy said. He pulled his finger out and looked at it. His cuticle, which had been split and torn, had healed. "This is great. Look."

Jody studied his cuticle. "It worked."

"Do another." He thrust another finger in her mouth.

She spit it out. "Stop that."

"Come on." He pushed at her lips. "Pleeeeze."

A big guy in a Forty-Niners sweatshirt leaned over from the table next to them and said, "Buddy, do you mind? I've got my kids here."

"Sorry," Tommy said, wiping vampire spit on his shirt. "We were just experimenting."

"Yeah, well, this isn't the place for it, okay?"

"Right," Tommy said.

"See?" Jody whispered. "I told you."

"Let's go home," Tommy said. "I've got a blister on my big toe."

"No fucking way, writer-boy."

"It's low in calories," Tommy coaxed, prodding her foot with his sneaker. "Good, and good for you."

"Not a chance."

Tommy sighed in defeat. "Well, I guess we've got more to worry about than my toe or your weight problem."

"Like what?"

"Like the fact that last night I saw a guy in the store parking lot that I think was the other vampire."

CHAPTER 16

Heartwarming and UL-Approved

There was a bum sleeping on the sidewalk across the street from the loft when they returned. Tommy, full of fast food and the elation of being twice laid, wanted to give the guy a dollar. Jody stopped him and pushed him up the steps. "Go on up," she said. "I'll be there in a minute."

She stood in the doorway watching the bum for movement. There was no heat signature around him and she assumed the worst. She waited for him to roll over and start laughing at her again. She was feeling strong and a little cocky from the infusion of Tommy's blood, so she had to fight the urge to confront the vampire, to get dead in his face and scream. Instead she just whispered, "Asshole," and closed the door. If his hearing was as acute as her own, and she was sure it was, he had heard her.

She found Tommy in bed, fast asleep.

Poor guy, she thought, running all over town doing my business. He probably hasn't slept more than a couple of hours since we met.

She pulled the covers over him, kissed him on the forehead, and went to the window in the front room to watch the bum across the street.

• • •

Tommy was dreaming of bebop-driven sentences read by a naked redhead when he woke to find her sleeping next to him. He threw his arm over her and pulled her close, but there was no response, no pleasant groan or reciprocal snuggle. She was out.

He pushed the light button on his watch and checked the time. It was almost noon. The room was so dark that the watch dial floated in his vision for a few seconds after he released the button. He went to the bathroom and fumbled around until he found the light switch. A single fluorescent tube clicked and sputtered and finally ignited, spilling a fuzzy green glow through the door into the bedroom.

She looks dead, he thought. Peaceful, but dead. Then he looked at himself in the bathroom mirror. I look dead too.

It took him a minute to realize that it was the fluorescent lighting that had sucked the life out of his face, not his vampire girlfriend. He affected a serious glare and thought about how they would describe him in a hundred years, when he was really famous and really dead.

Like so many great writers before him, Flood was known for his troubled countenance and sickly pallor, especially under fluorescent lighting. Those who knew him said that even in those early years they could sense that this thin, serious young man would make his presence known as a great man of letters as well as a sexual dynamo. His legacy to the world was a trail of great books and broken hearts, and although it is well known that his love life was his downfall, he felt no regret, as illustrated in his Nobel Prize acceptance speech: "I have followed my penis into hell and returned with the story."

Tommy bowed deeply before the mirror, careful to keep the Nobel Prize medal from banging the sink, then began to interview himself, speaking clearly and slowly into his toothbrush.

"I think it was shortly after my first successful bus transfer that I realized the City was mine. Here I would produce some of my greatest work, and here I would meet my first wife, the lovely but deeply disturbed Jody . . ."

Tommy waved the microphone/toothbrush away as if the memories were too painful to recall, but actually he was trying to remember Jody's last name. I should know her maiden name, he thought, if just for historical purposes.

He glanced into the bedroom where the lovely but deeply disturbed Jody was lying naked and half-covered on the bed. He thought, She won't mind if I wake her up. She doesn't have to be at work or anything.

He approached the bed and touched her cheek. "Jody," he whispered. She didn't stir.

He shook her a bit. "Jody, honey."

Nothing.

"Hey," he said, taking her shoulders. "Hey, wake up." She didn't respond.

He pulled the covers off her as his father used to do to him on cold winter mornings when he wouldn't get up to go to school. "Up and at 'em, soldier—ass in the air and feet on the floor," he said in his best drill-sergeant bark.

She looked really great lying there naked in the half-light from the bathroom. He was getting a little turned on.

How would I feel, he thought, if I woke up and she was making love to me? Why, I believe that I would be pleasantly surprised. I think that would be better than waking up to frying bacon and the Sunday funnies. Yes, I'm sure she'll be pleased.

He crawled into bed with her and ventured a tentative kiss. She was a little cold and didn't move a muscle, but he was sure she liked it. He ran a finger down the valley between her breasts and over her stomach.

What if she didn't wake up? What if we do it and she doesn't wake up at all? How would I feel if I woke up and she told me that we had done it while I slept? I'd be fine with it. A little sad that I missed things, but I wouldn't be mad. I'd just ask her if I had a good time. Women are different, though.

He tickled her just to get a reaction. Again, she didn't move.

She's so cold. With her not moving at all it might be a little morbid. Maybe I should wait. I'll tell her that I thought about it and decided that it wouldn't be courteous. She'll like that.

He sighed deeply, got out of bed and pulled the covers over her. I should buy her something, he thought.

Jody snapped into consciousness and bit down on something hard. She opened her eyes and saw Tommy sitting on the edge of the bed. She smiled.

"Good morning," he said.

She reached for whatever was in her mouth.

Tommy caught her hand. "Don't bite down. It's a thermometer." He checked his watch, then pulled the thermometer out of her mouth and read it. "Ninety-five point two. You're on your way."

Jody sat up and looked at the thermometer. "On my way to what?"

He smiled bashfully. "On your way to body temperature. I bought you an electric blanket. It's been on for like six hours."

She ran her hand over the blanket. "You've been warming me up?"

"Pretty cool, huh?" Tommy said. "I went to the library and got books too. I've been reading all afternoon." He picked up a stack of books and began to shuffle through them, reading the titles and handing each to her in turn. "*A Reader's Guide to Vampirism; Vampire Myths and Legends; Those That Stalk the Night*—kind of an ominous title, huh?"

She held the books as if they were made of wormy fruit. The covers depicted monstrous creatures rising from coffins, attacking women in various states of undress, and hanging around castles perched on barren mountains. The letters in the titles dripped blood. "These are all about vampires?"

"That's just the nonfiction that they had on hand. I ordered a bunch more through the library exchange. Check out some of the fiction." He picked up another stack from the floor.

"*A Feast of Blood; Red Thirst; Fangs; Dracula; Dracula's Dream; Dracula's Legacy; Fevre Dream; The Vampire Lestat*—there must have been a hundred novels."

Jody, a little overwhelmed, stared at the books. "There seems to be a theme here on the covers."

"Yeah," Tommy said. "Vampires seem to have an affinity for lingerie. Do you have any particular craving for sexy nightgowns?"

"Not really." Jody had always thought it a little silly to spend a lot of money on something that you only put on long enough for someone to take it off you. Evidently, though, if you went by these book covers, vampires looked at lingerie as garnish.

"Okay," Tommy said, picking up a notebook from the floor and making a check mark. "No lingerie fetish. I've made a list of vampire traits with boxes to check either 'fact' or 'fiction.' Since you missed the lecture, I guess we'll have to just test them."

"What lecture?"

Tommy put down his pen and looked at her as if she'd gotten into the express lane with a cartful of groceries and a two-party check. "Everybody knows that there's always an orientation lecture in vampire books. Usually it comes from some old professor guy with an accent, but sometimes it's another vampire. You obviously missed the lecture."

"I guess so," Jody said. "I must have been busy chasing women in lingerie."

"That's okay," Tommy said, returning to the list. "Obviously you don't have to sleep in your native soil." He checked it off. "And we know that everyone you bite doesn't necessarily turn into a vampire."

"No, a jerk, maybe . . ."

"Whatever," Tommy said, moving on in the list. "Okay, sunlight is bad for you." He made a check mark. "You can enter a house without being invited. How about running water?"

"What about it?"

"Vampires aren't supposed to be able to cross running water. Have you tried crossing any running water?"

"I've taken a couple of showers."

"Then that would be fiction. Let me smell your breath." He bent close to her.

She turned her head and shielded her mouth. "Tommy, I just woke up. Let me brush my teeth first."

"Vampires are supposed to have the 'fetid breath of a predator,' or, in some cases, 'breath like the rotting smell of the charnel house.' C'mon, give us a whiff."

Jody reluctantly breathed in his face. He sat up and considered the list.

"Well?" she asked.

"I'm thinking. I need to get the dictionary out of my suitcase."

"What for?"

"I'm not sure what a charnel house is."

"Can I brush my teeth while you look?"

"No, wait, I might need another whiff." He went to his suitcase and dug out the dictionary. While he looked up "charnel house," Jody cupped her hand and smelled her own breath. It was pretty foul.

"Here it is," he said, putting his finger on the word. "'Noun. A mausoleum or morgue. A structure where corpses are buried or stored. See *morning breath*.' I guess that we check 'fact' on that one."

"Can I brush my teeth now?"

"Sure. Are you going to shower?"

"I'd like to. Why?"

"Can I help? I mean, you're much more attractive when you're not room temperature."

She smiled. "You really know how to charm a girl." She got out of bed and went into the bathroom. Tommy waited on the bed.

"Well, come on," she said as she turned on the water.

"Sorry," he said, leaping to his feet and wrestling out of his shirt.

She stopped him at the bathroom door with a firm hand on the chest. "One second, mister. I have a question for you."

"Shoot."

"Men are pigs: fact or fiction?"

"Fact!" Tommy shouted.

"Correct! You win!" She leaped into his arms and kissed him.

CHAPTER 17

This Month's Makeover: The Faces of Fear

Simon McQueen had once climbed onto the back of a ton of pissed-off beef named Muffin and been promptly stomped into mush in front of an amazed rodeo crowd, and still managed to pinch the bottom of a female paramedic as he was carried away on a stretcher, singing a garbled version of "I've Got Friends in Low Places." Simon McQueen had once picked a fight with a gang of skinheads and managed to render three of them unconscious before a knife in the stomach and a jackboot to the head rendered him helpless. Simon had jumped out of an airplane, fallen off the roof of a Lutheran church, run over a police car in his pickup truck, smuggled a thousand pounds of marijuana across the border from Mexico inside a stuffed cow, and swum halfway to Alcatraz Island on a dare before the Coast Guard fished him out of the bay and revived him. Simon had done all these things without the slightest tic of fear. But tonight, laid out across register 3 in his skintight Wranglers and his endangered-species Tony Lama boots with the silver spurs, his black Stetson pulled down over his face, Simon McQueen was frightened.

Frightened that one of his two great secrets was about to become known.

The other Animals were sharing tales of their weekend adventures, exaggerating aspects of binges and babes, while Clint professed to God that they knew not what they did.

Simon sat up, pushed back his Stetson, and said, "Y'all wouldn't know a piece of ass if it sloshed upside your head."

The Animals fell silent, each trying to formulate a new and exciting way to tell Simon to fuck off, when Tommy came through the door.

"Fearless Leader!" Lash exclaimed.

Tommy grinned and faked a tap-dance step. "Gentlemen," he said. "I have reached out and touched the face of God—film at eleven."

Simon was wildly irritated by this added distraction from his worrying. "What happened, you go down to Castro Street and get converted?"

Tommy waved the comment away. "No, Sime—I can call you Sime, can't I? You see, last night, about this time"—he checked his watch—"there was a naked redhead hanging from the ceiling of my new loft, reading Kerouac aloud to me. If I die now, it was not all in vain. I'm ready to throw stock. How's the truck?"

"A big one," Troy Lee answered. "Three thousand cases. But the bitch is, the scanner is broken. We have to use the order books."

Troy's comment jabbed Simon like bad gas pain. He considered going home sick, but without his help the Animals would never be able to finish the truck before morning. A lump of fear rose in his throat. He couldn't use the order books. Simon McQueen couldn't read.

"Let's get to it then," Tommy said.

The Animals threw themselves into their work with an abandon they usually reserved for partying. Razor box-cutters whizzed, price guns clicked, and cardboard piled up in shoulder-high drifts at the ends of the aisles.

In addition to throwing the extra-large load, they had to allow an extra hour to write their stock orders. Normally the orders were done with a bar-code scanner, but with the scanner down, each man would have to go through a huge loose-leaf order book, writing in items by hand. By 5 A.M. they had most of the stock on the shelves and Simon McQueen was considering letting his box-cutter slip and cutting his leg so he could escape to the emergency room. But that might reveal a secret worse than illiteracy.

Tommy came into Simon's aisle carrying the order book. "You better get started, Sime." He held out the book and a pencil.

"I still got a hundred cases to throw," Simon said, not looking up. "Let someone else start."

"No, you've got the biggest section. Go ahead." Tommy bumped Simon on the shoulder with the book.

Simon looked up, then dropped his cutter and slowly took the book from Tommy. He opened the book and stared at the page, then at the shelf, then at the book.

Tommy said, "Order light on the juices, we've got a lot of stock in the back room."

Simon nodded and looked at the book, then at the shelf of vegetables before him.

Tommy said, "You're on the wrong page, Simon."

"I know," Simon snapped. "I'm just finding my place." He flipped through the pages, then stopped on a page of cake mixes and began looking at the shelf of vegetables. He could feel Tommy's gaze on him and wished that the skinny-little-faggot-book-reading-prick-bastard would just go away and leave him alone.

"Simon."

Simon looked up, his eyes pleading.

"Give me the book," Tommy said. "I think I'm going to order everybody's section tonight. It'll give you guys more time to throw stock and I need to get more familiar with the store anyway."

"I can do it," Simon said.

"I know," Tommy said, taking the book. "But why waste your talent on this bullshit?"

As Tommy walked away, Simon took his first deep breath of the night. "Flood," he called, "I'm buying the beers after shift."

Tommy didn't look back. "I know," he said.

Jody stood by the window in the dark loft watching the sleeping bum who lay on the sidewalk across the street and cursing under her breath. Go away, you bastard, she thought. Even as she thought it, she felt a measure of security in knowing exactly where her enemy was. As long as he lay on the sidewalk, Tommy was safe at the grocery store.

She had never felt the need to protect someone before. She had always been the one looking for protection, for a strong arm to lean on. Now she was the strong arm, at least when the sun was down. She had walked Tommy down the steps and waited with him until the cab arrived to take him to work. As she watched the cab pull away, she thought, This must be how my mother felt when she put me on the school bus that first time—except that Tommy doesn't have a Barbie lunch box. She kept an eye on the vampire lying on the sidewalk across the street.

Hours passed at the window and she asked the same questions over and over again, coming up with no solution to her problem, and no logic to the vampire's behavior. What did he want? Why had he killed the old woman and left her in the dumpster? Was he trying to frighten her, threaten her, or was there some kind of message to it all?

"You're not immortal. You can still be killed."

If he was going to kill her, why didn't he just do it? Why pretend to be a sleeping bum, watching her, waiting?

He has to find shelter before daylight. If I can just outlast him, maybe . . . Maybe what? I can't follow him or I'll be caught in the sunlight too.

She went to the bedroom and dug the almanac Tommy had given her out of her backpack. The sun would rise at 6:12 A.M. She checked her watch. She had an hour.

She waited at the window until six o'clock, then headed out of the loft to confront the vampire. As she went through the door she instinctively reached out to click off the lights, only to realize that she hadn't turned any on. If I live through this, she thought, I'm going to save a fortune on utilities.

She left the door at the top of the stairs unlocked, then went down the steps and propped the big fire door open with a soda can she found on the landing. She might have to get back in fast, and she didn't want to be slowed down by keys and locks.

Her muscles buzzed as she approached the vampire, the fight-or-flee instinct running through her like liquid lightning. A few feet away she picked up a foul smell, a rotting smell coming from the vampire. She stopped and swallowed hard.

"What exactly is it that you want?" she asked.

The vampire didn't move. His face was covered by the high collar of his overcoat.

She took another step forward. "What am I supposed to be doing?"

The smell was stronger now. She concentrated on the vampire's hands, trying to sense some movement that would warn her of an attack. There was none.

"Answer me!" she demanded. She stepped up and pulled the collar away from his face. She saw the glazed eyes and a bone jutting from the neck just as a hand clamped across her face and jerked her back off her feet.

She tried to reach behind her to claw her attacker's face but he jerked her to the side. She opened her mouth to scream and two of his fingers slipped into her mouth. She bit down hard. There was a scream and she was free.

She wheeled on her attacker, ready to fight, his severed fingers still in her mouth.

The vampire stood before her, cradling his bloody hand.

"Bitch," he said. Then he grinned.

Jody swallowed his fingers and hissed at him. "Fuck you, ass-hole. Come on." She fell into a crouch and waved him on.

The vampire was still grinning. "The taste of vampire blood has made you brave, fledgling. Don't take it too far."

His hand had stopped spurting blood and was scabbing over as she watched. "What do you want?"

The vampire looked at the sky, which was turning pink, threatening dawn.

"Right now I want to find a place to sleep," he said too calmly. He ripped the scab from his fingers and slung a spray of blood in her face. "Until we meet again, my love." He wheeled and ran across the street into an alley.

Jody stood watching and shaking with the need for a fight. She turned and looked at the dead bum: the decoy. She couldn't leave him here to attract police—not this close to the loft.

She glanced at the lightening sky, then hoisted the dead bum onto her back and headed back to the loft.

Tommy ran up the stairs and burst into the loft eager to share his discovery about Simon's illiteracy, but once through the door, he was knocked back by a stinging rotten odor like bloated roadkill.

What's she done now? he thought.

He opened the windows to air the place out and went to the bedroom, careful to open the door just wide enough to slip through without spilling sunlight on the bed. The smell was much stronger here and he gagged as he turned on the light.

Jody was lying on the bed with the electric blanket pulled up to her neck. Dried blood was crusted over her face. A wiggling wave of the willies ran up Tommy's spine, stronger than any he had felt since his father had first told him the secret of ball-park hot dogs. ("Snouts and butt holes," Dad had said, during the seventh-inning stretch. "I've got the willies," said Tommy.)

There was a note on the pillow by Jody's head. Tommy crept forward and snatched it off the pillow, then backpedaled to the door to read it.

Tommy,

Sorry I'm such a mess. It's almost dawn and I don't want to get stuck in the shower. I'll explain tonight.

Call Sears and have them deliver the largest chest freezer that they have. There's money in my backpack.
I missed you last night.

Love,
Jody

Tommy backed out of the room.

CHAPTER 18
Bugeater of the Barbary Coast

Tommy woke up on the futon feeling as if he had been through a two-day battle. The loft was dark but for the streetlights spilling through the windows and he could hear Jody running the shower in the other room. The new freezer was humming away in the kitchen. He rolled off the futon and groaned. His muscles creaked like rusty hinges and his head felt as if it were stuffed with cotton—like a low-grade hangover—not from the few beers he had shared with the Animals after work, but from the verbal beating he had taken from the appliance salesman at Sears.

The salesman, a round hypertensive named Lloyd, who wore the last extant leisure suit on the planet (powder blue with navy piping), had begun his assault with a five-minute lament on the disappearance of double knits (as if a concerted effort by a Greenpeace team in white vinyl shoes and gold chains might bring double knits back from the brink of extinction), then segued into a half-hour lecture on the tragedies visited on those poor souls who failed to purchase extended warranties on their Kenmore Freezemasters. "And so," Lloyd concluded, "he not only lost his job, his home, and his family, but that frozen food that could have saved the children at the orphanage spoiled, all because he tried to save eighty-seven dollars."

"I'll take it," Tommy said. "I'll take the longest warranty you have."

Lloyd laid a fatherly hand on Tommy's shoulder. "You won't regret this, son. I'm not one for high pressure myself, but the guys that sell these warranties after delivery are like the Mafia—they'll call you at all hours, they'll hound you, they'll find you wherever you go and they will ruin your life if you don't give in. I once sold a microwave to a man who woke up with a horse's head in his bed."

"Please," Tommy begged, "I'll sign anything, but they have to deliver it right now. Okay?"

Lloyd pumped Tommy's hand to start the flow of cash. "Welcome to better living through frozen food."

Tommy sat up on the futon and looked at the behemoth freezer that was humming in the half-light of the kitchen. Why? he thought. Why did I buy it? Why did she want it? I didn't even ask for an explanation from her, I just blindly followed her instructions. I'm a slave, like Renfield in *Dracula*. How long before I start eating bugs and howling at night?

He got up and walked, in his underwear and one sock, into the bedroom; the smell of decay was strong enough to make him gag. It was the smell that had driven him to sleep on the futon in the living room rather than crawl into bed with Jody. He'd fallen asleep reading Bram Stoker's *Dracula* to get some perspective on the love of his life.

She's the devil, he thought, staring at the steam creeping out from under the bathroom door. "Jody, is that you?" he asked the steam. The steam just crept.

"I'm in the shower," Jody said from the shower. "Come on in."

Tommy went to the bathroom and opened the door. "Jody, we need to talk." The bathroom was thick with steam—he could barely make out the shower doors.

"Close the door; it smells in there."

Tommy moved closer to the shower. "I'm worried about the way things are going," he said.

"Did you get the freezer?"

"Yes, that's part of what I wanted to talk to you about."

"You got the biggest one they had, right?"

"Yes, and a ten-year extended-service agreement."

"And it's a chest model, not an upright?"

"Yes, dammit, but Jody, you didn't even tell me why I was buying it and I just did it. Since I met you, it's like I have no will of my own. I've been sleeping all day. I'm not doing any writing. I hardly even see daylight anymore."

"Tommy, you work midnight to eight. When do you think you would sleep?"

"Don't twist my words. I will not eat bugs for you." She's the devil, he thought.

"Will you do my back?" She slid the shower door open and Tommy was transfixed by the water cascading between her breasts. "Well?" she said, cocking a hip.

Tommy slipped out of his briefs, pulled off his sock, and stepped into the shower. "Okay, but I'm not eating any bugs."

After a mad naked dash through the bedroom they sat on the futon toweling off and looking at the new freezer.

"It certainly is large," Jody said.

"I bought a dozen TV dinners so it wouldn't look so empty."

Jody said, "You'll have to take them out; put them in the regular fridge."

"Why? I don't think they'll fit."

"I know, but I have something to put in there and I don't think you'll want your TV dinners in there with it."

"What?"

"Well, you know that bad smell in the bedroom?"

"I was going to mention that. What is it?"

"It's a body."

"You killed someone?" Tommy slid away from her on the futon.

"No, I didn't kill anyone. Let me explain."

She told him about the bum, about creeping up on him thinking he was the vampire, and of the battle that ensued.

Tommy said, "Do you think he was trying to kill you?"

"I don't think so. It's as if he wants to show me how superior he is or something. Like he's testing me."

"So you bit off his fingers?"

"I didn't know what else to do."

"What was it like?"

"Honestly?"

"Of course?"

"It was a rush. It was an incredible rush."

"Better than drinking my blood?"

"Different."

Tommy turned his back on her and began to pout. Jody moved to him and kissed his ear.

"It was a fight, Tommy. I didn't come or anything, but I swear, I felt stronger after I . . . after I swallowed."

"So that's why you were all crusty with blood when I got home?"

"Yes, it was almost dawn when I got the body upstairs."

"That's another thing," Tommy said. "Why did you bring that stinky thing up here?"

"The police already found one body at the motel, and they have my name. Now they find another that was killed in the same way right next to where we live. I don't think they'd understand."

"So we're going to keep it in the freezer?"

"Just until I figure out what to do with him."

"I'm not comfortable with you calling it 'him.'"

"Just until I figure out what to do with *it,* then."

"There's a big bay out there."

"And how would you suggest that we get it down there without being seen?"

"I'll think about it."

Jody stood, wrapped a towel around herself, and walked back to the bedroom. "I'm going to put it in now; you might want to transfer your TV dinners." She paused at the door. "And I'm out of clean clothes. You're going to need to go to the Laundromat."

"Why don't you go?"

Jody regarded him gravely. "Tommy, you know I can't go out during the day."

"Oh no," Tommy said. "Don't pull that. I don't know of a single Laundromat that's not open all night. Besides, I can't be your slave full-time. I have to have some time to get some writing done. And I might be taking on a student."

"What kind of student?"

"A guy at work—Simon—he can't read. I'm going to offer to teach him."

"That's sweet of you," Jody said. She shook her hair out, let her towel fall to the floor, and struck a centerfold pose. "Are you sure you don't want to do the laundry?"

"No way. You have no power over me."

"Are you sure?" She licked her lips sensually. "That's not what you said in the shower."

I will resist her evil, Tommy thought. I will not give in. He stood and started gathering his clothes. "Don't you have a body to move?"

"All right then," Jody snapped. "I'll do the laundry while you're at work tonight." She turned and went into the bedroom.

"Good. I'll be out here looking for some tasty bugs," Tommy whispered to himself.

Midnight found Jody trudging down the steps with a trash bag full of laundry slung across her back. As she stepped onto the sidewalk and turned to lock the door she realized that she hadn't the slightest idea where to find a Laundromat in this neighborhood. The rolling steel door to the foundry was open and the two burly sculptors were working inside, bracing a man-sized plaster mold for pouring. She considered asking them for directions, but thought it might be better to wait and meet them when she was with Tommy. The interior of the foundry was glowing red with the heat from the molten bronze in the crucible, making it appear to her heat-sensitive vision like hell's own studio.

She stood for a moment watching waves of heat spill out the

top of the door, to swirl and dissipate in the night sky like dying paisley ghosts. She wanted to turn to someone and share the experience, but of course there was no one, and if there had been, they wouldn't have been able to see what she saw.

She thought, In the kingdom of the blind, a one-eyed man can get pretty lonely.

She sighed heavily and was starting toward Market Street when she heard a sharp staccato tapping of toenails at her heels. She dropped the laundry and wheeled around. A Boston terrier growled and snorted at her, then backed away a few feet and fell into a yapping fit that bordered on canine apoplexy, his bug eyes threatening to pop out of his head.

"Bummer, stop that!" came a shout from the corner.

Jody looked up to see a grizzled old man in an overcoat coming toward her wearing a saucepan on his head and carrying a wickedly pointed wooden sword. A golden retriever trotted along beside him, a smaller saucepan strapped to his head and two garbage-can lids strapped to his sides, giving the impression of a compact furry Viking ship.

"Bummer, come back here."

The little dog backed away a few more steps, then turned and ran back to the man. Jody noticed that the little dog had a miniature pie pan strapped over his ears with a rubber band.

The old man picked up the terrier in his free hand and trotted up to Jody. "I'm very sorry," he said. "The troops are girded for battle, but I fear they are a bit too eager to engage. Are you all right?"

Jody smiled. "I'm fine. Just a little startled."

The old man bowed. "Allow me to introduce myself . . ."

"You're the Emperor, aren't you?" Jody had been in the City for five years. She'd heard about the Emperor, but she'd only seen him from a distance.

"At your service," said the Emperor. The terrier growled suspiciously and the Emperor shoved the little dog, head first, into the oversized pocket of his overcoat, then buttoned the flap. Muffled growls emanated from the pocket.

"I apologize for my charge. He's long on courage, but rather short on manners. This is Lazarus."

Jody nodded to the retriever, who let out a slight growl and backed away a step. The garbage-can lids rattled on the sidewalk.

"Hi. I'm Jody. Pleased to meet you."

"I hope you will forgive my presumption," the Emperor said, "but I don't think it's safe for a young woman to be out on the street at night. Particularly in this neighborhood."

"Why this neighborhood?"

The Emperor moved closer and whispered. "I'm sure that you've noticed that the men and I are dressed for battle. We are hunting a vicious, murdering fiend that has been stalking the City. I don't mean to alarm you, but we last saw him on this very street. In fact, he killed a friend of mine right across the street not two nights ago."

"You saw him?" Jody asked. "Did you call the police?"

"The police will be of no help," the Emperor said. "This is not the run-of-the-mill scoundrel that we are used to in the City. He's a vampire." The Emperor lifted his wooden sword and tested the point against the tip of his finger.

Jody was shaken. She tried to calm herself, but the fear showed on her face.

"I've frightened you," the Emperor said.

"No—no, I'm fine. It's just . . . Your Majesty, there are no such things as vampires."

"As you wish," the Emperor said. "But I think it would be prudent for you to wait until daylight to do your business."

"I need to do my laundry or I won't have any clean clothes for tomorrow."

"Then allow us to escort you."

"No, really, Your Majesty, I'll be fine. By the way, where is the nearest Laundromat?"

"There is one not far from here, but it's in the Tenderloin. Even during the day you wouldn't be safe alone. I really must insist that you wait, my dear. Perhaps by then we will have exterminated the fiend."

"Well," Jody said, "if you insist. This is my apartment, right here." She dug the key out of her jeans and opened the door. She turned back to the Emperor. "Thank you."

"Safety first," the Emperor said. "Sleep well." The little dog growled in his pocket.

Jody went inside and closed the door, then waited until she heard the Emperor walk away. She waited another five minutes and went back onto the street.

She shouldered the laundry and headed toward the Tenderloin, thinking, This is great. How long before the police actually listen to the Emperor? Tommy and I are going to have to move and we haven't even decorated yet. And I hate doing laundry. I hate it. I'm sending our laundry out if Tommy won't do it. And we're going to have a cleaning lady—some nice, dependable woman who will come in after dark. And I'm not buying toilet paper. I don't use it and I'm not going to buy it. And something has to be done about this asshole vampire. God, I hate doing laundry.

She had gone two blocks when a man stepped out of a doorway in front of her. "Hey momma, you need some help."

She jumped in his face and shouted, "Fuck off, horndog!" with such viciousness that he screamed and leaped back into the doorway, then meekly called "Sorry" after her as she passed.

She thought, I'm not sorting. It all goes in warm. I don't care if the whites do go gray; I'm not sorting. And how do I know how to get out bloodstains? Who am I? Miss Household Hints? God, I hate laundry.

The clothes jumped and played and dived over each other like fabric dolphins. Jody sat on a folding table across from the dryer watching the show and thinking about the Emperor's warning. He'd said, "I don't think it's safe for a young woman to be out on the street at night." Jody agreed. Not long ago she would have been terrified if she'd found herself in the Tenderloin at night. She couldn't even remember coming down here during the day. Where had that fear gone? What had happened to her that she could face off with a vampire, bite off his fingers, and carry a dead body up a flight of stairs and shove it under the bed without even a flinch? Where was the fear and loathing? She didn't miss it, she just wondered what had happened to it.

It wasn't as if she were without fear. She was afraid of daylight, afraid of the police discovering her, and of Tommy rejecting her and leaving her alone. New fears and familiar fears, but there was nothing in the dark that frightened her, not the future, not even the old vampire—and she knew now, having tasted his blood, that he was old, very old. She saw him as an enemy, and her mind casted for strategies to defeat him, but she was not really afraid of him anymore: curious, but not afraid.

The dryer stopped—fabric dolphins dropped and died as if caught in tuna nets. Jody jumped off the table, opened the dryer, and was feeling the clothes for dampness when she heard footsteps on the sidewalk outside the Laundromat. She turned to see the tall black man she had chased into the doorway coming into the Laundromat, followed by two shorter men. All three wore silver L.A. Raiders jackets, high-top shoes, and evil grins.

Jody turned back to the dryer and started stuffing her clothes into the trash bag. She thought, I should be folding these.

"Yo, bitch," the tall man said.

Jody looked to the back of the Laundromat. The only door was in the front, behind the three men. She turned and looked up at them. "How about those Raiders?" she said with a smile. She felt a pressure in the roof of her mouth: the fangs extending.

The three men split up and moved around the folding table to surround her. In another life, this had been her worst nightmare. In this life she just smiled as two of them grabbed her arms from behind.

She saw a bead of sweat on the tall man's temple as he approached her and reached out to tear the front of her shirt. She ripped her right arm loose and caught the tall man's wrist as the sweat bead began to drip. She snapped his forearm and bones splintered though skin and muscle as she swung him, headfirst, through the glass door of the dryer. She reached over her shoulder and grabbed one of the Raider fans by the hair and smashed his face into the floor, then wheeled on her last attacker and shoved him back into the edge of the folding table, snapping his spine just above the hips and sending him spinning backward over a deck of washing machines. The bead of sweat hit the floor near the man with the smashed face.

Amid the hum of fluorescent lights and the moans of the man with the broken back, Jody loaded the rest of her laundry into the trash bag. She thought, This stuff is going to be nothing but wrinkles by the time I get home. Tommy's doing the laundry next time.

As she reached the door she ran her tongue over her teeth and was relieved to find her fangs had retracted. She looked over her shoulder at the carnage and shouted, "Forty-fucking-Niners!" The man with the broken back moaned.

CHAPTER 19
Jody's Delicate Condition

For the first few weeks Tommy was uncomfortable having a dead guy in the freezer, but after a while the dead guy became a fixture, a familiar frosty face with every TV dinner. Tommy named him Peary after another arctic explorer.

During the day, after he came home from work and before he crawled into bed with Jody, Tommy puttered around the loft talking first to himself, then, when he became comfortable with the idea, to Peary.

"You know, Peary," Tommy said one morning after he had pounded out two pages of a short story on his typewriter, "I am having a little trouble finding my voice in this story. When I write about the little farm girl in Georgia walking barefoot to school on the dirt road, I sound like Harper Lee, but when I write about her poor father, unjustly sentenced to a chain gang for stealing bread for his family, I start to sound a little like Mark Twain. But when the little girl grows up to become a Mafia don, I'm falling into more of a Sydney Collins Krantz style. What should I do?"

Peary, safe with his lid closed and his light off, did not answer.

"And how am I supposed to concentrate on literature when I'm reading all these vampire books for Jody? She doesn't understand that a writer is a special creature—that I'm different from everyone else. I'm not saying I'm superior to other people, just more sensitive, I guess. And did you notice that she never does any of the shopping? What does she do all night while I'm at work?"

Tommy was making an effort to understand Jody's situation, and had even devised a series of experiments from his reading to try and discover the limitations of her new situation. In the evening when they woke, after they shared a shower and a tumble or two, the scientific process would begin.

"Go ahead, honey, give it a try," Tommy said, shortly after he'd read *Dracula*.

"I am trying," Jody said. "I don't know what I'm supposed to try to do."

"Concentrate," Tommy said. "Push."

"What do you mean, push? I'm not giving birth, Tommy. What am I supposed to push on?"

"Try to grow fur. Try to make your arms change into wings."

Jody closed her eyes and concentrated—strained, even—and Tommy thought a little color came into her face.

Finally she said, "This is ridiculous." And it was determined that Jody could not turn into a bat.

"Mist," Tommy said. "Try to turn into mist. If you forget your key sometime, you can just ooze under the door to get in."

"It's not working."

"Keep trying. You know how your hair gathers in the shower drain? Well, if it gets clogged, you can just flow down there and dig out the clog."

"There's some motivation."

"Give it a try."

She tried and failed and the next day Tommy brought some Drano home from the store instead.

"But I could take you to the park and throw a Frisbee for you."

"I know, but I can't."

"I'll buy you all kinds of chew toys—a squeaky duck if you want."

"I'm sorry, Tommy, but I can't turn into a wolf."

• • •

"In the book, Dracula climbs down the castle wall face down."

"Good for him."

"You could try it on our building. It's only three stories."

"That's still a long way to fall."

"You won't fall. He doesn't fall in the book."

"And he levitates in the book, doesn't he?"

"Yeah."

"And we tried that, didn't we?"

"Well, yeah."

"Then I'd say that the book is fiction, wouldn't you?"

"Let's try something else; I'll get the list."

"Mind reading. Project your thoughts into my mind."

"Okay, I'm projecting. What am I thinking?"

"I can tell by the look on your face."

"You might be wrong, what am I thinking?"

"You'd like me to stop badgering you with these experiments."

"And?"

"You want me to take our clothes to the Laundromat."

"And?"

"That's all I'm getting."

"I want you to stop rubbing garlic on me while I'm sleeping."

"You can read thoughts!"

"No, Tommy, but I woke up this evening smelling like a pizza joint. Stop it with the garlic."

"So you don't know about the crucifix?"

"You touched me with a crucifix?"

"You weren't in any danger. I had a fire extinguisher right there in case you burst into flames."

"I don't think it's very nice of you to experiment on me while I'm sleeping. How would you feel if I rubbed stuff on you while you were sleeping?"

"Well, it depends. What are we talking about?"

"Just don't touch me while I'm sleeping, okay? A relationship is based on mutual trust and respect."

"So I guess the mallet and the stake are out of the question?"

"Tommy!"

"Kmart had a sale on mallets. You were wondering if you were immortal. I wasn't going to try it without asking you."

"How long do you think it will take for you to forget what sex feels like?"

"I'm sorry, Jody. Really, I am."

The question of immortality did, indeed, bother Jody. The old vampire had said that she could be killed, but it was not the sort of thing that you could easily test. It was Tommy, of course, after a long talk with Peary while trying to avoid working on his little Southern-girl story one morning, who came up with the test.

Jody awoke one evening to find him in the bathroom emptying ice cubes out of a tray into the big claw-foot tub.

He said, "I was a lifeguard one summer in high school."

"So?"

"I had to learn CPR. I spent half the summer pumping pissy pool water out of exhausted nine-year-olds."

"So?"

"Drowning."

"Drowning?"

"Yeah, we drown you. If you're immortal, you'll be fine. If not, the cold water will keep you fresh and I can revive you. There's about thirty more trays of ice stacked up on Peary. Could you grab some?"

"Tommy, I'm not sure about this."

"You want to know, don't you?"

"But a tub of ice water?"

"I've run all the possibilities down—guns, knives, an injection of potassium nitrate—this is the only one that can fail and not really kill you. I know you want to know, but I don't want to lose you to find out."

Jody, in spite of herself, was touched. "That's the sweetest thing anyone ever said to me."

"Well, you wouldn't want to kill me, would you?" Tommy was a little concerned about the fact that Jody had been feeding on him every four days. Not that he felt sick or weak; on the contrary, he found that each time she bit him he was energized, stronger, it seemed. He was throwing twice as much stock at the store and his mind seemed sharper, more alert. He was making good progress on his story. He was starting to look forward to being bitten.

"Come on then," he said. "In the tub."

Jody was wearing a silk nighty that she let drop to the floor. "You're sure if this doesn't work . . ."

"You'll be fine."

She took his hand. "I'm trusting you."

"I know. Get in."

Jody stepped into the cold water. "Brisk," she said.

"I didn't think you could feel it."

"I can feel temperature changes, but they don't bother me."

"We'll experiment on that next. Under you go."

Jody lay down in the tub, her hair spread across the water like crimson kelp.

Tommy checked his watch. "After you go under, don't hold your breath. It's going to be hard, but suck the water into your lungs. I'll leave you under for four minutes, then pull you out."

Jody took deep breaths and looked at him, a glint of panic in her eyes. He bent and kissed her. "I love you," he said.

"You do?"

"Of course." He pushed her head under the water.

She bobbed back up. "Me too," she said. Then she went under.

She tried to make herself take in the water but her lungs wouldn't let her and she held her breath. Four minutes later Tommy reached under her arms and pulled her up.

"I didn't do it," she said.

"Christ, Jody, I can't keep doing this."

"I held my breath."

"For four minutes?"

"I think I could have gone hours."

"Try again. You've got to inhale the water or you'll never die."

"Thanks, coach."

"Please."

She slipped under the water and sucked in a breath of water before she could think about it. She listened to the ice cubes tinkling on the surface, watched the bathroom light refracting through the water, occasionally interrupted by Tommy's face as he looked down on her. There was no panic, no choking—she didn't even feel the claustrophobia that she had expected. Actually, it was kind of pleasant.

Tommy pulled her up and she expelled a great cough of water, then began breathing normally.

"Are you okay?"

"Fine."

"You really did drown."

"It wasn't that bad."

"Try it again."

This time Tommy left her under for ten minutes before pulling her up.

After the cough, she said, "I guess that's it."

"Did you see the long tunnel with the light at the end? All your dead relatives waiting? The fiery gates of hell?"

"Nope, just ice cubes."

Tommy turned around and sat down hard on the bathroom rug with his back to the tub. "I feel like I was the one that got drowned."

"I feel great."

"That's it, you know. You are immortal."

"I guess so. As far as we can test it. Can I get out of the tub now?"

"Sure." He handed her a towel over his shoulder. "Jody, are you going to leave me when I get old?"

"You're nineteen years old."

"Yeah, but next year I'll be twenty, then twenty-one; then I'll be eating strained green beans and drooling all over myself and asking you what your name is every five seconds and you'll be twenty-six and perky and you'll resent me every time you have to change my incontinence pants."

"That's a cheery thought."

"Well, you will resent it, won't you?"

"Aren't you jumping the gun a little? You have great bladder control; I've seen you drink six beers without going to the bathroom."

"Sure, now, but . . ."

"Look, Tommy, could you look at this from my point of view? This is the first time I've had to really think about this as well. Do you realize that I'll never have blue hair and walk with tiny little steps? I'll never drive really slow all the time and spend hours complaining about my ailments. I'll never go to Denny's and steal all the extra jelly packets and squirrel them away in a giant handbag."

Tommy looked up at her. "You were looking forward to those things?"

"That's not the point, Tommy. I might be immortal, but I've lost a big part of my life. Like French fries. I miss eating French fries. I'm Irish, you know. Ever since the Great Potato Famine my people get nervous if they don't eat French fries every few days. Did you ever think about that?"

"No, I guess I didn't."

"I don't even know what I am. I don't know why I'm here. I was made by some mystery creature and I don't have the slightest idea why, or what he wants from me, or what I am supposed to be doing. Only that he's messing with my life in ways I can't understand. Do you have any idea what that is like?"

"Actually, I know exactly what that's like."

"You do?"

"Of course, everybody does. By the way, the Emperor told me that they found another body today. In a Laundromat in the Tenderloin. Broken neck and no blood."

CHAPTER 20
Angel

If Inspector Alphonse Rivera had been a bird, he would have been a crow. He was lean and dark, with slick, sharp features and black eyes that shone and shifted with suspicion and guile. Time and again his crowlike looks landed him in the undercover role of coke dealer. Sometimes Cuban, sometimes Mexican, and one time Colombian, he had driven more Mercedes and worn more Armani suits than most real drug dealers, but after twenty years in narcotics, on three different departments, he had transferred to homicide, claiming that he needed to work among a better class of people—namely, dead.

Oh, the joys of homicide! Simple crimes of passion, most solved within twenty-four hours or not at all. No stings, no suitcases of government money, no pretense, just simple deduction—sometimes very simple: a dead wife in the kitchen; a drunken husband standing in the foyer with a smoking thirty-eight; and Rivera, in his cheap Italian knock-off suit, gently disarming the new widower, who could only say, "Liver and onions." A body, a suspect, a weapon, and a motive: case solved and on to the next one, neat and tidy. Until now.

Rivera thought, If my luck could be bottled, it would be classified a chemical weapon. He read through the coroner's report again. "Cause of death: compression fracture of the fifth and sixth vertebrae (broken neck). Subject had lost massive amounts of blood—no visible wounds." On its own, it was a uniquely enigmatic report, but it wasn't on its own. It was the second body in a month that had sustained massive blood loss with no visible wounds.

Rivera looked across the desk to where his partner, Nick Cavuto, was reading a copy of the report.

"What do you think?" Rivera said.

Cavuto chewed on an unlit cigar. He was a burly and balding, gravel-voiced, third-generation cop—six degrees tougher than his father and grandfather had been because he was gay. He said, "I think if you have any vacation time coming, this would be the time to take it."

"So we're fucked."

"It's too early for us to be fucked. I'd say we've been taken to dinner and slipped the tongue on the good-night kiss."

Rivera smiled. He liked the way Cavuto tried to make everything sound like dialogue from a Bogart movie. The big detective's pride and joy was a complete set of signed first-edition Dashiell Hammett novels. "Give me the days when police work was done with a snub nose and a lead sap," Cavuto would say. "Computers are for pussies."

Rivera returned to the report. "It looks like this guy would have been dead in a month anyway: 'a ten-centimeter tumor on the liver.' Malignancy the size of a grapefruit."

Cavuto shifted the cigar to the other side of his mouth. "The old broad at the Van Ness Motel was on her way out too. Congestive heart disease. Too weak for a bypass. She ate nitro pills like they were M&M's."

"The euthanasia killer," Rivera said.

"So we're assuming this was the same guy?"

"Whatever you say, Nick."

"Two killings with the same MO and no motive. I don't even like the sound of it." Cavuto rubbed his temples as if trying to milk anxiety out through his tear ducts. "You were in San Junipero during the Night Stalker killings. We couldn't take a piss without tripping over a reporter. I say we lock this down. As far as the papers are concerned, the victims were robbed. No connection."

Rivera nodded. "I need a smoke. Let's go talk to those guys that got hit at the Laundromat a couple of weeks ago. Maybe there's a connection."

Cavuto pushed himself out of the chair and grabbed his hat off the desk. "Whoever voted for nonsmoking in the station house should be pistol-whipped."

"Didn't the President sponsor that bill?"

"All the more reason. The pussy."

Tommy lay looking at the ceiling, trying to catch his breath and extricate his right foot from a hopeless tangle in the sheets. Jody was drawing a tic-tac-toe in the sweat on his chest with her finger.

"You don't sweat anymore, do you?" he asked.

"Don't seem to."

"And you're not even out of breath. Am I doing something wrong?"

"No, it was great. I only get breathless when . . . when I . . ."

"When you bite me."

"Yeah."

"Did you . . ."

"Yes."

"Are you sure?"

"Are you?"

"No, I faked." Tommy grinned.

"Really?" Jody looked at the wet spot (on her side, of course).

"Why do you think I'm so winded? It's not easy to fake the ejaculation part."

"I, for one, was fooled."

"See."

He reached down and unwrapped the sheet from his foot, then he lay back and stared at the ceiling. Jody began to twist the sweaty locks of his hair into horns.

"Jody," Tommy said tentatively.

"Hmmm?"

"When I get old, I mean, if we're still together . . ."

She yanked on his hair.

"Ouch. Okay, we'll still be together. Have you ever heard of satyriasis?"

"No."

"Well, it happens to real old guys. They run around with a per-petual hard-on, chasing teenage girls and humping anything that moves until they have to be put in restraints."

"Wow, interesting disease."

"Yeah, well, when I get old, if I start to show the symp-toms . . ."

"Yeah?"

"Just let it run its course, okay?"

"I'll look forward to it."

Rivera held a plastic cup of orange juice for the mass of plaster and tubes that was LaOtis Small. LaOtis sipped from the straw, then pushed it away with his tongue. The body cast ran from be-low his knees to the top of his head, with holes for his face and outgoing tubes. Cavuto stood by the hospital bed taking notes.

"So you and your friends were doing laundry when an un-armed, redheaded woman attacked you and put all three of you in the hospital? Right?"

"She was a ninja, man. I know. I get the kick-boxing channel on cable."

Cavuto chomped an unlit cigar. "Your friend James says that she was six-four and weighed two hundred pounds."

"No, man, she was five-five, five-six."

"Your other buddy"—Cavuto checked his notepad for the name—"Kid Jay, said that it was a gang of Mexicans."

"No, man, he dreamin'; it was one ninja bitch."

"A five-and-a-half-foot woman put the three of you big strong guys in the hospital?"

"Yeah. We was just mindin' our own bidness. She come in and axed for some change. James tell her no, he got to put a load in the dryer, and she go fifty-one-fifty on him. She a ninja."

"Thank you, LaOtis, you've been very helpful." Cavuto shot Rivera a look and they left the hospital room.

In the hallway Rivera said, "So we're looking for a gang of red-headed, ninja Mexicans."

Cavuto said, "You think there's a molecule of truth in any of that?"

"They were all unconscious when they were brought in, and obviously they haven't tried to match up their stories. So if you throw out everything that doesn't match, you end up with a woman with long red hair."

"You think a woman could do that to them and manage to snap the neck of two other people without a struggle?"

"Not a chance," Rivera said. His beeper went off and he checked the number. "I'll call in."

Cavuto pulled up. "Go ahead, I'm going back in to talk to LaOtis. Meet me outside emergency."

"Take it easy, Nick, the guy's in a body cast."

Cavuto grinned. "Kind'a erotic, ain't it?" He turned and lumbered back toward LaOtis Small's room.

Jody walked Tommy up to Market Street, watched him eat a burger and fries, and put him on the 42 bus to work. Killing the time while Tommy worked was becoming tedious. She tried to stay in the loft, watched the late-night talk shows and old movies on cable, read magazines, and did a little cleaning, but by two in the morning the caged-cat feeling came over her and she went out to wander the streets.

Sometimes she walked Market among the street people and the convention crowds, other times she took a bus to North Beach and hung out on Broadway watching the sailors and the punks stagger, drunk and stoned, or the hookers and the hustlers running their games. It was on these crowded streets that she felt most lonely. Time and again she wanted to turn to someone and point out a unique heat pattern or the dark aura she sensed around the sick; like a child sharing the cloud animals flying through a summer sky. But no one else could see what she saw, no one heard the whispered propositions, the pointed refusals, or the rustle of money exchanging hands in alleys and doorways.

Other times she crept through the back streets and listened to the symphony of noises that no one else heard, smelled the spectrum of odors that had long ago exhausted her vocabulary. Each night there were more nameless sights and smells and sounds, and they came so fast and subtle that she eventually gave up trying to name them.

She thought, This is what it is to be an animal. Just experience—direct, instant, and wordless; memory and recognition, but no words. A poet with my senses could spend a lifetime trying to describe what it is to hear a building breathe and smell the aging of concrete. And for what? Why write a song when no one can play the notes or understand the lyrics? I'm alone.

Cavuto came through the double doors of the emergency room and joined Rivera, who was standing by the brown, City-issue Ford smoking a cigarette.

"What was the call?" Cavuto asked.

"We got another one. Broken neck. South of Market. Elderly male."

"Fuck," Cavuto said, yanking open the car door. "What about blood loss?"

"They don't know yet. This one's still warm." Rivera flipped his cigarette butt into the parking lot and climbed into the car. "You get anything more out of LaOtis?"

"Nothing important. They weren't doing their laundry, they went in looking for the girl, but he's sticking with the ninja story."

River started the car and looked at Cavuto. "You didn't rough him up?"

Cavuto pulled a Cross pen out of his shirt pocket and held it up. "Mightier than the sword."

Rivera cringed at the thought of what Cavuto might have done to LaOtis with the pen. "You didn't leave any marks, did you?"

"Lots," Cavuto grinned.

"Nick, you can't do that kind of—"

"Relax," Cavuto interrupted. "I just wrote, 'Thanks for all the information; I'm sure we'll get some convictions out of this,' on his cast. Then I signed it and told him that I wouldn't scratch it out until he told me the truth."

"Did you scratch it out?"

"Nope."

"If his friends see it, they'll kill him."

"Fuck him," Cavuto said. "Ninja redheads, my ass."

Four in the morning. Jody watched neon beer signs buzzing color across the dew-damp sidewalks of Polk Street. The street was deserted, so she played sensory games to amuse herself— closing her eyes and listening to the soft scratch of her sneakers echoing off the buildings as she walked. If she concentrated, she could walk several blocks without looking, listening for the streetlight switches at the corners and feeling the subtle changes in wind currents at the cross streets. When she felt she was going to run into something, she could shuffle her feet and the sound would form a rough image in her mind of the walls and poles and wires around her. If she stood quietly, she could reach out and form a map of the whole City in her head—sounds drew the lines, and smells filled in the colors.

She was listening to the fishing boats idling at the wharf a mile away when she heard footsteps and opened her eyes. A single figure had rounded the corner a couple of blocks ahead of her and was walking, head down, up Polk. She stepped into the doorway of a closed Russian restaurant and watched him. Sadness came off him in black waves.

His name was Philip. His friends called him Philly. He was twenty-three. He had grown up in Georgia and had run away to the City when he was sixteen so he wouldn't have to pretend to be something he was not. He had run away to the City to find love. After the one-night stands with rich older men, after the bars and the bathhouses, after finding out that he wasn't a freak, that there were other people just like him, after the last of the confusion and shame had settled like red Georgia dust, he'd found love.

He'd lived with his lover in a studio in the Castro district. And in that studio, sitting on the edge of a rented hospital bed, he had filled a syringe with morphine and injected it into his lover and held his hand while he died. Later, he cleared away the bed pans and the IV stand and the machine that he used to suck the fluid out of his lover's lungs and he threw them in the trash. The doctor said to hold on to them—that he would need them.

They buried Philly's lover in the morning and they took the embroidered square of fabric that was draped on the casket and folded it and handed it to him like the flag to a war widow. He got to keep it for a while before it was added to the quilt. He had it in his pocket now.

His hair was gone from the chemotherapy. His lungs hurt, and his feet hurt; the sarcomas that spotted his body were worst on his feet and his face. His joints ached and he couldn't keep his food down, but he could still walk. So he walked.

He walked up Polk Street, head down, at four in the morning, because he could. He could still walk.

When he reached the doorway of a Russian restaurant, Jody stepped out in front of him and he stopped and looked at her.

Somewhere, way down deep, he found that there was a smile left. "Are you the Angel of Death?" he asked.

"Yes," she said.

"It's good to see you," Philly said.

She held her arms out to him.

CHAPTER 21
Angel Dust

The bed of Simon's pickup was full of beer-sodden Animals enjoying the morning fog and speculating on the marital status of the new cashier. She had smiled at Tommy when she arrived, driving the Animals into a psychosexual frenzy.

"She looked like she was being towed through the store by two submarines," said Simon.

"Major hooters," said Troy Lee. "Major-league hooters."

Tommy said, "Can't you guys see more in a woman than T and A?"

"Nope," said Troy.

"No way," said Simon.

"Spoken like a guy who has a live-in girlfriend," said Lash.

"Yeah," Simon said. "How come we never see you with the little woman?"

"Seagull!" shouted Barry.

Simon pulled a pump shotgun from under a tarp in the truck bed, tracked on a seagull that was passing over, and fired.

"Missed again!" shouted Barry.

"You can't kill them all, Simon," Tommy said, his ears ringing from the blast. "Why don't you just cover your truck at night?"

Simon said. "You don't pay for twenty coats of hand-rubbed lacquer to cover it up."

The shotgun went under the tarp and the manager came through the front doors of the store. "What was that? What was that?" He was scanning the parking lot frantically as if he expected to see someone with a shotgun.

"Backfire," Simon said.

The manager looked for the offending car.

"They were heading toward the Marina," Tommy said.

"Well, you tell me if they come back," the manager said. "There's a noise ordinance in this city, you know." He turned to go back into the store.

"Hey, boss," Simon called. "The new girl, what's her name?"

"Mara," the manager said. "And you guys leave her alone. She's had a rough time of it lately."

"She single?" Troy asked.

"Off limits," the manager said. "I mean it. She lost a child a few months ago."

"Yes, boss," the Animals said in unison. The manager entered the store.

Simon ripped a beer from a six-pack ring. He held another out to Tommy. "Fearless Leader, another brew?"

"No, I've got to get home."

"Me too," said Simon. "I've got to clean the bird shit off the beast. You need a ride?"

"Sure, can we stop in Chinatown? I want to pick something up for Jody."

Simon shook his head. "You worry me, son. Men have been pussy-whipped to death, you know." He downed his beer and crushed the can. "Out of the truck, girls; Fearless Leader and I have to shop for tampons."

"Pull!" Troy shouted.

A half dozen beer cans arced into the air. The shotgun came out and Simon pumped out two quick shots. The beer cans fell to the parking lot unharmed. The shotgun went under the tarp. The manager came through the front door.

Simon said, "I saw it, boss. Was a baby-blue '72 Nova with a stuffed gerbil on the aerial. Call it in."

• • •

Jody's hands were covered with a greasy dust: the remains of Philly. The body had decomposed to dust in seconds after she finished drinking, leaving a pile of empty clothes. After staring at the pile for a moment, she shook off the shock and gathered the clothes into a bundle, which she carried into a nearby alley.

The blood-high raced through her like an espresso firehose. She leaned against a dumpster, holding the clothes to her breast like a security blanket. The alley tilted in her vision, then righted, then spun until she thought she would be sick.

When the alley stopped moving, she fumbled through the clothing until she found a wallet. She opened it and pulled out the contents. This bundle of rags had been a person; "Phillip Burns," the license said. He carried crinkled photos of friends, a library card, a dry-cleaning receipt, a bank card, and fifty-six dollars. Phillip Burns in a convenient, portable package. She pocketed the wallet, threw the clothes into the dumpster, then wiped her hands on her jeans and stumbled out of the alley.

I killed someone, she thought. My God, I killed someone. What should I feel?

She walked for blocks, not really looking where she was going, but listening to the rhythm of her own steps under the roar of the blood-high in her head. Philly had spilled into her shoes and she stopped and sat on the curb to dump him out.

What is this? she thought. This isn't anything. This isn't what I was before I was a vampire. What *is* this? This is impossible. This isn't a person. A person can't reduce to dust in seconds. What is this?

She took off her socks and shook them out.

This is fucking magic, she thought. This isn't some story out of one of Tommy's books. This isn't something you can experiment with in the bathroom. This is not natural, and whatever I am, it isn't natural. A vampire is magic, not science. And if this is what happens when a vampire kills, then how are the police finding bodies? Why is there a guy in my freezer?

She put on her shoes and socks and resumed walking. It was starting to get light and she quickened her pace, checked her watch, then broke into a run. She'd made a habit of checking the time of sunrise every morning in the almanac so she wouldn't be caught too far from home. Five years in the City had taught her the streets, but if she was going to run she had to learn the alleys and backstreets. She couldn't let anyone see her moving this fast.

As she ran, a voice sounded in her head. It was her voice, but not her voice. It was the voice that put no words to what her senses told her, yet understood. It was the voice that told her to hide from the light, to protect herself, to fight or flee. The vampire voice.

"Killing is what you do," the vampire voice said.

The human part of her was revolted. "No! I didn't want to kill him."

"Fuck him. It is as it should be. His life is ours. It feels good, doesn't it?"

Jody stopped fighting. It did feel good. She pushed the human part of her aside and let the predator take over to race the sun for her life.

Nick Cavuto paced around the chalk outline of the body as if he were preparing to perform a violent hopscotch on the corpse. "You know," Cavuto said, looking over at Rivera, who was trying to fend off a reporter from the *Chronicle* at the yellow crime-scene tape, "this guy is pissing me off."

Rivera excused himself from the reporter and joined Cavuto by the body. "Nick, keep it down," he whispered.

"This stiff is making my life difficult," Cavuto said. "I say we shoot him and take his wallet. Simple gunshot wound, robbery motive."

"He didn't have a wallet," said Rivera.

"There you have it, robbery. Massive blood loss from gunshot wound, broke his neck when he hit the ground."

The reporter perked up. "So it was a robbery?"

Cavuto glared at the reporter and put his hand on his thirty-eight. "Rivera, what do you say to a murder-suicide? Scoop over there killed this guy, then turned the gun on himself—case closed and we can go get some breakfast."

The reporter backed away from the line.

Two coroner's assistants moved to the body, pushing a gurney with a body bag on it. "You guys done here?" one of them asked Cavuto.

"Yeah," Cavuto said. "Take him away."

The coroners spread the body bag out and hoisted the body onto it. "Hey, Inspector, you want to bag this book?"

"What book?" Rivera turned. A paperback copy of Kerouac's *On the Road* was lying in the chalk line where the body had been. Rivera slipped on a pair of white cotton gloves and pulled an evidence bag from his jacket pocket. "Here you go, Nick. The guy was a speed reader. Snapped his neck on a meaningful passage."

Jody glanced at the lightening sky, ducked down an alley, and fell into a trot. She was only a block from home, she'd make it in long before sunrise. She leaped over a dumpster, just to do it, then high-stepped through a pile of crates like a halfback through fallen defenders. She was strong in the blood-high, quick and light on her feet, her body moved, dodged, and leaped on its own—no thought, just fluid motion and perfect balance.

She'd never been athletic in life: the last kid to be picked for kickball, straight C's in phys ed, no chance as a cheerleader; the self-conscious, one-step dancer with the rhythmic sense of an in-bred Aryan. But now she reveled in the movement and the strength, even as her instincts screamed for her to hide from the light.

She heard the policemen's voices before she saw the blue and red lights from their cars playing across the walls at the end of the alley. Fear tightened her muscles and she nearly fell in mid-step.

She crept forward and saw the police cars and coroner's wagon parked in front of the loft. The street was full of milling cops and reporters. She checked her watch and backed down the alley. Five minutes to sunrise.

She looked for a place to hide. There was the dumpster, even a few large garbage cans, three steel doors with massive locks, and a basement window with steel bars. She ran to the window and tried the bars. They moved a bit. She checked her watch. Two minutes. She braced her feet against the brick wall and pulled on the bars with her legs. Rusty bolts tore out of the mortar and the bars moved another half inch. She tried to peer into the window, but the wire-reinforced glass was clouded with dirt and age. She yanked on the bars again and they screamed in protest and came loose. She dropped the grate and was drawing back to kick out the glass when she heard movement behind the window.

Oh my God, there's someone inside!

She looked around to the dumpster, some fifty feet away. She looked at her watch. If it was right, the sun was up. She was . . .

The glass shattered behind her. Two hands came through the window, grabbed her ankles, and pulled her inside as she went out.

"These here turtles are defective," Simon said.

"It's okay, Simon," said Tommy.

They were in a Chinatown fish market, where Tommy was trying to purchase two massive snapping turtles from an old Chinese man in a rubber apron and boots.

"You no know turtle!" the old man insisted. "These plime, glade-A turtle. You no know shit about turtle."

The turtles were in orange crates to immobilize them. The old man sprayed them down with a garden hose to keep them wet.

"And I'm telling you, these turtles are defective," Simon insisted. "Their eyes are all glazed over. These turtles are on drugs."

Tommy said, "Really, Simon, it's okay."

Simon turned to Tommy and whispered, "You have to bargain with these guys. They won't respect you if you don't."

"Turtle's not on dlugs," said the old man. "You want turtle, you pay forty bucks."

Simon pushed his black Stetson back on his head and sighed. "Look, Hop Sing, you can do time for selling drugged turtles in this city."

"No dlugs. Fuck you, cowboy. Forty bucks or go away."

"Twenty."

"Thirty."

"Twenty-five and you clean 'em."

"No," Tommy said. "I want them alive."

Simon looked at Tommy as if he had farted in neon. "I'm trying to negotiate here."

"Thirty," said the old man. "As is."

"Twenty-seven," Simon said.

"Twenty-eight or go home," said the old man.

Simon turned to Tommy. "Pay him."

Tommy ticked off the bills and handed them to the old man, who counted them and put them in his rubber apron. "You' cowboy friend no know turtle."

"Thanks," Tommy said. He and Simon picked up the crates with the turtles and loaded them into the bed of Simon's truck.

As they climbed into the cab, Simon said, "You got to know how to deal with those little fuckers. Ever since we nuked them, they got a bad attitude."

"We nuked the Japanese, Simon, not the Chinese."

"Whatever. You should'a made him clean them for you."

"No, I want to give them to Jody alive."

"You're a charmer, Flood. A lot of guys would've just paid the ransom with candy and flowers."

"Ransom?"

"She's got your nooky held hostage, ain't she?"

"No, I just wanted to get her a present—to be nice."

Simon sighed heavily and rubbed the bridge of his nose as if fighting a headache. "Son, we need to talk."

• • •

Simon had distinctive ideas about the way women should be handled, and as they drove to SOMA he waxed eloquent on the subject while Tommy listened, thinking, If they knew about him, Simon would be elected the *Cosmo* Nightmare Man for the next decade.

"You see," Simon said, "when I was a kid in Texas, we used to walk through the watermelon fields kickin' each of them old melons as we went until one was so ripe and ready that it busted right open. Then we'd reach in and eat the heart right out of it and move on to the next one. That's how you got to treat women, Flood."

"Like kicking watermelons?"

"Right. Now you take that new cashier. She wants you, boy. But you're thinkin', I got me a piece at home so I don't need her. Right?"

"Right," Tommy said.

"Wrong. You got one at home that you're buying presents for and saying sweet things and tiptoeing around the house so as not to upset her and generally acting like a spineless nooky slave. But if you put it to that new cashier, then you got one up on your old lady. You can do what you want, when you want, and if she gets pissy and don't put out, you go back to your cashier. Your old lady has to try harder. There's competition. It's supply and demand. God bless America, it's nooky capitalism."

"I'm lost. I thought it was like watermelon farming."

"Whatever. Point is, you're whipped, Flood. You can't have no self-respect if you're whipped. And you can't have no fun." Simon turned on Tommy's street and pulled the truck over to the curb. "Something going on here."

There were four police cars parked in the street in front of the loft and a coroner's van was pulling away.

"Wait here," Tommy said. He got out of the car and walked toward the cops. A sharp-featured Hispanic cop in a suit met Tommy in the middle of the street. His badge wallet hung open from his belt; he was holding a plastic bag. Inside it Tommy saw a dog-eared copy of *On the Road*. He recognized the coffee stains on the cover.

"This street is closed, sir," the cop said. "Crime investigation."

"But I just live right there," Tommy said, pointing to the loft.

"Really," the cop said, raising an eyebrow. "Where are you coming from?"

"The fuck's going on here, pancho?" Simon said, coming up behind Tommy. "I got a truckful of dyin' turtles and I ain't got all damn day."

"Oh Christ," Tommy said, hanging his head.

CHAPTER 22
A Nod to the Queen of the Damned

It only took five minutes to convince the police that Tommy had been at work all night and had seen nothing. Simon had done most of the talking. Tommy was so shocked to see his book in the cop's hand that he couldn't find the answers to even the simplest questions. He was, however, able to convince the cop that his shocked state came from a body having been found outside his apartment. Sometimes it paid to play on the "I just fell off the turnip truck from Indiana" image.

They hauled the turtles up the steps and set the crates on the floor in the kitchen area.

"Where's the little woman?" Simon asked, eyeing the huge chest freezer.

"Probably still sleeping," Tommy said. "Grab yourself a beer out of the fridge. I'll check on her."

Tommy palmed open the bedroom door, then slipped through and closed it behind him. He thought, I've got to keep Simon out of here. He's going to want Jody to get up and . . .

The bed was empty.

Tommy ran to the bathroom and looked in the tub, thinking

that Jody might have been caught there at sunrise, but except for a rust ring, the tub was empty. He looked under the bed, found nothing but an old sock, then tore open the closet door and pushed the hanging clothes aside. Panic rose in his throat and came out in a scream of "No!"

"You okay in there?" Simon said from the kitchen.

"She's not here!"

Simon opened the door. "You got a nice crib here, Flood. You inherit some money or something?" Simon said. Then he spotted the panic on Tommy's face. "What's the matter?"

"She's not here."

"So, she probably went out early to get a doughnut or something."

"She can't go out during the day," Tommy said before he realized what he was saying. "I mean, she never goes out early."

"Don't sweat it. I thought you were going to teach me to read. Let's drink some beers and read some fucking books, okay?"

"No, I have to go look for her. She could be out in the sun . . ."

"Chill, Flood. She's fine. The worst that could happen is she's out with another guy. You might be a free man." Simon picked up a book from the stack by the bed. "Let's read this one. What's this one?"

Tommy wasn't listening. He was seeing Jody's burned body lying in a gutter somewhere. How could she let it happen? Didn't she check the almanac? He had to look for her. But where? You can't search a city the size of San Francisco.

Simon threw the book back on the stack and headed out of the bedroom, "Okay then, Slick, I'm out of here. Thanks for the beer."

"Okay," Tommy said. Then the idea of spending the day alone, waiting, threw him into another wave of panic. "No, Simon! Wait. We'll read."

"That one on the top of the stack," Simon said. "What's that one?"

Tommy picked it up. "*The Vampire Lestat,* by Anne Rice. I hear it's good."

"Then grab a beer and let's get literate."

• • •

Rivera, bleary-eyed and looking as if he had slept in his suit, sat at his desk looking over his notes. No matter how he shuffled them, they didn't make sense, didn't show a pattern. The only link between the victims was the way they had died: no motive. They wouldn't get the autopsy report for another twelve hours, but there was no doubt that the same person had done the killings.

Nick Cavuto came through the squad room door carrying a box of doughnuts and a copy of the *San Francisco Examiner.* "They fucking named him. The *Examiner* is calling him the Whiplash Killer. Once they name the killer, our problems double. You got anything?"

Rivera waved to the notes spread over his desk and shrugged. "I'm out of it, Nick. I can't even read my own writing. You take a look."

Cavuto took a maple stick from the box and sat down across from Rivera. He grabbed a handful of papers and began leafing through them, then stopped and flipped back. He looked up. "You talked to this Flood kid this morning, right?"

Rivera was looking at the doughnuts. His stomach lurched at the thought of eating one. "Yeah, he lives across the street from where we found the body. He works at the Marina Safeway—was working at the time of the murder."

Cavuto raised an eyebrow. "The kid was staying at the motel where we found the old lady."

"You're kidding."

Cavuto held out the notes for Rivera to read. "List of guests. A uniform talked to the kid, said he was at work, but no one confirmed it."

Rivera looked up apologetically. "I can't believe I missed that. The kid was a little squirrelly when I talked to him. His friend did most of the talking."

Cavuto gathered up the papers. "Go home. Shower and sleep. I'll call the manager of the Safeway and make sure the kid was working at the time of the murders. We'll go there tonight and talk to the kid."

"Okay, then let's ask him how he's getting the blood out of the bodies."

Tommy had spent two hours trying to explain the difference between vowels and consonants to Simon before he gave up and sent the cowboy home to wax his truck and watch "Sesame Street." Maybe Simon wasn't meant to read. Maybe he was meant to be all instinct and no intelligence. In a way, Tommy admired him. Simon didn't worry, he took things at face value as they happened. Simon was like the strong, free and easy Cassady to Tommy's introspective, overanalytical Kerouac. Maybe he would put Simon in his story of the little girl growing up in the South. The story he would be working on if he weren't worrying about Jody.

He sat all day on the couch, reading *The Vampire Lestat* until he couldn't concentrate anymore, then he paced the apartment, checking his watch and railing to Peary, who listened patiently from the freezer.

"You know, Peary, it's inconsiderate of her not to leave me a note. I don't have any idea what she does while I'm at work. She could be having a dozen affairs and I wouldn't even know."

He checked the almanac eight times for the time the sun would set.

"I know, I know, until I met Jody, nothing really ever happened to me. That's why I came here, right? Okay, I'm being unfair, but maybe I'd be better off with a normal woman. Jody just doesn't understand that I'm not like other guys. That I'm special. I'm a writer. I can't handle stress as well as other guys—I take it personal."

Tommy heated up a frozen dinner and left the freezer lid open so Peary could hear him better.

"I have to look to the future, you know. When I'm a famous writer I'm going to have to go on book tours. She can't go with me. What can I say, 'No, I'm sorry, but I can't go. If I go away my wife will starve to death'?"

He paced around the turtles, who were struggling in their crates. One of them raised his spiny head and considered Tommy.

"I know how you guys feel. Just waiting for someone to eat you. You think I don't know how that feels?"

When he could no longer look them in the eye, he carried the turtles into the bathroom, then returned to the living room and tried to get through a few more chapters of *The Vampire Lestat.*

"This is wrong," he said to Peary. "It says that vampires don't have sex after they are turned. Of course it only talks about male vampires. What if she's been faking? You know, she could be frigid except for when she drinks my blood."

He was working himself into a frenzy of sexual insecurity— something that felt familiar and almost comfortable—when the phone rang. He yanked it off the cradle.

"Hello."

A woman's voice, surprised but trying to not to show it, said, "Hello. I'd like to speak to Jody, please."

"She's not here," Tommy said. "She's at work," he added quickly.

"I called her at work and they said she left her job over a month ago."

"Uh, she has a new job. I don't know the number."

"Well, whoever you are," the woman said, losing the pretense of politeness, "would you tell her that she still has a mother. And tell her that it is common courtesy to tell your mother when you change your phone number. And tell her that I need to know what she is going to do for the holidays."

"I'll tell her," Tommy said.

"Are you the stockbroker? What was it . . . Kurt?"

"No, I'm Tommy."

"Well, it's only two weeks until Christmas, Tommy, so if you're still around, we'll be meeting."

"I'll look forward to it," Tommy said. Like I look forward to a root canal, he thought.

Jody's mom hung up. Tommy put down the phone and checked his watch. Only an hour to sunset. "She's alive," he said to Peary, "I'm sure of it. If she survived her mother, she can survive anything."

She heard steam rushing through pipes, rats scurrying in shredded paper, the spinnerets of spiders weaving webs, the footsteps of a heavy man, and the padding and panting of dogs. She opened her eyes and looked around. She was on her back on the basement floor, alone. Cardboard boxes were scattered about the room. Moonlight and sounds of movement spilled through the broken window.

She got up and stepped up on a crate to look out the window. She was met by a yap and a snort and the growling countenance of a bug-eyed dog with a pan strapped to his head.

"Ack!" She wiped the slime from her cheek.

The Emperor fell to his knees and reached through the window. "Oh goodness, are you all right, dear?"

"Yes, I'm fine. I'm fine."

"Are you injured? Shall I call the police?"

"No, thank you. Could you give me a hand?" She would have leaped through the window, but it wasn't a good idea in front of the Emperor. She took his hand and let him pull her through the window.

Once on her feet in the alley, she dusted off her jeans. Bummer had fallen into a yapping fit. The Emperor picked up the little dog and stuffed him into his oversized coat pocket.

"I must apologize for Bummer's behavior. There's no excuse for it, really, but he is a victim of inbreeding. Being royalty myself, I make allowances. If it's any consolation, it was only on Bummer's insistence that we ventured down this alley and found you."

"Well, thanks," Jody said. "I don't know exactly what happened."

"Check your valuables, dear. You've obviously been accosted by some ne'er-do-well. Perhaps we should find you some medical attention."

"No, I'm just a little shaken up. I just need to get home."

"Then please allow me and my men to escort you to your door."

"No, that's okay. My loft is just at the end of the alley."

The Emperor held up his finger to caution her. "Please, my dear. Safety first."

Jody shrugged. "Well, all right. Thanks." Bummer was squirming and snorting inside the Emperor's buttoned pocket like—well, like a pocketful of dog. "Can he breathe in there?"

"Bummer will be fine. He's just a bit overexcited since we've gone to war. His first time in the field, you know."

Jody eyed the Emperor's cruelly pointed wooden sword. "How goes the battle?"

"I believe we are closing in on the forces of evil. The fiend will be vanquished and victory will soon be ours."

"That's nice," Jody said.

When Tommy heard her coming up the stairs he threw his book across the room, ran to the loft door, and yanked it open. Jody was standing on the landing.

"Hi," she said.

Tommy was torn between taking her in his arms and pushing her down the steps. He just stood there. "Hi," he said.

Jody kissed him on the cheek and walked passed him into the loft. Tommy stood there, trying to figure out how to react. "Are you okay?" Once he was sure she wasn't hurt, he'd tear into her for staying out all day.

She fell onto the futon like a bag of rags. "I had a really bad night."

"Where were you?"

"I was in a basement, about half a block from here. I would have called, but I was dead."

"That's not funny. I was worried. They found a body out front last night."

"I know, I saw the cops all over the place outside, just before dawn. That's why I couldn't get back."

"The cops had my copy of *On the Road* in an evidence bag. I think I'm in trouble."

"Was your name in it?"

"No, but obviously my fingerprints were all over it. How did it get there?"

"The vampire put it there, Tommy."

"How did he get it? It was here in the loft."

"I don't know. He's trying to freak us out. He's leaving the bodies near us so the police will connect us to the killings. He doesn't have to leave bodies at all, Tommy. He's killing these people in a way that leaves evidence."

"What do you mean, he doesn't have to leave bodies at all?"

"Tommy, come here. Sit down. I have to tell you something."

"I don't like the tone of your voice. This is bad news, isn't it? This is the big letdown, isn't it? You were with another guy last night."

"Sit down and shut up, please."

Tommy sat and she told him. Told him about the killing, about the body turning to dust, and about being dragged into the basement.

When she had finished, Tommy sat for a moment looking at her, then moved away from her on the futon. "You took the guy's money?"

"It seemed wrong to throw it away."

"And killing him didn't seem wrong?"

"No, it didn't. I can't explain it. It felt like I was supposed to."

"If you were hungry you should have told me. I don't mind, really."

"It wasn't like that, Tommy. Look, I don't know how to file this—emotionally, I mean. I don't feel like I killed someone. The point I'm trying to make is that the body crumbled to dust. There was no body. The people the vampire is killing aren't dying from his bite. He's breaking their necks before they die. He's doing all this on purpose to scare me. I'm afraid he might hurt you to get at me. I've suspected it for a long time, but I didn't want to say anything to you. If you want to leave, I'll understand."

"I didn't say anything about leaving. I don't know what to do. How would you feel if I told you *I* had killed someone?"

"It would depend. This guy wanted to die. He was in pain. He was going to die anyway."

"Do you want me to leave?"

"Of course not. But I need you to try and understand."

"I am trying. That's all I've been doing. Why do you think I've been doing all these experiments? You act like this is easy for me. I've been a mess all day worrying about you and you're in a basement a few steps away. What about that? Who dragged you into the basement?"

"I don't know."

"Whoever it was saved your life. Was it the vampire?"

"I said, I don't know."

Tommy went across the room and pick up the paperback of *The Vampire Lestat*. "This guy, Lestat, he can tell when there's another vampire around. He can sense it. Can't you sense it?"

"Right, and that's why we have a dead guy in the freezer. No, I can't sense it."

Tommy held up the book. "There's a whole history of the vampire race in here. I think this Anne Rice knows a real vampire or something."

"That's what you thought about Bram Stoker, too. And I spent an hour standing on a chair trying to turn into a bat."

"No, this is different. Lestat isn't evil, he likes humans. He only kills murderers that are without remorse. He knows when there are other vampires around. Lestat can fly."

Jody jumped up and ripped the book out of his hand. "And Anne Rice can write, Tommy, but I'm not throwing that in your face."

"You don't have to get personal."

"Look, Tommy, maybe there's some truth in one of these books that you're reading, but how do we know which one? Huh? Nobody gave me a fucking owner's manual when I got these fangs. I'm doing the best that I can."

Tommy looked away from her, then at his shoes. "You're right, I'm sorry. I'm confused and I'm a little scared. I don't know what I'm doing either. Hell, Jody, you might have AIDS now, we don't know."

"I don't have AIDS. I know I don't."

"How do you know? It's not like we can send you down to the clinic to test you or anything."

"I know it, Tommy. I could feel it if I did. Except for sunlight and food, I'm not even allergic to anything anymore. Hand lotions and soaps I couldn't get near before without breaking into a rash don't affect me. I've done a few experiments of my own. My body won't let anything hurt me. I'm safe. Besides . . ." Jody paused and grinned, waiting for him to ask.

"Besides what?"

"He was wearing a condom."

Tommy resumed staring at his shoes, said nothing, then looked up at her and laughed. "That's incredibly sick, Jody."

She nodded and laughed.

"I love you," he said, moving to her and taking her in his arms.

"Me too," she said, hugging him back.

"That's really sick, you know that?"

"Yep," she said. "Tommy, I don't want to break this beautiful moment, but I have to take a shower." She kissed him and pushed him away gently, then headed into the bathroom.

"Uh, Jody," he called after her, "I got a present for you in Chinatown today."

There's an explanation for this, she thought, standing in the bathroom, looking at the turtles. There is a perfectly good reason why there are two huge snapping turtles in my tub.

"Do you like them?" Tommy was standing in the doorway behind her.

"These are for me, then?" She tried to smile. She really did.

"Yeah, Simon helped me get them home. I didn't think I could carry them on the bus. Aren't they great?"

Jody looked in the tub again. The turtles were trying to crawl on top of each other. Their claws screeched on the porcelain when they moved.

"I don't know what to say," Jody said.

"I thought that we could feed them fish and stuff, and you'd have a blood supply right here at home. Besides me, I mean."

She turned and regarded Tommy. Yes, he was serious. He was really serious. "You haven't . . ."

"Their names are Scott and Zelda. Zelda is missing a toe on her back foot. That's how you tell them apart. Do you like them? You seem a little reticent."

A little, she thought. You couldn't have brought me flowers or jewelry, like most guys. You had to say it with reptiles. "I don't suppose there's any chance that you saved the receipt?"

Tommy's face avalanched into disappointment. "You don't like them."

"No, they're fine. But, I really wanted to take a shower. I'm not sure I want to be naked in front of them."

"Oh," Tommy said, brightening. "I'll take them into the living room."

He pulled a towel off the rod and began maneuvering over the tub, trying to get a drop on Zelda. "You have to be careful; they can take off a finger in those jaws."

"I see," Jody said. But she didn't see at all. The idea of biting one of the spiny creatures in the tub gave her an industrial-size case of the creeps.

Tommy lunged and came up with Zelda, wrapped in swaddling clothes and snapping at his face. "She hates being picked up." Zelda's claws tore at the towel and Tommy's shirt as she attempted to swim through midair. He set the turtle on her back on the bathroom floor and readied the towel to lunge into the tub for Scott. "Lestat can call animals to him when he's hungry. Maybe you can train them."

"Stop it with the Lestat stuff, Tommy. I'm not sucking turtles."

He turned to her and slipped, falling into the tub. Scott snapped, barely missing Tommy's arm, and latched on to the sleeve of his denim shirt. "I'm okay. I'm okay. He didn't get me."

Jody pulled him from the tub. Scott was still attached to his sleeve and was determined not to let go.

Turtles hate heights. They don't even like being a few feet off the ground. It's the main reason they have resisted evolution for so long—fear of heights. Turtle thinking goes thus: Sure, first our scales turn into feathers and the next thing you know we're fly-ing and chirping and perching on trees. We've seen it happen. Thanks, but we're staying right here in the mud where we be-long. You're not going to see us flying full-tilt boogie into a slid-ing glass door."

Scott was not letting go of the sleeve, not as long as Tommy was standing. "Help me," Tommy said. "Pry him off."

Jody looked for a place on the turtle to grab—reached out and pulled back several times. "I don't want to touch him."

The phone rang.

"I'll get it," Jody said, running out of the bathroom.

Tommy dragged Scott to the doorway, keeping his feet safely away from Zelda's jaws. "I forgot to tell you . . ."

"Hello," Jody said into the phone. "Oh, hi, Mom."

CHAPTER 23
Mom and Terrapin Pie

"She's in town," Jody said. "She's coming over in a few minutes."
Jody lowered the phone to its cradle.

Tommy appeared in the bedroom doorway, Scott still dangling from his sleeve. "You're kidding."

"You're missing a cuff link," Jody said.

"I don't think he's going to let go. Do we have any scissors?"

Jody took Tommy by the sleeve a few inches above where Scott was clamped. "You ready?"

Tommy nodded and she ripped his sleeve off at the shoulder. Scott skulked into the bedroom, the sleeve still clamped in his jaws.

"That was my best shirt," Tommy said, looking at his bare arm.

"Sorry, but we've got to clean this place up and get a story together."

"Where did she call from?"

"She was at the Fairmont Hotel. We've got maybe ten minutes."

"So she won't be staying with us."

"Are you kidding? My mother under the same roof where people are living in sin? Not in this lifetime, turtleboy."

Tommy took the turtleboy shot in stride. This was an emergency and there was no time for hurt feelings. "Does you mother use phrases like 'living in sin'?"

"I think she has it embroidered on a sampler over the telephone so she won't forget to use it every month when I call."

Tommy shook his head. "We're doomed. Why didn't you call her this month? She said you always call her."

Jody was pacing now, trying to think. "Because I didn't get my reminder."

"What reminder?"

"My period. I always call her when I get my period each month—just to get all the unpleasantness out of the way at one time."

"When was the last time you had a period?"

Jody thought for a minute. It was before she had turned. "I don't know, eight, nine weeks. I'm sorry, I can't believe I forgot."

Tommy went to the futon, sat down, and cradled his head in his hands. "What do we do now?"

Jody sat next to him. "I don't suppose we have time to redecorate."

In the next ten minutes, while they cleaned up the loft, Jody tried to prepare Tommy for what he was about to experience. "She doesn't like men. My father left her for a younger woman when I was twelve, and Mother thinks all men are snakes. And she doesn't really like women either, since she was betrayed by one. She was one of the first women to graduate from Stanford, so she's a bit of a snob about that. She says that I broke her heart when I didn't go to Stanford. It's been downhill since then. She doesn't like that I live in the City and she has never approved of any of my jobs, my boyfriends, or the way I dress."

Tommy stopped in the middle of scrubbing the kitchen sink. "So what should I talk about?"

"It would probably be best if you just sat quietly and looked repentant."

"That's how I always look."

Jody heard the stairwell door open. "She's here. Go change your shirt."

Tommy ran to the bedroom, stripping off his one-sleeler as he went. I'm not ready for this, he thought. I have more work to do on myself before I'm ready for a presentation.

Jody opened the door catching her mother poised to knock.

"Mom!" Jody said, with as much enthusiasm as she could muster. "You look great."

Frances Evelyn Stroud stood on the landing looking at her youngest daughter with restrained disapproval. She was a short, stout woman dressed in layers of wool and silk under an eggshell cashmere coat. Her hair was a woven gray-blond, flared and lacquered to expose a pair of pearl earrings roughly the size of Ping-Pong balls. Her eyebrows had been plucked away and painted back, her cheekbones were high and highlighted, her lips lined, filled, and clamped tight. She had the same striking green eyes as her daughter, flecked now with sparks of judgment. She had been pretty once but was now passing into the limbo-land of the menopausal woman known as handsome.

"May I come in," she said.

Jody, caught in the half-gesture of offering a hug, dropped her arms. "Of course," she said, stepping aside. "It's good to see you," she said, closing the door behind her mother.

Tommy bounded from the bedroom into the kitchen and slid to a stop on stocking feet. "Hi," he said.

Jody put her hand on her mother's back. Frances flinched, ever so slightly, at the touch. "Mother, this is Thomas Flood. He's a writer. Tommy, this is my mother, Frances Stroud."

Tommy approached Frances and offered his hand. "Pleased to meet you . . ."

She clutched her Gucci bag tightly, then forced herself to take his hand. "Mrs. Stroud," she said, trying to head off the unpleasantness of hearing her Christian name come out of Tommy's mouth.

Jody broke the moment of discomfort so they could pass into the next one. "So, Mom, can I take your coat? Would you like to sit down?"

Frances Stroud surrendered her coat to her daughter as if she were surrendering her credit cards to a mugger, as if she didn't want to know where it was going because she would never see it again. "Is this your couch?" she asked, nodding toward the futon.

"Have a seat, Mother; we'll get you something to drink. We have . . ." Jody realized that she had no idea what they had. "Tommy, what do we have?"

Tommy wasn't expecting the questions to start so soon. "I'll look," he said, running to the kitchen and throwing open a cabinet. "We have coffee, regular and decaf." He dug behind the coffee, the sugar, the powdered creamer. "We have Ovaltine, and . . ." He threw open the refrigerator. "Beer, milk, cranberry juice, and beer—a lot of beer—I mean, not a lot, but plenty, and . . ." He opened the chest freezer. Peary stared up at him through a gap between frozen dinners. Tommy slammed the lid. ". . . that's it. Nothing in there."

"Decaf, please," said Mother Stroud. She turned to Jody, who was returning from balling up her mother's cashmere coat and throwing it in the corner of the closet. "So, you've left your job at Transamerica. Are you working, dear?"

Jody sat in a wicker chair across the wicker coffee table from her mother. (Tommy had decided to decorate the loft in a Pier 1 Imports cheap-shit motif. As a result it was only a ceiling fan and a cockatoo away from looking like a Thai cathouse.)

Jody said, "I've taken a job in marketing." It sounded respectable. It sounded professional. It sounded like a lie.

"You might have told me and saved me the embarrassment of calling Transamerica only to find out that you had been let go."

"I quit, Mother. I wasn't let go."

Tommy, trying to will himself invisible, bowed his way between them to deliver the decaf, which he had arranged on a wicker tray with cream and sugar. "And you, Mr. Flood, you're a writer? What do you write?"

Tommy brightened. "I'm working on a short story about a little girl growing up in the South. Her father is on a chain gang."

"You're from the South, then?"

"No, Indiana."

"Oh," she said, as if he had just confessed to being raised by rats. "And where did you go to university?"

"I, um, I'm sort of self-educated. I think experience is the best teacher." Tommy realized that he was sweating.

"I see," she said. "And where might I read your work?"

"I'm not published yet." He squirmed. "I'm working on it, though," he added quickly.

"So you have another job. Are you in marketing as well?"

Jody intervened. She could see steam rising off Tommy. "He manages the Marina Safeway, Mother." It was a small lie, nothing compared to the tapestry of lies she had woven for her mother over the years.

Mother Stroud turned a scalpel gaze on her daughter. "You know, Jody, it's not too late to apply to Stanford. You'd be a bit older than the other freshmen, but I could pull a few strings."

How does she do this? Jody wondered. How does she come into my home and within minutes make me feel like dirt on a stick? Why does she do it?

"Mother, I think I'm beyond going back to school."

Mother Stroud picked up her cup as if to sip, then paused. "Of course, dear. You wouldn't want to neglect your career and family."

It was a verbal sucker punch delivered with polite, extended-pinky malice. Jody felt something drop inside her like cyanide pellets into acid. Her guilt dropped through the gallows' trap and jerked with broken-neck finality. She regretted only the ten thousand sentences she had started with, "I love my mother, but . . ." You do that so people don't judge you cold and inhuman, Jody thought. Too late now.

She said, "Perhaps you're right, Mother. Perhaps if I had gone to Stanford I would understand why I wasn't born with an innate knowledge of cooking and cleaning and child-rearing and managing a career and a relationship. I've always wondered if it's lack of education or genetic deficiency."

Mother Stroud was unshaken. "I can't speak for your father's genetic background, dear."

Tommy was grateful that Mother Stroud's attention had turned from him, but he could see Jody's gaze narrowing, going from hurt to anger. He wanted to come to her aid. He wanted to make peace. He wanted to hide in the corner. He wanted to wade in and kick ass. He weighed his polite upbringing against the anarchists, rebels, and iconoclasts who were his heroes. He could eat this woman alive. He was a writer and words were his weapons. She wouldn't have a chance. He'd destroy her.

And he would have. He was taking a deep breath to prepare to light into her when he saw a swath of denim disappearing slowly under the frame of the futon: his dismembered shirt sleeve. He held his breath and looked at Jody. She was smiling, saying nothing.

Mother Stroud said, "Your father was at Stanford on an athletic scholarship, you know. They would have never let him in otherwise."

"I'm sure you're right, Mother," Jody said. She smiled politely, listening not to her mother, but to the melodic scraping of turtle claws on carpet. She focused on the sound and could hear the slow, cold lugging of Scott's heart.

Mother Stroud sipped her decaf. Tommy waited. Jody said, "So how long will you be in the City?"

"I just came up to do some shopping. I'm sponsoring a benefit for the Monterey Symphony and I wanted a new gown. Of course I could have found something in Carmel, but everyone would have seen it already. The bane of living in a small community."

Jody nodded as if she understood. She had no connection to this woman, not anymore. Frances Evelyn Stroud was a stranger, an unpleasant stranger. Jody felt more of a connection with the turtle under the futon.

Under the futon, Scott spotted a pattern of scales on Mother Stroud's shoes. He'd never seen Italian faux-alligator pumps, but he knew scales. When you are lying peacefully buried in the muck at the bottom of a pond and you see scales, it means food. You bite.

Frances Stroud shrieked and leaped to her feet, pulling her right foot free of her shoe as she fell into the wicker coffee table. Jody caught her mother by the shoulders and set her on her feet. Frances pushed her away and backed across the room as she watched the snapping turtle emerge from under the futon merrily chomping on the pump.

"What is that? What is that thing? That thing is eating my shoe. Stop it! Kill it!"

Tommy hurdled the futon and dived for the turtle, catching the heel of the shoe before it disappeared. Scott dug his claws into the carpet and backed off. Tommy came up with heel in hand.

"I got part of it."

Jody went to her mother's side. "I meant to call the exterminator, Mother. If I'd had more notice . . ."

Mother Stroud was breathing in outraged yips. "How can you live like this?"

Tommy held the heel out to her.

"I don't want that. Call me a cab."

Tommy paused, considered the opportunity, then let it pass and went to the phone.

"You can't go out without shoes, Mother. I'll get you something to wear." Jody went to the bedroom and came back with her rattiest pair of sneakers. "Here, Mom, these will get you back to the hotel."

Mother Stroud, afraid to sit down anywhere, leaned against the door and stepped into the sneakers. Jody tied them for her and slipped the uneaten pump into her mother's bag. "There you go." She stepped back. "Now, what are we going to do for the holidays?"

Mother Stroud, her gaze trained on Scott, just shook her head. The turtle had wedged himself between the legs of the coffee table and was dragging it around the loft.

A cab pulled up outside and beeped the horn. Mother Stroud tore her gaze away from the turtle and looked at her daughter. "I'll be in Europe for the holidays. I have to go now." She opened the door and backed out through it.

"'Bye, Mom," Jody said.

"Nice meeting you, Mrs. Stroud," Tommy called after her.

When the cab pulled away, Tommy turned to Jody and said, "Well, that went pretty well, didn't it? I think she likes me."

Jody was leaning against the door, staring at the floor. She looked up and began to giggle silently. Soon she was doubled over laughing.

"What?" Tommy said.

Jody looked up at him, tears streaming her face. "I think I'm ready to meet your folks, don't you?"

"I don't know. They might be sort of upset that you're not a Methodist."

CHAPTER 24
The Return of Breakfast

The Emperor lay spread-eagle on the end of a dock in the Saint Francis Yacht Club Marina, watching clouds pass over the bay. Bummer and Lazarus lay beside him, their feet in the air, dozing. The three might have been crucified there, if the dogs hadn't been smiling.

"Men," the Emperor said, "it seems to me now that there is, indeed, a point to that Otis Redding song about sitting on the dock of the bay. After a long night of vampire hunting, this is a most pleasant way to spend the day. Bummer, I believe a commendation is in order. When you led us down here, I thought you were wasting our time."

Bummer did not answer. He was dreaming of a park full of large trees and bite-sized mailmen. His legs twitched and he let out a sleepy ruff each time he crunched one of their tiny heads. In dreams, mailmen taste like chicken.

The Emperor said, "But pleasant as this is, it tastes of guilt, of responsibility. Two months tracking this fiend, and we are no closer to finding him than when we started. Yet here we lay, enjoying the day. I can see the faces of the victims in these clouds."

Lazarus rolled over and licked the Emperor's hand.

"You're right, Lazarus, without sleep we will not be fit for battle. Perhaps, in leading us here, Bummer was wiser than we thought."

The Emperor closed his eyes and let the sound of waves lapping against the piers lull him to sleep.

Lying at anchor, a hundred yards away, was a hundred-foot motor yacht registered in the Netherlands. Belowdecks, in a watertight stainless steel vault, the vampire slept through the day.

Tommy had been asleep for an hour when pounding on the door downstairs woke him. In the darkness of the bedroom he nudged Jody, but she was out for the day. He checked his watch: 7:30 A.M.

The loft rocked with the pounding. He crawled out of bed and stumbled to the door in his underwear. The morning light spilling though the loft's windows temporarily blinded him and he barked his shin on the corner of the freezer on his way through the kitchen.

"I'm coming," he yelled. It sounded as if they were using a hammer on the door.

He did a Quasimodo step and slid down the stairs, holding his damaged shin in one hand, and cracked the downstairs door. Simon peeked through the crack. Tommy could see a ball-peen hammer in his hand, poised for another pound.

Simon said, "Pardner, we need to have us a sit-down."

"I'm sleeping, Sime. Jody's sleeping."

"Well, you're up now. Wake up the little woman, we need breakfast."

Tommy opened the door a little wider and saw Drew dazzling a stoned and goofy grin behind Simon. "Fearless Leader!"

All the Animals were there, holding grocery bags, waiting.

Tommy thought, This is how Anne Frank felt when the Gestapo came to the door.

Simon pushed through the door, causing Tommy to hop back a step to avoid having his toes skinned. "Hey."

Simon looked at Tommy's erection-stretched jockey shorts. "That just a morning wood, or you in the middle of something?"

"I told you, I was sleeping."

"You're young, it could still grow some. Don't feel bad."

Tommy looked down at his insulted member as Simon breezed past him up the stairs, followed by the rest of the Animals. Clint and Lash stopped and helped Tommy to his feet.

"I was sleeping," Tommy said pathetically. "It's my day off."

Lash patted Tommy's shoulder. "I'm cutting class today. We thought you needed moral support."

"For what? I'm fine."

"Cops came by the store last night looking for you. We wouldn't give them your address or anything."

"Cops?" Tommy was waking up now. He could hear beers being popped open in the loft. "What did the cops want with me?"

"They wanted to see your time cards. They wanted to see if you were working on a bunch of nights. They wouldn't say why. Simon tried to distract them by accusing me of leading a black terrorist group."

"That was nice of him."

"Yeah, he's a sweetheart. He told that new cashier, Mara, that you were in love with her but were too shy to tell her."

"Forgive him," Clint said piously. "He knows not what he does."

Simon popped out onto the landing. "Flood, did you drug this bitch? She won't wake up."

"Stay out of the bedroom!" Tommy shook off Lash and Clint and ran up the stairs.

Cavuto chewed an unlit cigar. "I say we go to the kid's house and lean on him."

Rivera looked up from a stack of green-striped computer printout. "Why? He was working when all the murders happened."

"Because he's all we've got. What about the prints on the book; anything?"

"There were half a dozen good prints on the cover. Nothing

the computer could match. Interesting thing is, none of the prints were the victim's. He never touched it."

"What about the kid; a match?"

"No way to tell, he's never been printed. Let it go, Nick. That kid didn't kill these people."

Cavuto ran his hand over his bald head as if looking for a bump that would hold an answer. "Let's arrest him and print him."

"On what charges?"

"We'll ask him. You know what the Chinese say, 'Beat a kid every day; if you don't know why, the kid will.'"

"You ever think about adopting, Nick?" Rivera flipped the last page of the printout and threw it into the wastebasket by his desk. "Justice doesn't have shit. All the unsolved murders with massive blood loss involve mutilation. No vampires here."

For two months they had avoided using the word. Now, here it was. Cavuto took out a wooden match, scraped it against the bottom of his shoe, and moved it around the tip of his cigar. "Rivera, we will not refer to this perp by the V-word again. You don't remember the Night Stalker. This fucking Whiplash Killer thing the press has picked up is bad enough."

"You shouldn't smoke in here," said Rivera. "The sprout eaters will file a grievance."

"Fuck 'em. I can't think without smoking. Let's run sex offenders. Look for priors of rapes and assaults with blood draining. This guy might have just graduated to killing. Then let's run it with cross-dressers."

"Cross-dressers?"

"Yeah, I want to put this thing with the redhead to bed. Having a lead is ruining our perfect record."

She woke to a miasma of smells that hit her like a sockful of sand: burned eggs, bacon grease, beer, maple syrup, stale pot smoke, whiskey, vomit and male sweat. The smells carried memories from before the change—memories of high school keggers and drunken surfers face-down in puddles of puke. Hangover memories. Coming as they did, right after a visit from her mother, they carried shame and loathing and the urge to fall back into bed and hide under the covers.

She thought, I guess there's a few things about being human that I don't miss.

She pulled on a pair of sweatpants and one of Tommy's shirts and opened the bedroom door. It looked as if the good ship *International Pancakes* had run aground in the kitchen. Every horizontal surface was covered with breakfast jetsam. She stepped through the debris, careful not to kick any of the plates, frying pans, coffee cups, or beer cans that littered the floor. Beyond the freezer and the counter she spotted the shipwreck survivor.

Tommy lay on the futon, limbs akimbo, an empty Bushmill's bottle by his head, snoring.

She stood there for a moment running her options over in her head. On one hand, she wanted to fly into a rage; wake Tommy up and scream at him for violating the sanctity of their home. A justifiable tantrum was strongly tempting. On the other hand, until now Tommy had always been considerate. And he *would* clean everything up. Plus, the hangover he was about to experience would be more punishment than she could dole out in a week. Besides, she wasn't really that angry. It didn't seem to matter. It was just a mess. It was a tough decision.

She thought, Oh heck, no harm, no foul. I'll just make him coffee and give him that "I'm-so-disappointed-in-you" look.

"Tommy," she said. She sat down on the edge of the futon and jostled him gently. "Sweetheart, wake up; you've destroyed the house and I need you to suffer for it."

Tommy opened one bloodshot eye and groaned. "Sick," he said.

Jody heard a convulsive sloshing in Tommy's stomach and before she could think about it she had caught him under the armpits and was dragging him across the room to the kitchen sink.

"Oh my God!" Tommy cried, and if he was going to say anything else it was drowned out by the sound of his stomach emptying into the sink. Jody held him up, smiling to herself with the satisfaction of the self-righteously sober.

After a few seconds of retching, he gasped and looked up at her. Tears streamed down his face. His nose dripped threads of slime.

Cheerfully, Jody said, "Can I fix you a drink?"

"Oh my God!" His head went back into the sink and the body-wrenching heaves began anew. Jody patted his back and said "Poor baby" until he came up for air again.

"How about some breakfast?" she asked.

He dived into the sink once again.

After five minutes the heaves subsided and Tommy hung on the edge of the sink. Jody turned on the faucet and used the dish sprayer to hose off his face. "I guess you and the guys had a little party this morning, huh?"

Tommy nodded, not looking up. "I tried to keep them out. I'm sorry. I'm scum."

"Yes, you are, sweetheart." She ruffed his hair.

"I'll clean it up."

"Yes, you will," she said.

"I'm really sorry."

"Yes, you are. Do we want to go back to the futon and sit down?"

"Water," Tommy said.

She ran him a glass of water and steadied him while he drank, then aimed him into the sink when the water came back up.

"Are you finished now?" she asked.

He nodded.

She dragged him into the bathroom and washed his face, rubbing a little too hard, like an angry mother administering an abrasive spit-bath to a chocolate-covered toddler. "Now you go sit down and I'll make you some coffee."

Tommy staggered back to the living room and fell onto the futon. Jody found the coffee filters in the cupboard and began to make the coffee. She opened the cupboard to look for a cup but the Animals had used them all. They were strewn around the loft, tipped over or half full of whisky diluted by melted ice.

Ice?

"Tommy!"

He groaned and grabbed his head. "Don't yell."

"Tommy, did you guys use the ice from the freezer?"

"I don't know. Simon was bartending."

Jody brushed the dishes and pans from the lid of the chest freezer and threw it open. The ice trays, the ones Tommy had bought for the drowning experiment, were empty and scattered around the inside of the freezer. Peary's frosty face stared up at her. She slammed the lid shut and stormed across the room to Tommy.

"Dammit, Tommy, how could you be so careless?"

"Don't yell. Please don't yell. I'll clean it up."

"Clean it up my ass. Someone was in the freezer. Someone saw the body."

"I think I'm going to be sick."

"Did they come into the bedroom while I was sleeping? Did they see me?"

Tommy cradled his head as if it would crack at any moment and spill his brains onto the floor. "They had to get to the bathroom. It's okay; I covered you up so the light wouldn't get to you."

"You idiot!" She snatched up a coffee cup and prepared to throw it at him, then caught herself. She had to get out of here before she hurt him. She shook as she set the cup on the counter.

"I'm going out, Tommy. Clean up this mess." She turned and went to the bedroom to change.

When she emerged, still shaking with anger, Tommy was standing in the kitchen looking repentant.

"Will you be home before I leave for work?"

She glared at him. "I don't know. I don't know when I'll be back. Why didn't you just put a sign on the door, 'See the Vampire'? This is my life you're playing with, Tommy."

He didn't answer. She turned and walked out, slamming the door.

"I'll feed your turtles for you," he called after her.

PART III
Hunters

CHAPTER 25
All Dressed Up

Tommy stormed around the loft collecting beer cans and breakfast plates and carrying them to the kitchen. "Bitch!" he said to Peary. "Shark-faced bitch. It's not like I have any experience at this. It's not like there's *Cosmo* articles on how to take care of a vampire. Bloodsucking, day-sleeping, turtle-hating, creepy-crawling, no-toilet-paper-buying, inconsiderate bitch!"

He slammed an armload of dishes into the sink. "I didn't ask for this. A few friends come over for breakfast and she goes batshit. Did I make a fuss when her mother came over with no notice? Did I say a word when she brought a dead guy home and shoved him under the bed? No offense, Peary. Do I complain about her weird hours? Her eating habits? No, I haven't said a word."

"It's not like I came to the City saying, 'Oh, I can't wait to find a woman whose only joy in life is sucking out my bodily fluids.' Okay, well, maybe I did, but I didn't mean this."

Tommy tied up a trash bag full of beer cans and threw it in the corner. The crash reverberated through his head, reminding him of his hangover. He cradled his throbbing temples and went to the bathroom, where he heaved until he thought his stomach would turn inside out. He pushed himself up from the bowl and wiped his eyes. Two snapping turtles regarded him from the tub.

"What are you guys looking at?"

Scott's jaw dropped open and he hissed. Zelda ducked under the foot of fouled water and swam against the corner of the tub.

"I need a shower. You guys are going to have to roam around for a while."

Tommy found a towel and wrestled the turtles out of the tub, then stepped in and ran the shower until the water went cold. As he dressed he watched Scott and Zelda wandering around the bedroom, bumping into walls, then backing up and slumping off until they hit another wall.

"You guys are miserable here, aren't you? No one appreciates you? Well, it doesn't look like Jody's going to use you. Whoever heard of a vampire with a weak stomach? There's no reason for all of us to be miserable."

Tommy had been using the milk crates he'd carried Scott and Zelda in as laundry baskets. He dumped the dirty laundry on the floor and lined the crates with damp towels. "Let's go, guys. We're going to the park."

He put Scott in a crate and carried him down the steps to the sidewalk. Then went back up for Zelda and called a cab. When he returned to the street, one of the biker/sculptors was standing outside of the foundry, blotting sweat out of his beard with a bandanna.

"You live upstairs, right?" The sculptor was about thirty-five, long-haired and bearded, wearing grimy jeans and a denim vest with no shirt. His beer belly protruded from the vest and hung over his belt like a great hairy bag of pudding.

"Yeah, I'm Tom Flood." Tommy set the crate on the sidewalk and offered his hand. The sculptor clamped down on it until Tommy winced with pain.

"I'm Frank. My partner's Monk. He's inside."

"Monk?"

"Short for Monkey. We work in brass."

Tommy massaged his crushed hand. "I don't get it."

"Balls on a brass monkey."

"Oh," Tommy said, nodding as if he understood.

"What's with the turtles?" Frank asked.

"Pets," Tommy said. "They're getting too big for our place, so I'm going to take a cab over to Golden Gate Park and let them go in the pond."

"That why your old lady left all pissed off?"

"Yeah, she doesn't want them in the house anymore."

"Fucking women," Frank said in sympathy. "My last old lady was always on me about keeping my scooter in the living room. I still have the scooter."

Obviously, in Frank's eyes, Tommy should be carrying Jody out in a crate. Frank thought he was a wimp. "No big deal," Tommy said with a shrug, "they were hers. I don't really care."

"I could use a couple of turtles, if you want to save cab fare."

"Really?" Tommy hadn't relished the idea of loading the crates into a cab anyway. "You wouldn't eat them, would you? I mean, I don't care, but—"

"No fucking way, man."

A blue cab pulled up and stopped. Tommy signaled to the driver, then turned back to Frank. "I've been feeding them hamburger."

"Cool," Frank said. "I'm on it."

"I have to go." Tommy opened the cab door and looked back at Frank. "Can I visit them?"

"Anytime," Frank said. "Later." He bent and picked up the crate containing Zelda.

Tommy got in the cab. "Marina Safeway," he said. He would be a couple of hours early for work, but he didn't want to stay at the loft and risk another tirade if Jody returned. He could kill the time reading or something.

As the cab pulled away he looked out the back window and watched Frank carrying the second crate inside. Tommy felt as if he had just abandoned his children.

Jody thought, I guess not everything changed when I changed. Without realizing how she got there, Jody found herself at Macy's in Union Square. It was as if some instinctual navigator, activated by conflict with men, had guided her there. A dozen times in the past she had found herself here, arriving with a purse full of tear-smeared Kleenex and a handful of credit cards tilted toward their limit. It was a common, and very human, response. She spotted other women doing the same thing: flipping through racks, testing fabrics, checking prices, fighting back tears and anger, and actually believing salespeople who told them that they looked stunning.

Jody wondered if department stores knew what percentage of their profits came from domestic unrest. As she passed a display of indecently expensive cosmetics, she spotted a sign that read: "Mélange Youth Cream—Because he'll never understand why you're worth it." Yep, they knew. The righteous and the wronged shall find solace in a sale at Macy's.

It was two weeks until Christmas and the stores in Union Square were staying open late into the evening. Tinsel and lights were festooned across every aisle, and every item not marked for sale was decorated with fake evergreen, red and green ribbon, and various plastic approximations of snow. Droves of package-laden shoppers trudged through the aisles like the chorus line of the cheerful, sleigh-bell version of the Bataan Death March, ever careful to keep moving lest some ambitious window dresser mistake them for mannequins and spray them down with aerosol snow.

Jody watched the heat trails of the lights, breathed deep the aroma of fudge and candy and a thousand mingled colognes and deodorants, listened to the whir of the motors that animated electric elves and reindeer under the cloak of Muzak-mellowed Christmas carols—and she liked it.

Christmas is better as a vampire, she thought.

The crowds used to bother her, but now they seemed like . . . like cattle: harmless and unaware. To her predator side, even the women wearing fur, who used to grate on her nerves, seemed not only harmless, but even enlightened in this heightened sensual world.

I'd like to roll naked on mink, she thought. She frowned to herself. Not with Tommy, though. Not for a while, anyway.

She found herself scanning the crowds, looking for the dark

aura that betrayed the dying—prey—then caught herself and shivered. She looked over their heads, like an elevator rider avoiding eye contact, and the gleam of black caught her eye.

It was a cocktail dress, minimally displayed on an emaciated Venus de Milo mannequin in a Santa hat. The LBD, Little Black Dress: the fashion equivalent of nuclear weapons; public lingerie; effective not because of what it was, but what it wasn't. You had to have the legs and the body to wear an LBD. Jody did. But you also had to have the confidence, and that she'd never been able to muster. Jody looked down at her jeans and sweatshirt, then at the dress, then at her tennis shoes. She pushed her way through the crowd to the dress.

A rotund, tastefully dressed saleswoman approached Jody from behind. "May I help you?"

Jody's gaze was trained on the dress as if it were the Star of Bethlehem and she was overstocked with frankincense and myrrh. "I need to see that dress in a three."

"Very good," the woman said. "I'll bring you a five and a seven as well."

Jody looked at the woman for the first time and saw the woman looking at her sweatshirt as if it would sprout tentacles and strangle her at any moment.

"A three will be fine," Jody said.

"A three might be a bit snug," the woman said.

"That's the idea," Jody said. She smiled politely, imagining herself snatching out handfuls of the woman's tastefully tinted hair.

"Now let's get the item number off of that," the woman said, making a show of holding the tag so that Jody could see the price. She sneaked a look for Jody's reaction.

"He's paying," Jody said, just to be irritating. "It's a gift."

"Oh, how nice," the woman said, trying to brighten, but obviously disgusted. Jody understood. Six months ago she would have hated the kind of woman she was pretending to be. The woman said, "This will be lovely for holiday parties."

"Actually, it's for a funeral." Jody couldn't remember having this much fun while shopping.

"Oh, I'm sorry." The woman looked apologetic and held her hands to her heart in sympathy.

"It's okay; I didn't know the deceased very well."

"I see," the woman said.

Jody lowered her eyes. "His wife," she said.

"I'll get the dress," the woman said, turning and hurrying away.

Tommy had only been in the Safeway once before when it was still open: the day he applied for the job. Now it seemed entirely too active and entirely too quiet without the Stones or Pearl Jam blasting over the speakers. He felt that his territory had been somehow violated by strangers. He resented the customers who ruined the Animals' work by taking things off the shelves.

As he passed the office he nodded to the manager and headed to the breakroom to kill time until it was time to go to work. The breakroom was a windowless room behind the meat department, furnished with molded plastic chairs, a Formica folding table, a coffee machine, and a variety of safety posters. Tommy brushed some crumbs off a chair, found a coffee-stained *Reader's Digest* under an opened package of stale bear claws, and sat down to read and sulk.

He read: "A Bear's Got Mom!: Drama in Real Life" and "I Am Joe's Duodenum"; and he was beginning to feel a pull toward the bathroom and the Midwest, both things he associated with *Reader's Digest,* when he flipped to an article entitled: "Bats: Our Wild and Wacky Winged Friends" and felt his duodenum quiver with interest.

Someone entered the breakroom, and without looking up, Tommy said, "Did you know that if the brown bat fed on humans instead of insects, that one bat could eat the entire population of Minneapolis in one night?"

"I didn't know that," said a woman's voice.

Tommy looked up from the magazine to see the new cashier, Mara, pulling a chair out from the table. She was tall and a little thin, but large-breasted; a blue-eyed blonde of about twenty. Tommy had been expecting one of the box boys and he stared at her for a second while he changed gears. "Oh, hi. I'm Tom Flood. I'm on the night crew."

"I've seen you," she said. "I'm Mara. I'm new."

Tommy smiled. "Nice to meet you. I came in a little early to catch up on some paperwork."

"*Reader's Digest*?" She raised an eyebrow.

"Oh, this? No, I don't normally read it. I just spotted this article on bats and decided to check it out. They're our wild and wacky winged friends, you know?" He looked at the page as if to confirm his interest. "For instance, did you know that the vampire bat is the only mammal that has been successfully frozen and thawed out alive?"

"I'm sorry, bats give me the creeps."

"Me too," Tommy said, throwing the magazine aside. "Do you read?"

"I've been reading the Beats. I just moved here and I want to get a feeling for the City's literature."

"You're kidding. I've only been here a few months myself. It's a great city."

"I haven't had a chance to look around much. Moving and everything. I left a bad situation back home and I've been trying to adjust."

She didn't look at him when she talked. Tommy assumed at first that it was because she found him disgusting, but after studying her he realized that she was just shy.

"Have you been to North Beach? The Beats all lived there in the fifties."

"No, I don't know my way around yet."

"Oh, you have to go to City Lights Books, and Enrico's. And the bars up there all have pictures of Kerouac and Ginsberg on the walls. You can almost hear the jazz playing."

Mara finally looked up at him and smiled. "You're interested in the Beats?" Her eyes were wide, bright, and crystal-blue. He liked her.

"I'm a writer," Tommy said. It was his turn to look away. "I mean, I want to be a writer. I used to live in Chinatown, it's right next to North Beach."

"Maybe you could give me directions to some of the hot spots."

"I could show you," Tommy said. As soon as he said it he wanted to retract the offer. Jody would kill him.

"That would be wonderful, if you wouldn't mind. I don't know anyone in the City except the other cashiers, and they all have home lives."

Tommy was confused. The manager had said that she had recently lost a child. He assumed that she was married. He didn't want it to appear that he was trying to make a move on her. He didn't really want to make a move on her. But if he were still single, unattached . . .

No, Jody wouldn't understand. Having never had a girlfriend before, he'd never been tempted to stray. He had no idea how to deal with it. He said, "I could show you and your husband around a little and the two of you could have a night on the town."

"I'm divorced," Mara said. "I wasn't married very long."

"I'm sorry," Tommy said.

Mara shook her head as if to dismiss his sympathy. "It's a short story. I got pregnant and we got married. The baby died and he left." She said it without feeling, as if she had distanced herself emotionally from the experience—as if it had happened to someone else. "I'm trying to make a new start." She checked her watch. "I'd better get back up front. I'll see you."

She stood and started to leave the room.

"Mara," Tommy called and she turned. "I'd love to show you around if you'd like."

"I'd like that. Thanks. I'm working days for the rest of the week."

"No problem," Tommy said. "How about tomorrow night? I don't have a car, but we can meet in North Beach at Enrico's if you want."

"Write down the address." She took a slip of paper and a pen from her purse and handed it to him. He scribbled the address and handed it back to her.

"What time?" she asked.

"Seven, I guess."

"Seven it is," she said, and left the breakroom.

Tommy thought: I'm a dead man.

Jody turned in front of the mirror, admiring the way the LBD fit. It was cut down to the small of her back and had a neckline that plunged to the sternum, but was held together at her cleavage with a transparent black mesh. The saleswoman stood beside her, frowning, holding larger sizes of the same dress.

"Are you sure you don't want to try the five, dear?"

Jody said, "No, this one is fine. I'll need some sheer black nylons to go with it."

The saleswoman fought down a grimace and managed a professional smile. "And do you have shoes to match?"

"Suggestions?" Jody asked, not looking away from her reflection. She thought, I wouldn't have been caught dead in something like this a few months ago. Oh hell, I'm caught dead in everything now.

Jody laughed at the thought and the saleswoman took it personally and dropped her polite smile. An edge of disgust in her voice, she said, "I suppose you could complete the look with a pair of Italian fuck-me pumps and some maroon lipstick."

Jody turned to the dowdy woman and gave her a knowing smile. "You've done this before, haven't you?"

After a visit to the shoe department, Jody found herself at the cosmetics counter where an ebullient gay man talked her into "doing her colors" on the computer. He stared at the screen in disbelief.

"Oh my goodness. This is exciting."

"What?" Jody said impatiently. She just wanted to buy some lipstick and get out. She'd satisfied her shopping Jones by reducing the woman in evening wear to tears.

"You're my first winter," said Maurice. (His name was Maurice; it said so on his badge.) "You know, I've done a thousand autumns, and I get springs out the yin-yang, but a winter . . . We *are* going to have fun!"

Maurice began piling samples of eye shadow, lipstick, mascara, and powder on the counter next to the winter color palette. He opened a tube of mascara and held it next to Jody's face. "This one's called Elm Blight, it approximates the color of dead trees in the snow. It complements your eyes wonderfully. Go ahead, dear, try it."

While Jody brushed the mascara onto her lashes, using the magnifying mirror on the counter, Maurice read from the Winter Woman's profile.

"'The Winter Woman is as wild as a blizzard, as fresh as new snow. While some see her as cold, she has a fiery heart under that ice-queen exterior. She likes the stark simplicity of Japanese art and the daring complexity of Russian literature. She prefers sharp to flowing lines, brooding to pouting, and rock and roll to country and western. Her drink is vodka, her car is German, her analgesic is Advil. The Winter Woman likes her men weak and her coffee strong. She is prone to anemia, hysteria, and suicide.'" Maurice stepped back from the counter and took a deep bow, as if he had just finished a dramatic reading.

Jody looked up from the mirror and blinked, the lashes on her right eye describing a starlike *Clockwork Orange* pattern against her pale skin. "They can tell all of that from my coloring?"

Maurice nodded and brandished a sable brush. "Here, dear, let's try some of this blush to bring up those cheekbones. It's called American Rust, it emulates the color of a '63 Rambler that has been driven on salted roads. Very winter."

Jody leaned on the counter to allow Maurice access to her cheeks.

A half hour later she looked in the mirror, rotated now to the non-magnified side, and pursed her lips. For the first time she really looked like a vampire.

"I wish we had a camera," Maurice gushed. "You are a winter masterpiece." He handed her a small bag filled with cosmetics. "That will be three hundred dollars."

Jody paid him. "Is there somewhere I can change? I'd like to see how I look with my new outfit."

Maurice pointed across the store. "There's a changing room over there. And don't forget your free gift, dear, the Needless Notions Lotion Collection, a fifty-dollar value." Maurice held up a plastic faux-Gucci gym bag full of bottles.

"Thanks." Jody took the bag and sulked off toward the changing room. Halfway across the store she picked up the sound of the dowdy saleswoman from evening wear and turned to see her talking to Maurice. Jody focused and could hear what they were saying over the crowd and Christmas Muzak.

"How did it go?" asked the woman.

Maurice grinned. "She went away looking like a Donner Party Barbie."

The woman and Maurice exchanged a gleeful high five.

Bitches, Jody thought.

CHAPTER 26
At the End of the Night . . .

The Emperor worked a wooden match around the end of a Cuban cigar, drawing and checking until the tip glowed like revolution.

"I don't agree with their ideology," said the Emperor, "but we must give the Marxists their due—they roll a fine cigar."

Bummer snorted and growled at the cigar, then shook himself violently, spraying the Emperor and Lazarus with a fine wet mist.

The Emperor scratched the Boston terrier behind the ears. "Settle down, little one, you needed a bath. If we vanquish our enemy, it will be through gallantry and courage, not the stench of our persons."

Shortly after sunset a member of the yacht club had given the Emperor the cigar and had invited him to use the club showers. Much to the chagrin of the club custodian, the Emperor shared his shower with Bummer and Lazarus, who left the drain hopelessly clogged with the fluff, stuff, and filth such as heroes are made of. Now they were passing the evening on the same dock on which they had slept, the Emperor savoring his cigar while the troops stood watch.

"Where do we go from here? Must we wait for the fiend to kill again before we pick up the trail?"

Bummer considered the questions, working the words over in

his doggy brain looking for a "food" word. Not finding it, he began to lick his balls to remove the annoying odor of deodorant soap. Once he achieved the desired balance (of both his ends smelling roughly the same), he padded around the dock marking the mooring posts against seabound invaders. With the borders of the realm firmly established, he went in search of something dead to roll in to remove the last evidence of the shower. The right smell was near, but it was coming in off the water.

Bummer went toward the smell until he stood at the end of the dock. He saw a small white cloud bubbling out over the gunwale of a yacht moored a hundred yards away. Bummer barked to let the cloud know to stay away.

"Settle down, little one," said the Emperor.

Lazarus shook some water out of his ears and joined Bummer at the end of the dock. The cloud was halfway between the yacht and the dock, pulsating and bubbling as it moved across the water toward them. Lazarus lowered his head and growled. Bummer added a high whine to the harmony.

"What is it, men?" the Emperor asked. He put his cigar out on the sole of his shoe and secured the remains in his breast pocket before limping, stiff from sitting, to the end of the dock.

The cloud was almost to the dock. Lazarus bared his teeth and snarled at it. Bummer backed away from the edge of the dock, not sure whether to bolt or stand his ground.

The Emperor looked out over the water and saw the cloud. It was not wispy at the edges, but sharply defined, more like a solid mass of gel than water vapor. "It's just a bit of fog, men, don't . . ."

He spotted a face forming in the cloud that changed as he watched to the shape of a giant hand, then bubbled into the head of a dog.

"Although weather is not my specialty, I would venture to guess that that is no ordinary fog bank."

The cloud undulated into the shape of a huge viper that reared up, twenty feet over the water, as if preparing to strike. Bummer and Lazarus let go with a fusillade of barking.

"Gents, let us away to the showers. I've left my sword by the sink." The Emperor turned and ran down the dock, Bummer and Lazarus close at his heels. When he reached the clubhouse he turned to see the cloud creeping over the lip of the dock. He stood, watching transfixed, as the cloud began to condense into the solid form of a tall, dark man.

The Animals began drifting into the store around midnight, and to Tommy's delight they all seemed at least as hung over as he was. Drew, tall, gaunt, and deadly earnest, had them sit on the register counters and wait for his medical diagnosis. He walked from man to man, looking at their tongues and the whites of their eyes. Then he walked toward the office and seemed to lose himself in concentration. After a moment he went into the office and came back with the truck manifest.

Drew noted the number of cases, then nodded to himself and removed a bottle of pills from his shirt pocket and handed it to Tommy. "Take one and pass it down. Who drank the tequila?"

Simon, who had pulled his black Stetson over his eyes, raised his hand with a slight moan.

"You take two, Simon. They're Valium number fives."

"Housewife heroin," said Simon.

Drew announced, "Everyone drink a quart of Gatorade, a slug of Pepto, three aspirin, some B vitamins, and two Vivarin."

Barry, the balding scuba diver, said, "I don't trust that over-the-counter stuff."

"I'm not finished," Drew said. From his shirt pocket he pulled an aluminum cigar tube, unscrewed the cap, and tipped it into his hand. A long, yellow paper cone slid out. He held it out to Tommy. It smelled like a cross between a skunk and a eucalyptus cough drop. Tommy raised an eyebrow to Drew. "What is it?"

"Don't worry about it. It's recommended by the Jamaican Medical Association. Anybody got a light?"

Simon pitched his Zippo to Drew, who handed it to Tommy.

Tommy hesitated before lighting the joint and looked at Drew. "This is just pot, right? This isn't some weird designer kill-the-family-with-a-chain-saw-and-choke-to-death-on-your-own-vomit drug, right?"

"Not if used as directed," Drew said.

"Oh. Okay." Tommy sparked the Zippo, lit the joint, and took a deep hit. Holding in the smoke—his eyes watering, his face scrunched in gargoyle determination, his limbs contorted as if he had contracted a case of the instant creeping geeks—he offered the joint to Lash, the black business major.

There was a thump on the front door, followed by an urgent pounding that rattled the windows. Tommy dropped the joint and coughed, expelling a blast of smoke and spittle in Lash's face. The Animals shouted and turned, not so much startled by the noise, but tortured by the assault on their collective hangover.

Outside the double automatic doors the Emperor pounded on the frame with his wooden sword. The dogs jumped around his feet barking and leaping as if they had treed a raccoon on the roof of the store.

Tommy, still gasping for breath, dug into his pocket for the store keys and made his way to the door. "It's okay. I know him."

"Everybody knows him," Simon said. "Crazy old fuck."

Tommy turned the key and pulled the doors open. The Emperor fell into the store. Bummer and Lazarus leaped over their master and disappeared down an aisle.

The Emperor thrashed around on the floor and Tommy had to step back to keep from having his shins whacked by the wooden sword.

"Calm down," Tommy said. "You're okay."

The Emperor climbed to his feet and grabbed Tommy by the shoulders. "We have to marshal our forces. The monster is at hand. Quickly now!"

Tommy looked back at the Animals and grinned. "He's okay, really." Then, to the Emperor, "Just slow down, okay. Can I get you something to eat?"

"There's no time for that. We must take the battle to him."

Simon called, "Maybe Drew has something to mellow him

out." Drew had recovered the joint and was in the process of re-lighting it.

Tommy closed and locked the door, then took the Emperor by the arm and led him toward the office. "See, Your Majesty, you're inside now. You're safe. Now let's go sit down and see if we can sort this out."

"Locked doors won't stop him. He can take the form of mist and pass through the smallest crack." The Emperor addressed the Animals. "Arm yourself, while there is still time."

"Who?" Asked Lash. "Who's he talking about?"

Tommy cleared his throat. "The Emperor thinks that there's a vampire stalking the City."

"You're shittin' me," Barry said.

"I've just seen him," the Emperor said, "at the marina. He changed from a cloud of vapor to human form as I watched. He's not far behind me, either."

Tommy patted the old man's arm. "Don't be silly, Your Highness. Even if there were vampires, they can't turn into vapor."

"But I saw it."

"Look!" Tommy said. "You saw something else. I know for a fact that vampires can't change into vapor."

"You know that for a fact?" Simon drawled.

Tommy looked at Simon, expecting to see the usual grin, but Simon was waiting for an answer.

Tommy shook his head. "I'm trying to get things under control here, Simon. You want to give me a break?"

"How do you know?" Simon insisted.

"It was in a book I was reading. You remember, Simon, you read that one too."

Simon looked as if he had just been threatened, which he had. "Yeah, right," he said, pushing his Stetson back down over his eyes and leaning back on the register. "Well, you ought to just call the loony-bin boys for your friend there."

"I'll take care of him," Tommy said. "You guys get started on the truck." He opened the office door and nudged the Emperor toward it.

"What about the men?" asked the Emperor.

"They're safe. Come on in and tell me about it."

"But the monster?"

"If he wanted to kill me, I'd be dead already." Tommy shut the office door behind them.

Big hair, Jody thought. Big hair is the way to go with this outfit. After all these years of trying to tame my hair, all I had to do was dress like an upscale hooker and I would have been fine.

She was walking up Geary Street, her fake Gucci bag of free cosmetics still in hand. There was a new club down here somewhere and she needed to dance, or at least show off a little.

A panhandler wearing a cardboard sign that read, "I am Unemployed and Illiterate (a friend wrote this for me)," stopped her and tried to sell her a free weekly newspaper.

Jody said, "I can pick that up anywhere. It's free."

"It is?"

"Yes. They give it away in every store and café in town."

"I wondered why they were laying out there for the taking."

Jody was angry with herself for being pulled into this exchange. "It says 'free' right there on the cover."

The bum pointed to the sign hanging around his neck and tried to look tragic. "Maybe you could give me quarter for it anyway."

Jody started to walk away. The bum followed along beside her. "There's a great article on recovery groups on page ten."

She looked at him.

"Someone told me," he said.

Jody stopped. "I'll give you this if you'll leave me alone." She held out the cosmetics bag.

The bum acted as if he had to think about it. He looked her up and down, pausing at her cleavage before looking her in the eye. "Maybe we could work something out. You must be cold in that dress. I could warm you up."

"Normally," Jody said, "if I met a guy who was unemployed and illiterate who hadn't bathed in a couple of weeks, I'd be standing in a puddle with excitement, but I'm sort of in a bad mood tonight, so take this bag and give me the fucking paper before I pop your little head like a zit." She pushed the bag into his chest, knocking him back against the window of a closed camera store.

The bum offered her the paper tentatively and she snatched it from his hand.

He said, "You're a lesbian, aren't you?"

Jody screamed at him: a high, explosive, unintelligible expulsion of pure inhuman frustration—a Hendrix high note sampled and sung by a billion suffering souls in Hell's own choir. The window of the camera shop shattered and fell in shards to the sidewalk. The store alarm wailed, paltry in comparison to Jody's scream. The bum covered his ears and ran away.

"Cool," Jody said, more than a bit satisfied with herself. She opened the paper and read as she walked up the street to the club.

Outside the club Jody got in line with a crowd of well-dressed wannabees and resumed reading her paper, enjoying the stares of the men on line in her peripheral vision.

The club was called 753. It seemed to Jody that all of the new, trendy clubs had eschewed names for numbers. Kurt and his broker buddies had been big fans of the number-named clubs, which made for Monday-morning recount conversations that sounded more like equations: "We went to Fourteen Ninety-Two and Ten Sixty-Six, then Jimmy drank ten Seven-Sevens at Nineteen Seventeen, went fifty-one fifty and got eighty-sixed." Normally, that many numbers in succession would have had Kurt diving for his PC to establish trend lines and resistance levels. Jody glazed over at the mention of numbers, which would have made living with the broker a bit of an ordeal even if he hadn't been an asshole.

She thought, I wonder if Kurt will be here. I hope so. I hope he's here with the little well-bred, breastless wonder. Oh, she won't care, but he'll die a thousand jealous deaths.

Then she heard the alarm sounding down the street and thought, Maybe I should learn to channel some of this hostility.

"You, in the LBD!" said the doorman.

Jody looked up from her paper.

"Go on in," the doorman said.

As she walked past the other people on line she was careful to avoid eye contact. One single guy reached out and grabbed her arm.

"Say I'm your date," he begged. "I've been waiting for two hours."

"Hi, Kurt," Jody said. "I didn't see you."

Kurt stepped back. "Oh. Oh my God. Jody?"

She smiled. "How's your head?"

He was trying to catch his breath. "Fine. It's fine. You look . . ."

"Thanks, Kurt. Good to see you again. I'd better get inside."

He clawed the air after her. "Could you say I'm your date?"

She turned and looked at him as if she had found him in the back of the refrigerator with green growing on him.

"I have been chosen, Kurt. You, on the other hand, are an untouchable. I don't think you'd be appropriate for the image I'm trying to project."

As she walked into the club she heard Kurt say to the next guy in line, "She's a lesbian, you know."

Jody thought, Yep, I've got to work on controlling my hostility.

The theme of 753 was Old San Francisco; actually, Old San Francisco burning down, which is largely what Old San Francisco used to do. There was an antique hand-pump fire engine in the middle of the dance floor. Cellophane flames leaped from pseudowindows driven by turbine fans. Nozzles in the ceiling drizzled dry-ice smoke over a crowd of young professionals arrhythmically sweating in layers of casual cotton and wool. A flannel-clad grunge rocker here; a tie-dyed and dreadlocked Rastafarian there; some neo-hippies; a sprinkling of black-eyed, white-faced New Wave holdovers—looking alienated—contemplating the next body part to have pierced; a few harmless suburban homeboys—here to bust a move, def and phat, in three-hundred-dollar giant gel-filled, glow-in-the-dark, pneumatic, NBA-endorsed sneakers. The doorman had tried to make a mix, but with fashionable micro-brewery beer going for seven bucks a bottle, the crowd was bound to overbalance to the side of privilege and form a thick yuppie scum. Cocktail waitresses in fireman helmets served reservoirs of imported water and thanked people for not smoking.

Jody slinked onto a barstool and opened her paper to avoid eye contact with a droopy-eyed drunk on the next stool. It didn't work.

"'Scuse me, I couldn't help noticing that you were sitting down. I'm sitting down too. Small world, huh?"

Jody looked up briefly and smiled. Mistake.

"Can I buy you a drink?" the drunk asked.

"Thanks, I don't drink," she said, thinking, Why did I come here? What did I hope to accomplish?

"It's my hair, isn't it?"

Jody looked at the guy. He was about her age and balding, not quite finished with what looked like a bad hair-transplant job. His scalp looked as if it had been strafed with a machine gun full of plugs. She felt bad for him.

"No, I really don't drink."

"How about a mineral water?"

"Thanks. I don't drink anything."

From the stool behind her a man's voice. "She'll drink this."

She turned to see a glass filled with a thick, red-black liquid being pushed in front of her by a bone-white hand. The index and middle finger seemed a little too short.

"They're still growing back," the vampire said.

Jody recoiled from him so hard she nearly went over backward on her barstool. The vampire caught her arm and steadied her.

"Hey, buddy," said Hair Plugs, "hands off."

The vampire let go of Jody's arm, reached across to put his hand on Hair Plugs's shoulder, and held him fast to his seat. The drunk's eyes went wide. The vampire smiled.

"She'll rip out your throat and drink your blood as you die. Is that what you want?"

Hair Plugs shook his head violently. "No, I already have an ex-wife."

The vampire released him. "Go away."

Hair Plugs slid off the stool and ran off into the crowd on the dance floor. Jody leaped to her feet and started to follow him. The vampire caught her arm and wheeled her around.

"Don't," he said.

Jody caught his wrist and began to squeeze. A human arm would have been reduced to mush. The vampire grinned. Jody locked eyes with him. "Let go."

"Sit," he said.

"Murderer."

The vampire threw his head back and laughed. The bartender, a burly jock type, looked up, then looked away. Just another loud drunk.

"I can take you," Jody said, not really believing it. She wanted to break loose and run.

The vampire, still smiling, said, "It would make an interesting news story, wouldn't it? 'Pale Couple Destroys Club in Domestic Disagreement.' Shall we?"

Jody let go of his wrist but stayed locked on his eyes. They were black, showing no iris. "What do you want?"

The vampire broke the stare and shook his head. "Little fledgling, I want your company, of course. Now sit."

Jody climbed back onto the stool and stared into the glass before her.

"That's better. It's almost over, you know. I didn't think you would last this long, but alas, it must come to an end. The game has become a bit too public. You have to break from the cattle now. They don't understand you. You are not one of them anymore. You are their enemy. You know it, don't you? You've known it since your first kill. Even your little pet knows it."

Jody started to shake. "How did you get into the loft to get Tommy's book?"

The vampire grinned again. "One develops certain talents over time. You're still young, you wouldn't understand."

Part of Jody wanted to slam her fist into his face and run, yet another part wanted answers to all the questions that had been running through her mind since the night she was changed.

"Why me? Why did you do this to me?"

The vampire stood up and patted her on the shoulder. "It's almost over. The sadness of having a pet is that they always die on you. At the end of the night, you are alone. You'll know that feeling very soon. Drink up." He turned and walked away.

Jody watched him leave, relieved that he was gone, but at the same time disappointed. There were so many questions.

She picked up the glass, smelled the liquid, and nearly gagged. The bartender snickered. "I never had an order for a double of straight grenadine before. Can I get you something else?"

"No, I've got to go catch him."

She picked up her paper, got up, ran up the steps and out of the club. She found that if she stayed on the balls of her feet, she could actually run in the high-heeled pumps. Chalk one up for vampire strength, she thought.

She grabbed the doorman by the shoulder and swung him around. "Did you see a thin, pale guy in black just leave?"

"That way." The doorman pointed east on Geary. "He was walking."

"Thanks," Jody tossed over her shoulder as she took to the sidewalk, waiting to break into a run until she was out of sight from the club. She ran a block before taking off the pumps and carrying them. The street was empty; only the buzz of wires and the soft padding of her feet on the sidewalk broke the silence.

She'd run ten blocks when she spotted him, a block away, leaning against a lamppost.

He turned and looked at her as she pulled up.

"So, fledgling, what are you going to do when you catch me?" he asked in a soft voice, knowing she would hear. "Kill me? Break off a signpost and drive it though my heart? Rip my head from my shoulders and play puppet with it while my body flops around on the sidewalk?" The vampire pantomimed flopping, rolled his eyes, and grinned.

Jody said nothing. She didn't know what she was going to do. She hadn't thought about it. "No," she said. "How can I stop you from killing Tommy?"

"They always betray you, you know. It's in their nature."

"What if I leave? Don't tell him where I'm going?"

"He knows we exist. We have to hide, fledgling. Always. Completely."

Jody felt strangely calm. Perhaps it was hearing the "we." Maybe it was talking in a normal voice to someone a block away. Whatever it was, she wasn't afraid, not for herself, anyway. She said, "If we have to hide, why all the killings?"

The vampire laughed again. "Did you ever have a cat bring you a bird it had killed?"

"Why?"

"Presents, fledgling. Now if you are going to kill me, please do. If not, go play with your pet while you can."

He turned and walked away.

"Wait!" Jody called. "Did you pull me through the basement window?"

"No," the vampire said without looking back. "I am not interested in saving you. And if you follow me, you will find out exactly how a vampire can be killed."

Gotcha, asshole, Jody thought. He *had* saved her.

CHAPTER 27
Bridging the Boredom

Half past midnight. He stood at the top of the southwest tower of the Oakland Bay Bridge, some fifty stories above the gunmetal-cold bay, thinking, Jump or dive? He wore a black silk suit and he paused for a moment, regretting that the suit would be ruined. He liked the feel and flow of silk on his skin. Oh well.

Two miles away Jody was walking up Market Street wishing that she could just get drunk and pass out. I wonder, she thought, if I found someone who was really drunk and drank his blood? No, this damn system of mine would probably identify alcohol as a poison and fight the effects. So many questions. If only I'd remembered to ask them.

She stopped at a phone booth and called Tommy at the store.

"Marina Safeway."

"Tommy, it's me."

"Are you still mad?"

"Not mad enough, I guess. I just wanted to tell you to stay in the store until after daylight. Don't go outside for any reason. And stay around the other guys if you can."

"Why? What's the matter?"

"Just do as I say, Tommy."

"I cleaned up the loft. Mostly, anyway."

"We'll talk about it tomorrow night. Stay at home until I wake up, okay?"

"Are you still going to be pissed?"

"Probably. I'll see you then. Good-bye." She hung up. How could he be so smart sometimes and so ignorant other times? Maybe the vampire was right, a human could never understand her. She suddenly felt very lonely.

She ducked into an all-night diner and ordered a cup of coffee as rent on a booth. She still could enjoy the smell of coffee, even if she couldn't keep it down.

She opened the paper she had bought from the bum with her cosmetics bag and began to read through the personals. "Men Seeking Women," Women Seeking Men," "Men Seeking Men," "Women Seeking Women," "Men Seeking Small Fuzzy Animals"; there was a wide selection of categories. She scanned over the more mundane entries until her eye settled on one under "Support Groups." "Are You a Vampire? You don't have to face your problem alone. Blood Drinkers Anonymous can help. Mon.–Fri. Midnight. Rm. 212 Asian Cultural Center, Non-Smoking."

It was Friday. It was midnight. She was only ten minutes from the Asian Cultural Center. Could it be this simple?

The first thing she noticed when she walked into room 212 of the Asian Cultural Center is that all of the people sitting in a circle in molded plastic chairs, all twenty of them, were giving off heat signatures. They were all human.

She was backing out of the door when a pear-shaped woman in a leotard and black cape intercepted her and took her hand.

"Welcome," said the woman. She sported a set of rather wicked-looking fangs that caused her to lisp. "I'm Tabitha. We're just getting ready to start. Come on in. There's coffee and cookies."

She led Jody to an orange plastic chair and urged her to sit down. "It's hard the first time, but everyone here has been where you are."

"Not bloody likely," Jody said, wiping a speck of Tabitha's spittle from her cheek.

Tabitha pointed to a plastic medallion that hung from her neck by a heavy silver chain. "See this chip? I've been clean and bloodless for six months. If I can do it, so can you. One night at a time."

Tabitha squeezed her arm, then threw her cape over her shoulder, turned dramatically, and stalked across the room to the cookie table, her cape billowing behind her.

Jody looked at the other occupants of the room. All were talking, most were sneaking looks at her between sips of coffee. The men were all tall and thin with protruding Adam's apples and bad skin. Their dress ranged from business suits to jeans and flannel. They might have been a chess club out for the evening if not for the capes. To a man, they wore capes. Four of seven had fangs. Two sets of four were made of glow-in-the-dark plastic.

Jody focused on two of them whispering in the corner. "I told you, this is a babe-fest. Did you see the redhead?" He sneaked a look. His partner said, "I think I saw her at Compulsive Cleaners last week."

"Compulsive Cleaners, I was going to try that. How are the odds?"

"Lots of gay guys, but a few babes. Mostly they smell like Pine Sol, but it's hot if you like latex gloves."

"Cool, I'll check it out. I think I'm going to quit going to Adult Children of Alcoholics, everybody's looking to blame, no one's looking to get laid."

Jody thought, I don't know if I want to hear quiet desperation this clearly. She changed her focus to the women in the room.

A six-foot-two brunette woman in a black choir robe and Kabuki-like makeup was complaining to a washed-out blonde wearing a tattered wedding dress. "They want to be tied up, I tie them up. They want to be spanked, I spank them. They want to be called names, I call them names. But try and drink a little of their blood, and they scream like babies. What about my needs?"

"I know," said the blonde. "I asked Robert to sleep in the coffin one time and he left."

"You have a coffin? I want a coffin."

Christ, Jody thought, I've got to get out of here.

Tabitha clapped her hands. "Let's get the meeting started!"

Those who were standing found seats. Several men tried to shove their way into the seats next to Jody. A skinny geek with peanut-butter breath leaned in to her and said, "I was on 'Oprah' on Halloween. 'Men who drink blood and the women who find them disgusting.' If you want, you can come by my place and watch the tape after the meeting."

"I'm out of here," Jody said. She jumped up and headed for the door.

Behind her she heard Tabitha saying, "Hi, I'm Tabitha and I'm a bloodsucking fiend."

"Hi, Tabitha," the group said in chorus.

Outside Jody looked up and down the street wondering which way to go, what to do. She paused by a phone booth, realizing that there was no one she could call. Tears welled in her eyes. Why even bother to hope? The only person who had the slightest idea how she felt was the vampire who had made her. And he had made it clear that he wasn't interested in helping her—the evil fucker.

I should set him up with my mother, she thought, then the two of them can look down on humanity together. The thought made her smile.

Then the phone rang. She looked at it for a second, looked around for someone else who would answer it, but except for a guy standing by his car a couple of blocks away, the street was empty.

She picked up the phone. "Hello."

A man's voice said, "I thought you would show up here eventually."

"Who is this?" Jody asked. The man sounded young, his voice was unfamiliar.

"I can't tell you that yet."

"Okay," Jody said. "'Bye."

"Wait, wait, wait, don't hang up."

"Well?"

"You're the one, aren't you? You're real. I mean, you are a real vampire."

Jody held the phone away, stared at the receiver as if it were an alien object. "Who is this?"

"I don't want to tell you my name. I don't want you to be able to find me. Let's just say that I'm a friend."

"That's how most of my friends are," Jody said. "They don't tell me their names or how to find them. It keeps my social calendar pretty clear." Who was this guy? Who could possibly know that she was here, right now?

"Okay, I guess I owe you something. I'm a med student at . . . at a local college. I did some research on one of the bodies . . . one of the bodies of the people you killed."

"I didn't kill anyone. I don't know what you're talking about. If I am who you think I am, how did you know I'd be here? I didn't even know I would be here until an hour ago."

"I've been waiting, watching every night for a couple of weeks. I had a theory that you wouldn't have any noticeable body heat, and you don't."

"What are you talking about? No one notices anybody's body heat."

"Look up the street. By the white Toyota. It's running, by the way. If you make a move to come toward me, I'm gone."

Jody looked more closely at the person up the street standing by a white car. The car was running. The man was holding a cell phone and looking at her through some very large binoculars.

"I see you," she said. "What do you want?"

"I'm looking at you through infrared glasses. You're not giving off any body heat, so I know you're the one. My theory was right."

"Are you a cop?"

"No, I told you, I'm a medical student. I don't want to turn you in. In fact, I think I might be able to help you, if you're interested in being helped."

"Talk," Jody said. She held her hand over the phone and focused on the guy by the car. She could hear him talking into the cell phone.

"They gave one of the cadavers to our department after the coroner was done with it. It was a male, about sixty years old, the third victim, I think. I noticed that there was a clean spot on his neck, as if it had been washed. The coroner hadn't put that in his report. I took a tissue sample and put it under a microscope. The tissue in that area was living. Regenerating. I cultured it and it started to die, until I added something on a hunch."

"What?" Jody asked. She didn't know what to think. This man knew she was a vampire, and strangely, she felt an urge to attack. Some protective instinct wanted her to hurt him. Kill him. She fought to stay calm.

"Hemoglobin. I added some human hemoglobin and the tissue started to regenerate again. I ran it through the sequencer. It's not human DNA. It's close, but not human. It doesn't produce heat, doesn't seem to burn fuel the same way that mammalian cells do. The coroner said that he was the one that had drained the blood from the body, but he'd never done that before. And I knew that the guy had been murdered. I made a guess. I saw the ad in the *Weekly* for a vampire support group, so I've been watching."

Jody said, "Suppose I believe what you're saying. Suppose I believe that you believe this bullshit, how could you help me? Supposing I wanted to be helped?"

"My major is gene therapy. There's a chance I could reverse the process."

"This isn't science. I'm not saying that you're right about your theory. There are a lot of things that you don't know, that can't be explained by science. If you don't know that by now, you will. What you're talking about is magic."

"Magic is just science that we don't know yet. Do you want me to help or not?"

"Why would you want to do that? As far as you know, I kill people."

"So does cancer, but I still work on it. Do you have any idea what kind of competition there is for jobs in my field? It's an all-or-nothing field. I could end up getting my PhD and giving saccharine enemas to rats for five bucks an hour. What I learn from you would put my résumé at the top of the stack."

Jody didn't know what to say. Part of her wanted to drop the phone and go after him. Another part wanted to accept his help.

She said, "What do you want me to do?"

"Nothing yet. How can I get hold of you?"

"I can't tell you that. I'll call you. What's your number?"

"I can't tell you that."

Jody sighed. "Look, Mr. Scientific Genius, figure out something. And by the way, I really didn't kill those people."

"Then why are you even listening to me?"

"I guess this conversation is over. Get in your car and get comfortable with asking rats to bend over. Good-bye."

"Wait, we could meet somewhere. Tomorrow. Someplace public."

"No, it has to be at night. Someplace private. You could have cops everywhere." She watched him as she talked. He had put the binoculars down and she could see that he was Asian.

"You're the killer here. Would *you* meet you someplace private and dark?"

"All right. Tomorrow night. Seven o'clock, at Enrico's on Broadway. That public enough for you?"

"Sure. Can I bring a blood-sample kit? Would you let me?"

"Would you let me?" she asked.

He didn't answer.

"Just kidding," she said. "Look, I don't want to hurt you, but I don't want to get hurt either. When you leave here, drive like hell and take an indirect route home."

"Why?"

"Because I really didn't kill those people, but I know who did, and he's been following me. If he's seen you, you're in danger."

The line was quiet for a minute, just the ghost voices of a cellular connection. Jody watched the Asian guy watching her.

Finally he cleared his throat. "How many of you are there?"

"I don't know," she said.

"I know that all of the victims don't change. It couldn't work. The geometric progression would have the entire human race turned to vampires in a month." He sounded more confident now that he had brought the conversation back to science.

"I'll tell you what I know tomorrow. But don't expect much. I don't know much. Or I'll tell you now if you want to talk face to face, but I don't think it's a good idea to talk about this with you on a cell phone."

"Yeah, you're right. Not now, though. Not here. You understand, don't you?"

Jody nodded, exaggerating the gesture so he could see. "The longer you stand there, the better chance you have of being seen by . . . by the other one. Tomorrow night, then. Seven o'clock."

"Will you be wearing that dress?"

Jody smiled. "Do you like it? It's new."

"It's great. I didn't think you would be a woman."

"Thanks. Go now."

She watched him climb into the Toyota, the cell phone still in hand. "Promise not to try and track me down?"

"I know where you'll be tomorrow night, remember?"

"Oh yeah. By the way, my name's Steve."

"Hi, Steve. I'm Jody."

"'Bye," he said. He disconnected. Jody hung up the phone and watched him drive away.

She thought, Great, another one to worry about.

It hadn't occurred to her that her condition might be reversible. But then, the med student didn't know about how the body had turned to dust. Science indeed.

Jump or dive, he thought. The silk suit whipped about his legs in the chill wind. The tower's aircraft warning light flashed red across his face and he could see heat swirling off it, dissolving over the bay.

His name was Elijah Ben Sapir. He stood five feet ten inches tall and he had been a vampire for eight hundred years. In human life he had been an alchemist and had spent his time mixing noxious chemicals and chanting arcane incantations trying to turn lead into gold and tap the secret of eternal life. He hadn't been a particularly good alchemist. He had never been able to pull off the gold transformation, although by a bizarre miscalculation of chemistry he did manage to invent Teflon some eight hundred years before DuPont would find a use for it. (It should be noted, though, that archaeologists recently uncovered a Viking rune stone in Greenland that mentions a Jew who entered the palace of Constantine the Magnificent in 1224 selling a line of nonstick hot pokers for the Emperor's torture chamber and was promptly given the bum's rush to the city gates. The accuracy of the story has been questioned, however, as it begins, "I never believed that your letters were true until Gunner and I . . ." and goes on to recount the sexual exploits of two Vikings and a harem of brown-skinned Byzantine babes.)

Ben Sapir's search for eternal life had been somewhat more successful. Granted, it came with the side effects of drinking human blood and staying out of sunlight, but he had gotten used to that. It was the loneliness that he couldn't abide. Perhaps, after all these years, it would end. He was afraid to hope.

It had been a hundred years since a fledgling had lasted this long. She had been a Yanomamo woman in the Amazon Basin and she had hunted the jungle for three months before she returned to her village and turned her sister. The sisters declared themselves gods and demanded sacrifices from the village. He found them by the river feeding on an old woman, and he took no pleasure in killing them. Perhaps the redhead, perhaps she would be the one.

Dive, he decided. He leaped away from the tower, jackknifed into a dive, and plunged fifty stories to the black water. The challenge was to avoid changing to mist before hitting the water. That was too easy.

The impact of the water ripped the clothes off his back; the stitching of his shoes exploded with the pressure. He surfaced, naked except for one sock that had strangely survived the impact, and began the long swim back to his yacht thinking, I shouldn't have saved her from the sunlight. I must be desperate for entertainment.

CHAPTER 28
Is That a Blackjack in Your Pocket?

Tommy booted the Emperor out of the store at dawn. It had been a long night trying to keep the crazed ruler away from the Animals while throwing stock and trying to figure out the logistics of his meeting with Mara, all while under the influence of Dr. Drew's polio weed, which seemed to affect the part of the brain that motivates one to sit in the corner and drool while staring at one's hands. When the shift ended, he declined the Animal's invitation for beers and Frisbee in the parking lot, swiped a baguette from the bread-delivery man, and caught the bus home, intent on going straight to bed. He knew his plan was foiled when Frank, the biker/sculptor, met him outside their building holding a familiar-looking bronze turtle.

"Flood, check it out." Frank held up the turtle. "It worked!"

"What worked?" Tommy asked.

"Thick electroplating process. Come on in, I'll show you." Frank turned and led Tommy through the roll-up door into the foundry.

The foundry took up the entire bottom floor of the building. There was a huge furnace making a muffled rumbling sound.

There were several large pits filled with sand, and plaster-of-Paris molds lay in them in various states of completion. In the back, near the only windows, stood wax figures of naked women, Indians, Buddhas, and birds, waiting to be cut up and placed in plaster of Paris.

Frank said, "We've been doing a lot of statues for people's gardens. Buddhas are big with the koi-pond types. That's what we needed the turtles for. Monk already sold one of them to a woman in Pacific Heights for five hundred bucks. Sight unseen."

"My turtles?" Tommy said. He looked more closely at the bronze turtle Frank was holding. "Zelda!"

"Can you believe it?" Frank said. "We did them both in less than eight hours. Lost-wax process would have taken days. I'll show you."

He led Tommy to the other side of the shop where a short, portly man in leather and denim was working beside a tall Plexiglas tank filled with a translucent green liquid.

Frank said, "Monk, this is our neighbor, Tom Flood. Flood, this is my partner Monk."

Monk grunted, not looking up from a compressor that he seemed to be having trouble with. Tommy could see how he had gotten his name. He had a large bowl-shaped bald spot with a fringe of hair around it: the Benedictine version of Easy Rider, Friar Tuck on wheels.

"This," said Frank, gesturing toward the ten-foot tank, "as far as we know, is the biggest electroplating tank on the West Coast."

Tommy didn't know quite how to react. He was still stunned by seeing the bronze likeness of Zelda. "That's just spiffy," he said finally.

"Yeah, dude. We can do anything we can find. No molds, no wax carvings. You just dunk and go. That's how we did your turtles."

Tommy was beginning to get it. "You mean that that is not a sculpture? You covered my turtles with brass?"

"That's it. That liquid is supersaturated with dissolved metal.

We sprayed the turtles with a thin metal-based paint that would conduct current. Then we attached a wire to them and dipped them in the tank. The current draws the metal out of the water and it fuses to the paint on the turtle. Leave it a long time and the coating gets thick enough to have structural integrity. *Voilà*, a bronze garden turtle. I don't think anybody's ever done it before. We owe you, man."

Monk grunted in gratitude.

Tommy didn't know whether to be angry or depressed. "You should have told me you were going to kill them."

"I thought you knew, man. Sorry. You can have this one, if you want." Frank presented the bronzed Zelda.

Tommy shook his head and looked away. "I don't think I could look at her." He turned and walked away.

Frank said, "C'mon, man, take it. We owe you one. If you need a favor or something . . ."

Tommy took Zelda. How would he explain to Jody? "By the way, I've turned your little friends into statues." And this right after they'd had a big fight. He slunk up the steps feeling completely lost.

Jody had left him a note on the counter:

Tommy:

Imperative that you are here when I wake up. If you go out you are in serious, life-threatening trouble. I mean it. I have some very important things to tell you. No time now, I'm going to go out any second. Be here when I wake up.

Jody

"Great," Tommy said to Peary. "Now what do I do about Mara? Who does Jody think she is, threatening me? What does she think she's going to do if I'm not here? I can't be here. Why don't you keep her busy until I get home." Tommy patted the chest freezer and an idea came to him.

"You know, Peary, scientists have frozen vampire bats and

thawed them completely unharmed. I mean, how would she know? How many times has she thought it was Tuesday when it was really Wednesday?"

Tommy went to the bedroom and looked in on Jody, who had made it to bed, but not in time to change out of her black dress.

Wow, Tommy thought, she never dresses like that for me.

She looked so peaceful. Sexy, but peaceful.

She'll be angry if she finds out, but she's angry now. It won't really hurt her. I can just take her out tomorrow morning and put her under the electric blanket. By sundown she'll be thawed out and I'll have handled the Mara thing. I can tell Mara that I'm involved. I can't start something new until this is finished. Maybe with the extra time, Jody will have chilled a little.

He smiled to himself.

He opened the lid of the freezer, then went into the bedroom to get Jody. He carried her into the kitchen and laid her in the freezer on top of Peary. As he tucked her into the fetal position he felt a twinge of jealousy. "You guys behave now, okay?" He tucked a few TV dinners around her nice and snug under her arms, then kissed her on the forehead and gently closed the lid.

As he crawled into bed he thought, If she ever finds out about this, she's really going to be pissed.

Tommy had been asleep three hours when the pounding started. He rolled out of bed, stumbled across the dark bedroom, and was blinded when he opened the door into the loft. He was just regaining his eyesight when he opened the fire door and Rivera said, "Are you Thomas Flood, Junior?"

"Yes," Tommy said, bracing himself against the doorjamb.

"I'm Inspector Alphonse Rivera from the San Francisco Police Department." He held up a badge wallet. "You're under arrest"—Rivera pulled a warrant from his jacket pocket—"for abandoning a vehicle on a public street."

"You're kidding," Tommy said.

Cavuto stepped through the door and grabbed Tommy by the shoulder, whipping him around as the big cop pulled his handcuffs from his belt. "You have the right to remain silent . . ." Cavuto said.

Two hours later Tommy had been processed, probed, and printed, and as Cavuto had expected, Tommy's fingerprints matched those on the copy of *On the Road* that they had found under the dead bum. It was enough for them to get a search warrant issued for the loft. Five minutes after they entered the loft a mobile crime lab was dispatched along with a forensics team and two coroners' trucks. As far as crime scenes went, the loft in SOMA was the mother lode.

Cavuto and Rivera left the crime scene to the forensics team and returned to the station, where they took Tommy from a holding cell and put him in a pleasantly pink interrogation room furnished with a metal table and two chairs. There was a mirror on one wall and a tape recorder sat on the table. Tommy sat staring at the pink wall, remembering something about how pink was supposed to calm you down. It didn't seem to be working. His stomach was tied in knots.

Rivera had done dozens of interrogations with Cavuto and they always took the same roles: Cavuto was the bad cop, and Rivera was the good cop. Actually Rivera never felt like the good cop. More often he was the I-am-tired-and-overworked-and-I'm-being-nice-to-you-because-I-don't-have-the-energy-to-be-angry cop.

"Would you like a smoke?" Rivera asked.

"Sure," Tommy said.

Cavuto jumped in his face. "Too bad, punk. There's no smoking in here." Cavuto took great pleasure in being the bad cop. He practiced in front of the mirror at home.

Rivera shrugged. "He's right. You can't smoke."

Tommy said, "That's okay, I don't smoke."

"How about a lawyer then?" asked Rivera. "Or a phone call?"

"I have to be at work at midnight," Tommy said. "If it looks like I'm going to be late, I'll use my call then."

Cavuto was pacing the room, timing his path so he could wheel on Tommy with every statement. He wheeled. "Yeah, kid, you're going to be late, about thirty years late, if they don't fry you."

Tommy pushed back in his chair with fright.

"Good one, Nick," Rivera said.

"Thanks." Cavuto smiled around an unlit cigar and backed away from the table where Tommy sat.

Rivera moved up. "Okay, kid, you don't want an attorney. Where do you want to start? We've got you hands-down on two murders and probably three. If you tell us the story, tell us everything, about all the other murders, we might be able to waive the death penalty."

"I didn't kill anybody."

"Don't be cute," Cavuto said. "We found two bodies in your freezer. We've got your fingerprints all over a book that we found under a third body outside your apartment. We've got you staying at the motel where we found a fourth body. And we've got you with a closetful of women's clothing and eyewitnesses that put a woman near where we found a fifth body . . ."

Tommy interrupted, "Actually, there's only one body in the freezer. The other is my girlfriend."

"You sick fuck." Cavuto drew back as if to hit Tommy. Rivera moved to restrain him. Tommy cowered in his chair.

Rivera led Cavuto to the far side of the room. "Let me take this for a minute." He left Cavuto grumbling to himself and went to the seat across from Tommy.

"Look, kid, we've got you cold, so to speak, on two murders. We've got circumstantial evidence on another. You are going to jail for a very long time, and at this point, the death penalty is looking pretty good. Now if you tell us everything, and don't leave anything out, we might be able to help you out, but you have to give us enough to close all the cases. Do you understand?"

Tommy nodded. "But I didn't kill anybody. I put Jody in the freezer, which I admit is inconsiderate, but I didn't kill her."

Cavuto growled. Rivera nodded in mock acceptance of the

story. "Fine, but if you didn't kill them, who did? Did someone you know force you into this?"

Cavuto exploded, "Oh Christ, Rivera! What do you need, a videotape? This little bastard did it."

"Nick, please. Give me a minute here."

Cavuto moved to the table and leaned over it until his face was next to Tommy's. He whispered, raspy and gruff, "Flood, don't think you can use a wiggle and a wink to get yourself out of this. That might work down on Castro, but I'm immune to it here, you got me? I'm going to leave now, but when I come back, if you haven't told my partner your story, I'm going to cause pain. Lots of it, and I won't leave a mark on you." He stood up, smiled, then turned and left the room.

Tommy looked at Rivera. "A wiggle and a wink?"

"Nick thinks you're cute," Rivera said.

"He's gay?"

"Completely."

Tommy shook his head. "I would have never guessed."

"He's a Shriner, too." Rivera tapped a cigarette out of his pack and lit it. "Looks can be deceiving."

"Hey, I didn't think you were allowed to smoke in here."

Rivera blew smoke in Tommy's face. "You had two people in your freezer, and you're giving me shit about smoking."

"Good point."

Rivera sat down and leaned back in the chair. "Tommy, I'm going to give you one more chance to tell me how you killed those people, then I'm going to let Nick back in here and I'm going to leave. He really likes you. This room is soundproof, you know."

Tommy swallowed hard. "You're not going to believe me. It's a pretty fantastic story. There's supernatural stuff involved."

Rivera rubbed his temples. "Satan told you to do it?" he said wearily.

"No."

"Elvis?"

"I told you, it's supernatural."

"Tommy, I'm going to tell you something I've never told anyone before. If you repeat it, I'll deny I said it. Five years ago I saw a white owl with a seventy-foot wingspan swoop out of the sky and pluck a demon off a hillside and take off into the sky."

"I heard that cops get the best drugs," Tommy said.

Rivera got up. "I'm going to bring Nick in."

"No, wait. I'll tell you. It was a vampire. You can thaw Jody out and ask her."

Rivera reached over and turned on the tape recorder. "Now slow down. Start at the beginning and go until we walked you into this room."

An hour later Rivera met Cavuto behind the one-way mirror. Cavuto was not happy. "You know, I'd rather you just threaten that I would beat him up."

"It worked, didn't it?"

"There's nothing there we can use. Not a thing. If he sticks with that story he'll get off on insanity. It's too wild. I want to know how he got the blood out of the bodies."

"The kid thinks he's a writer. He's showing off his imagination. Let's let him sit awhile and get something to eat. I want to find the Emperor."

"That wacko?"

"He's been reporting seeing a vampire for weeks. Maybe he saw the kid doing one of the murders."

CHAPTER 29
Paying Respects

Gilbert Bendetti liked his job, really liked his job. It was a government job, of sorts, so the benefits were good and the work easy. He liked working nights, too, it was quiet and he was usually in the morgue by himself, so he didn't have to feel self-conscious about his weight or his bad skin. He liked playing with computers and the lab equipment, and he liked answering the phone and acting official. Being the night man at the coroner's office would have been a great job even if he didn't get to fuck the dead, but with that, it was heaven.

Tonight Gilbert was bubbling with anticipation. They had wheeled Miss Right in that afternoon and left him explicit instructions not to put her away, but to let her sit out to thaw for the autopsy. Some psycho had put her in a freezer. Sick bastard had put TV dinners under her arms. Now she was curled up on a gurney, teasing him. That cocktail dress, that red hair—he could hardly wait.

He checked the log and locked his skin books in the desk drawer, then loosened his lab coat and went down the hall to test her for flexibility. The last time he checked she'd started to get a little flexibility, but he knew that inside she was—well—frigid, despite the Salisbury-steak gravy dripping from under her arms.

He pushed through the glass door into the holding room and

there she was, just as he had left her, her pouty lips beckoning to him, her lovely legs curled up behind her.

"My angel," Gilbert said, "shall I help you with those pesky panty hose?"

He straightened her legs on the gurney and pushed her skirt up. She was still a little chilly, but she was movable. Good, once rigor mortis set in, passion could put you into positions that would challenge a yoga master. Gilbert had thrown his back out more than once.

Her panty hose were sheer black, but except for her right big toe, her feet were dusty. She must have been walking in her stocking feet. Indulging himself in some foreplay, Gilbert had sucked her big toe clean shortly after they brought her in. Foreplay, sorta.

He considered testing her with the meat thermometer, but she was so perfect, he didn't want to mark that lovely body. He reached up under her skirt, grabbed the waistband of her panty hose, and began to work them down.

"Black lace panties, my goodness . . ." He tried to remember her name, then checked her toe tag. "My goodness, Jody, how did you know I liked black lace?"

He peeled her panty hose off, stopping to loosen the toe tag first, then ran his hands up her thighs after the lace panties.

"And a natural redhead," Gilbert said, dropping the panties on the floor. He stepped back a moment to admire her and slip out of his lab coat. He locked the wheels on the gurney, pulled the TV dinners out from under her arms, and unzipped his pants.

"This is going to be so good. So good." He climbed over the end of the gurney, careful to stay balanced. Nothing ruined the mood more than toppling to the linoleum and bashing your skull.

He licked a path up the inside of her leg.

"Tommy, that tickles," she said.

Gilbert looked up. No, it's my imagination. He returned to his pleasure.

"No, let me shower first," she said. She sat up.

Gilbert pushed himself backward so violently that the gurney went up on its end, dumping Jody on the floor. Gilbert backed away from her holding his chest, his breath refusing to come, his withering willy waving in front of him.

Jody climbed to her feet. "Who are you?"

Gilbert couldn't talk. He couldn't breathe. It felt as if barbed wire had been looped around his heart and was being yanked by a team of horses. He backed into a rack of drawers, banging his head.

Jody looked around. "How did I get here? Answer me."

Gilbert gasped and fell to his knees.

"Where's Tommy? And where the fuck are my panties?"

Gilbert was shaking his head. He rolled on his side, took two more tortured breaths, and died.

"Hey!" Jody said. "I need some answers here."

Gilbert didn't answer. Jody watched the black aura of his dying fade away, leaving only the residual heat signature of his body.

"Sorry," she said.

She looked around: the gurney, the big file drawers of the dead, the instruments of dissection—this sure looked like the morgues in the movies. Something had gone seriously wrong while she slept.

She checked her watch, but it was gone. The wall clock over Gilbert's body read 1 A.M.

Why did I wake up so late? I've got to find Tommy and find out what happened.

She picked up her panties from the floor and wiggled into them. The panty hose she left where they lay, instead looking around for her shoes. She didn't see them. She didn't see her purse anywhere either.

Money. I'm going to need cab fare.

She crouched by Gilbert's body and rifled through his pockets, coming up with thirty dollars and some change. Almost as an afterthought she tucked his exposed member back into his pants and zipped him up.

"I did that for your family, not for you," she said. Then thought, I'm getting worse than Tommy, talking to dead people.

She started toward the door, then stopped and looked at the wall of drawers. The scenario came over her like a sudden sneeze.

Tommy is probably in one of those drawers. The vampire killed him, and when the coroner came, they thought I was dead too. But why did he spare me? And why did it take so long to wake up? Maybe it was that med student. Maybe when I missed the meeting he told the cops where to find me. But he didn't know how to find me.

She went though the glass doors and down the hall where she stopped at the phone and called the loft. No answer. She dialed the Marina Safeway's number.

"Marina Safeway." She recognized Simon McQueen's drawl.

"Simon, this is Jody. I need to talk to Tommy."

"Who? Who did you say you were?"

"It's Jody. Tommy's girlfriend. I need to speak to him."

Simon was quiet for a moment. When he finally spoke, his voice was an octave lower. "You don't know where Flood is?"

"He's not there?"

"Nope."

"Is he okay?"

"In a manner of speakin', he's okay. What about you? You feelin' all right?"

"Yes, Simon, I'm fine. Where's Tommy?"

"Well, ain't you a wonder. You're sure you feel okay?"

"Yes. Where's Tommy?"

"I can't tell you over the phone. I'll come get you. Where are you?"

"I'm not sure; just a second." Jody ran to the front door. The address was printed on the glass. She went back to the phone and gave Simon an address two blocks away.

"Let me get someone to cover my section. I'll be there in a half hour."

"Thanks, Simon." Jody hung up. What in the hell was going on?

• • •

While she waited for Simon to arrive, Jody parried the propositions of two guys in a Mercedes who had mistaken her for a hooker. Not an unreasonable mistake considering she was standing barefoot on a back street in a low-cut cocktail dress on a cold San Francisco night. Finally, when she told them she was an undercover cop, their resolve softened and they drove off hanging their heads.

Simon rounded the corner five minutes later and skidded to a stop in a cloud of smoking rubber and testosterone. He threw the door open for her.

"Get in."

Jody leaped into the passenger seat. Simon seemed a little surprised that she hadn't used the two steps mounted under the door. "You're steppin' high tonight, darlin'," Simon said.

Jody closed the door. "Where's Tommy?"

"Hold your horses, I'll take you to him." Simon put the truck in gear and roared off. "You sure you're feeling all right?"

"Yes, I'm fine. Why couldn't you tell me what happened to Tommy on the phone?"

"Well, he's hiding out. Seems the police want him for some murders."

"The Whiplash murders?"

"Those be the ones." Simon looked at her. "Ain't you cold?"

"Oh, I lost my coat."

"And shoes?"

"Yes, and shoes. Some guys were chasing me." Jody knew she didn't sound very convincing.

They were headed down Market toward the Bay Bridge. Simon grinned and pushed his black Stetson back on his head. "You don't get cold, do you, darlin'?"

"What do you mean?"

Simon hit the electric-lock button; Jody heard the lock go thunk at her side. Simon said, "You don't get hot either, do you? Or sick. Do you get sick?"

Jody hugged the door handle. "What are you getting at, Simon?"

Simon reached inside his jacket and came out with a Colt Python revolver. He pointed it at her and cocked it. "Now I know bullets might not kill you, but I'll bet they hurt like hell. And I put some little wood pegs in the hollow points just in case that does the job."

Jody had no idea what a bullet would do to her and she didn't want to find out. "What do you want, Simon?"

Simon pulled the truck into an alley and switched off the engine. "Couple of things. I don't know which I want first until you answer some questions."

"Whatever you want, Simon. You're Tommy's friend. You don't have to be a hard-ass, just ask."

"That's right sweet of you, darlin'. Now tell me, do you get sick?"

"Everybody gets sick, Simon. I get a cold every now and then."

Simon dug the gun into her ribs. "Don't bullshit me now. I know what you are."

Jody looked closely at Simon for the first time. He was burning up, the heat coming off him in red waves, even in the relative warmth of the truck cab. But below the heat aura she saw something else that she hadn't seen the first night she'd met him. Maybe because she hadn't known what to look for. Under the heat signature Simon was ringed by a thin black corona, as she had seen on other people—the death aura, but thinner, as if it was just growing.

She said, "Are you sure you're not just being an asshole again, Simon? Holding up your friend's girlfriend?"

"Don't get slippery on me, Red. I saw you sleeping that day we partied at your house. I touched you. You're cold as a witch's titty. And Flood always complainin' about you sleeping all day. And how he had to have them turtles alive. But I didn't put it all together until the Emperor started screaming about vampires and the cops took Flood away."

"You're nuts, Simon. None of that proves anything. There's no such thing as vampires."

"Oh yeah? Well, you know why they arrested Tommy?"

"No, I didn't know . . ."

"Because they found you dead in the freezer, that's why. He's in for your murder, missy. I still had some doubts until you called just now. You'll be my first dead piece of ass, not counting the time I choked my chicken over a picture of Marilyn."

Jody was stunned. A wave of panic swept through her, the inner voice shouting, *Kill him, hide; kill him, hide.* She fought it back. "You're doing this because you want sex?"

"Well, that's part of it. You see, I ain't been well laid for five years—since I picked me up this bug. It's kinda hard to get yourself into a good three-toweler when you got the dick of death. I ain't no ass bandit, though. I let some whore from Oakland fix me up with a speedball. Six of us shared the needle."

"You're dying of AIDS?" Jody asked.

"No need to candy-coat it, darlin'. Just come right out and say it."

"Sorry, Simon, but when someone has a gun on me and tells me he's going to rape me, I forget my manners."

"Ain't going to be no rape unless you want it. The other thing is more important."

"Other thing?"

"I want you to change me into a vampire."

"No, you don't, Simon. You don't know what it's like."

"I don't need to know, darlin'. I know I'm going to die if you don't. It ain't just HIV anymore, it's full-blown. I can hardly get my boots on and off from the sores. The doctor's got me on enough pills to choke a horse. Now do it."

Jody felt for him. For all his arrogant cowboy panache, she could tell he was afraid. "I don't know how, Simon. I don't know how I was changed. It just happened."

He dug the barrel of the gun up under her breast and slid across the seat next to her. "You just bite my damn neck. Now do it!"

"That doesn't work. That would just kill you. I don't know how to turn you into a vampire."

Simon took the gun out of her ribs and held it against her

thigh. "I'm going to count to three, then I'm going to shoot you in the leg if you don't start turning me. Then I'm going to count to three and shoot you in the other leg. I didn't want to do this, but you got to see."

Jody could see tears welling up in Simon's eyes. He didn't want to do this, but she knew he would. She wondered even if she knew how to turn him if she would do it. "Simon, please, I really don't know how to turn you. Let me go. Maybe I'll find out."

"I don't have the time, darlin'. If I have to trade the daylight for a lifetime of nights, I'll take the nights. I'm counting now. One!"

"Simon, don't. Just wait."

"Two!"

Jody watched a tear roll out of his eye. She felt his body tense and looked down at the gun. The tendons in his hand were tightening. He was going to do it.

"Three!"

Jody shot out her right hand, palm open, and hit Simon under the chin while sweeping the gun away from her leg with her right. The gun went off, sending a bullet through the floorboard. The explosion covered the noise of Simon's neck snapping but she could feel the crunch against her palm. Simon slumped back in the seat, his head thrown back and mouth open as if he were frozen in a laugh. Over the ringing in her ears Jody could hear his last breath squeaking out of his lungs. The black aura around him faded away.

She reached over and straightened his Stetson. "God, Simon, I'm sorry. I'm so sorry."

Rivera drove. Cavuto sat in the passenger seat smoking and talking on the radio. He keyed the mike. "If anyone sees the Emperor tonight, detain him and call Rivera and Cavuto. He's wanted for questioning but he's not, I repeat *not,* a suspect. In other words, don't scare him."

Cavuto hung the mike on the dash and said to Rivera, "You really don't think that this is a waste of time?"

"Like I said, Nick, homicide and the coroner are the only ones who know about the blood loss. Our guys wouldn't leak, but even if there was a leak in the coroner's office, I can't imagine anyone telling the Emperor. Whoever did these murders is behaving like a vampire. Maybe he thinks he's a vampire. So to catch him, we have to pretend we're tracking a vampire."

"That's bullshit. We've got enough evidence on the kid to get an indictment right now, and by the time forensics gets done with his apartment we'll have enough for a conviction."

"Yeah," Rivera said, "except for one thing."

Cavuto rolled his eyes. "I know, you don't think he killed anyone."

"And neither do you."

Cavuto chomped his cigar and looked out the car window at a group of winos milling on a corner by a liquor store.

"Do you?" Rivera insisted.

"He knows who did. And if I have to walk his cute little ass right up to the chair to get him to tell, I will."

A call came over the radio. "Go ahead," Cavuto said into the mike.

The dispatcher's voice crackled over the speaker. "Unit ten is holding the Emperor at Mason and Bay. Do you want them to bring him in?"

Cavuto turned to Rivera and raised his eyebrows. "Well?"

"No, tell them we'll be there in five."

Cavuto keyed the mike. "Negative, we're on our way."

Three minutes later Rivera pulled the unmarked Dodge into a red zone behind the cruiser. The two uniformed officers were playing with Lazarus and Bummer, whose armor rattled and clanged as they frisked. The Emperor stood by, his wooden sword still in hand.

Rivera got out of the car first. "Good evening, Your Majesty."

"Give me a fucking break," Cavuto said under his breath as he hoisted his bulk out of the car.

"And a good early morning to you, Inspector." The Emperor bowed. "I see the fiend has us all burning the midnight oil."

Rivera nodded to the uniforms. "We got it, guys, thanks." One of the uniforms was a woman. She shot Rivera a dirty look as she headed for the cruiser.

Rivera turned his attention back to the Emperor. "You've been busy calling in reports of a vampire in the City."

The Emperor frowned. "And I must say, Inspector, I'm a bit disappointed with the lack of promptness of your response."

"Eat me," said Cavuto.

"We've been busy," Rivera said.

"Well, you're here at last." The Emperor waved to Bummer and Lazarus, who were waiting at his heel. "You know the men?"

"We've met," Rivera said with a wave. "Your Majesty, you reported seeing a vampire"—Rivera pulled a notebook out of his jacket pocket—"three different times over the last month and a half." Rivera took a copy of Tommy's mug shot from his notebook and held it out to the Emperor. "Is this the man you saw?"

"Heavens no. That's my friend C. Thomas Flood, aspiring author. A fine, if confused, lad. I arranged for his employment at the Marina Safeway."

"But he's not the man you reported as being a vampire."

"No. The fiend is older, and has sharp features, of Arab descent, I would guess, if he were not so pale."

Cavuto stepped up and took the picture from Rivera. "You reported the body they found in SOMA, but you said you didn't see anything. Did you see this man anywhere near the scene?"

"The victim was a friend of mine, Charlie. He left his mind in Vietnam, I'm afraid, but a good soul just the same. He had been dead for some time when I found him, though. The fiend left him there to rot."

Cavuto bristled. "But you didn't see this vampire guy at the scene either."

"I have seen him in the financial district, once in Chinatown, and at the marina last night. In fact, that young man gave me sanctuary at the Safeway."

Cavuto's beeper went off. He ignored it. "You saw Flood and this vampire guy together?"

"No, I ran from the wharf when the fiend materialized out of mist."

"I'm outta here," Cavuto said, throwing up his hands. He checked his beeper and went back to the car.

Rivera held his ground. "I'm sorry, Your Majesty, my partner needs to learn some manners. Now, if you can just tell me . . ."

Cavuto beeped the horn and hung his head out the window. "Rivera, come on. They found another one. Let's go."

"Wait a second." Rivera took a business card out of his wallet and gave it to the Emperor. "Highness, could you call me tomorrow, around noon? I'll come get you wherever you are—buy you and the men some lunch."

"Of course, my son."

Cavuto yelled out the car window, "Let's go, this one's fresh."

"Be careful," Rivera said to the Emperor. "Watch your back, okay?"

The Emperor grinned. "Safety first."

Rivera turned and walked to the car. He was still shutting the door as Cavuto pulled away from the curb. Cavuto said, "Another snapped neck. Body's in a pickup off of Market. Uniforms found it five minutes ago."

"Blood loss?"

"They knew enough not to say over the radio. But there's a witness."

"Witness?"

"Homeless guy sleeping in the alley saw a woman leaving the scene. There's an all-points out for a redheaded female in a black cocktail dress."

"You're bullshitting."

Cavuto turned and looked him in the eye. "The Laundromat ninja returns."

"Santa Fucking Maria," Rivera said.

"I love it when you speak Spanish."

The radio crackled again, the dispatcher calling their unit number. Rivera grabbed the mike and keyed it.

"What now?" he said.

CHAPTER 30
Cops and Corpses

"This guy is pissing me off," Cavuto said, expelling a blue cloud of cigar smoke against the file drawers of the dead. "I hate this fucking guy." He was standing over the body of Gilbert Bendetti, who had a thermometer sticking out of the side of his abdomen.

"Inspector, there's no smoking allowed in here," said a uniformed officer who had been called to the scene.

Cavuto waved to the drawers. "Do you think they mind?"

The officer shook his head. "No, sir."

Cavuto blew a stream of smoke at Gilbert. "And him, do you think he minds?"

"No, sir."

"And you, Patrolman Jeeter, you don't mind, do you?"

Jeeter cleared his throat. "Uh . . . no, sir."

"Well, good," Cavuto said. "Look on the side of the car, Jeeter. It says 'Protect and Serve,' not 'Piss and Moan.'"

"Yes, sir."

Rivera came through the double doors, followed by a tall, six-tyish man in a lab coat and silver wire-frame glasses.

Cavuto looked up. "Doc, this guy done, or what?"

The doctor pulled a surgical mask over his face as he approached the body. He bent over Gilbert and checked the thermometer. "He's been dead about four hours. I'd put the time of death between one and one-thirty I won't be able to tell for sure until I finish the postmortem, but offhand I'd say myocardial infarction."

"I hate this guy," Cavuto repeated. He looked down at Jody's toe tag, which was lying on the linoleum with a chalk circle drawn around it. "Any chance this guy misplaced the redhead?"

The coroner looked up. "None at all. Someone removed the body."

Rivera had his notebook out and was scribbling as the doctor talked. "Any news on the one that just came in, the cowboy? Any blood loss?"

"Again, I can't say for sure, but it looks like a broken neck is the cause of death. There may have been some blood loss, but not as much as we've seen with the others. Since he was sitting up, it could just be settling."

"What about the wound on the throat?" Rivera asked.

"What wound?" the coroner said. "There was no wound on the throat; I checked the body myself."

Rivera's arms fell to his sides, his pen clattered on the linoleum. "Doctor, could you check again? Nick and I both saw distinct puncture wounds on the right side of the neck."

The doctor stood up and walked to the rack of drawers and pulled one out. "Check for yourself."

Cavuto and Rivera moved to either side of the drawer. Rivera turned Simon's head to the side while inspecting his neck. He looked up at Cavuto, who shook his head and walked away.

"Nick, you saw it, right?"

Cavuto nodded.

Rivera turned to the doctor. "I saw the wounds, Doc, I swear. I've been doing this too long to get something like that wrong."

The coroner shrugged. "When was the last time you two slept?"

"Together, you mean?" said Cavuto.

The coroner frowned.

Rivera said, "Thanks, Doc, we've got some more work at the other crime scene. We'll be back. Let's go, Nick."

Cavuto was standing over Gilbert again. "I hate this guy, and I hate that cowboy in the drawer. Did I mention that?"

Rivera tuned on his heel and started toward the doors, then stopped and looked down. There was a distinct footprint on the linoleum in brown gravy. Made by a small foot, a woman's bare foot.

Rivera turned to the coroner. "Doc, you got any women working here?"

"Not down here. Only in the office."

"Fuck! Nick, come on, we need to talk." Rivera stormed through the double doors, leaving them swinging.

Cavuto ambled after him. He paused at the doors and turned back to the coroner. "He's moody, Doc."

The coroner nodded.

"Nothing to the press about the blood loss, if there was any. And nothing about the missing body."

"Of course not. I have no desire to advertise that my office is losing bodies," the coroner said.

Rivera was waiting in the hallway when Cavuto came through the doors. "We've got to cut the kid loose, you know that."

"We can hold him another twenty-four hours."

"He didn't do it."

"Yeah, but he knows something."

"Maybe we should let him go and follow him."

"Give me one more shot at him. Alone."

"Whatever. We've got something else to consider too. You saw those puncture marks on the cowboy's throat the same as I did, right?"

Cavuto chewed his cigar and looked at the ceiling.

"Well?"

Cavuto nodded.

"Then maybe the others had wounds too. Maybe they had wounds that went away. And did you see the footprint?"

"I saw it."

"Nick, do you believe in vampires?"

Cavuto turned and walked down the hall. "I need a stiff one."

"You mean a drink?"

Cavuto glared over his shoulder and growled.

Rivera grinned. "I owed you that one."

Tommy guessed the temperature in the cell to be about sixty-five, but even so, his cellmate, the six-foot-five, two-hundred-fifty-pound, unshaven, unbathed, one-eyed psychopath with the Disney-character tattoos, was dripping with sweat.

Maybe, Tommy thought, as he cowered in the corner behind the toilet, it's warmer up there on the bunk. Or maybe it's hard work trying to stare at someone menacingly, without blinking, for six hours when you only have one eye.

"I hate you," said One-Eye.

"Sorry," said Tommy.

One-Eye stood up and flexed his biceps; Micky and Goofy bulged angrily. "Are you making fun of me?"

Tommy didn't want to say anything, so he shook his head violently, trying to make sure that nothing remotely resembling a smile crossed his face.

One-Eye sat down on the bunk and resumed menacing. "What are you in for?"

"Nothing," Tommy said. "I didn't do anything."

"Don't fuck with me, ass-wipe. What were you arrested for?"

Tommy fidgeted, trying to work his way into the cinder-block wall. "Well, I put my girlfriend in the freezer, but I don't think that's a crime."

One-Eye, for the first time since he'd been put in the cell, smiled. "Me either. You didn't use an assault weapon, did you?"

"Nope, a Sears frost-free."

"Oh, good; they're really tough on crimes with assault weapons."

"So," Tommy said, venturing an inch out of the corner, "what are you in for?" Thinking baby-stomping, thinking cannibalism, thinking fast-food massacre.

One-Eye hung his head. "Copyright infringement."

"You're kidding?"

One-Eye frowned. Tommy slid back into his corner, adding, "Really? That's bad."

One-Eye pulled off his ratty T-shirt. The Seven Dwarfs danced across his massive chest between knife and bullet scars. On his stomach, Snow White and Cinderella were locked in a frothy embrace of mutual muffin munching.

"Yeah, I made the mistake of walking around without a shirt. A Disney executive who was up here on vacation saw me down by the wharf. He called their legal pit bulls."

Tommy shook his head in sympathy. "I didn't know they put you in jail for copyright infringement."

"Well, they don't, really. It was when I ripped the guy's shoulders out of their sockets that the police got involved."

"That's not a crime either, is it?"

One-Eye rubbed his temples as if it was excruciating to remember. "It was in front of his kids."

"Oh," Tommy said.

"Flood, on your feet," a guard said from the cell door. Inspector Nick Cavuto stood behind him.

"C'mon, cutie," Cavuto said. "We're going for a last walk."

The blood-high wasn't racing through her with flush and fever as it always had before. No, it was more like the satisfying fullness of a lasagna dinner chased with double espressos. Still, the strength sang in her limbs; she ripped the loft-door dead bolts through the metal doorjamb as easily as she had torn the plastic crime-scene tape the police had put across the door.

Strange, she thought, there *is* a difference in drinking from a living body.

Her remorse over killing Simon had passed in seconds and the predator mind had taken over. A new aspect of the predator had reared up this time, not just the instinct to hide and hunt, but to protect.

If Tommy was in jail for putting her in the freezer, it meant that the police had also found Peary, and they would try to connect Tommy to the other murders. But if they found another victim while Tommy was behind bars, they would have to set him free. And she needed him to be free, first so that she could find out why he had frozen her, but more important, because it was time to turn the tables on the other vampire, and the only safe way to hunt him was to do it during daylight.

She had bit Simon's neck and used the heel of her hand to pump his heart as she drank. There was no guilt or self-consciousness in the act; the predator mind had taken over. She found herself thinking about the burly fireman who had come to Transamerica to teach the employees earthquake preparedness, which had included a course in CPR. What would he think of one of his students' using his technique to pump lifeblood from the murdered? "I'm sorry, Fireman Frank, I sucked like an Electrolux, but it just wasn't enough. If it's any consolation, I didn't enjoy it."

What little strength she had gained from Simon's blood seemed to evaporate as she walked into the loft. It was in worse shape than the day the Animals had come for breakfast. The futon was bundled against the wall; the books had been taken out of their shelves and spread out on the floor; the cabinets hung open, their contents tumbled across the counters; and a fine patina of fingerprint powder covered every surface. She wanted to cry.

It reminded her of the time she had lived with a heavy-metal bass player for two months, who had torn their apartment apart looking for money for drugs. Money?

She ran to the bedroom and to the dresser where she had stashed the remaining cash the old vampire had given her. It was gone. She threw open the drawer where she kept her lingerie. She'd kept a couple thousand rolled up in a bra, a holdover habit from the days of hiding cash from the bass player. It was there. She had enough for a month's rent, but then what? It wouldn't matter if Tommy didn't stop the other vampire. He was going to kill them both, she was sure of it, and he was going to do it soon.

As she weighed the rolls of bills in her hand, she heard someone open the stairwell door, then footfalls on the steps. She went to the kitchen and waited, crouched behind the counter.

Someone was in the loft. A man. She could hear his heart—smell sweat and stale deodorant coming off him. Tommy's deodorant. She stood up.

"Hi," Tommy said. "Boy, am I glad to see you."

CHAPTER 31

He Was an Ex-Con, She Was Defrosted . . .

She started to lean over the counter to give him a hug, then stopped herself. "You look awful," she said.

He was unshaven, his hair stuck out in greasy tufts, and his clothes looked as if he'd slept in them. He hadn't. He hadn't slept at all.

"Thanks," he said. "You look a little tattered yourself."

She raised her hand to her hair, felt a tangle, and let it drop. "And I thought my red hair went so well with freezer burn."

"I can explain that."

She came around the counter and stood before him, not knowing whether to hold him or hit him.

"That's a great dress. Is it new?"

"It was a great dress before the gravy and cobbler melted all over it. What happened, Tommy? Why was I frozen?"

He reached out to touch her face. "How are you? I mean, are you okay?"

"Good time to ask." She glared at him.

He looked in her eyes, then away. "You're very beautiful, you know that?" He crumpled to the floor and sat with his back against the counter. "I'm so sorry, Jody. I didn't want to hurt you. I was just . . . sort of lonely."

She felt tears welling in her eyes and wiped them away. He was genuinely sorry, she could tell. And she had always been a sucker for pathetic apologies, going back as far as the time the bass player she was seeing hocked her stereo. Or had that been the construction worker? "What happened?" she pressed.

He stared at the floor and shook his head. "I don't know. I wanted someone to talk about books with. Someone who thought I was special. I met a girl at work. I was just going to meet her for coffee, nothing else. But I didn't think you'd understand. So I . . . well, you know."

Jody sat down on the floor in front of him. "Tommy, you could have killed me."

"I'm sorry!" he screamed. "I'm afraid of you. You scare the hell out of me sometimes. I didn't think it would hurt you or I wouldn't have done it. I just wanted to feel special, but you're the special one. I just wanted to talk to someone who sees things the way I do, who can understand how I feel about things. I want to take you out and show you off, even during the day. I've never really had a girlfriend before. I love you. I want to share things with you."

He looked down, would not meet her gaze.

Jody took his hand and squeezed it. "I know how you feel. You don't know how well I know. And I love you too."

Finally he looked at her, then pulled her into his arms. They held each other for a long time, rocking each other like crying children. A half hour passed, ticked off with tear-salty kisses, before she said, "Do you want to share a shower? I don't want to let go of you, and it'll be dawn soon."

Warmed and cleaned by the shower, they danced, still wet, though the dark bedroom, to fall together on the bare mattress. For Tommy, being with her, in her, was like coming to a place where he was safe and loved, and those dark and hostile things that walked the world outside were washed away in the smell of her damp hair, a soft kiss on the eyelid, and mingled whispers of love and reassurance.

It had never been like this for Jody. It was escape from worry and suspicion and from the predator mind that had been rising for days like a shark to blood. There was no urge to feed, but a different hunger drove her to hold him deep and long and still, to envelop and keep him there forever. Her vampire senses rose to the touch of his hands, his mouth—as if finally her sense of touch had grown to feel life itself as pleasure. Love.

When they finished she held his face against her breast and listened to his breathing becoming slow as he fell asleep. Tears crept from the corners of her eyes as dawn broke, releasing her from the night's last thought: I'm loved at last, and I have to give it up.

Tommy was still sleeping at sundown. She kissed him gently on the forehead, then nipped his ear to wake him. He opened his eyes and smiled. She could see it in the dark; it was a genuine smile.

"Hey," he said.

She snuggled against him. "We've got to get up. There's things to do."

"You're cold. Are you cold?"

"I'm never cold." She rolled out of bed and went to the light switch. "Eyes," she warned as she flipped on the light.

Tommy shielded his eyes. "For the love of God, Montressor!"

"Poe?" she said. "Right?"

"Yep."

"See? I can talk books."

Tommy sat up. "I'm sorry. I didn't give you a chance. I guess we were always talking about—about your condition."

She smiled and snatched a pair of jeans and a flannel shirt from the pile of clothes on the floor.

"I talked to the other vampire the other night. That's why I left the note."

Tommy was wide awake now. "You talked to him? Where?"

"In a club. I was mad at you. I wanted to go out. Show off."

"What did he say?"

"He said it's almost over. Tommy, I think he's going to try and kill you, maybe both of us."

"Well, that sucks."

"And you've got to stop him."

"Me? Why me? You're the one with X-ray vision and stuff."

"He's too strong. I get the feeling he's really old. He's clever. I think that the longer that you're a vampire, the more you can do. I'm starting to feel . . . well, sharper as time goes on."

"He's too strong for you, but you want me stop him? How?"

"You'll have to get to him while he's sleeping."

"Kill him? Just like that? Even if I could find him, how would I kill him? Nothing hurts you guys—unless you have some kryptonite."

"You could drag him into the sunlight. Or cut his head off—I'm sure that would do it. Or you could totally dismember him and scatter the pieces." Jody had to look away from him when she said this. It was as if someone else was talking.

"Right," Tommy said, "just shovel him into a garbage bag and get on the forty-two bus. Leave a piece at every stop. Are you nuts? I can't kill anyone, Jody. I'm not built that way."

"Well, I can't do it."

"Why don't we just go to Indiana? You'll like it there. I can get a union job and make my mom happy. You can learn to bowl. It'll be great—no dead guys in the freezer, no vampires . . .

"By the way, how'd you . . . I mean, where did you thaw out?"

"In the morgue. With a pervert all ready to live out his wet dreams on me."

"I'll kill him!"

"Not necessary."

"You killed him? Jody, you can't keep—"

"I didn't kill him. He just sort of died. But there's something else."

"I can't wait."

"The vampire killed Simon."

Tommy was shaken. "How? Where?"

"The same way as the others. That's why the cops let you go."

Tommy took a minute to digest this, sat for a moment looking at his hands. He looked up and said, "How did you know I was in jail?"

"You told me."

"I did?"

"Of course. You were so tired last night. I'm not surprised you don't remember." She buttoned up the flannel shirt. "Tommy, you've got to find the vampire and kill him. I think Simon was his last warning before he takes us."

Tommy shook his head. "I can't believe he got Simon. Why Simon?"

"Because he was close to you. Come on, I'll make you coffee." She started into the kitchen and tripped over the brass turtle. "What's this?"

"Long story," Tommy said.

Jody looked around, listened for the sound of turtle claws. "Where's Scott and Zelda?"

"I set them free. Go make coffee."

Rivera and Cavuto sat in an unmarked cruiser in the alley across the street from the loft, taking turns dozing and watching.

It was Rivera's turn to watch while Cavuto snored in the driver's seat. Rivera didn't like the way things were going. Weird shit just seemed to follow him. His job was to find evidence and catch bad guys, but too often, especially in this case, the evidence pointed to a bad guy who wasn't a guy at all: wasn't human. He didn't want to believe that there was a vampire loose in the City, but he did. And he knew he'd never convince Cavuto, or anybody, for that matter. Still, he'd dug out his mother's silver crucifix before he left the house. It was in his jacket pocket next to his badge wallet. He had been tempted to take it out and say a rosary, but Cavuto, despite his growling snore, was a light sleeper, and Rivera didn't want to endure the ridicule should the big cop wake up in the middle of a Hail Mary.

Rivera was getting ready to wake Cavuto and catch a nap when the lights went on in the loft.

"Nick," he said. "Lights are on."

Cavuto woke, instantly alert. "What?"

"Lights are on. The kid's up."

Cavuto lit his cigar. "And?"

"I just thought you'd want to know."

"Look, Rivera, the lights coming on is not something happening. I know that after ten or twelve hours it seems like something, but it's not. You're losing your edge. The kid leaving, the kid strangling someone, that's something happening."

Rivera was insulted by the admonition. He'd been a cop as long as Cavuto and he didn't have to take crap like that. "Eat shit, Nick. It's my turn to sleep anyway."

Cavuto checked his watch. "Right."

They watched the windows for a while, saying nothing. Shadows moved inside the loft. Too many shadows.

"There's someone else up there," Rivera said.

Cavuto squinted at the shadows and grabbed a pair of binoculars from the seat. "Looks like a girl." Someone passed by the window. "A redhead with a lot of hair."

Tommy took a sip of his coffee and sighed. "I don't even know where to start. This is a big city and I don't know my way around that well."

"Well, we could just wait here for him to come get us." Jody looked at his cup, watched the heat waves coming off the coffee. "God, I miss coffee."

"Can't you just wander around until you feel something? Lestat can . . ."

"Don't start with that!"

"Sorry." He took another sip. "The Animals might help. They'll want revenge for Simon. Can I tell them?"

"You might as well. Those guys do just enough drugs that they might believe you. Besides, I'm sure the story was in the paper this morning."

"Yeah, I'm sure it was." He put his cup down and looked at her. "How did you know about Simon?"

Jody looked away. "I was in the morgue when they brought him in."

"You saw him?"

"I heard the cops talking. I slipped out during the excitement when they found the dead pervert."

"Oh," Tommy said, not quite sure of himself.

She reached out and took his hand. "You'd better go. I'll call a cab."

"They took all the money," Tommy said.

"I have a little left." She handed him two hundred-dollar bills.

He raised his eyebrows. "A little?"

Jody grinned. "Be careful. Stay around people until it gets light. Don't get out of the cab unless there are a lot of people around. I'm sure he doesn't want any witnesses."

"Okay."

"And call me if anything happens. Try to be back here by sundown tomorrow, but if you can't, call and leave me a message where you are."

"So you can protect me?"

"So I can *try* to protect you."

"Why don't you come with me?"

"Because there's two cops in the alley across the street watching the loft. I saw them from the window. I don't think we want them to see me."

"But it's dark in the alley."

"Exactly."

Tommy took her in his arms. "That is so cool. When I get back, will you read to me naked, hanging from the ceiling beam in the dark?"

"Sure."

"Dirty limericks?"

"Anything."

"That's so cool."

• • •

Five minutes later Tommy stood at the bottom of the stairs with the fire door cracked just enough to see when his cab arrived. When the blue-and-white DeSoto cab pulled up, he opened the fire door and a furry black-and-white comet shot past him.

"Bummer! Stop!" the Emperor shouted.

The little dog skipped up the steps with a yap and a rattle every step of the way; his pie-pan helmet was hanging upside down by the chin strap, hitting the edge of each step. He stopped at the top of the stairs and commenced a leaping, barking, scratching attack on the door.

Tommy leaned against the wall holding his chest. He thought, Good, a heart attack will sure mess up the vampire's murder plans.

"Forgive him," the Emperor said. "He always seems to do this when we pass your domicile." Then, to Lazarus, "Would you be so kind as to retrieve our comrade-in-arms?"

The golden retriever bounded up the stairs and snatched Bummer out of the air in mid-leap, then carried him down by the scruff of the neck as the rat dog struggled and snarled.

The Emperor relieved Lazarus of his squirming charge and shoved the smaller soldier into the oversized pocket of his coat. He buttoned the flap and smiled at Tommy. "Dogged enthusiasm in a handy reclosable package."

Tommy laughed, more nervous than amused. "Your Highness, what are you doing here?"

"Why, I am looking for you, my son. The authorities have been asking after you in regard to the monster. The time to act is at hand." The Emperor waved his sword wildly as he spoke.

Tommy stepped back. "You're going to put someone's eye out with that thing."

The Emperor held his sword at port arms. "Oh, quite right. Safety first."

Tommy signaled to the cabdriver over the Emperor's shoulder. "Your Highness, I agree, it's time to do something. I'm on my way to get some help."

"Recruits!" the Emperor exclaimed. "Shall we join forces against evil? Call the City to arms? Drive evil back to the dark crevice from whence it came? Can the men and I share your cab?" He patted his still squirming pocket.

Tommy eyed the cabdriver. "Well, I don't know." He pulled open the rear door and leaned in. "Dogs and royalty okay?" he asked the cabbie.

The driver said something in Farsi that Tommy took for a yes. "Let's go." Tommy stepped back and motioned for the Emperor to get in.

Lazarus jumped into the back seat with a rattle of armor, followed by the Emperor and Tommy. As soon as the cab had gone a block, Bummer settled down and the Emperor let him out of his pocket. "Something about your building vexes him. I don't understand it."

Tommy shrugged, thinking about how he was going to tell the Animals about Simon's death.

The Emperor rolled down the window and he and his men rode through the City with their heads out the window, squinting into the wind like mobile gargoyles.

Cavuto slapped Rivera on the shoulder, startling him out of sleep. "Wake up. Something's going down. A cab just pulled up and that old wacko just came around the corner with his dogs."

Rivera wiped his eyes and sat up. "What's the Emperor doing here?"

"There's the kid. How in the hell did he get hold of the old wacko?"

They watched as Tommy and the Emperor talked, Tommy glancing from time to time at the cabdriver. A few minutes passed and they loaded into the cab.

"Here we go," Cavuto said as he started the car.

"Wait, let me out."

"What?"

"I want to see where the girl goes. Who she is."

"Just go ask her."

"I'm out of here." Rivera picked up the portable radio from the seat. "Stay in touch. I'll send for another car."

Cavuto was rocking in the driver's seat, waiting to go. "Call me on the cell phone if you see the girl. Keep it off the radio."

Rivera stopped halfway out of the car. "You think it's the girl from the morgue, don't you?"

"Get out," Cavuto said. "He's leaving."

The cab pulled away. Cavuto let them get a block away, then pulled out after them, leaving Rivera standing in the dark alley fingering the crucifix in his pocket.

Four stories above him, on the roof of a light industrial building, Elijah Ben Sapir, the vampire, looked down on Rivera, noting how much heat the policeman was losing though the thinning spot in his hair. "Jump or dive?" he said to himself.

CHAPTER 32

All for One, and . . .
Well, You Know

They might have been the Magnificent Seven or the Seven Samurai. If each of them had been a trained professional, a gunfighter with a character flaw, or a broken warrior with a past—or if each had a secret reason for joining a suicide mission, an antihero's sense of justice, and a burning desire to put things right—they might have become an elite fighting unit whose resourcefulness and courage would lead them to victory over those who would oppose or oppress. But the fact was, they were a disorganized bunch of perpetual adolescents, untrained and unprepared for anything but throwing stock and having fun: the Animals.

They sat on the registers as Tommy paced before them telling them about the vampire, about Simon's death, and giving them the call to action while the Emperor stood by quoting passages from Henry the Fifth's speech at the Battle of Agincourt.

"The cops aren't going to believe it, and I can't do it alone," Tommy said.

The Emperor said, "'We few, we lucky few . . .'"

"So who's with me?"

The Animals didn't say a word.

"Barry," Tommy said, "you're a scuba diver. You've got some balls, right? Sure, you're balding and going to fat, but this is a chance to make a difference."

Barry looked at this shoes.

Tommy jumped to Drew, who hung his head so that his greasy blond hair covered his face. "Drew, you have the most complete knowledge of chemistry of anyone I've ever met. It's time to use it."

"We've got a truck to unload," Drew said.

Tommy moved to Clint; stared into his thick glasses, ruffled his curly black hair. "Clint, God wants you to do this. This vampire is evil incarnate. Sure, you're a little burned out, but you can still strike a blow for righteousness."

"Blessed are the meek," said Clint.

"Jeff!" Tommy said. The big jock looked up, as if the key to the universe lay in the fluorescent lights. "Jeff, you're big, you're dumb, your knee is blown out, but hey, man, you look good. We might be able to use that."

Jeff began whistling.

Tommy moved on. "Lash, your people have been oppressed for hundreds of years. It's time to strike back. Look, you don't have your MBA yet—they haven't completely juiced you of your usefulness yet. Would Martin Luther King back down from this challenge? Malcolm X? James Brown? Don't you have a dream? Don't you feel good, like you knew that you would, now?"

Lash shook his head. "I have to study in the morning, man."

"Troy Lee? Samurai tradition? You're the only trained fighter here."

"I'm Chinese, not Japanese."

"Whatever. You're a kung-fu guy. You can reach into a guy's pocket and take his wallet before he knows it's gone. No one has reflexes like you."

"Okay," Troy said.

Tommy stopped on his way to the next man. "Really?"

"Sure, I'll help you. Simon was a good friend."

"Wow," Tommy said. He looked to Gustavo. "Well?"

Gustavo shook his head.

"Viva Zapata!" Tommy said.

"Leave him alone," Troy Lee said. "He's got a family."

"You're right," Tommy said. "Sorry, Gustavo."

Troy Lee got up and stood in front of the other Animals. "But you fuckers. You worthless bags of dog meat. If Simon could see you he'd shoot every one of you. This could be the best party we ever had."

Drew looked up. "Party?"

"Yeah," Troy Lee said, "party. We drink some brews, kick some ass, dismember some monsters—maybe pick up some babes. Christ, Drew, who knows what kind of shit we could get into. And you're going to miss it."

"I'm in," said Drew.

"Me too," said Barry.

Troy looked at Jeff and Clint. "Well?" They nodded.

"Lash, you in?"

"Okay," Lash said without conviction.

"Okay," Tommy said. "Let's throw the truck. We can't start until morning anyway. We'll figure out a plan and get some weapons then."

Troy Lee held up a finger. "One thing. How do we find the vampire?"

Tommy said, "Okay, let's get to work."

Morning found the Animals in the Safeway parking lot, drinking beer and discussing the strategy for finding and disposing of a monster.

"So, as far as you know, drugs don't affect them?" Drew asked.

"I don't think so," Tommy said.

"Well, no wonder he's pissed off," Drew said.

"What about guns?" Jeff asked. "I've got Simon's shotgun at my house."

Tommy thought for a moment before answering. "They *can* be hurt; I mean, damaged. But Jody heals incredibly fast—this guy might even be faster. Still, I'd rather have a twelve-gauge against him than nothing."

Barry said, "A stake through the heart always works in the movies."

Tommy nodded. "It might work. We could try it. If we get that far, we can cut him up, too."

"Spearguns," Barry said. "I've got three of them. A CO_2 model and two that use elastics. They won't shoot far, but they might pin him down while we cut him up."

"I've got a couple of short fighting swords," Troy Lee interjected. "Razor sharp."

"Good," Tommy said. "Bring 'em."

"I'll bring the Word," Clint said. He'd been shouting "Get thee behind me, Satan," all night, putting the Animals on edge.

"Why don't you just go home and pray," Lash said, giving Clint a push. "We need some action here." He turned from Clint and addressed the group. "Look, guys, spearguns and swords are great, but how do we find this guy? The cops have been looking for him for three months, and they obviously haven't had any luck. If he's really after Tommy, then the best thing we can do is ambush him at Tommy's apartment. And I'm not sure I want to face him when he's awake. Simon was my friend too, but he was also one of the quickest people I ever met and the vampire took him out like he was a baby. And the paper said that he was armed. I don't know . . ."

"He's right," Drew said. "We're fucked. Anyone want to catch the ferry to Sausalito and terrorize some yuppie artists? I've got mushrooms."

"Shrooms! Shrooms! Shrooms!" the Animals chanted.

Suddenly there was a staccato clanging, like someone banging on a garbage-can lid with a stick, which is pretty much what it was. The Emperor, who had been silent all night, stepped into the circle. "Before your spines go to jelly, men, take heart. I've been thinking."

"Oh, no!" someone shouted.

"I think I have a way to find the fiend and dispose of him before sundown."

"Right," Drew said sarcastically. "How?"

The Emperor picked up Bummer and held out the little dog as

if he were displaying the Holy Grail, "Pound for pound, a better soldier never marched, and a better tracker never sniffed out a sewer rat. I've been so stupid."

"Beg your pardon, Your Majesty," Tommy said. "But what the fuck are you talking about?"

"Until last night I didn't know that the lovely young woman with whom you share your abode was a vampire. Yet every time we passed your building Bummer went into a frenzy. He's been the same each time we've encountered the fiend himself. I believe he has a special sensitivity for the smell of vampires."

They all stared at him, waiting.

"Gather your courage and your weapons, good fellows. We'll meet here in two hours and remove this evil from my city. And a little dog shall lead us."

The Animals looked at Tommy, who shrugged and nodded. They had a new leader now. "Two hours, guys," Tommy said. "The Emperor's in charge."

Cavuto watched the Animals disperse though his field glasses. He was sitting in the parking lot at Fort Mason, a hundred yards from the Safeway. He put down the binoculars and dialed Rivera's number on his cellular phone.

"Rivera."

"Anything happening there?" Cavuto asked.

"No, I don't think that anything will now that it's daylight. The lights stayed off after the kid left, but I could hear a vacuum cleaner running. The girl's up there but she didn't turn on the light."

"So she likes to clean in the dark."

"I think she can see in the dark."

"I don't want to talk about it," Cavuto said. "Anything else?"

"Not much. Some kids were dropping pebbles on me from the roof. The guys in the foundry below the kid's apartment are moving around now. A couple of bums are doing some close-order public urinating in the alley. What's happening there?"

"The kid worked all night, drank some beers with the crew;

they just split up but the kid and the wacko are still here."

"Why don't you call in some relief?"

"I don't want this out of our hands until we know more. Stay by the phone."

"Anything from the coroner?"

"Yeah, just got off the phone with him. Massive blood loss from the guy in the truck. None from the guy in the morgue. Heart attack. They still haven't found the girl's body."

"That's because she was cleaning house all night."

"Gotta go," Cavuto said.

Tommy and the Emperor were waiting in the parking lot when the Animals returned in Troy Lee's Toyota and began unloading equipment.

"Stop, stop, stop," Tommy said. "We can't run all over the City with spearguns and swords."

"And shotguns," Jeff said proudly, jacking a shell into the chamber of Simon's shotgun.

"Put that back in the car."

"No problem," Drew said, holding up a roll of Christmas wrap. "Dallas, November 22, 1963."

"What?" Tommy said.

"Lee Harvey Oswald walks into the book depository with a venetian blind. Minutes later Jackie's scooping brains off the trunk of a Lincoln. Anybody asks, we're all giving venetian blinds to our moms for Christmas."

"Oh," Tommy said. "Okay."

Clint climbed out of the Toyota wearing a choir robe, a half dozen crosses hung around his neck. He held a Baggie full of crackers in one hand, a squirt gun in the other. "I'm ready," he said to Tommy and the Emperor.

"Snacks," Tommy said, nodding to the Baggie. "Good thinking."

"The Heavenly Host," Clint said. He brandished the squirt gun. "Loaded with holy water."

"That stuff doesn't work, Clint."

"O ye of little faith," Clint said.

Bummer and Lazarus had left the Emperor's side and were nosing up to Clint. "See, they know the power of the Spirit."

Just then Bummer jumped and snatched the Baggie, then took off around the corner of the store, followed closely by Lazarus, Clint, and the Emperor.

"Stop him," Clint shouted at an old man coming out of the store. "He's taken the body of Christ."

"Don't hurt him," the Emperor shouted. "He's the only hope for saving the City."

Tommy took off after them. As he passed the bewildered old man, Tommy said, "Last week they were playing cards with Elvis. What can I say?"

The old man seemed to accept this and hurried off.

Tommy caught up with them behind the store, where the Emperor was holding Bummer in one hand and fending off Clint with his wooden sword with the other, while Lazarus licked the last few crumbs out of the torn plastic bag.

"He ate the blessed Savior!" Clint wailed. "He ate the blessed Savior!"

Tommy caught Clint around the waist and pulled him away. "It's okay, Clint. Bummer's a Christian."

Jeff rounded the corner, his size-fourteen Reeboks clomping like a quarter horse. He looked at the empty Baggie. "Oh, I get it. They freeze-dried him, right?"

Drew came around the corner, followed by Lash and Troy Lee. "Do we have a partying platoon, or what?" Drew said.

Jeff said, "I never knew that they freeze-dried Jesus, did you?"

Lash checked his watch. "We've got less than six hours before it gets dark. Maybe we should get started."

Tommy released Clint and the Emperor lowered his sword.

"We need something to give Bummer the scent," the Emperor said. "Something that the fiend has touched."

Tommy dug into his jeans pocket and pulled out one of the hundreds that Jody had given him. "I'm pretty sure that he touched this, but it's been a while."

The Emperor took the hundred and held it to Bummer's nose. "It shouldn't matter. His senses are keen and his heart is righteous." To Bummer he said, "This is the scent, little one. Find this scent."

He put Bummer down and the little dog was off with a yap and a snort. The vampire hunters followed, losing sight of Bummer as he rounded the store. When they came around to the front of the store, the manager was coming out, holding a snarling Bummer in his arms.

"Flood, is this your dog?"

"He's his own man," the Emperor said.

"Well, he just ran in and blew snot all over the cash in register eight. You train him to find money?"

The Emperor looked down to the hundred-dollar bill in his hand, then at Tommy. "Perhaps we should find something else to put him on the scent."

"Where was the last place you saw the vampire?" Tommy asked.

The gate guard at the Saint Francis Yacht Club wasn't buying a word of it.

"Really," Tommy said. "We're here to decorate for the Christmas party." The Animals waved their gaily wrapped weapons to illustrate the point. "And the Archbishop has come along to perform midnight mass." Tommy pointed to Clint, who grinned and winked through his thick glasses.

"Deus ex machina," Clint said, exhausting his Latin. "Shalom," he added for good measure.

The guard tapped his clipboard. "I'm sorry, gentlemen, I can't let you through without a membership or a guest pass."

The Emperor cleared his throat royally. "Good man, each moment you delay may be paid for with human suffering."

The guard thought that he might have just been threatened, hoped, in fact, that he had, so he could pull his gun, and was just letting his hand drop to his gun belt when the phone in the gate booth rang.

"Stay here," he instructed the vampire hunters. He answered the phone and nodded at it, then looked across Marina Boulevard to where a brown Dodge was parked. He hung up the phone and came out of the booth.

"Go on in," he said, obviously not happy about it. He pushed a button, the gate rose, and the Animals went in, headed for the East Harbor. Two minutes later the brown Dodge pulled up and stopped by the gate. Cavuto rolled down the window and flashed his badge.

"Thanks," he said to the guard. "I'll keep an eye on them for you."

"No problem," said the guard. "You ever get to shoot anyone?"

"Not today." Cavuto said. He drove though the gate, staying just out of sight of the Animals.

At the end of the dock the Animals and the Emperor stared forlornly at the big white motor yacht moored a hundred yards out into the harbor. Bummer was in the midst of a yapping fit.

"You see," said the Emperor, "he knows that the fiend is aboard."

"You're sure that's the boat that he came off of?"

"Most definitely. It chills my spine to think of it—the mist forming into a monster."

"That's great," Tommy said, "but how do we get aboard?" He turned to Barry, who was applying sunscreen to his bald spot. "Can you swim it?"

"We could all swim it," Barry said. "But how do we keep the gun dry? I could go get my Zodiac and take us all out there, but it'll take a while."

"How long?"

"Maybe an hour."

"We've got four, maybe five hours until sunset," Lash said.

"Go," Tommy said. "Get it."

"No, wait," said Drew, looking at the rows of yachts in the nearby slips. "Jeff, can you swim?"

The big power forward shook his head. "Nope."

"Good," Drew said. He took the Christmas-paper-wrapped shotgun from Jeff, then grabbed him by the arm and threw him into the water. "Man overboard! Man overboard! We need a boat."

The few owners and crew members who were performing maintenance on the nearby boats looked up. Drew spotted a good-sized life raft on the stern of a sixty-footer. "There, you guys, get that."

The Animals scrambled after the raft. The yacht's crew helped them get it over the side into the water.

Jeff, flailing in the water, had slapped his way back to the dock. Drew pushed him away with the shotgun. "Not yet, big guy." Over his shoulder he shouted, "Hurry, you guys! He's drowning!"

Tommy, Barry, and Lash were paddling the rubber raft for all they were worth. The yachtsmen and the Emperor shouted instructions, while Drew and Troy Lee watched their friend trying not to drown.

"He's doing really well for a non-swimmer," Drew said calmly.

"Doesn't want to get his hair wet," said Troy with Taoist simplicity.

"Yeah, can't waste that two hours of blow-drying."

Tommy moved to the front of the raft and held his paddle out to Jeff. "Grab it."

Jeff flailed and thrashed, but didn't grab the paddle.

"If he stops paddling his head will go under," Troy called. "You'll have to grab him."

Tommy whacked Jeff on the head with the plastic paddle. "Grab it!" The power forward slipped under for a second and bobbed to the surface again.

"That's one!" Drew called.

"Now grab it," Tommy yelled. He raised the paddle as if to strike again. Jeff shook his head violently and reached for the paddle as he went under again.

"That's two!"

Tommy pulled the paddle up with Jeff on the end while Barry and Lash wrestled the big man into the boat.

"Well done, men," the Emperor said.

The yachtsmen stood at the end of the dock, watching in amazement. Drew turned to them. "We're going to need that raft for a while, okay?"

One of the crewmen started to protest and Drew jacked a shell into the shotgun, ripping the wrapping paper. "Big shark hunt. We need the raft."

The crewman nodded and backed away. "Sure, as long as you need it."

"Okay," Tommy called. "Everybody in the raft."

Drew and Troy Lee helped the Emperor get into the raft, then handed over Bummer and Lazarus and climbed in themselves. The Emperor stood at the front of the raft as they made their way across the harbor to the *Sanguine II*.

Twenty yards from the yacht Bummer began barking and bouncing around the raft. "The fiend is definitely on board," the Emperor said. He picked up Bummer and shoved him into his pocket. "Well done, little one."

It took five minutes to get everyone on board and the life raft secured to the stern. "How we doing on time, Lash?" Tommy asked.

"We're looking at four, maybe four and a half hours of daylight. Will he wake up at sunset or dark?"

"Jody usually wakes up right at sunset. So let's say four."

"Okay, everybody," Tommy said, "let's spread out and find the vampire."

"I don't know if that's a good idea," said Jeff. He was dripping and his lips had gone blue with the cold. The Animals looked at him. He was embarrassed by the attention. "Well, in all of the horror movies, the people split up and the monster picks them off one by one."

"Good point," Tommy said. "Everybody stay together; find this fucker and get it over with." He raised a gift-wrapped speargun in salute. "For Simon!"

"For Simon!" the Animals shouted as they followed Tommy below.

CHAPTER 33
Ship of Fools

Tommy led them down a narrow hallway and into a large room paneled in dark walnut and furnished with heavy, dark wood furniture. Paintings and bookshelves filled with leather volumes lined the walls; strands of gold wire running across the front of the shelves to hold the books in place in rough seas were the only evidence that they were on a boat. There were no windows; the only light came from small spotlights recessed into the ceiling that shone on the paintings.

Tommy paused in the middle of the room, fighting the urge to stop and look at the books. Lash moved to his side.

"See that?" Lash asked. He nodded toward a large painting—bright colors and bold shapes, squiggles and lines—that hung between two doors at the far end of the room.

Tommy said, "Looks like it should be hung on a fridge with ladybug magnets."

"It's a Miró," Lash said. "It must be worth millions."

"How do you know it's an original?"

"Tommy, look at this yacht; if you can afford a boat like this, you don't hang fakes." Lash pointed to another, smaller painting of a woman reclining on a pile of satin cushions. "That's a Goya. Probably priceless."

"So what's your point?" Tommy asked.

"Would you leave something like that unguarded? And I don't think that you can run a boat this size without a crew."

"Swell," Tommy said. "Jeff, let me have that shotgun."

Jeff, still shivering from his dunk, handed over the gun.

"Shell in the chamber," Jeff said.

Tommy took the gun, checked the safety, and started forward. "Keep your eyes open, guys."

They went through the door to the right of the Miró into another hallway, this one paneled in teak. Paintings hung along the walls between louvered teak doors.

Tommy paused at the first door and signaled for Barry to back him up with a speargun as he opened it. Inside, row upon row of suits and jackets hung on motorized tracks. Above the tracks, shelves were filled with hats and expensive shoes.

Tommy pushed aside some of the suits and peered between them, looking for a set of legs and feet. "No one here," he said. "Did anyone bring a flashlight?"

"Didn't think about it," Barry said.

Tommy backed out of the closet and moved to the next door. "It's a bathroom."

"A head," Barry corrected, looking around Tommy's shoulder into the room. "There's no toilet."

"Vampires don't go," Tommy said. "I'd say this guy had this boat built for him."

They moved down the hall checking each room. There were rooms full of paintings and sculpture, crated, labeled, and stacked in rows; another with oriental carpets rolled and stacked; a room that looked like an office, with computers, a copy machine, fax machines, and filing cabinets; and another head.

They followed the hallway around a gentle curve to the left, where it traced the line of the bow of the boat. At the apex there was a teak spiral staircase that led to a deck above and one below. Light spilled down from above. The hallway curved around the bow and back to the stern.

"The hallway must go back to that other door in that big room." Tommy said. "Lash, you, Clint, Troy, and Jeff check the rooms on that side. Your Majesty, Barry, Drew, come with me. Meet us back here."

"I thought we were going to stay together," Jeff said.

"I don't think you're going to find anything down there. If you do, yell like hell."

The Emperor patted Lazarus's head. "Stay here, good fellow. We shan't be long."

Tommy pointed upward with the shotgun and mounted the stairs. He emerged onto the bridge and squinted against the light coming through the windows. He stepped aside and looked around the bridge while the others came up the stairs behind him.

"It looks more like the bridge of a starship," Tommy said to the Emperor as he came up.

Low consoles filled with switches and screens ran along the front of the bridge under wide, streamlined windows. There were five different radar screens blipping away. At least a dozen other screens were scrolling figures and text; red, green, and amber lights glowed along the rows of toggle switches over three computer keyboards. The only thing that looked remotely nautical to Tommy was the chrome wheel at the front of the bridge.

"Anybody know what any of this stuff is?" Tommy asked.

Barry said, "I'd say that this is the crew that we were wondering about. This whole thing is automated."

Barry stepped up to one of the consoles and all the screens and lights winked out.

"I didn't touch anything," Barry said.

The foghorn on Alcatraz sounded and they looked out the window toward the abandoned prison. The fog was making its way across the bay toward shore.

"How's our time?" Tommy asked.

Drew checked his watch. "About two hours."

"Okay, let's check that lower deck."

As they came down the steps, Lash said, "Nothing. More art, more electronics. There's no galley, and I can't figure out where the crew sleeps."

"There is no crew," Tommy said as he started down the steps to the lower deck. "It's all run by machines."

The floor of the lower deck was made of diamond-plate steel; there were no carpets and no wood: pipes and wires ran around the steel bulkheads. A steel pressure hatch opened into a narrow passageway. Light from the bridge two decks above spilled a few feet into the passageway, then it was dark.

"Drew," Tommy said, "you got a lighter?"

"Always," Drew said, handing him a disposable butane lighter.

Tommy crouched and went through the hatch, took a few steps, and clicked the lighter.

"This must lead to the engines," Lash said. "But it should be bigger." He knocked on the steel wall, making a dull thud. "I think this is all fuel around us. This thing must have an incredible range."

Tommy looked at the lighter, then back at Lash, whose black face was just highlights in the flame. "Fuel?"

"It's sealed."

"Oh," Tommy said. He moved a few more feet and barked his elbow on the metal ring of a pressure hatch. "Ouch!"

"Open it," Drew said.

Tommy handed him the shotgun and lighter and grabbed the heavy metal ring. He strained against it but it didn't budge. "Help."

Lash snaked past Drew and joined Tommy on the ring. They put their weight on it and pushed. The wheel screeched in protest, then broke loose. Tommy pulled the hatch open and was hit with the smell of urine and decay.

"Christ." He turned away coughing. "Lash, give me the lighter."

Lash handed him the lighter. Tommy reached through the hatch and lit it. There were bars just inside the hatch, beyond that a rotting mattress, some empty food cans, and a bucket. Red-brown splotches smeared the gray walls, one in the shape of a handprint.

"Is it the fiend?" the Emperor asked.

Tommy moved back from the hatch and handed back the lighter. "No, it's a cage."

Lash looked in. "A prison cell? I don't get it."

Tommy slid down the bulkhead and sat on the steel floor, trying to catch his breath. "You said this thing had an incredible range. Could stay out to sea for months, probably?"

"Yeah," Lash said.

"He has to store his food somewhere."

Inside the vampire's vault, just above his face, a computer screen was scrolling information. A schematic of the *Sanguine II* lit up one side of the screen with nine red dots representing the vampire hunters and Lazarus. Green dotted lines traced the patterns of their movements since they had boarded the ship. Another area of the screen recorded the time they had boarded and another showed exterior views of the yacht: the raft tied up at the rear, the dock, fog sweeping over the Saint Francis clubhouse. Radar readouts showed the surrounding watercraft, the shoreline, Alcatraz, and the Golden Gate in the distance. Optical disk drives recorded all the information so the vampire could replay it upon awakening.

Motion detectors had, upon sensing Barry's presence near the console on the bridge, activated switches that rerouted all of the ship's control to the vault. The *Sanguine II* was wide awake and awaiting its master.

"How's our time, Lash?" Tommy asked.

"About an hour."

They were gathered at the stern of the yacht, watching the fog roll into shore. They had searched the entire ship, then gone back through it again, opening every closet, cupboard, and access panel.

"He's got to be here."

"Perhaps," said the Emperor, "we should go ashore and set Bummer on another trail."

At the mention of his name Bummer yapped and worked his head out of the Emperor's pocket. Tommy scratched his ears.

"Let him out."

The Emperor unbuttoned his pocket and Bummer leaped out, bit Tommy on the ankle, and shot through the hatch.

"Ouch!"

"Follow him," the Emperor said. "He's on the trail." He ran through the hatch, followed by the Animals and Tommy, limping slightly.

Five minutes later they were standing on the diamond-plate floor of the engine room. Bummer was scratching at the floor and whining.

"This is stupid," Barry said. "We've been through this area three times."

Tommy looked at the section of floor where Bummer was scratching. There was a rectangular seam, ten feet long by three feet wide, sealed with a rubber gasket. "We didn't look under the floor."

"It's water under the floor, isn't it?" Jeff said.

Tommy got down on his knees and examined the seam. "Troy, give me one of those swords."

Troy Lee handed him a fighting sword. Tommy worked the tip under the rubber gasket and the blade sank into the seam. "Get that other sword into this crack and help me pry it up."

Troy worked his sword into the seam and they counted to three. The edge of the panel popped up. The other Animals caught the edge and lifted. The floor panel came up, revealing a coffin-length stainless-steel vault two feet below the floor. Bummer leaped into the opening in the floor and began running around the vault, leaping and barking.

"Well done, little one," the Emperor said.

Tommy looked at the Animals, who were holding the floor panel up on its edge. "Gentlemen, I'd like you to meet the owner of this vessel."

Drew let go of the floor panel and jumped into the opening with the vault. There was just enough room in the opening for him to move sideways around the vault. "It's on hydraulic lifts.

And there's a shitload of cables running in and out of it."

"Open it," Troy Lee said, holding his sword at ready.

Drew pulled at the lid of the vault, then let go and knocked on the side. "This thing is thick. Really thick." He reached up and took Troy's sword, worked the blade under the lid, and pried. The sword snapped.

"Christ, Drew! That sword cost a week's pay."

"Sorry," Drew said. "We're not going to pry this baby open. Not even with a crowbar."

Tommy said, "Lash, how's our time?"

"Forty minutes, give or take five."

To Drew, Tommy said, "What do you think? How do we get it open? A torch?"

Drew shook his head. "Too thick. It'd take hours to get through this. I say we blow it."

"With what?"

Drew grinned. "Common items you can find in your own kitchen. Someone's going to need to go back to the store and get me some stuff."

Cavuto watched Troy Lee's Toyota turning around, put down his binoculars, and quickly backed the cruiser into a driveway behind the shower buildings. He hit the redial on his cell phone and the gate guard answered on the first ring.

"Saint Francis Yacht Club, gate."

"This is Inspector Cavuto again. I need to know the registered owner of the *Sanguine Two.*"

"I'm not supposed to give out that information."

"Look, I'm going to shoot some guys in a minute. You want to help, or what?"

"It's registered to a Dutch shipping company. Ben Sapir Limited."

"Have you seen anyone coming to or from that boat? Crew? Visitors?"

There was a pause while the guard checked his records. "No,

nothing since it came into harbor. Except that it fueled up last night. Paid cash. No signature. Man, that baby's got some fuel capacity."

"How long has it been here?"

Another pause. "A little over three months. Came in on September fifteenth."

Cavuto checked his notebook. The first body was found on the seventeenth of September. "Thanks," he said to the guard.

"Those guys you had me let in are causing trouble. They took a boat."

"They're coming back through the gate. Let them do what they want. I'll take responsibility."

Cavuto disconnected and dialed the number of Rivera's cell phone.

Rivera answered on the first ring. "Yeah."

"Where are you?" Cavuto could hear Rivera lighting a cigarette.

"Watching the kid's apartment. I got a car. You?"

"The kid and the night crew are on a big motor yacht at the Saint Francis yacht club—hundred-footer. Boat's called the *Sanguine Two*; registered to a Dutch shipping company. They've been out there a couple of hours. Two of them just left."

"He didn't seem like the yachting type."

"No shit. But I'm staying with the kid. The *Sanguine Two* pulled into port two days before the first murder. Maybe we should get a warrant."

"Probable cause?"

"I don't know—suspicion of piracy."

"You want to call in some other units?"

"Not unless something happens. I don't want the attention. Any movement from your girl?"

"No. But it's getting dark. I'll let you know."

"Just go knock on the damn door and find out what's going on."

"Can't. I'm not ready to interview a murder victim. I haven't had any experience in it."

"I hate it when you talk like that. Call me." Cavuto rung off and began rubbing a headache out of his temples.

Jeff and Troy Lee were running through the Safeway aisles, Troy shouting out items off Drew's list while Jeff pushed the cart.

"A case of Vaseline," Troy said. "I'll get it out of the stock-room. You grab the sugar, and the Wonder Grow."

"Got it," Jeff said.

They rendezvoused at the express lane. The cashier, a middle-aged woman with bottle-blond hair, glared at them over her rose-tinted glasses.

"C'mon, Kathleen," Troy said. "That eight-items-or-less bull-shit doesn't apply to employees."

Like everyone who worked days at the Safeway, Kathleen was a little afraid of the Animals. She sighed and began running the items over the scanner while Troy Lee shoved them into bags: ten five-pound bags of sugar, ten boxes of Wonder Grow fertilizer, five quarts of Wild Turkey bourbon, a case of charcoal lighter, a giant box of laundry detergent, a box of utility candles, a bag of charcoal, ten boxes of mothballs . . .

When she got to the case of Vaseline, Kathleen paused and looked up at Jeff. He gave her his best all-American-boy smile. "We're having a little party," he said.

She huffed and totaled the order. Jeff threw a handful of bills on the counter and followed Troy out of the store, pushing the cart at a dead run.

Twenty minutes later the Animals were scrambling through the *Sanguine II* with the bags of supplies for Drew, who was crouched in the opening with the stainless-steel vault. Tommy handed down the boxes of fertilizer.

"Potassium nitrate," Drew said. "No recreational value, but the nitrates make a nice bang." He tore the lid off a box and dumped the powder into a growing pile. "Give me some of that Wild Turkey."

Tommy handed down some bottles. Drew twisted the cap off

one and took a drink. He shivered, blinked back a tear, and emptied the rest of the bottle into the dry ingredients. "Hand me that broken sword. I need something to stir with."

Tommy reached for the sword and looked up at Lash. "How we doing?"

Lash didn't even look at his watch. "It's officially dark," he said.

CHAPTER 34
Hell Breaks Loose

A wave of anxiety washed over Jody as she woke up. "Tommy," she called. She leaped out of bed and went into the living area, not stopping to turn on the light.

"Tommy?"

The loft was quiet. She checked the answering machine: no messages.

I'm not going to do this again, she thought. I can't handle another night of worrying.

She'd cleaned up the mess from the police search the night before, put lemon oil on the wood, scrubbed out the sinks and the tubs, and watched cable TV until dawn. All the time she thought about what Tommy had said about sharing, about being with someone who could understand what you saw and how you felt. She wanted that.

She wanted someone who could run the night with her, someone who could hear the buildings breathe and watch the sidewalks glow with heat just after sundown. But she wanted Tommy. She wanted love. She wanted the blood-high and she wanted sex that touched her heart. She wanted excitement and she wanted security.

She wanted to be part of the crowd, but she wanted to be an

individual. She wanted to be human, but she wanted the strength, the senses, and the mental acuity of the vampire. She wanted it all.

What if I had a choice, she thought, if that medical student could cure me, would I go back to being human? It would mean that Tommy and I could stay together, but he would never know the feeling of being a god, and neither would I. Never again.

So I leave; what then? I'm alone. More alone than I've ever been. I hate being alone.

She stopped pacing and went to the window. The cop from the night before was out there, sitting in a brown Dodge, watching. The other cop had followed Tommy.

"Tommy, you jerk. Call me."

The cop would know where Tommy was. But how to get him to tell? Seduce him? Use the Vulcan nerve pinch? Sleeper hold?

Maybe I should just go up there and knock on the door, Rivera thought. "Inspector Alphonse Rivera, San Francisco PD. If you have a few minutes, I'd like to talk to you about being dead. How was it? Who did it? Did it piss you off?"

He adjusted himself in the car seat and took a sip from his coffee. He was trying to pace his smoking. No more than four cigarettes an hour. He was in his forties now and he couldn't handle the four-pack-a-night stakeouts—going home with his throat raw, his lungs seared, and a vicious ache in his sinuses. He checked his watch to see if enough time had passed since he'd last lit up. Almost. He rolled down the car window and something caught him by the throat, cutting off his breath. He dropped his coffee, feeling the scald in his lap as he reached in his jacket for his gun. Something caught his hand and held it like a bear trap.

The hand on his throat relaxed a bit and he sucked in a short breath. He tried to turn his head and the clamp on his throat cut off his breath again. A pretty face came through the window.

"Hi," Jody said. She loosened her grip on his throat a degree.

"Hi," Rivera croaked.

"Feel the grip on your wrist?"

Rivera felt the bear trap on his wrist tighten, his hand went numb, and his whole arm lit up with pain.

"Yes!"

"Okay," Jody said. "I'm pretty sure I can crush your windpipe before you could move, but I wanted you to be sure too. You sure?"

Rivera tried to nod.

"Good. Your partner followed Tommy last night. Do you know where they are now?"

Again Rivera attempted to nod. On the seat next to him, the cell phone chirped.

She released his arm, snatched the gun out of his shoulder holster, flipped off the safety, and pointed it at his head, all before he could draw a single breath. "Take me there," she said.

Elijah Ben Sapir watched the red dots moving around on the video screen above his face. He had awakened feeling gleeful about killing the fledgling's toy boy, then he saw that his home had been invaded. He was hit with an emotion so rare it took him a while to recognize it. Fear. It had been a long time since he'd been afraid. It felt good.

The dots on the screen were moving around on the stern of the boat, scrambling in and out of the main cabin above. Every few seconds a dot would disappear off the screen, then reappear. They were getting in and out of a raft at the stern.

The vampire reached up and flipped a series of toggle switches. The big diesels on either side of his vault roared to life. Another toggle and an electric winch began grinding in the anchor.

"Move, move, move!" Tommy shouted into the cabin. "The engines started."

Barry came through the hatch carrying a bronze statue of a ballerina. Tommy waited at the stern of the yacht with Drew. Troy Lee, Lash, Jeff, Clint, and the Emperor and his troops were already in the raft, trying to find room to move around the paintings and statues.

"Over," Tommy said, taking the statue from Barry as the squat diver went over the side into the arms of the waiting Animals, almost capsizing the raft. Tommy threw the statue down to the Emperor, who caught it and went to the floor of the raft with its weight.

Tommy threw a leg over the railing, and looked back. "Light it, Drew. Now!"

Drew bent and held his lighter to the end of a wax-coated strip of cloth that ran across the stern deck and through the hatch to the main cabin. He watched the flame follow the trail for a few feet, then stood and joined Tommy at the rail. "It's going."

They went over the rail backward and the Animals obliged them by stepping aside and letting them both hit the floor of the raft unimpeded. The raft lurched and righted itself. Tommy fought for breath to give a command.

"Paddle, men!" the Emperor shouted.

The Animals began to beat the water with their paddles. There was a loud clunking noise from the yacht as the transmission engaged and the raft was rocked as the twin screws engaged and began pushing the yacht away from them.

"Rivera," Rivera said into the cell phone.

"The yacht is moving," Cavuto said. "I think I just aided these guys in looting it." He unzipped a leather case on the car seat, revealing a huge chrome-plated automatic pistol, a Desert Eagle .50-caliber. It fired bullets roughly the weight of a small dog and kicked like a jackhammer. One shot could reduce a cinder block to gravel.

"I'm on my way," Rivera said.

"What about the girl?" Cavuto slammed a clip into the Desert Eagle, dropped another one into his jacket pocket.

"She's—she'll be fine. I'm at Van Ness and Lombard. I'll be there in about three minutes. Don't call in backup."

"I'm not—oh Jesus Christ!"
"What?"
"The fucking thing just blew up."

A fountain of flame shot from the stern of the *Sanguine II,* a second passed, and the rest of the yacht disappeared in a cloud of flame that rose into the sky above her. She had cleared the breakwater and was perhaps three hundred yards out into the bay when the fuse reached Drew's incendiary cocktail.

The raft had just made the dock when the explosion went off. Tommy leaped onto the dock and watched the mushroom cloud dissipate. The shock wave rolled in and Tommy reached back to the raft and caught the Emperor before he went into the water.

Debris rained down around them. A pool of fire and unexploded diesel fuel spread out across the water, illuminating the whole area with a dancing bright orange.

"Is this a party boat, or what?" Drew shouted.

The Animals scrambled out of the raft onto the dock and began handing up the objets d'art. Tommy stood aside and watched the burn. Bummer cowered in the Emperor's arms.

"Do you think we got him?"

Jeff handed the Degas ballerina to Troy and looked over his shoulder. "Fucking A, we got him. Nice mix, Drew."

Drew took a bow and almost went over the edge of the dock.

The Emperor said. "I can't help but think that the explosion may have attracted the attention of the authorities, gentlemen. I would recommend a speedy retreat."

Drew looked at the burning slick. "I wish I had some acid. This would be great on acid."

Jeff jumped down into the raft and handed up the last painting, the Miró. He looked past Troy Lee, who was wrestling up the heavy frame, and said, "Whoops."

"What?" Troy said.

Jeff nodded past him and the Animals turned around. Cavuto had a very large, very shiny pistol pointed at them.

"No one move!"

They didn't. The spearguns were stacked on the dock. Clint held the shotgun loosely at his side as he prayed. He dropped it.

"Drop it," Cavuto said.

"I did," said Clint.

"That's true, he did," Tommy said. "And before you asked. He should get extra credit for that."

Cavuto motioned with the pistol. "Everybody down. On your faces. Now!" The Animals dropped. Lazarus barked.

The Emperor stepped forward. "Officer, these young men have—"

"Now!" Cavuto screamed. The Emperor dropped to the dock with the Animals.

The screens went dark an instant before he was slammed against the side of the vault. He tumbled inside, feeling his flesh burn on the steel with every turn. The vault glowed red with the heat and had filled with smoke from the seared wires and the vampire's clothing.

After a few seconds the tumbling stopped. The vampire was jammed into one end of the vault, his face against his knees. His skin was stinging and he tried to will it to heal, but it had been days since he had fed, so the healing came slowly.

He located the lid by finding the smashed CRT and radar screens. Salt water sprayed in a fine mist from behind the screens. He pushed on the lid but it didn't move. He felt for the latches and released them, then heaved against the lid with force that would have crumpled a car fender, yet the lid stayed fast. The heat of the explosion had welded it shut.

I should have killed him last week, the vampire thought. This is what I get for indulging my pleasures.

He reached into the broken CRT, looking for the source of the spraying water, then concentrated his will and went to mist. The transition was slow, weak as he was, but when he had finally lost his solid form he followed the path of the water and wormed his way through the pinhole to the open ocean.

The vault lay on the bottom in a hundred and twenty feet of

water and as soon as the vampire escaped, the pressure of four atmospheres condensed him to his solid shape. He tried to force himself to mist, failed, then swam toward the orange glow at the surface, thinking, The boy dies first, then a new suit.

He broke the surface in the midst of the flame slick, then scissor-kicked hard enough to bring himself completely out of the water and tried to go to mist. His limbs dissolved in the air, their vapor whipped by the flame and standing out white in the rolling black diesel smoke, but he could not hold. He fell back into the water, followed by a vortex of vapor that condensed back to solid form under water. Frustrated and angry, he began the swim around the breakwater toward the yacht club.

Cavuto panned the Desert Eagle back and forth across the heads of the prostrated Animals as he moved forward to get their weapons. Lazarus growled and backed away as the big cop approached. Sirens sounded in the distance. Crew members and yacht owners were popping out of the hatches of nearby yachts like curious prairie dogs.

"Inside!" Cavuto shouted, and the yachters ducked for cover.

Cavuto heard footsteps on the dock behind him and swung quickly around. The gate guard, looking down the cavelike barrel of the Eagle, stopped as if he'd hit a force field. Cavuto swung back to cover the Animals.

Over his shoulder Cavuto said, "Go back to the gate and call nine-one-one. Tell them to send me some backup."

"Right," the guard said.

"All right, scumbags, you're under arrest. And if any of you even twitches, I'll turn you into a red stain. You have the right . . ."

The vampire came out of the water like a wet comet and landed on the dock behind the Animals. He was burned black and his clothes hung in sooty shreds. Cavuto fired without thinking and missed. The vampire looked up long enough to grin at him, then reached down and snatched Tommy by the back of his shirt and yanked him up like a rag doll.

Cavuto aimed and fired again. The second shot hit the vampire in the thigh, taking out a three-inch chuck of flesh. The vampire dropped Tommy, turned on Cavuto, and leaped. The third bullet caught the vampire in the abdomen, the impact spraying flesh and spinning him in the air like a football. He landed in a heap at Cavuto's feet. The big cop tried to back away to get another shot off, but before he could aim, the vampire snatched the gun out of his hand, taking most of the skin off his trigger finger. He leaped backward, clawing inside his jacket for his detective special as the vampire tossed the Desert Eagle over his shoulder and climbed to his feet. "You are a dead man," he growled.

Cavuto watched the gaping wounds in the vampire's leg and stomach pulsing, bubbling, and filling with smoke. He caught the butt of his revolver just as the vampire leaped, his fingers outstretched to drive into Cavuto's chest.

Cavuto ducked, heard a hiss and a loud thunk, and looked up, amazed that he was still alive. The vampire had stopped an inch from him. A gleaming spear through his leg had pinned him to the dock. The black kid stood a few yards away, a gas-powered speargun in hand.

The vampire wrenched himself around and clawed at the spear. Cavuto yanked out his gun, but with his damaged finger he ended up flinging it off the dock. He heard the sound of tires behind him, then a car coming down the dock. A second spear thunked through the vampire's shoulder.

Tommy threw the speargun aside. The Animals were all on their feet. "Troy, throw me the sword!"

Troy Lee picked up the fighting sword from the deck and threw it at Tommy. Tommy sidestepped; the sword whizzed by him and clattered on the dock near Cavuto, who was standing motionless, stunned at almost seeing his own death.

"Handle first, you doofus," Tommy said as he ran after the sword.

The vampire yanked the spear out of his shoulder and reached for the one in his leg.

The Emperor picked up his wooden sword from the deck and

charged the vampire. Lash caught him by the collar, yanking him aside as Barry fired a third spear, hitting the vampire in the hip. Jeff let go with a blast from the shotgun.

The vampire jerked with the impact of the shot and screamed.

Tommy dived for the fighting sword at Cavuto's feet. The big cop lifted him to his feet.

"Thanks," Tommy said.

"You're welcome," Cavuto said.

"I didn't kill those people."

"I'm figuring that out," Cavuto said.

A brown car skidded to a stop on the dock. Tommy looked up for an instant, then turned and headed toward the vampire, who was clawing at the spear in his leg. His wounds bubbled and seethed with vapor; his body was trying to heal even as new damage was inflicted on it.

Tommy raised the sword over the vampire's head and closed his eyes.

"No!" It was Jody's voice.

Tommy opened his eyes. Jody was on her knees, shielding the vampire, who had given up the struggle and was waiting for the final blow. "No," Jody said. "Don't kill him."

Tommy lowered the sword. Jody looked at Jeff, who still held the shotgun. "No," she said. Jeff looked at Tommy, who nodded. Jeff lowered the shotgun.

"Kill the fiend, now!" cried the Emperor, still struggling against Lash's hold on his coat.

"No," Jody said. She pulled the spear out of the vampire's leg and he screamed. She patted his head. "One more," she said quietly. She yanked the spear out of his hip and he gasped.

Jody propped the vampire up on her lap. The Animals and Cavuto stood watching, not sure what to do. Clint prayed quietly, barely audible over the approaching siren.

"Blood," the vampire said. He looked into Jody's eyes. "Yours."

"Give me that sword, Tommy." Jody said.

He hesitated and raised the sword to strike.

"No!" She covered the vampire with her body.

"But Jody, he's killed people."

"You don't know anything, Tommy. They were all going to die anyway."

"Get out of the way."

Jody turned to Cavuto. "Tell him. All the victims were terminally ill, weren't they?"

Cavuto nodded. "The coroner said that none of them had more than a few months."

Tommy was almost in tears. "He killed Simon."

"Simon had AIDS, Tommy."

"No way. Not Simon. Simon was the animal of the Animals."

"He was hiding it from you guys. He was scared to death. Now, please, give me the sword."

"No, get out of the way."

Tommy reared back for the killing blow. He felt a hand on his shoulder, then another one catch his sword arm and pull it down. He looked around to see the Emperor.

"Let him go, son. The measure of a man's power is the depth of his mercy. Give me the sword. The killing is over."

The Emperor worked the sword out of Tommy's grip and handed it to Jody. She took it, ran the blade across her wrist, then held the wound to the vampire's mouth. He took her arm in his hands and drank.

Jody looked at Cavuto. "Your partner is handcuffed to the wheel of the car. Get him and walk away before anyone else gets here. I need the car. I don't want to be followed either."

Cavuto dropped back into cop mode. "Bullshit."

"Go get your partner and go. Do you want to explain this?"

"What?"

"All this." Jody pulled her arm out of the vampire's mouth and gestured around the dock. "Look, the murders will stop. I promise. We're leaving and we're never coming back. So let it drop. And leave Tommy and these guys alone."

"Or what?" Cavuto said.

Jody cradled the old vampire and lifted him as she stood up. "Or we'll come back." She carried the vampire to the cruiser and put him in the back seat and crawled in with him. Rivera was sitting in the front seat. Cavuto came to the side of the car and handed his handcuff key through the window to Rivera.

"I told you," Rivera said.

Cavuto nodded. "We're fucked, you know? We have to let them go."

Rivera unlocked the handcuffs and got out of the car. He stood next to Cavuto, not sure what to do next.

Jody stuck her head out the back window of the cruiser. "Come on, Tommy, you drive."

Tommy turned to the Emperor, who nodded for him to go, then to the Animals. "You guys, get that stuff off the dock. In Troy's car. Get out of here. I'll call you at the store tomorrow."

Tommy shrugged, got in the car, and started it. "What now?"

"To the loft, Tommy. He needs a dark place to heal."

"I'm not comfortable with this, Jody. I want you to know that. I'd like to know what your relationship is to this guy."

The vampire moaned.

"Drive," she said.

They pulled off the dock, leaving the Animals scrambling around collecting the art and the two policemen staring at them in amazement.

She said, "I love you, Tommy, but I need someone who's like me. Someone who understands. You know how that is, right?"

"So you run off with the first rich older guy that comes along?"

"He's the only one, Tommy." She stroked the vampire's burned hair. "I don't have any choice. I hate being alone. And if he died, then I'd never know about what I am."

"So you two are going away? You're leaving me?"

"I wish I could think of some other way. I'm sorry."

"I knew you'd break my heart."

CHAPTER 35
Sculptures

Sunset cast a warm orange across the great Pyramid, while below, the Emperor enjoyed a cappuccino on a concrete bench and Bummer and Lazarus battled for the remains of a three-pound porterhouse.

"Men, would that I could let you, like Cincinnatus, retire like gentlemen soldiers to the country, but the City is still in need. The fiend is vanquished, but not the despair of my people. Our responsibility is legion."

A family of tourists passed the Emperor, hurrying to get to the cable-car stop at California Street before dark, and the Emperor tipped his cup in salute. The father, a balding fat man in an Alcatraz sweatshirt, took the Emperor's gesture as a request for spare change and said, "Why don't you get a job?"

The Emperor smiled. "Good sir, I have a job. I am Emperor of San Francisco and Protector of Mexico."

The tourist scrunched his face in disgust. "Look at you. Look at your clothes. You stink. You need a bath. You're nothing but a bum."

The Emperor looked down at the fraying cuffs of his dirty wool overcoat, his rib-worn gray corduroys, stained with splatters of vampire blood, the holes in his filthy sneakers. He raised an arm and took a sniff, then hung his head.

The tourists walked away.

• • •

Cavuto and Rivera sat in leather wingback chairs in front of the fireplace in Cavuto's Cow Hollow apartment. The fireplace was burning, the fire crackling and dancing as it fought off the damp chill of the bay. The room was furnished with rugged oak antiques, the bookshelves filled with detective novels, the walls hung with guns and posters from Bogart movies. Rivera drank cognac; Cavuto, Scotch. On the coffee table between them stood a three-foot-high bronze statue of a ballerina.

"So what do we do with it?" Cavuto asked. "It's probably stolen."

"Maybe not," Rivera said. "He might have bought it from Degas himself."

"The black kid says it's worth millions. You think he's right?"

Rivera lit a cigarette. "If it's authentic, yeah. So what do we do with it?"

"I've only got a couple of years before I retire. I've always wanted to own a rare-book shop."

Rivera smiled at the thought. "The wife wants to see Europe. I wouldn't mind having a little business of my own. Maybe learn to play golf."

"We could turn it in and just finish our time. They're going to move us out of homicide after this, you know that? We're too old for narcotics. Probably vice—night after night of screaming hookers."

Rivera sighed. "I'll miss homicide."

"Yeah, it was quiet."

"I've always wanted to learn about rare books," Rivera said.

"No golf," Cavuto said. "Golf is for pussies."

Tommy moved the futon so he could sit facing the two statues, then sat down to admire his handiwork. He'd worked all day in the foundry below, covering Jody and the vampire with the thin coat of conductive paint and putting them into the bronzing vats. The two biker sculptors had been more than happy to help, espe-

cially when Tommy pulled a handful of cash out of the grocery
bag that the Emperor had delivered.

The statues looked very lifelike. They should, they were still
alive under the bronze coating, except for Zelda, who stood
next to the two vampires. Tommy had put Jody in a leotard before he applied the paint. He'd dressed the vampire in a pair of
his own jockey shorts. It was amazing how fast the vampire had
healed after drinking Jody's blood. The worst part had been
waiting—waiting outside the bedroom where Jody had carried
the vampire, waiting for them to go out at sunrise, listening to
the soft murmur of their voices. What had they been talking
about?

Overall, the vampire looked pretty good. Almost all the damage to his body had healed by morning. Jody, even bronzed,
looked beautiful. The finishing touch had been to drill ear holes
through the thick bronze coating so he could talk to her.

"Jody, I know that you're probably really, really mad. I don't
blame you. But I didn't have a choice. It's not forever, it's just until I can figure out what to do. I didn't want to lose you. I know
you wanted to just go away and I think you would have, but *he*
wouldn't have. He would never have let me live."

Tommy waited, as if he would get some response from the
statue. He picked up the grocery bag of money from the floor
and held it up.

"By the way, we're rich! Cool, huh? I'll never make fun of Lash
for studying business again. In less than a day he fenced the art
from the yacht and got us ten cents on the dollar. Our cut's over
a hundred thousand. The guys flew to Vegas. We tried to give a
share to the Emperor, but he would only take enough to buy a
meal for Bummer and Lazarus. He said that money would distract him from his responsibilities. Great, huh?"

He dropped the money and sighed.

"Those two cops believed you. They're going to leave us alone.
They reported that the killer was on board the yacht when it
went up. Lash gave the gate guard some money to back up their
story. I couldn't believe they were going along with it. I think the
big cop kind of likes me.

"I'm going to write a book about this. I came here to find adventure and being with you sure has been that. And I don't want to give it up. I know we're not the same. And we shouldn't feel lonely when we have each other. I love you. I'm going to figure something out. I've got to sleep now. It's been days."

He got up and went to Jody. "I'm sorry," he said. He kissed the cold bronze lips and was turning to go into the bedroom when the phone rang.

"It's probably the Animals calling from some casino," he said as he picked up the phone.

"Hello."

"Uh, hi," a man's voice said. "Could I speak to Jody, please?"

Tommy pulled the phone away and looked at it, then put it to his ear and said, "Jody's . . . well . . . she's deceased."

"I know. Can I speak to her?"

"You sick fuck."

"Is this C. Thomas Flood? The guy from the paper?"

Who was this guy? "Look, buddy, that was a mistake. They got the guy who did those murders."

"Look, my name is Steve. I can't tell you my last name. Not until I'm sure it's safe. I'm a med student at Berkeley. I spoke to Jody the other night. We were supposed to meet the other night at Enrico's, but she never showed up. I'm kind of glad, I met a nice girl who works at the Safeway with you. Anyway, when I saw Jody's name in the paper I took a chance and looked up the number."

"If you saw the paper, you know what happened to Jody," Tommy said. "This isn't very funny."

The line was silent for a moment, then Steve said, "Do you know what she is?"

Tommy was shocked. "Do you?"

"So you do know?"

"She is, I mean *was*, my girlfriend."

"Look, I'm not trying to blackmail you or anything. I don't want to turn you in. I talked to Jody about reversing her condition. Well, I think I've found a way to do it."

"You're kidding."

"No. Tell her. I'll call you back tomorrow night. I know she's not up during the day."

"Wait," Tommy said. "Are you serious about this? I mean, you can make her human again?"

"I think so. It will probably take a few months. But I've been able to do it with cloned cells in the lab."

Tommy covered the mouthpiece and turned to the statue of Jody. "There's a guy here that says he can help you. We can be . . ."

Vapor was streaming out of the ear holes in the brass and swirling into a cloud in the middle of the room. Tommy dropped the phone and backed away from the cloud. He could hear Steve's voice calling for him on the phone.

Tommy backed against the counter in the kitchen. "Jody, is that you?"

The cloud was pulsating, sending out tendrils, or were they limbs? It was as if it was condensing into a solid shape.

Jody thought, Oh Tommy, you can't believe what I learned last night. You're going to have the adventure of your life, lover. And it's going to be such a long life. The things you'll see—I can't wait to show them to you.

She became solid, stood before him, naked, smiling.

Tommy held the phone to his chest. "You're pissed, aren't you?"

"I was never going to leave you, Tommy. I love you."

"But what about him?" Tommy pointed to the bronzed vampire.

"I had to make him think that I was going to go with him so I could find out what I needed to know. I've learned a lot, Tommy. I'm going to teach you." She started moving toward him.

"He taught you the mist thing, huh?"

"That, and how a vampire is made."

"No kidding. That could come in handy."

"And soon," she said. She looked back at the old vampire. "The bronzing was a pretty good trick. I didn't exactly know what I was going to do with him after I found out what I needed to know. Maybe later we can figure out a way to let him out and still be safe."

"So, you're not mad? You're really not leaving?"

"No. I thought I would have to leave, but I never wanted to. You and I are going to be together for a very long time."

Tommy smiled. "Great, this guy on the phone says . . ."

"Hang up, Tommy. And come here."

"But he says . . . he can change you back."

"Hang up." She took the phone from him and set it down on the counter, then moved into his arms and kissed him.

Author photo by Darren Westlund / Studio 3, Seattle; sculpture in author photo by Sherry Schuyler

CHRISTOPHER MOORE is the author of <u>Coyote Blue</u> and <u>Practical Demonkeeping</u>. He lives near Big Sur, California. Moore can be contacted by e-mail at BSFiends@AOL.com.

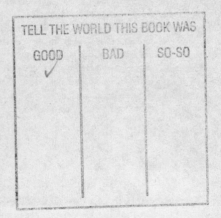

TELL THE WORLD THIS BOOK WAS

GOOD	BAD	SO-SO
✓		

BLOODSUCKING FIENDS
ISBN 0-380-72813-3 (paperback)

Jody never asked to become a vampire. But when she wakes up under an alley dumpster with a badly burned arm, an aching neck, superhuman strength, and a thirst for blood, she realizes the decision has been made for her. An eternity of nocturnal prowlings is going to take some getting used to, however, and that's where Tommy fits in. Biding his time night-clerking and frozen turkey bowling in a San Francisco Safeway, Tommy's world is turned upside-down when a beautiful, undead redhead walks through the door and proceeds to rock Tommy's live—and afterlife—in ways he never imagined possible.

"One of those rare writers who is laugh-out-loud funny." —*Santa Barbara Independent*

COYOTE BLUE
ISBN 0-380-72523-1 (paperback)

As a boy, he was Samson Hunts Alone—until a deadly misunderstanding with the law forced him to flee the Crow reservation at age fifteen. Now a successful Santa Barbara insurance salesman celebrating his thirty-fifth birthday and his hollow, invented life, destiny offers Samuel Hunter the dangerous gift of love in the exquisite form of Calliope Kincaid, *and* a curse in the unheralded appearance of an ancient Indian god. Coyote, the trickster, has arrived to transform tranquility into chaos, to reawaken the mystical storyteller within Sam…and to seriously screw up his existence in the process.

"Moore excels at putting a comic spin on cosmic issues." —*San Francisco Chronicle*

PRACTICAL DEMONKEEPING
ISBN 0-380-81655-5 (paperback)

Moore's ingenious debut novel introduces the reader to one of the most memorably mismatched pairs in the annals of literature. The good-looking one is one-hundred-year-old ex-seminarian and "road" scholar Travis O'Hearn. The green one is Catch, a demon with a nasty habit of eating most of the people he meets. Behind the fake Tudor facade of Pine Cove, California, Catch sees a four-star buffet. Travis, on the other hand, thinks he sees a way of ridding himself of his toothy traveling companion. The winos, Neo-pagans, and deadbeat Lotharios of Pine Cove, meanwhile, have other ideas.

"Moore is a very sick man, in the very best sense of the word." —Carl Hiaasen

• CUBE KID •

DIARY OF AN 8-BIT WARRIOR

QUEST MODE

Illustrations by Saboten

Andrews McMeel
PUBLISHING®

I stood **next to Breeze** in a small quartz room. A sea lantern illuminated the room with a **pale blue glow.** Against the center of one wall stood a **mysterious** object. It was **three yards tall, three yards wide,** and flat, like a banner. But instead of dyed wool, it was a surface like the calmest pool of water.

Breeze reached out with her right hand and **grazed her reflection.** She lowered her hand, and we continued staring at ourselves in silence. **In awe.** It was the first time we'd seen ourselves this way.

On top of that were <u>our outfits.</u>

Our clothes were sewn of spider silk. Puddles, the owner of the Clothing Castle, had worked with the humans for days to craft perfect re-creations of Earth fashion. Then, to make us look even more majestic, our cloaks had been modified to fall over our shoulders.

Poster children. Symbols of hope.
Villagetown's biggest stars.
That's what we've become.

Some would say it's sweet: a budding romance between two young heroes fighting valiantly against all odds. I'd say that's an exaggeration. Although Breeze and I are close, we haven't had much time for anything besides battle or preparations for the next. I guess the mayor wants to change that, though. He wants the people to have something to believe in. I suppose that's why he whisked us away in the middle of the dance.

And when we return, we're to smile,
hold hands, and raise them before a cheering crowd.

"You look so different from when we first met," I said.

"I suppose." Breeze stared **vacantly** ahead. "I wish we could have danced more."

"Me too."

I adjusted the collar of my shirt. We heard a **click,** and the door opened. In the reflection, I saw the mayor step in. As he studied us, particularly our outfits, the faintest trace of a smile appeared beneath his mustache.

"I apologize for taking you away like this," he said, gliding in. "I just wanted to make sure that you two are . . . looking your **very best** for the award ceremony."

"It's fine," Breeze said, still fixed on **her reflection.**

The mayor slid between us and ran his gnarled fingers along the edge of the object's smooth iron frame.

"So, what do you think? **Do you like it?**"

Breeze nodded. "It's . . . **amazing.** What is it called?"

"This is known as **a mirror.** This one is thousands of years old, crafted during the start of the **Second Great War.** As I understand, it came from an ancient temple. **The Tabernacle of Gloomfell Cove.** That's near the sea, beyond a vast mountain range to the northwest, far, far from here."

"I suppose it'd be **impossible to craft** such an object **ourselves,**" I said. "How did it wind up here, anyway?"

"Our records say a trader brought it here. Traders used to be quite common, back when it was **still safe to travel.** I was just a boy then. So many voyagers and vagabonds constantly visited our village. It seems like yesterday. . . ."

I nodded, vaguely recalling reading something about that in school. Only recently had our village learned of **the Eyeless One's** return, yet our scholars believe he's been gathering his strength and amassing his armies for a long time. The coming war is, perhaps, something he's been planning for at least fifty years. Before that, **monster attacks** were far from common. You could have traveled **the Overworld** for weeks without encountering one. And now . . .

After staring off **into nothingness** for a moment, the mayor raised his head and **smiled** again. Was that a tear in the corner of his eye?

"You two look so wonderful," he finally said. "Yes, you're **exactly** what our village **needs** right now." Another pause. "I . . . hope you can understand why **I'm asking all this of you.**"

I looked his **reflection** in the eye.
"Of course, sir."

We walked back in silence. Almost everyone was at the party, so the streets were mostly empty. Still, we could see distant **silhouettes** on the wall, spaced evenly—every hundred blocks, more or less. **Humans standing watch,** enchanted bows slung over their shoulders. There was, no doubt, at least one more up in the sky tower—**ready to activate** the note block alarm system should trouble arise—but I couldn't see into the tower's nest from here.

Upon reaching the **village hall,** things were mostly the same as when we left: **posters and banners, jukeboxes and cakes.** And a thousand or so people celebrating Villagetown's success. Even though **the Eyeless One** was still out there, his minions had been driven back.

For us, that was <u>enough.</u>
At this point, we'll take **any victory** we can get,
no matter how small.

I heard some **laughter** to my left: Breeze was already being swept away by a handful of human girls. They couldn't get over **her cloak.** Stump couldn't get over mine. After he slapped me on the back and flashed **a huge grin,** his gaze fell to my shoulders. "What's that about?"

"For the **award ceremony,** I guess." I glanced around at the jovial crowd of villagers and humans. "**So what's new?** Have you heard anything since I left?"

"Yeah. This kid—**Tucker,** I think—said he was playing on the wall the other morning and saw **a rabbit** on the plains. And not just any rabbit. He claims it was **a zombie.**"

Stump made **a spooky face,** then busted out laughing. "The imaginations of kids these days!"

"**Hmmm,**" I said. "Actually, I'd like to look into it. I'll speak to him **later.**"

"Also, I keep seeing **this weird old man,**" Stump said. "Red robes. Red hat. Black sunglasses. Huge white beard. Said his name is **Cocoa. Cocoa Witherbean.**"

"Cocoa Witherbean, huh?"

I **thought** for a moment, but the name didn't ring any bells, and neither did the description. That wasn't all that strange, though. New people have been showing up at our gate almost **every week. Survivors.** Usually, it's a small group of **clueless** villagers who've fled from some tiny, obscure town after being attacked in the middle of the night. Otherwise, it's a lone human who's been **wandering the Overworld** for months. We take them all in, show them around, and assign them some work to do.

"So this **Cocoa,**" I said, "is he one of the new arrivals from this morning?"

"Maybe. Whoever he is, **he's creepy.** I've seen him snooping around outside a **library,** too."

"Interesting. . . ." Once more I thought back but didn't remember seeing anyone who fit Stump's verbal sketch.

"All right, I'll **keep an eye out** for this guy," I said. "Anything else?"

"**Nope.** Not really."

"Well, keep up the **good work,**" I said. "And don't let your guard down. Even at a time like this"—I reached up and patted **my diamond sword,** which was now sheathed across my back—"we can't forget who we are."

Stump's smile **faded.** "Yes, **sir!**"

"**Hey!** You don't need to call me that."

"But they said I'm **supposed** to call you that, now that **you're a captain.**"

"**That doesn't matter.** We've been friends since we were just a single block tall. I'm just **Runt,** okay?"

"Sure thing," he said, frowning. "You know, Runt, you . . . you're acting **awfully serious** all of a sudden. What happened? Is anything wrong?"

I lowered my head, unsure what to say. What **could** I say? I couldn't stop thinking about what the mayor had said earlier. *You're a* warrior, Runt—a sworn defender of our village. And today, you must act the part. . . .

Of course, I didn't need to say anything to Stump. He understood. He understood **better than anyone.** He'd been there when hundreds of mobs breached the wall. So as I stood in silence, he didn't say anything, either—just gave me a **slow** nod. Perhaps he was recalling it as well. Several other villagers ran up, **laughing and joking** and handing us slices of **cake** . . . and the images quickly left our minds. For the moment.

For that matter, I was **so wrapped up** in the celebration that I almost failed to notice the villagers' clothes. Many of them were dressed in **human-style outfits** like me. Breeze was right. We really are becoming more and more like the **humans.** Then again, they're becoming more like us, too. One look at their leader was enough to convince you. There he was, **Kolbert21337,** He Who Hails from Earth, **Lord Commander of the Lost Legion** . . . dressed in a **villager's** robe.

"**PLEASE STOP** CALLING ME THAT," he yelled. "**KOLB** WILL DO **JUST FINE.** I really need to find another one of those enchanted name tags so I can change this silly name. . . . By the way—I have **an important announcement!** My best friend **Kaeleb** recently discovered how to craft **apple pie!** We'd like to **share** some with you guys! In return, we'd love to try some of **your famous** grass stew! We've heard it's a village delicacy, and we really want to know what it tastes like!"

He went on to explain how there's **a holiday on Earth** that celebrates a time when two vastly different groups of people shared food with each other. The humans wanted to start something like that here. **Unfortunately** for them, they had no idea what they were getting into. **Grass stew** is considered a village delicacy not because it **tastes good,** but because **it's hard to craft.** You need shears **enchanted with Silk Touch** to harvest grass. As for the taste, you're **better off** eating grass raw.

Poor Kolbert . . . uhh, "Kolb."
He **quickly** discovered this.

"Well, do you like it? I crafted it myself."

"It's, um . . . DELICIOUS."

"GREAT! Glad you liked it! How about some more?"

"Um . . . actually, it's the strangest thing. I suddenly feel very full!"

Finally, the mayor announced that it was **time for the award ceremony.** As we approached, we saw that in his palm he was holding **six tiny objects,** each **no bigger than a single seed.** Two resembled **hearts,** and another two resembled **swords.** The last pair, however, I didn't recognize. They were **gray** in color, **stone,** with flecks of **white-blue diamond** here and there. They almost looked like some kind of . . . um . . . **bird?**

10

"For this year's **graduates,**" the mayor called out, "we've crafted **various emblems** to signify their **achievements,** their chosen professions, and their titles."

He held one of the **birdlike emblems** in his right hand and raised it over his head. The bird's **diamond flecks** caught the setting sun, sparkling brilliantly. "This one specifically," he added, "the **Diamond Blockbird,** is crafted from a single piece of **diamond ore** to demonstrate its **rarity** and value. Thus, each emblem has been crafted to honor those who have **fought so hard to protect our village** in these dark and troubled times. And out of the many brave young graduates here, the two standing beside me have **fought the hardest.** For this reason, we've decided that they may both serve as **captains** and share leadership of **their group.**"

At this, a lot of people began **whispering,** but for Breeze and me, this was **no surprise.** The mayor had mentioned this earlier when he first took us to that room. He had said that he wanted our group to **stand out** above the rest. Since we've proven ourselves and all. . . . But I think there's more to it. He also told us that our group would be the **first** to **explore the Overworld.** When it comes to leading and making the right decisions, he probably trusts Breeze more than me. **That's understandable.** Sometimes I let **my emotions** get the best of me. Breeze, on the other hand, **never** loses her cool. So she'll be serving as, like . . . **my babysitter?** No, that's not how a heroic swordsman would say it. She'll be there to ensure I don't make any mistakes. **That's it.**

The mayor turned and **gave us a knowing nod.** Recalling our instructions, I **fell to one knee,** as did Breeze. Then he began fastening different emblems on the left shoulder of our cloaks, just above our **hearts.** They clung securely, like **sticky pistons.** Then he pulled out **another pair: little blue stars.** The official emblem of **a captain.** He **replaced** my original diamond badge with this.

As he fastened on each pair, one after another, he called out **their meaning** to the crowd. From what I understand, he had borrowed this from the **Lost Legion.** Every member of that clan is required to dedicate themselves to this thing called **role-playing.** Since they're supposed to be an order of **knights,** they have to carry themselves like knights. And whenever a clan member is promoted, it's through this special ceremony known as **knighting.**

"To our noblest of heroes, Breeze and Runt . . . you shall hereby be known as warriors, as well as . . .

"Defenders of
Villagetown . . ."

"Captains of
Night Watch . . ."

"and Explorers of
the Overworld."

I wanted to believe his words, but I **couldn't help feeling** that this whole thing was mostly **just an act** to boost village morale. I don't think of myself as **a hero. Not even close.** In many ways, I'm still **just a kid.** I **still** get scared at times. And I still have so much to learn.

Yet seeing hundreds of faces **light up,** tears being brushed away, it suddenly seemed that our survival **wasn't unimaginable** but **likely—even certain.** It was as if the **Wizard with No Eyes** was just another **low-level monster,** out there somewhere waiting to be farmed.

Below, whispers grew louder and louder, until they finally **erupted into cheers and screams.** But that seemed **so quiet** compared to the pounding in my chest. The more I watched them, the more **I felt this awful weight.** It grew heavier with each smile directed my way. Only then did I begin to fully realize what this all meant, how high the bar was. **The whole village was counting on me.** When I glanced at Breeze, though, that feeling went away.

No, I thought. They're not counting on me. . . .
They're counting on US.

What am I worrying about? As long as she's there, Villagetown has nothing to worry about.

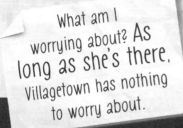

"May I have this dance?"

"Wow, they're actually dancing! Why don't we join them?"
"Um . . ."
"Err . . . Hello, Stump. Would you, um . . . well, would you like to dance?"
"Sure, but only if you can keep up. I'm about to unleash my newest move. I call it the Creeper Rush."

17

Without a doubt, today was the best day of my life.

The party was winding down, so I walked Breeze home. Her dad was already there when we arrived. I had noticed that he had **seemed a little off** the entire night . . . **gloomy . . .** but there, seeing him in front of the doorway, his attitude mirrored the **storm clouds** that were gathering above our heads: **somber and unnerving.** Something was bothering him.

Breeze didn't seem to notice, or at least she chose not to bring any attention to it. She turned **with a smile.**

"See you tomorrow, Runt. And make sure you **get some sleep**. We have a big day ahead of us."

Her father made a slight movement, like **a jolt?** I'm not quite sure.

"Good night," Breeze said, still smiling.

"Good night."

I was **exhausted** when I got home.

"Good night, **Son!**" my mom said.

"We're very proud of you," my dad added.

Yeah, it really was **the best day of my life.** And tomorrow is going to be **even better.** Tomorrow I begin my **first real adventure,** what I've been **dreaming** about for so long. In the morning, we'll start our first exploration outside the walls. We're supposed to head out in our groups, always staying **within sight** of the ramparts. **I can't wait.**

And **strangely,** it seemed like tomorrow couldn't wait for me, either. Knock! Knock! **Knock!**

Huh? Who's knocking? It must be Mom. I slept in. I'll be late for school.

I actually thought that, in **my deep sleep,** until my eyes flew open and I **sat straight up** in bed.

But there was no way someone could have been knocking at my door— I'd been so tired earlier that **I forgot to shut it.** That was when I saw the **shadowy figure** standing just outside my window. Okay, so I'm not **the brightest** person upon first waking up, but I knew it wasn't my mom.

No, whoever it was, **it was a human. . . .**

And when I looked closer . . . **yes—**

That human most definitely resembled Kolb.

"Come with me, **hero.**"

He took me to **his house,** to a **small dark room. A secret** library.

There, he told me **everything.**

How **we'd be attacked.**

How we couldn't possibly defend ourselves.

How we needed **better armor,** better **weapons,** and **better items** than the ones we had. How a standard crafting table **wouldn't** be enough.

He showed me a book, an **ancient** book, and a drawing of something thought to exist only in **legend**. An **aeon forge**—otherwise known as **an advanced crafting table**.

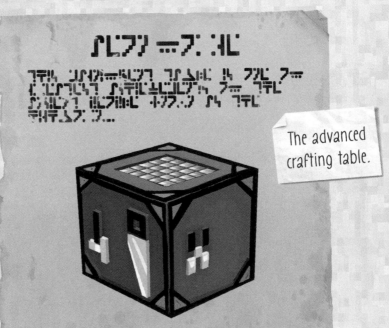

The advanced crafting table.

Weeks ago, **several members of the Lost Legion** went into the wilds in **search** of one. Tonight, they had returned **empty-handed, barely** hanging on. . . .

"I know you will succeed **where they have failed**," Kolb said. "You must go. **Tonight.**"

"Alone? What about **Breeze?**"

"She'll **talk you out of it.** You know that. As for the rest . . . they'll only **slow you down.**"

"I assume **there's a reason** you can't just go yourself?"

"**There is.** Members of **the Lost Legion** continue to fight among themselves. If I left now, **the clan would fall apart.** And even if I could leave, **I wouldn't make it** one night out there."

"What makes you so sure?"

"I'm . . . **being hunted.**"

"The Eyeless One's minions have been searching for me ever since I arrived in this world. I was on the run even before I arrived here. I changed my appearance, my armor, and even my name. . . ."

23

"If they discovered **who I really am**, every last one of them would rush to this area. So **I must stay hidden.**"

"**I don't get it.** Why are they looking for you?"

"They . . . see me as **a threat.** I'll just leave it at that."

"You probably can't read ancient script, huh? This loosely translates to '**Destroy him.**' What can I say? Monsters hate me. A lot."

So Kolb **really** is a high-level knight? One so **powerful** that **the Eyeless One's** servants are on his tail? And he's sending me on **a quest** to save my village? What does one say to that?

"**. . . You'll feed my pet slime** while I'm gone?" Kolb's instructions sounded **simple enough:**

"Head north, to the village of **Owl's Reach.** A librarian named **Feathers** has the table we need."

Then he gave me a map. **A map of Ardenvell,** the main continent.

"It isn't very **complete,** but it'll have to do. The other guys lost mine."

On the map, it looked **so close.** I was surprised when he said it would take **days** to get there. . . .

Of course, I should have **consulted** with the others before going on **some crazy quest** alone in the middle of the night . . .

but then, you know me.

It all happened so **fast.** Before I knew it, I'm on top of **a big white horse,** doing my best to hold on as the animal chugged full speed ahead.

A million questions are running through my mind right now. Was Kolb telling **the truth?** Why is he being hunted? **Who is he?** And this **crafting table . . .** will I really find one in some village called **Owl's Reach?**

Most important, **did I make the right decision?** It feels **so reckless** going out on my own like this. **I'm terrified.** The mayor's going to be **outraged. . . .**

What was I **supposed** to do? If I had talked to Breeze, she would have **stopped me. Anyone** would have stopped me. **Kolb had been right** about that. And if he's right about the upcoming attack, we really will need every advantage we can get.

I glance at **the map** again. Owl's Reach isn't marked, but it's there. **Somewhere. Some fifty thousand blocks away.** Okay, so my quest is pretty clear: all I have to do is head **somewhere,** talk to someone, and try not to get eaten by zombies along the way. **No problem.** But I really wish he'd given me a **better map.** Even if it's the most complete map Villagetown's libraries had to offer, that's not exactly saying much.

Most of the other maps, well . . .

It's actually
not so bad . . .

compared to this.

ZOMBIE CREEPER

ENDER RABBIT

(He gave me one of those maps, too. I'm . . . not sure why. Yeah, I can't fathom how so much villager knowledge has been lost over the generations, when we have such useful information at our disposal. . . .)

As far as supplies go, **I'm set:** Kolb gave me a stack of carrots, a stack of oak, half a stack of coal, a crafting table, a furnace, a bed. Also **332 emeralds** taken from his clan's **ender chest.** Plus, I have a full set of **stone tools** I crafted earlier and, of course, **my sword. There's just one problem.** I'm still wearing these clothes. Here's the thing about this outfit: although it makes me seem like a **rich noble** hailing from some **powerful kingdom**—a kingdom where **golden apples** are served in cafeterias and everyone drinks **healing potions** instead of water—it doesn't provide **any armor or stats** of any kind. And they're rather useful, armor and stats. **I like armor and stats. A lot.** I'd wear a big **beetroot sack** as long as it provided even a bit of armor or maybe increased my **movement speed**.

I'd somehow craft it into a shirt
and wear that thing with pride.

As I make my way **north,** I sometimes glance to the **south, toward home.** I decided earlier that if I see **any smoke** after sunrise, I'd head back to the village **as fast as possible.** Of course, by the time I'd make it back, it would already be **too late.** . . . .

I can't help but imagine **the mayor's face** upon hearing that I'm gone. It's kind of **ridiculous** when you think about it. Just a few hours after I was **hailed** as one of **Villagetown's heroes,** I vanished without a trace. So much for the mayor's plan of **boosting morale.** . . . I can almost hear **Emerald** cracking **some joke** about it. Something about how I got so wound up over the whole **"Explorer of the Overworld"** thing that I zoomed off without **any instructions.** Okay, I admit it— that's probably something I'd do.

All right. The sun's going down. I'm about to **make camp.** That is, dig an **emergency shelter.** I won't write about the process of **digging** a shelter here. **I've already gone over that.** Besides, I don't feel like dwelling on the fact that I'll be spending **the night in a dirt hole.** I still have a shred of **dignity.**

In a hole . . . next to a horse . . .
a horse whose name I don't even know . . .
a horse who slobbers all over me.

"No!
Those are the carrots;
these are my fingers."

I'm having trouble falling asleep.

Two blocks of dirt sit between me and fresh air, yet I still hear all kinds of **sounds.** Distant howls, **eerie calls.** Sounds not made by any **zombie,** but that's about all I know.

Back pressed against damp earth, in total darkness, **I wait. . . .** I listen to those cries, **thinking about home.** Family. Friends.

That reminds me—**that very heavy** book Max handed to me before he took off with Lola. I place a torch at my feet and turn the first page.

CHAPTER 1
RARE METALS

WE SHALL BEGIN THIS TOME WITH AN IN-DEPTH LOOK AT THOSE RELATIVELY RARE AND UNKNOWN METALS, THOUGHT BY MANY TO EXIST IN LEGEND ONLY. LET IT BE KNOWN THAT SUCH FANTASTIC METALS DO EXIST. SO FANTASTIC ARE THESE METALS, ONLY A PERSON OF GODLIKE POWER COULD DESIRE BETTER.

VOIDCRYSTAL   MYTHRIL   FIRE ELEMENTIUM

EARTH ESPER   ADAMANT   ORICAL

I've come across **a ruined village.** Maybe there was a **fire** here. Only cobblestone foundations remained. After searching around, I didn't find anything. No items. No signs of battle. No rubble, even.

The whole place is just . . .
empty.

I actually drew a picture of the place, along with a caption saying: "Actually, it's not so bad. Just put up some flowerpots, some carpet, maybe a painting. . . . Um, never mind."

Obviously, the joke was that **no amount** of decoration could cheer this place up. But **I threw the picture away,** because it felt wrong to joke about other people's **misfortunes.** This has to be one of the villages those survivors came from. **This was their home.** I still remember their faces when they showed up at our gate.

If I ever find out who did this . . .

The horse is gone. I didn't leash it when I went to check out the village because I don't have a leash. **Why didn't Kolb give me one? Seriously,** that horse was right there, no farther than fifteen or twenty blocks away, just nibbling on grass. I checked a few houses in the village, wrote in here, **came back, and . . . great.** The **weird thing** is that I can see for hundreds of blocks in every direction and there's **no horse** in sight. He must have really booked it. Was I really such a bad master? **As if!** I fed that thing more than I fed myself!

Great. Now Kolb's going to be angry with me, too. And traveling **on foot** is going to consume **way more energy.** I'm not sure if these carrots will last. I might have to **go hunting** at some point.

Oh **wait.** I stashed my bow in one of my **item chests** back home. **So glad I did that. . . .** See, this is where I've failed—a real warrior would have definitely anticipated a human randomly showing up in the middle of the night and sending said warrior to find an item that may or may not **actually exist.**

Okay. Let's stay positive. At least I'm not going to have to deal with **horse slobber** tonight. Horses eat **potatoes,** apparently. And apparently, **my nose** resembles one.

I wonder what's **everyone's doing back home.** What happened **after I left?** Kolb could be in **a lot of trouble** for sending me out here **on my own.** It's possible that this whole thing could undo the alliance. What if the humans got **kicked out?** What if the mayor **banished** him?

No, it must have played out differently than that. After all, before I left, Kolb said he would **handle everything.** He must have succeeded, because if **Breeze** found out I left, she would've taken a horse and come looking for me. **She would've caught up to me** by now. So everything must be continuing as **normal.** Everyone's getting their feet wet, exploring the Overworld just outside the wall. **Yeah, that's all.**

Breeze must be leading Max, Stump, Lola, and Emerald on **a field trip.** Finding **caves. Mapping the terrain.** Spending the night in a carefully constructed shelter that would—at least compared to the emergency shelter I just dug—look like **the royal suite in Snark's Tavern.** They must be thinking they're tough, eating stacks of bread and sharing ghost stories in the ruddy glow of a redstone torch placed on the ground. **Oooh, spooky.**

Note: I added the destroyed village to my map. Should I ever discover its name, I'll update it.

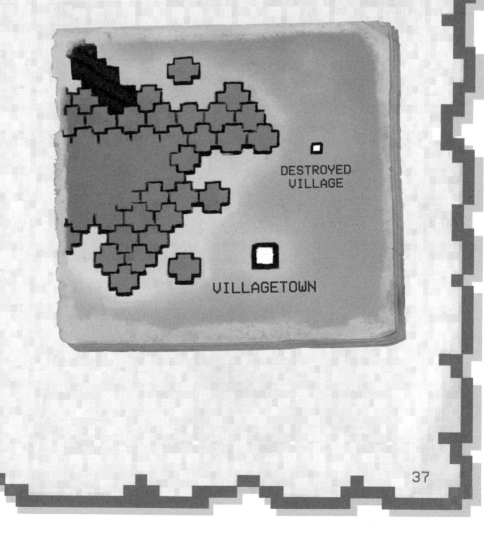

"Aetherstone. Adamant. Elementite. Endersteel. Orical. Redsteel. Mythril. Voidcrystal . . ."

In my new underground abode, **I recite these words out loud.** They're the names of some of the **rarest known materials,** or **elements,** of which there are many. Most only exist naturally in the **outer dimensions.** That is, **the dimensions beyond the End.** They're exceedingly **hard** to mine, even with an **obsidian pickax.** Others, such as redsteel and endersteel, don't exist naturally in any known dimension and therefore

cannot be mined. They're created by smelting other materials in an object known as **a crucible**—basically **an advanced furnace.**

I find it confusing that this so-called **elementite** has at least **five different types: fire, earth, air, water, and shadow.** According to the author of this book, a villager named **Theonius** who lived some five hundred years ago, scholars believed there are several more types of elementite. The scholars also argued about what it should be called: **elementite** or **elementium.**

Huh . . . interesting . . . Zzzzz.

Back to reading, even if this book is **slightly boring.** I still can't **sleep.** A zombie has been walking around overhead for the past hour or so. Earlier, I heard this strange sound: *thunk, thunk, thunk.* My imagination went wild. I couldn't picture anything other than some horrible monster, **half tree, half . . .** But no, it was just that zombie, walking into the trunk of an oak tree. **Facepalm.** Some real nice monsters you have there, Herobrine.

What am I even doing out here?
All we have to do is plant trees all around the village and . . .
BINGO! Attack thwarted.

The morning consisted of **walking** and eating carrots. **Mostly. I know. Pretty** thrilling. I like to **start off my mornings** in the Overworld real intense like that.

The highlight of the day was when I came across **an arrow** lodged in the side of a small stone cliff. Okay, so that alone **isn't very interesting,** but it wasn't **a normal arrow.** The tip was made of **obsidian,** with **a creepy** ghostlike face. The face had an odd expression, both **sad and angry,** like someone had just stolen a muffin that he was about to eat. **Which would definitely make me sad and angry.**

Needless to say, I've **never seen** an arrow like that before. I can only assume it's **poisoned.** Or **enchanted** with some horrible debuff that makes Wither look like **slight mining fatigue.** Being **the curious explorer** that I am, I almost wanted to **poke myself** with it just to see what would happen. But I quickly realized that a zombie, a pigman, or perhaps a creeper would be **a much better** test **subject.**

Do you see it?
The creepy face?
Like, part creeper, part ghast, and both sad and angry at the same time?

Or am I just imagining things again?

"**Nah,** this arrow totally isn't enchanted with **Noob Melting VII.** It was obviously crafted out of **sheer love and happiness.**"

In fact, if it struck a grass block, it would probably sprout **thousands of flowers.**

I spotted **a forest** in the middle of the plains. In its very center was a **grotto-like** area with **a cliff** and **a waterfall.**

It was a **beautiful** scene, inviting, with fragrant blossoms and multicolored leaves and mossy stone under streams of **brilliant blue water**—golden sunlight pouring down. *Come on in,* this place seemed to say. *Just go for a little swim. You don't need to worry. There are no creepers here.* **Promise.** *Ignore that slight rustling sound behind you. Ignore the hissing. Focus on the water.*

Maybe that was why **I cautiously approached,** expecting **the worst.** But there was nothing. No **giant squid** surging from the depths. No zombies rising from the ground.

Only **tranquility,** loveliness, a gentle breeze . . . and a most <u>unusual-looking</u> girl.

Upon seeing her, I actually gasped.

"Are you . . . **an NPC?**" she asked, stepping back slightly.

". . ."

Here we go again, I thought. *As if I haven't already heard enough of that back at the village. Wait, does that mean she's a human? No, she can't be. She looks nothing like one.*

"My name is **Runt,**" I said, approaching.

She **nearly tripped** as she backed up. Then, after another **uneasy glance** in my direction, she **darted into the forest.** Apparently, I'm the **scariest villager** who ever lived.

43

"Hey! **Wait! C**ome back!"

But she was already gone.

I **stood there** for a moment, completely stunned. **Who was she? What was she?** What was up with **her sword?** It was **thin** but **longer** than any sword I'd ever seen.

"Well, she's **definitely** not a human," I muttered. "Not with ears like that."

And suddenly I realized that I'd been talking to myself **an awful lot** lately. Asking myself questions out loud. I never **really** thought about it, but you're **truly alone** when it comes to the Overworld. Sure, I'd heard that it was **barren.** Still, you don't quite understand just how empty it is until you **see it with your own eyes.**

After living in a village my entire life, I find the silence **rather unsettling.**

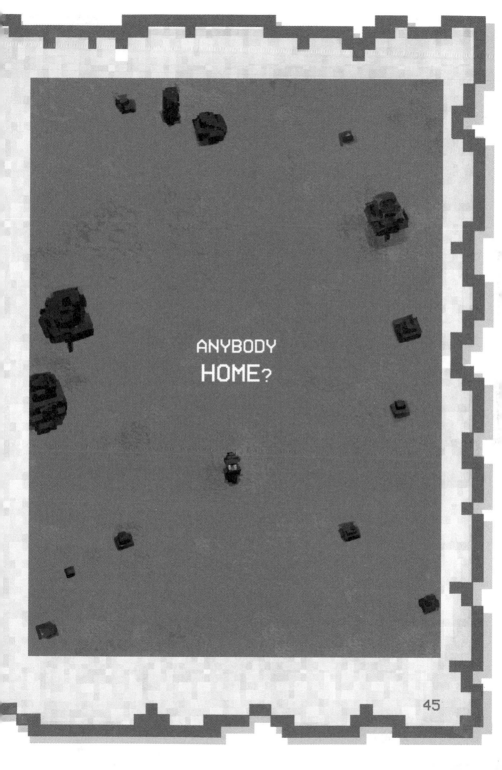

TUESDAY—UPDATE I

*"The Overworld. The Nether. The End. The Void. The Aether.
The Cleft. The Shadowlands. The Veil. The Maelstrom. The Abyss.
The Channel. The Pinnacle. The Zone. Icerahn . . ."*

More self-assigned reading in a temporary underground home. I'm reviewing **dimensions** this time. Before reciting them, I was reading about one in particular: **the Void.** It's this **mysterious** place with **crystalline** plants, pools of water that bestow **magical** effects, and a race of people known as **mycons.** Known for their crafting ability, they are to villagers as **mooshrooms** are to cows.

Maybe I'll visit that place **someday.** There's a path in the Overworld that leads to it; it's **a gigantic chasm** in a forest far to the west. Furthermore, the book says gateways may exist **between the Nether and the Void.** That's pretty useless information for me, since I personally have **no intention** of setting foot in a place where everything **breathes fire.**

All right. **Back to studying.**

THE AETHER

THE FIFTH DIMENSION, THE AETHER, CONSISTS OF VAST ISLES OF AETHERSTONE SUSPENDED IN A BLACK, STAR-FILLED VOID.

MANY DIFFERENT RACES INHABIT THE LARGER ISLES, MOST NOTABLY THE FISHMEN AND THE BIRDMEN, THE NAMES OF WHICH HAVE BEEN LOST THROUGH THE AGES. ALTHOUGH THESE PEOPLE ARE PEACEFUL, IT SHOULD BE NOTED THAT THEY ARE PERFECTLY CAPABLE OF DEFENDING THEMSELVES.

AS THE DISTANCE BETWEEN EACH ISLE CAN BE VAST, THE MOST EFFICIENT METHOD OF TRAVELING BETWEEN THEM IS THROUGH THE USE OF A FLYING MOUNT, PARTICULARLY A SPECTRAL RAVEN: A BIRD NATIVE TO THIS DIMENSION, FOUND ON MANY OF THE LARGEST ISLES AND QUITE EASILY TAMED WITH BEETROOTS OR SUGAR. THE FASTEST AMONG THEM CAN RIVAL AN ENDER DRAGON IN SPEED.

Uh, giant ghost chickens that you can ride like horses? Why did I have to be born in the Overworld?! Whyyy?!?!

This morning I encountered more people: five humans riding in a **V-shaped formation.** Both they and their black horses were covered in **black armor,** and they were riding **fast.** Those mounts had to be at least **twice as quick** as Kolb's.

The one in front spotted me, too. **Was he their leader?** He didn't wave, just **turned back** as they tore across the plains from the east to the west—from my right to my left—fifty or so blocks up ahead. Wherever they were going, they were in a **big hurry.** And they were **serious.** As if the **fate of the world** rested on their shoulders. The way they dressed almost reminded me of **the Legion.** Of Kolb. Were they part of that clan?

"Stop! **Wait!** Seriously, why does everyone keep running away from me?! I . . . just want someone to talk to."

WEDNESDAY—UPDATE I

In other news, I'm running low on carrots. That's the **optimistic** version. . . . In reality, I have **two carrots** left. Something just dawned on me. **It's been what—five days?** But I haven't seen many animals. I spotted **a chicken** on the first day. A **cow** on the second. But I still had a ton of carrots at that point—and a horse.

This is bad. Are animals really this **rare** in the Overworld? Are they like **diamonds** with legs? Now I can't even find 1 chicken. **Not even 1!** I wrote "**1**" instead of "one" to conserve my food bar. **It's less tiring.**

UPDATE: Never mind, writing in here doesn't appear to be draining my food bar. Or hunger bar. I don't even know what to call it. . . . All I know is that my stomach starts **growling** when I get down to two chicken thighs.

Actually, what was it that Max once said in class? Only **strenuous activities** affect the food bar. Therefore, once starvation creeps up on me, all I have to do is **stop moving.** My food bar won't decrease at all. I can wait days, if needed, until some pig comes along, then **boom**—a nice cooked pork chop sizzling away on an open furnace, sautéed with mushrooms, seasoned with bits of dandelion and possibly some grass torn from a grass block and sprinkled on top the way Stump decorates his cakes at . . .

Oh!
I can taste it now!

Huh? What's that? No, I'm not starving! **How could you even suggest such a thing?** A dashing **gentleswordsman** such as myself would never fall into such a desperate and sad situation! I'm just planning ahead! **Believe me!**

Tonight I read about **Ardenvell.** The largest city, also known as the **capital,** is called **Aetheria City.** It's far to the west. It sounds like **paradise.** The book speaks of magnificent white towers reaching up to the sky. It's home to some of the greatest blacksmiths in all the land. **The Knights of Aetheria,** too. It's an ancestral order that goes way back, to the time of the **Second Great War.**

Aetheria City

I saw a chicken. A chicken!

On any other day, this wouldn't have made the news. But today, it was everything. I literally could have just left this entry like that—*I saw a chicken*—and it still would have been the single most important entry in the Overworld, the Nether, the End, the Void, the Aether, the Cleft, the Shadowlands . . . okay, I forgot the rest.

But I digress. Back to the chicken. Without a bow, I had to chase it down. I ate my last carrot to do so—you can't sprint when your food bar is too low. And as the furnace crackled away, with the smell of roast chicken drifting through the air, I heard a distant cluck, followed by another. Suddenly, it seemed like chickens were raining from the sky. They were fluttering around everywhere, crazily flapping their wings. One even flew into my face.

What's their problem? I thought. *Is there a wolf or something?*

I chased after them all, catching six in total. And here's where things get weird. (Sigh.)

I ran up to the last one. Sword held over my head. More than ready to turn that animal into tomorrow's lunch and hopefully one-third of an arrow. Then I . . . well, I noticed something odd: the chicken's feathers, instead of being mostly white, were dark gray, sickly green, even yellow-brown. . . .

I'll have you know that I, being the **thoughtful warrior** that I am, was well aware that this chicken could have been an **unknown** species or could have originated from some special biome, perhaps **the savanna to the west.** . . . Maybe chickens in savanna biomes have different-colored feathers than most—I don't know, do I look like a chicken expert? But the thing was, **this chicken,** it, um . . . well, I mean it, it kind of . . . it had no . . . **you see,** it, um . . . okay, okay, I'll just say it up front, sure, yeah, and **if you get scared,** that's totally not my fault. **Deep breath,** here goes:

This chicken,
it . . .
it didn't have eyes!

No, whenever someone refers to the "Eyeless One" . . . this is not who they're talking about.

It was a zombie. **A zombie chicken.** So Tucker was right! As **unbelievable** as it may seem, there really **are** zombie animals. But how could **a zombie chicken** survive in the sun? More important, why didn't **anyone** tell us about this in school? Maybe the teachers thought it was best that we didn't know; maybe they figured some of the students would just start **crying** and someone would ask, sobbing, "D-d-does that mean F-Fluffy can turn into a **z-zombie?**"

Or maybe the teachers **don't know.** Is it a new phenomenon? **Caused by what, though? Magic?** Some kind of hideous curse placed by **He Who Never Blinks?** Who could do such a thing to such a poor, **defenseless little animal?** It tried attacking me but moved much slower than an ordinary zombie, its little legs moving awkwardly, **robotically,** like a tiny golem. All I had to do was step back every now and then, no real hurry. A little flap of its wings. One step forward—no, it **stopped. Okay, there it went**—never mind, it stopped **again.** So sad. No, this couldn't go on.

"**Sorry,** chicken."

The chicken's undead state appeared to make it tougher, for it took **two swings of my diamond sword** to bring that thing down. The meat it dropped did not appear to be what one might call . . . **edible.** Besides by **a pigman named Urg,** that is. *(What? Don't look at me like that! He's the hero of this series I came across in the library: Urg the Barbarian. He'll eat anything. In the second book, he survived in the Overworld by eating a **zombie's shoes.**)*

*But **even Urg** wouldn't eat something like this*, I thought, staring down at the ground. Mind wandering, I left **the rotten food** where it had dropped and moved onward, **onward, forever onward . . .** over highlands and valleys, mounds and hillocks, low outcroppings of stone, and gravel, gravel—dark gray patches that were once, of course, **a very long time ago,** incredibly safe and well-traveled roads.

A massive wall of cobblestone. I staggered forward, one wobbling foot in front of the other.

Voices.
Distant chatter.

My jaw dropped like an anvil.
I wasn't dreaming. **It wasn't a mirage.**

(Look at those little owl banners. How cool is that? What is that, the sigil of this village? I might not know what they are, exactly, but they're cool and I want some. I'll try crafting a few when I get back.)

58

Owl's Reach.
I'd found it.

Without a word, the three lookouts **waved from above.** Iron blocks gave way to **gravel streets, wooden houses, and so many people**—no two of them the same. Everywhere I looked, **villagers** were bumbling about, building homes, farming crops, and trading with everyone else. **Humans, mostly.** Others **resembled that girl** I saw, with **light-gray skin and the longest ears.** Some looked **even weirder.** There was truly every kind of person imaginable.

59

They ranged from fairly normal looking, such as this human wizard girl . . .

"Just one more level and I'll have that spell."

. . . to those known as "dark dwarves," with light-blue skin.

"Hey! Watcha staring at, noob?!"

63

From what I gather, **Owl's Reach** serves as a crossroads for **explorers** like myself. Inns and item shops abound, **catering** to all those who wished to rest and **resupply** before heading out on their next epic adventure. And the level of construction here is simply **staggering.** Roaming those streets, I soon **forgot about my quest.** I reeled around in awe, **taking everything in. . . .**

I **wasn't surprised** to hear all kinds of odd names. **ReindeerGirl. Mr. Pasta. EnderLord80000, KraftyKreeper.** As odd and **varied** as their appearances. But some had **normal-sounding** names. Harold. Alex. Jake. Rebecca. Sarah. Emma.

Anyway—seeing all those people made me recall something Kolb once said. **In that game the humans used to play,** there were these things called **skins.** A skin **altered one's appearance.** So a player could become pretty much anything. Knights. Wizards. Elves. Dwarves. Ninjas. Faeries. Princesses. **Even animal-people.** So maybe these strange people **used to be players** from that game. After all, they spoke just like the humans back home. Even so, there were times when I **couldn't quite follow** their conversations. They used **unfamiliar** words, like "**mod**" and "**server.**" Of course, there were many more I did understand. Quest. NPC. Dungeon. Loot. Boss. Armor. Stat. My time **hanging around the Legion** had paid off somewhat.

One conversation in particular caught my attention. A dark dwarf was chatting up a girl with large catlike ears.

"Man, we really **crushed that boss!**" the dwarf exclaimed. "That stone golem **didn't stand a chance!** Honestly, the dungeons around here are **way too easy!**"

"Yeah, well, the **patrols** are another story," Cat-Ears said. "Those pigmen are **pretty tough.** What are they looking for, anyway? Why are there so many of them in this area? Maybe we should **head back west.** I'm sick of dealing with them every time we hit **the plains.**"

(Note: She must have been talking about the monsters looking for Kolb. So he wasn't lying. He said they ambushed his clan mates before they even arrived at the Reach. But they probably aren't looking for a villager like me. Maybe that's why he sent me. . . .)

"**Aww, come on!**" the dwarf said. "Just **think of the loot,** huh? Every dungeon we've cleared so far has been **absolutely loaded!**"

I **cleared my throat** and approached the odd duo.

"**Err,** excuse me. I'm a bit lost. Do you know where I could—"

The dwarf glared at me. "What do we look like, the **Lost Legion?!** Go ask **one of them** for help!"

"In fact, **I just saw one,**" said Cat-Ears. She pointed down a sun-filled street. "I thought I saw her go into that library **over there.**" She drew closer and smiled. "**I was a noob once,** too. Don't worry, eh? You'll get the hang of it. **Here's a little tip.** The Lost Legion has **a lot of codes,** and its members must follow them at all times. One is **protecting noobs** from **trolls, griefers,** and aggressive **monsters.**

65

Another is offering assistance to any player who asks. So whenever you see a Legionnaire, use that to your advantage."

The dwarf laughed. "Ah, **what a sight!** A high-ranking member of the **Boss Wizards,** handing out advice **like an NPC in a starting zone!**"

"It's **his lucky day,**" she said with a shrug. "I'm in a **good mood.**" Then she fixed her gaze **toward the sky,** toward the **dark clouds** that warned of a coming storm and the distant lightning that was already **flashing** above the mountains. "All right," she said, "we are not **going out in that.** Remember last time?"

"Aye. Let's hit **an inn** and wait it out." The dwarf patted me on the shoulder. "**Good luck, kid.**"

With that, the pair **took off,** leaving me **even more** confused than before. So **the Lost Legion** had a code of honor, huh? Seems like they **forgot all about that** when they first showed up at my village. And who were the **Boss Wizards, anyway?** I decided I'd better hit that **library.** If someone from the Legion was there, they'd **surely** help me out. **Hmmm.** But if they really were in the Legion, why weren't they **with Kolb?**

A torch lit up above my head. **Library.** I zoomed down the street, in the direction Cat-Ears had pointed, and spotted it immediately: *The Quill & Feather.*

It really is my lucky day, I thought, glancing at the clouds. But I didn't want to **push it.** I didn't feel like being turned into a witch just yet. Potion brewing is **so boring.** *Hey! Wait a minute,* I thought. *Why is it called **The Quill & Feather?** Aren't quills and feathers pretty much the same thing?*

The storm was **already raging** by the time I reached the door. That wasn't odd—that's just how it is in the Overworld. One second it's all sunshine, not a cloud in the sky, and **the next** it's pouring rain, the lightning so frequent you can only cower indoors. And **not due to thunder,** or the chance of being struck, but knowing those hills are most likely filled with enough **charged creepers** to blast through **an obsidian** door.

I burst through the library's door **like a human in Villagetown. Unfortunately,** there was only one person inside, and that person was no member of the Legion. Nor was it **Feathers.** It couldn't have been. From what Kolb told me, **Feathers was not only a librarian** also but **a wizard** who specialized in **ancient lore** and **antiquities.** Thus, I expected Feathers to be like the things he studied: ancient and dusty, with a huge white beard, bushy white eyebrows, billowing blue robes, and a gnarled staff. **You know, a cliché wizard or something.** The person who stood before me, however, was **nothing of the sort.**

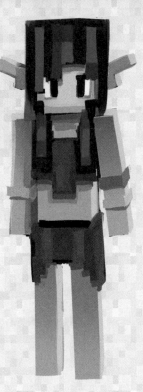

Until yesterday, I thought pigmen looked weird. Upon seeing **a girl with light green skin,** thoughts of **advanced crafting tables** and saving my village once again vanished from my mind. Only **a single question** remained:

"Are you a . . . **zombie?**"

She gave me the **strangest** look. "You've never seen a **limoniad** before?" At my **obvious confusion,** she added: "**Ah.** First time **away** from home, I take it. Well, you've come to the right place. I have a little something that just might **help you.**" She grabbed **a tome** off a nearby shelf and thrust it forward **violently,** as if she were to **knock me out** with it. "**On the house,**" she said with a smile. "You'd better brush up on your **mythology.**"

Great. As if I needed another book. With a **mental sigh,** I stared down at the red leather cover. *Races of Aetheria.*

"Oh," she said, "**I'm Feathers,** by the way."

She then gave me a lecture on how **a limoniad** is a type of **nymph** with ties to meadows—a natural being similar to elves, dryads, or faeries. Which explained her **skin color,** hair, and bracelets of woven **flower petals.** As for the people with gray skin, they're called **moon elves.** The humanoid wolves are **lupins.** I'd already figured out **dark dwarves** because I heard some people talking about them back there in the street. *(That, and I'm just really, really smart.)*

Okay, enough of this, I thought. *I'm on a quest, not some school trip.*

I glanced at the two **strange-looking** blocks nearby. Feathers had been **fiddling around** with them when I'd first entered. They didn't really look like that crafting table Kolb had shown me, but it was a solid start and **way better** than talking about faeries.

"So, what are those things?" I asked.

"**Command blocks,**" she said, turning to them. "Picked them up at an auction on the cheap. In fact, I was the only one to place a bid. No one wanted them because they seemed worthless, but I think it's only because no one knows **how to operate** them. They're over **three thousand years old!**"

Fearing another lecture, I decided to get straight to the point: "How about **an advanced crafting table?** Do you have one of those?"

"Advanced crafting table? Oh. You mean **aeon forge?**" She smiled again. "Looking to do **some real crafting,** huh? You're in luck, then. I have one for sale. **Only twenty-five hundred emeralds,** too."

My mind **overheated** when she said two things:
1.) **Only.**
2.) <u>**Twenty-five hundred** emeralds.</u>

I almost wanted to **inform her** of proper **trading etiquette:** when stating the price of an item, **1.)** and **2.)** may **never** be used in the same sentence.

"Is there any way you can **lower** the price? **Student discount,** perhaps?" I did my best to **look pitiful.** "It's for a **class project.** Those teachers, they said I'll never pass **Crafting VIII** until I craft **a powder keg.**" I wiped away **imaginary tears. Sniffled.** "No, without that table, **I just can't go on!**"

"Sorry," she said. "The price is **not negotiable.** Do you know how in-demand those things are? **No one** knows how to craft them.

Not anymore, at least. It's a **lost art.** Which means there are a limited number of them left in the world. And every time someone carrying one slips and **falls into a pool of lava,** well, that number gets **closer to zero.**"

So <u>**that's**</u> how it's gonna be. . . .

Summoning all my **wit,** I crafted the following response in my mind: "I see."

That was **all I had.** Seeing all those weird people had **taken a lot out of me.** Nothing would have helped, anyway. She was **clearly proud** of her wares. I had one last idea, though.

Long story short, I **left** and **came back** minutes later with a piece of paper in my hand. I slapped that thing onto the floating carpet that served as a table. *Boom, **boom.** (I didn't make that sound, although looking back, I should have. For dramatic effect.)*

"Nice try. By the way, you spelled 'approve' wrong."

ADVANCED CRAFTING TABLE
90% OFF

REDEEMABLE AT THE QUILL & FEATHER

"MY NAME IS FEATHERS, AND I TOTALLY APROVE OF THIS COUPON."
—FEATHERS

USE SHEERS ON THE DOTTED LINE

I roamed the streets after leaving.
Forlorn. Wallowing in self-pity.
Rubbing my chin as I thought about my situation.

Man, my **trading** skills were useless back there! That girl was clearly a pro. **Twenty-five hundred emeralds. . . .** Do people actually walk around with **that many precious stones** in their pocket? And why did Kolb give me so few? **Was that really all he had?**

My food bar was at two. There was a villager **peddling bread** nearby, so I traded twenty-five oak blocks for five loaves. A **bad trade,** but I didn't care. *(Little did that guy know, the joke was on him: I would have traded the entire stack for one.)*

Then I hit up a nearby shop. It specialized in **arms and armor,** judging by the signs.

I don't know why I went in there.
Guess I just **needed** information.

The dwarven blacksmith didn't greet me. Actually, he flat-out **ignored** me. To him, I **didn't exist.** He clearly had a well-trained eye for **low-level emerald-pinchers** such as myself. Which was fine. I just wanted to look at the various **sets,** particularly the leather, **dyed red and enchanted with Fire Protection,** and the two full sets of **diamond.** I'd never seen armor of such quality back home.

Nor these kinds of prices: <u>**8,000 emeralds**</u>
for the diamond set . . . **gulp!**

So it's official, I thought. *Around here, emeralds apparently* ~~grow on trees~~ *—err, drop from leaf blocks like apples.*

That was when I saw an **endersteel** breastplate. It was straight out of that book **Max** gave me. **Diamond has nothing** on armor like that. You could probably **tank an ender dragon** in that thing.

I approached this **wondrous** item, staring at it, gazing at it, studying it . . . it, and its price: **27,000 emeralds.**

This sight . . . the sight of this **masterfully crafted** item, just hanging there on that stand like some ordinary armor despite costing a fortune . . . this sight **undid the fabric of my existence.** It **destroyed** my world. My carefully crafted little universe—so sheltered, so innocent—**shattered,** just like that. I realized that my home village, the place I've lived my entire life . . . is, for lack of a better word, a **noobtown.** There was no doubt in my mind: I knew absolutely nothing of this world and **had nothing, was nothing.**

But that's good, right? Isn't that what I've always looked for, always **wanted?** There I was, a budding adventurer on the open road, surrounded by unknowns, nearly **a hundred thousand blocks** from home, five hundred emeralds to my name, and a newfound desire for more. **I stood up** straighter. Nodded to myself. I had to do this. No moping, **no crying.** My village was counting on me. Just me. **Breeze** was no longer here to hold my hand. But where would I begin? My diamond sword was worth only a small fraction of what I'd need.

How could I possibly get enough to buy that table?

As I stood in the armor shop, **pondering** this question in dismay, I soon found that things often have a strange way of working out. For the answer to my problems **walked right through the door.**

A young man, with **tattered** leather armor and **rusted** iron sword, timidly approached the counter, where he threw down **an assortment of flowers.** Blue orchids, daisies, morningcrest. Several others I didn't recognize. The blacksmith beamed **like a glowstone block.**

"**Thank you!** You don't know **how much** this means to me! Oh, it looks like I'll be able to craft that set of armor **in time for the king's birthday** after all! **What a joyous day!**"

Flowers used in a crafting recipe for armor?

I forgot about this immediately when the blacksmith threw down **a pile of emeralds** on the counter.

Whaaaaat?! My jaw weighed **a ton.** That had to be at least one hundred and fifty, or **two hundred,** no . . .

"**Two hundred fifty,**" the blacksmith said. "As promised."

Without a word, the swordsman scooped the emeralds into his belt pouch, turned around, and headed for the door. **He stopped.** Right next to me. Turned **slowly.** Stared at me. Opened his mouth. **Closed it.** Opened it and closed it again. **A cube of sweat** formed upon his brow, and he **exhaled.** If I had to describe him in a single word, it would be "**lost.**" That's all I saw in his eyes. Perhaps he had only **recently arrived** in our world, **torn from his own** like all the rest. Or perhaps he hadn't yet come to terms with living here.

"**H-hey,**" he finally said.

"Hey," was my reply. "**Um** . . . I have a question." Fearing **the blacksmith** might overhear me, I glanced over my shoulder before whispering, "Why **so many emeralds** for a bunch of flowers?"

A raised eyebrow. "You . . . don't know? **It was a quest.**"

"Is that **like a job?**"

Another **strange** look. "Quests were one of the things included in the **last server update.**" The more he spoke, the steadier his voice became. "Most NPCs **will give you one** if you talk to them long enough. Especially in this town."

"So I just **ask them about quests?**"

"**Something** like that. Come here. I'll show you."

I trailed behind him as he approached the counter once more.

"This guy's **looking for some work,**" he said to the smith. "Do you have anything he could **help you with?**"

"Why, **yes,**" the blacksmith said. "I'm looking for some **glowmoss.** You'll find some in **a tomb** to the southwest of here. **The Tomb of the Forgotten King.** Retrieve this rare crafting ingredient, and I will pay you most handsomely: **seven hundred fifty emeralds.**"

Upon hearing this, **my heart sank** like a zombie in a waterfall. That was less than **a third** of what I needed. **However . . .**

The swordsman **nudged** me. "**Take it,**" he whispered. "Seven hundred fifty is **pretty good,** and dungeons are usually **loaded with loot.** The items you'd collect could be worth **thousands.**"

Suddenly, the zombie in my chest **chugged a Flying Potion** and was now dancing upon the clouds.

"**I accept,**" I said. "Just show me that dungeon, and **I'll show you** some glowmoss in no time."

"Glad to hear it," the blacksmith said. "**Do you have a map?** I can mark it for you." He took my map and added **the Tomb's location.**

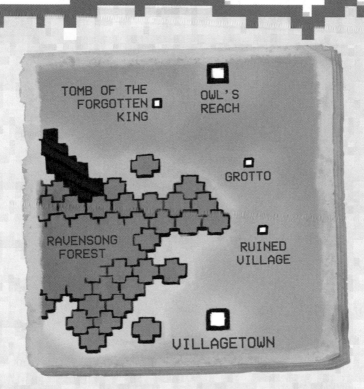

TOMB OF THE
FORGOTTEN ☐
KING

OWL'S
REACH

GROTTO

RAVENSONG
FOREST

RUINED
VILLAGE

VILLAGETOWN

"So I just go there and retrieve **your glowmoss? That's it?**"

The blacksmith smiled. "**That's it!** An easy task for a fine young warrior like yourself! Of course, before you take off, you'll be needing **this.**" He slid **a strange item** across the counter. "**Best of luck,** young man. Now, if you'll excuse me, I have **a birthday present** to craft. **Armor fit for a king!**"

I stared down at the bizarre object. I'd never seen **anything like it** before.

"What do I do **with this?**" I asked the human, whose name I still didn't know.

"**Seriously?** You don't know what **a key** is? **Wow.** Never thought I'd meet someone who knew **less** than I do. . . ."

And so I received **another lecture.** This time, about dungeons and keys.

"**Dungeons** were another part of the last update," he said. "They can be anything now, from your typical **underground maze** to a **small castle,** or even an **entire town.** And here's the craziest part. They can't be modified. When you're in a dungeon, **you can't mine or place anything.** Oftentimes, you need to use **a key** to open a dungeon's front door, and these keys are usually provided by NPCs. Beyond that, **monsters** sometimes drop them."

"I don't get it," I said. "**Why can't dungeons be mined?**"

"Because **the Builders** made them," he said. "If you could just run around mining everything, it would **undo** all their hard work. Plus, trolls could place **obsidian blocks** over the front doors to prevent noobs from entering. Or you could just **tunnel your way to the final boss** without first dealing with the minions, puzzles, and traps—what would be **the point?** Dungeons were built for the players to provide **challenges,** places to explore."

<u>Whoa.</u> Information overload.
But hey, at least he wasn't calling me an NPC.

Although I didn't understand everything he said, I got the **general idea.** In a dungeon, you have to **play by the rules.** You have to explore it the way the Builders intended. **But who are these so-called Builders?** Why would they go out of their way to create challenges for other people? So mysterious.

I must have seemed **extremely confused,** because the swordsman gave me that **funny look** again.

"I'm guessing you used to play a lot of **single-player,**" he said. "Was it your first time playing on **the Aetheria server?** You were connected, right? When the server **crashed?**"

"**Um,** well, I . . . I mean . . ."

"How'd you even **survive** this long? Have you been hiding in this city the whole time?" When I failed to respond, he followed up with **even more** questions.

"Do you even remember what happened? **The crash? The event?**"

I had **no idea** what he was talking about. It must have had something to do with what the humans back home always argued about. "**Interface**" this, "**MindLink**" that. A virtual world that had **turned real.** He thought I was one of them. A person **from Earth.**

"I kind of don't really, um . . . Err, I'm what some might call **an NPC.**"

"**Oh.**"

What followed were **ten long seconds of silence.**

"**It's the outfit,**" he said. "I've never seen an NPC villager wear something like that, so I just assumed . . . **Yeah.** Feeling a little noob right now. Anyway, I guess it's about time **I made friends with an NPC.**"

He smiled and extended a hand.

"**My name's Eto.**"

"Runt," I said. "**Runt** Ironfurnace.**"

We made small talk for a bit after that. Where I came from. Why I'm here. He'd only recently arrived from **the capital,** where he'd accepted **a quest** from some townsperson—a series of errands that had eventually sent him here. He told me how a quest can be **anything**. They're often **mundane,** like his flower-hunting quest. Other times, a single quest could involve traveling to **all four corners of the world.**

Eto stared ahead, as if looking at something **a million blocks away.**

"**Like you,** I haven't explored all that much. I only recently gathered up enough **courage** to leave **the safety** of the capital. But I met this guy a few days ago. Good guy. **Great player.** He's been exploring since day one. While most of us were still **cowering** in **fear,** he was setting out. The **tales** he had, of the places he's been, things he's seen . . . ships, airships, and an underground city that **puts the capital to shame. . . .** Calls himself **a treasure** hunter."

"When you say ship, you mean **boat,** right?"

"No. I'm talking about real vessels, with sails and cabins and everything. **And this guy has one.** Or so he claimed. He and some villager were eventually going to set sail and explore the ocean. And maybe **the continent to the north.**"

"You mean there's **more than one continent?**"

"That's what he said."

Another. Continent. It felt like I'd been **struck by lightning** again. Except I hadn't turned into a witch . . . at least then I could have brewed a potion of some kind that would increase my intelligence enough to understand what this guy was saying. **It took seven days,** on foot, to travel a tiny little distance on that map. There could be thousands of villages on Ardenvell—and just as many towns, cities, and castles. And now some human is telling me there's **more than one continent?!**

"It's pretty **strange,** though," he said. "Despite his **accomplishments,** that guy can't even remember **his own name.** He only knows his name starts with an **S.**"

"That is **pretty strange.**"

"Yeah. . . ." He glanced at the door. "Speaking of friends, I have to get going. I'm supposed to meet up with someone."

"All right. I guess I should say thanks. For everything."

He nodded. "And hey. If you decide to try that dungeon, I suggest getting someone to tag along. Never go solo. See ya around!"

And just like that, my new friend took off, leaving me with plenty of unanswered questions.

I couldn't stop thinking about what he had told me. I envisioned a ship sailing across countless ocean biomes, airships skipping across the clouds, and an underground city filled entirely with dwarves.

But none of that was quite as wonderful as the small obsidian key in my hand.

The storm had mostly cleared by the time I left the shop. I made my way to the **village square,** since plenty of people seemed to enjoy hanging out there. I soon bumped into the cat-eared girl and loud-mouthed dwarf from earlier. They were replenishing their food bars. When I asked if they could help me out, they **spit out bits of cake.**

"**Let me get this straight,**" the dwarf said. "You want us to join you on a dungeon quest."

"**That's right.**"

"And you've . . . never actually **been in a dungeon.**"

"**I haven't,**" I said, "but I'll do my very best! I'm a **quick learner!** I can **carry** stuff, too! Think of me as an extra inventory. **And** an extra pair of **arms.** Whenever you need a healing potion, **I'll be right there!** Potion support, **at your service!** I'll uncork those potions so fast, those zombies will think you have **ten life bars!**" I sighed. "Basically, I just . . . **really need** emeralds."

The dwarf **chuckled.** "I'm **sure** you do, but dungeons are **no place** for noobs. I'd feel **guilty** if something happened to ya."

"I'm afraid **he's right,**" the girl with the cat ears said. "Dungeons are full of **powerful monsters.** They're much stronger than what you find in the Overworld. And they're nothing compared to **the traps.** . . . If you set one off, **that's it.** Someone will probably find **your items** on the ground a day or two later, and they'll know exactly where **not** to step."

"**Oh.** Okay. Well, um, thanks. Yeah, see you. **Good luck.**"

After they left, I stood around for a few minutes, looking for a possible companion. Surely I could find someone. But practically **nobody** was alone, and the few I approached avoided eye contact or **politely declined.**

"Dungeon? **Nope.** I'm waiting for someone."

"**Nah.** I don't do dungeons."

"Maybe **some other time.**"

My face must have revealed **a wide variety** of emotions. **Confusion. Frustration. Helplessness. Despair. Doubt.** Imagine a pigman who had been zapped by lightning **eight times** in the same week. Imagine how crazy he felt after that eighth time. Imagine his face. That was **pretty much my face.**

It was beginning to feel like everything I'd learned in school was useless. **At least out here.** The Overworld is totally different from what I'd read about, thought about, and dreamed about all this time. **A noob.** I've really become a noob **all over again.** Which wouldn't be so bad, if I didn't have to be a noob by myself. . . . They say misery loves company; well, noobishness loves company, too.

On top of that, my luck was **running out.** I became acutely aware of this when I heard a deep grunt, like a monstrous pig, directly behind me.

I <u>slowly turned around.</u>

"**You!** Villager! **Ogre dare!**"

(*Ogre dare? Um, I think he meant over there.*)

Far off, past a hundred or so other people chatting away, a **pigman** was approaching. A pigman in **black leather armor** covered in **crude iron spikes.** I knew it must've been one of **the monsters hunting** Kolb, so I turned away and started **walking.** Until I felt **a hand** upon my shoulder. I **whirled around** to face **beady black eyes** and a square pink nose. And breath so **hideous** it probably could have broken though **netherrack.**

"**Hey!**" the pigman said. "**I was talking to you!**"

"You were? **Are you sure?** I thought I heard you calling for some villager."

"Is that not what you are?"

I looked down at myself. "Do I **look** like a villager to you? Do you see a robe?"

"**No,** but your . . ." He pointed to his nose. "**Enough!** I am **Reh,** servant of the **great and powerful god-king** known as **the Eyeless One,** the **Forever Eternal,** the **One True** Wizard, He Who . . ." He **paused,** as though he'd forgotten the rest, then **grunted** angrily. "You are to come with me to **Stormgarden Keep** for questioning!"

God-king? So that's what they call him, huh? Yeah, and what about this guy's name? His name is **Reh**? That's not a monster name. All things considered, he's lucky I'm such a **nice guy.** A less composed warrior would have already attacked this ridiculously named pigman *as a matter of principle!*

"First of all," I said, "**that's an amazing title.** Really. God-king, **One True Wizard . . .** just wow. Admittedly, **'Forever Eternal'** is a bit **redundant,** but still, it does have a certain ring to it. Anyway, I'd love to go with you, **I would,** but . . . it really depends."

"**On what?**"

"Well . . . during the **interrogation,** will you be serving milk and cookies?"

He grumbled and drew **his obsidian sword.** He didn't like milk and cookies! **What sacrilege!** And here I thought we could be friends!

Suddenly, I heard **Kolb's voice** in my mind. A speech he once gave to his fellow clan members:

You are members of the Lost Legion! **You are OP!** *The* **hardest** *of the hard core! The bravest souls in all the land! Walking tanks destined to* **crush** *the armies of He Who Would Never Wear Sunglasses! Without fear!* **Without mercy!**

I drew my sword with the **glass-like ring** of diamond.

An **epic battle** ensued. All you could hear were the sounds of our swords clashing against each other over and over, along with pig-like grunts and shouts from the surrounding people, more and more of whom were gathering by the second now, asking one another:

88

"Am I **seeing this right?** Are those **two NPCs** fighting?"

I blocked **so many** of my opponent's attacks. I'd been working on my block moves **for weeks.** Now, one nanosecond after that sword came flying at me, I put up my own to the clash of diamond on obsidian. It was **kind of boring.**

I blocked. He blocked. I blocked. He blocked. Okay, **cool**—he didn't block. I only had to **repeat this** thirty or so times to inch his life bar down, half a heart at a time, until it was nothing but a line of **empty hearts.**

That's right.

I, being the **noble and talented gentleswordsman** that I am—possessing far superior wit and consummate skill at arms—**rid the world** of this foul, netherrack-wilting **stench.**

The humanoid pig sank with a low, sad moan. "**Urggguuu!**"

I returned my sword to its **scabbard** before he hit the ground. *(A total pro move, by the way. I heard a farmer let out a little gasp. At least one person was impressed!)*

Glowing **experience orbs** flew toward me, and I felt the familiar rush of **XP** gain. An eerie silence lingered. The monster **dissolved** into a cloud of smoke. The onlookers begain rambling to one another. Many of them **were armed.** Adventurers, **explorers** . . .

Couldn't they have **helped me out?!**

"What's happening?" someone asked.

"Is this part of a quest event?" asked someone else.

"Maybe it is," said a third. "I say we stick around and find out!"

But they weren't asking the right questions.
Where's the pigman's armor?
And his sword?

His items had evaporated into nothingness, like the pigman himself.
Pretty rude. Aspiring evil wizards, **take note:** If you're going to send your **minions** after someone, make sure they don't drop **any items.** This way, if your underlings fail, the person you're after won't have anything to show for it. They'll just be wasting time. So **the Eyeless One** really is as terrible as they say . . . more like **Heartless One!** That pigman could have **at least** dropped an emerald or something!

Moments later, **five more pigmen** charged from the crowd and surrounded me, **swords drawn.** All right, I admit it: at this point, I was definitely contemplating going with them. Even if they weren't serving milk and cookies, surrendering would at least mean **living** to enjoy milk and cookies another day.

"Hey, guys." My gaze swept across so many square pink faces. "**How are you?** About that interrogation. I—"

Suddenly, I heard the **sound of hooves** on gravel. They were approaching **fast.** I struggled to get a better look across the crowd, but I couldn't see past the hats and helmets and ridiculous hairstyles.

At last, I saw her. Breeze rode into view confidently, gracefully, as though she'd been riding **all her life.**

As though she <u>belonged</u> out here.
As though there was
no better place for her to be.

"Thought you might need some help."

She leapt from her horse and **drew two blades,** one in each hand. It was then that I noticed the faint, colorful motes **swirling in the air** around her—the visual effects of **multiple potions.** But I was far more **shocked** by her expression: her face showed **anger** instead of its usual **sweetness and innocence.**

The pigmen slowly **turned toward her,** grunting. They had no idea what was in store for them. If they had, they would've thrown down their weapons on the spot and **denounced their beloved "god-king."**

"Herobrine?!" they would've said. "What are you talking about?! Is that **some kind of pickle?!**"

Instead, two of them **pointed at her** and bent over, clutching their stomachs. **They were laughing.**

That's one of Breeze's strengths. **Pebble** once said that, after class. They'd been assigned as dueling partners. The duel started with him turning back to his friends and **smirking.** It ended with him facedown **in the mud.** You'd never think a wooden sword could be **so dangerous** until you saw one in her hands.

All right, I take back what I said about that first battle. **This one was truly epic.** The way we moved **together,** swords **flashing . . .** it was something out of a fairy tale. And it felt just like the old days, when we had fought back to back, uncertain whether we would **survive.** We took them down one by one, until there weren't any monsters left— only gravel and cobblestone. And a sea of people **cheering.**

"After this," someone said, "maybe those pigmen will finally **leave us alone.**"

"**Yeah,**" said another, "but it's strange to see NPCs handling things. It really must be some kind of **quest event.** Maybe **a secret one.** Let's hang around this village for a little longer, huh?"

And in the middle of them all were **two villagers** named **Breeze and Runt.** I still **couldn't believe** she was here.

"How did you **find** me?" I asked.

"The mayor told me **everything,**" she said. "They were keeping it **a secret.**"

So Kolb must have told the council, I thought. And the council decided to **keep the mission a secret?** They probably wanted to avoid widespread chaos. Knowing villagers, they would have definitely **panicked.**

"I'm **really** glad to see you," I said.

"**Me too.**" She gave me a **hug.** "So . . . what happened?"

"**Long story** on that. In short, I'm on **a quest,** and we're going to a dungeon."

"**A dungeon?**"

"I'll tell you on the way. First, we need to buy **some supplies.** C'mon. Most of the shops are that way."

She grabbed me by the shoulder.

"**My horse is over there.**"

"Oh." I grimaced.

How embarrassing. I hope she doesn't ask about . . .

"By the way," she said, "where's Meadow?"

"Who's Meadow?"

"Um, Kolb's horse? A rare charger with an enchanted saddle?"

Charger? Is that a type of horse? Well, that horse didn't look so special to me. And was that saddle really enchanted? It had felt really comfortable, like sitting on a block of feathers.

Another grimace.

. . . Embarrassing.

Atop Breeze's gilded horse, **Shybiss,** we set out to do some trading. I needed **armor** and **potions,** after all, and both of us needed more **food.** At least one shopkeeper was about to have **a good day.**

I went over **everything** I'd experienced and learned so far. My **strange** encounters on the road. **Feathers.** The **absurd** price of an advanced crafting table. **The absurd price of everything.** What that human had told me about quests, dungeons, and keys. As for **Villagetown,** it was just as **I'd thought:** the mayor had told everyone that I was **in trouble** and that I wouldn't be seen again until I was done filling **five double chests** with potato-based food items. Okay, so I didn't expect **that,** exactly, but I did call that he would lie to avoid a **total panic.**

"What am I supposedly **being punished** for?" I asked.

"The paper."

"The paper? **Oh. Yeah.** The paper."

I'd forgotten all about that paper. We were supposed to write **twenty pages** on why we'd chosen our **profession.** It was due the very same morning I'd set out. Of course, I, being **the studious warrior-scholar** that I am, finished writing that paper. The night I left, just before falling asleep, I filled each of those twenty pages with **one single, massive word—or letter.** Well, the last two pages were drawings. One of the monsters' forest **burning,** another of a zombie **crying.** But still, **twenty pages.**

"Of course, I couldn't help feeling that **something** was wrong," Breeze said. "It was **odd.** Why would they **lock you up in a house** for that? I didn't learn **the truth** until two days ago, when I overheard Kolb speaking to **the mayor and my father.** I stormed up to them and demanded the truth. They **told me everything** and sent me to go find you. Said you **should have been back** by now."

"Yeah? How was I supposed to know **horses just run off** like that?" I sighed. "Okay, what about **the others?** Is anyone else coming?"

"**No.** I'm the only one who knows. **They're all training.** Exploring. We've already spent **several nights** outside. Some of the humans made **watchtowers. Beacons,** they call them. Also . . ."

Breeze told me how she'd **traded** for some new items for her journey. **The outfit** she was wearing now. A **black wool** tunic, black wool skirt, and black leather boots. The wool provided as much armor as leather, but it gave **bonuses to stealth and speed.** The boots had similar stats, as well as a bonus to **jump height.** Such bonuses suited her, since Breeze was the type who cherished **mobility.** That was her style, a style she employed **to full effect.**

"I also traded for this," she said, drawing an **emerald sword** from its scabbard. That was one of the swords she'd **wielded earlier,** but I hadn't noticed the **color.** It looked just like a diamond sword, only **brilliant green.**

"It's a bit **better** than diamond," she said. "**Same average damage** but with a slightly **faster** attack speed." She glanced back at me and **smiled.** "After making friends with a few human girls, I found they have **a lot** of interesting items like this."

"How about **those arrows?**" I asked. "Did you trade for those, too?"

"No. **Sophia** and **Talia** gave them to me. I almost **declined** but figured **weakness arrows** could come in handy out here."

"**Huh.** Where'd they find all that stuff?"

"**Dungeons,** I guess. Before they arrived at Villagetown."

"That's **good to know.** Hopefully the one we're going to will be **filled** with items like that. We really need an **equipment upgrade.** Those pigmen were—"

Breeze **stirred** in the saddle. "What's that?"

I followed **her gaze** to a building that resembled **a temple.** It seemed to be constructed entirely of **white quartz.**

At first, I thought it was **a church** of some kind. Breeze did, too. A sign above the door read: **"Temple of Entity."** Another sign read: **"Donation Pit Inside."** I had no idea what a **donation** pit was, but I knew it had something to do with **charity.** As in, giving things away. **Offerings** for the poor. And guess who was currently **the poorest person** in Owl's Reach? Surely they could **spare** a handful of emeralds for this **humble peasant.**

"Should we check it out?" Breeze asked.

"I think that's **an excellent idea,**" I said, glancing at the sign once more.

In my mind, it no longer read "Donation Pit"
but "Free Cool Stuff."

"Yes, **excellent** idea."

Austere. Majestic.
Breathtaking.

The Temple of Entity was all these things **and more.** The double spruce doors gave way to a **vast** chamber filled with sunlight and opalescent stained glass. I couldn't stop asking myself how such a thing could be built, with **chiseled quartz columns** towering far above to a lofty ceiling. What kind of **scaffolding** had been used? Dirt blocks?

Red carpet stretched between countless ancient pews, and far away, on either wall, were **vast murals** of **legendary battles.** One mural depicted an **army of knights** against **monstrous hordes,** rays of light descending from the heavens, and **fires** erupting from below. Farther inside, the windows ended, and redstone torches served as the only light source. Many of these torches surrounded **a black altar, a massive slab of obsidian** whose surfaces were sculpted with various reliefs.

Breeze stepped in first, her footsteps **echoing.** Mine were noticeably **louder.** We stared at every mural, every statue, and every etched relief. The farther we ventured inside, the darker it became, until it was **almost gloomy.**

We stopped before **a statue** of a robed man with **two pairs of feathery wings.** There was no face under the hood of the robe, and he held a weapon that I can only describe as a **farming tool,** except **much larger** than any I'd seen.

"The White Shepherd," Breeze said softly, running her fingers across the statue's arm. "Entity."

". . ."

Entity. . . . He was a character in a **fairy tale,** wasn't he? Yes, my mom used to read me that story when I was **little.** Back when all we had to worry about was our **harvest.** He was a **godlike** figure, an **Immortal,** who lived during the time of the **Second Great War.** The world was nearly torn apart then, and when things grew worse, Entity crafted **twelve weapons of indescribable power** and chose **twelve heroes** to wield them. With them, the world had a fighting **chance.**

"What **happened** during that final battle?" I asked. "I forget how it went. **Both sides** fell, didn't they?"

"The knights managed to **destroy the Eyeless One,**" she said, "although not completely. **They fell** to his minions afterward, vastly outnumbered. They **sacrificed** themselves. Their weapons were then **destroyed**—shattered—yet they survived . . . in some form. **Fragments.** Those knights were to be reborn someday, in order to restore their original weapons and help save the world. **For good,** this time."

"You sure know your **fairy tales.**" I glanced around the temple once more and felt **a little chill.** "Looks like they take them pretty **seriously** around here, huh?"

Her expression suddenly grew **dark.** Or had she been that way ever since we'd approached this statue? Perhaps there was **some truth** to the legend. Maybe a bunch of knights really did end up fighting some **evil** wizard with weapons of **divine** origin. And maybe Entity really did exist, so very long ago. Did any of that matter now?

Hey, what is that?

Eyes **lighting up,** I pointed to a doorway.

"Now there's something I can believe in!"

According to the sign, the door led to **the donation pit.** Call me **disrespectful,** but I practically started **running.** The doorway led to a much smaller chamber, and the donation pit was . . . never mind. **Forget it.** I'm just going to **draw** a picture. Because no words could capture the sheer **amazingness** of what I was seeing.

Items. A pool of them, one block deep. The majority of them **were gold,** but I spotted several pieces of **enchanted leather and iron armor.** A **diamond** sword. Saddles. Potions. Even accessories such as belts, rings, bracelets. . . . I leapt in and **rummaged** around like a dragon wallowing in its **treasure hoard.**

Giddy with delight, I picked up an iron breastplate. **Free!** And an extra diamond sword—**free!** And look at those potions, just waiting to be **chugged!** Why would one go to a shop to trade for items when they could just come **here?!**

Hold on. Hollllllld on. Hold on like a noob holding on to a ladder over a lava pit. This doesn't make any sense. People clearly left all this great stuff here, **but why?**

My smile **faded** bit by bit. Indeed, this piece of armor, shimmering faintly with a soft **violet** light, contained a low-level enchantment. But the enchantment was one I'd never heard of before, and it didn't **sound** like much of an enchantment **at all.**

I turned to Breeze. "**Burden II . . . ?** What is that?"

"It decreases your **attack speed** and **movement speed**," she said. "By 33%, I think."

"Decreases . . . **not increases?**"

She nodded. "A **negative** enchantment. Otherwise known as **a curse.**"

"But who . . . **why** . . . how can such a thing be possible?! I've never heard of **negative enchantments!**"

"That's because you **never spent much time** at an enchanting table," she said, wading up to me. "It happens sometimes. For whatever reason, **an enchanting attempt fails,** and . . ."

No, I thought, *this can't be right.* Then it started to dawn on me, and I examined the items in the **gleaming, glittering** mountain.

Everything here was indeed enchanted, from saddles to horse armor to the most beautiful of golden rings. . . . But each of those enchantments had names like "Dullness," "Breaking," or "Vulnerability."

"Dullness **reduces** a weapon's damage," Breeze said. "Breaking multiplies **durability loss.** And Vulnerability **reduces** an armor's protective value."

"What about this one?" I asked, holding up a diamond sword with **Unblocking V.**

"That reduces the effectiveness of blocking," she said. "I think level V is **100% reduction.** So blocking with it wouldn't reduce damage **at all.**"

"**Whoa!** That definitely doesn't meet my standards of item quality."

I **casually** tossed that sword over my shoulder and retrieved another sword—iron, with **Lifedrain III.**

"And this?" I asked.

"Lifedrain? Let's see . . . I think that **damages you over time.**"

"**Frozen Nether!**" I dropped that sword as if it were a miniature creeper ready to explode.

"And **don't even touch** that one," Breeze said. She pointed at an iron sword with her foot. It had **Binding II.** "If you equip something that has **Binding,** you **can't remove it** unless you use a specific potion."

"Yeah, I get it now," I said, glancing around **in despair.** "That's why everyone **left this stuff** here. We're standing in a **trash pile.**"

"Not exactly," Breeze said. "Many of these items would be of use to someone with nothing at all. An iron sword with Dullness I is **still better** than a normal wooden sword."

"How do you explain all the stuff with Binding and Lifedrain, then? And that dead bush? **Trolls? Griefers?**"

"Most likely." Scanning the items once more, she bent down and picked up a necklace. "**Nice.** I guess **not everything** here is bad."

A necklace, huh. . . .

Like bracelets, necklaces fall under the class of items known as **accessories.** Many different types of accessories can be worn at the same time. It's sort of like **a second set** of armor. It includes one belt, two rings, two bracelets, and one necklace.

FAERIE CHARM
ACCESSORY
REGENERATION I

The effect it gave was **small. Regeneration I,** when applied to a piece of armor or an accessory, doesn't heal **very much** over time, as each level of Regeneration is approximately 10% of a person's natural healing rate. Still, **it was free**—and better than **nothing.** She must have arrived at the same conclusion, because she equipped **the faerie charm**—or rather, wore it around her neck.

At this discovery, and perhaps **a little jealous** of her find, I began sifting through the items again. I **desperately needed** armor. "Breaking III, Slowness VI . . . **oh!** Here's one with every single negative enchantment I've seen so far. Hmm. How about this . . . ? Yeah, this one isn't so bad."

I picked up **an iron breastplate.** Strangely, it had either been **renamed** or had been generated with the following name: **Tarnished Breastplate.** It was covered in spots of brown rust, and **it only** had Burden I, which, according to Breeze, reduced attack speed and movement speed by only **10%.**

I stress "**only**"
because everything else was **worse.**

In the end, I wound up with a **matching** set of **Burden I** armor. Some leggings and a pair of boots, anyway—all **covered in rust.** Next, I examined all the shields. The best had **Unblocking I, a 20% reduction** in blocking effectiveness. That wasn't **the worst** thing in the world. It wasn't even the worst thing about the shield. It had an **owl sigil** on the front that wasn't exactly intimidating. How was I supposed to **scare monsters** with a giant owl on my shield?

"Whatever," I muttered to myself, strapping it on.

Finally, a gray cap with a white feather replaced the outlandish **red-and-purple thing** I'd been wearing. **Moldy Cap.** What a name! But **the look** it gave: the white feather provided a gentle accent to the grays of my armor, a smooth flow of color, **subtle.** And the bits of **green mold** really brought out the color of **my eyes. Just kidding.** What do you think this is, **Celebrity Villager** or something? I only cared about the +1 armor **bonus.**

Wait. What's this **Resilience I** enchantment?

Breeze **noticed** it as well. "**Nice** find. Each level of Resilience reduces damage taken from **critical hits** by 5%."

"You mean the damage **I take?**"

"Yes. It's **not** a negative enchantment."

"Thank you, **teacher.**"

Thoroughly **pleased** at this news, I inspected myself.

I almost felt like **a real warrior.**
A low-level one, surely,
but a **warrior** nonetheless.

TARNISHED
BREASTPLATE

+5 ARMOR

BURDEN I

DIAMOND
SWORD

ATTACK
SPEED 1.6

AVERAGE
DAMAGE 7

UNBREAKING I

MOLDY CAP

+1 ARMOR

RESILIENCE I

VEIL OF THE
VICTORIOUS

SUREFOOTED II

SAFEGUARD I

(+1 UNKNOWN
MODIFIER)

TARNISHED
LEGGINGS

+4 ARMOR

BURDEN I

TARNISHED
BOOTS

+2 ARMOR

BURDEN I

OWL'S REACH
BUCKLER

+1 ARMOR

UNBLOCKING I

Look out,
monsters! Momma
didn't raise no noob.

109

Breeze **giggled.** "You know, if you swapped that shield for **a red one,** you could almost pass for **a Legionnaire.**"

"**Yeah?** Too bad I'll never be able to join them."

"**Why not?**"

"I asked Kolb like **five times** already. And Kaeleb. And ObsidianDude. Everyone I asked said **the Legion** has **strict requirements.** You have to be a **human.**"

"**Maybe they'll change** that in the future."

"Maybe."

Scanning the items once more, Breeze picked up a belt made of **iron cubes.** It was the only other **accessory** that had **positive enchantments.** The rest had curses or **nothing at all,** offering no benefit beyond **style.**

She offered **the belt** to me. "You want it?"

"No, **it's fine.** I think I'm set. Besides, you need some armor, too."

With a brief **nod,** she threw the belt around her waist. "**All right,**" she said. "Guess I'm good to go. **Oh, hmm.**" She picked up **a green circlet** and threw it on as well. "**There.** How do I look?"

EMERALD SWORD
ATTACK SPEED 1.5
AVERAGE DAMAGE 7
UNBREAKING I

DIAMOND SWORD
ATTACK SPEED 1.6
AVERAGE DAMAGE 7
UNBREAKING I

ARROWS OF WEAKNESS
DEBUFF 30 SEC
−4 ATTACK DAMAGE

FAERIE CHARM
REGENERATION I

ZEPHYR BOOTS
+2 ARMOR
LEAPING I
STEALTH I
SWIFTNESS II
FEATHER FALLING I

IVY CIRCLET
+1 ARMOR
REGENERATION I

NIGHTSONG TUNIC
+3 ARMOR
STEALTH I
SWIFTNESS I
THORNS II

NIGHTSONG SKIRT
+2 ARMOR
STEALTH I
SWIFTNESS I

VEIL OF THE VICTORIOUS
SUREFOOTED II
SAFEGUARD I
1 (UNKNOWN MODIFIER)

OPAL CHAIN BELT
+1 ARMOR
FIRE RESISTANCE I

Okay, those boots are OP. I really need to trade with Kaeleb when I get back.

111

"**Fabulous,**" I said. "A true **dungeoneer.**"

Of course, looking at the stats of our **many items** might seem **overwhelming.** But to the **experienced,** it was like reading another language, which translated into:

I'd **sacrificed** the ability to move and attack quickly in return for **a strong defense.** With a shield capable of blocking most **frontal** attacks, I could withstand an incredible amount of punishment. In short, I was set up to be a great **frontline combatant. A wall.** Even so, a **10%** reduction to attack speed **didn't mean** my diamond sword was worthless.

Meanwhile, Breeze had chosen **another strategy: high mobility.** If injured, she could easily **retreat,** switch to **her bow,** and attack from a distance while slowly **healing** from her Regeneration effects. And if we encountered a particularly dangerous threat, her **weakness arrows** would reduce its damage. Combined with my high armor, damage could be **cut by half** or more.

"Looks like most of the potions are just **poisons,**" Breeze said. "Trolls have been **hard at work** here. They're not entirely **useless,** though. We could turn them into splash potions. All we need is some **gunpowder.**"

"**Good idea,**" I said, and helped her collect the bottles. "Yknow, if **Emerald** were here right now, I know exactly what she'd say. She'd suggest we haul this stuff to the nearest trader and try selling everything for **one emerald each.**"

"I highly doubt anyone would pay even one emerald for half these items," Breeze said. "And who knows what might happen if someone caught us? I'm pretty sure this donation pit isn't meant to be **raided** like this. Besides, that isn't what she'd say."

"**Oh?** What would she say, then?"

"She'd say it's **time to go shopping,** I mean. And she'd show us this." Breeze held up **a stack of emeralds.**

"What?! Where'd you get that?"

"I asked Emerald for **a loan.** Didn't say what for, of course."

"And she agreed, **just like that?** How much did she give you?"

"**One hundred fifty.** And Kolb gave me **another hundred.** I know he had to trade away most of his stuff to do so. Including **his other horse.**"

Whaaaaat?! His other horse?!

Oh, **this is bad! Really bad!** Kolb is going to be so angry. I don't even want to go back home! Okay, there has to be way out of this. **Think. Think!**

Maybe I can just buy him a new horse? **Yeah!** And when he asks why "**Meadow**" looks different, I'll just say that I . . . **um . . .** enchanted her fur? **How genius is that?!**

"Come on," Breeze said. She was standing in the doorway by now. "I know I'm going to sound like Emerald when I say this, but . . . shopping is actually **kinda fun.**"

113

Moomoo Alpha's
Survival Shop

A **strange energetic music** came from a jukebox in the corner of the room. There were so many enchanted items behind the counter that **the wall glowed.**

Moomoo, the dwarven shopkeeper, flashed **a wide grin.** He gave us a line that seemed straight out of a **shopkeeper manual:**

"Go on, **treat yourself!**"

Then another:

"See anything **ya like?**"

I swear. . . . Was there anything on that wall someone wouldn't mind having? There was a diamond sword with **Unbreaking V.** A **gold** breastplate with so many enchantments it actually **surpassed diamond** in value. **A leash** for monsters. A bed that gave **a strength buff** for an entire day. Even an **enchanted name tag.**

Yet one of the **most ordinary** items caught my eye. A simple **potion of Healing I.** We needed **as many** as we could get. Sadly, with **582 emeralds** between us, and each healing potion costing **twenty-five . . .**

"Twenty-five emeralds," I muttered. "We could get them for **five** back home."

"Maybe we should go somewhere else," Breeze said.

She said this openly, **so the shopkeeper would hear.** I played along:

"**Oh, that's right.** That other guy was selling them for **fifteen,** wasn't he?"

"**Ten, I think.** Or was it nine?" She tilted her head **thoughtfully,** eyes to the side, one finger on her chin.

Yeah, that **Moomoo** should've been **sweating ghast tears.** But he didn't look **nervous.** Still, I figured that was just an act. Yeah, what do you think about that, bud—two real traders just rolled into your fancy little shop.

Here's the thing, though: **it wasn't an act.**

"I believe **you two are mistaken**," he said with a slight grin, "for every major shop in Owl's Reach follows the **Aetherian Item Index.** This Index is a list compiled in the capital annually and used as **a strict guideline** for determining the base value of an item. Accordingly, you'll find most common items going for the same price **everywhere.** Of course, you are more than welcome to take a look at our town's many other fine establishments. I'm sure you'll find my statement **accurate.**"

Breeze and I exchanged glances. The look on my face was probably a cross between "What did he just say?" and "**That means we can't haggle him down, right?**"

Meanwhile, her face said: "**Don't worry. We've got this.**"

"Then we'll take **fifteen bottles,**" she said, winking at me. Those were **one emerald each.**

With a **slight nod,** Moomoo retrieved the bottles from an ender chest and placed them onto the counter. "Anything else, **young lady?**"

"**Nether wart,**" she said. "An equal number."

Three emeralds each. I **realized** where she was going with this. Nether wart was required to craft a **base potion.** A base potion was like the foundation for almost every other potion. We were going to brew **our own healing potions** to save money. Even without haggling, Breeze had found a way around the **absurd** prices of that smug little dwarf.

He realized this as well.

"I guess you'll be needing some **melons** and **gold nuggets**," he said, "as those are the ingredients for a healing potion. **Unfortunately,** I am out of stock for both. I've been receiving **many adventurers** lately who've been looking to do their own brewing. **It's the strangest thing.**"

"Do you know where we might find some?" Breeze asked.

We were treated to **another smile** from Moomoo. "I'd say your best bet would be asking other adventurers. You'll most likely find some with **a surplus** of ingredients to trade. You might try an inn. There's a big one just down the street. **The Enchanted Dragon.** Can't miss it."

"Thanks a lot," Breeze said. "Oh, we need **gunpowder,** too."

She answered my question before I could ask: "We can use gunpowder to make **splash potions,** remember? Splash healing potions are useful because they heal in an **area of effect,** or AoE."

"You mean **a single potion** can heal **both of us** with its splash?" I asked.

She nodded. "**As long as we're close together.** We just throw them at our feet. On top of that, it's **faster** than drinking one. I believe the healing effect would **wound** any nearby undead as well. And all it will take is a pinch of **gunpowder.**"

"**Amazing,**" I said. "Although, I don't recall ever learning this in school. Did **your dad** teach you this stuff?"

"Nope. **Lola.**"

"I might have known."

Thanks, Lola. Even though you aren't here, it's as if . . .

I went over **the numbers** with Breeze. If we wanted to craft **fifteen splash healing potions,** we needed **fifteen bottles** at ◆ 1 each, **fifteen pieces of nether wart** at ◆ 3 each and **fifteen handfuls of gunpowder,** also at ◆ 3.

◆ 15 + ◆ 45 + ◆ 45 – **a total of ◆ 105.**

The shopkeeper told us that **a gold nugget** goes for around ◆ 2, a **slice of melon** ◆ 1. We needed eight nuggets and one slice of melon per potion.

In short, we determined that it would cost roughly ◆ **360** for fifteen splash healing potions. **The alternative** would be spending ◆ 375 on fifteen **normal** healing potions, without the AoE effect.

"**Booyah!**" I said to Breeze.

The dwarf looked **a little annoyed.**

"**Yes,** you can surely craft your own healing potions," he said, "and you'll save some emeralds. But if you buy from me, you'll save something **far more valuable: time** and **energy.** Both of you are clearly **tired.** Why would you complicate things? Buy my healing potions, and spend **the rest of your night relaxing.**" He **patted** one of his ender chests. "I have three stacks right in here."

"No thanks," I said. "**We're good.**"

"We'll have **at least two hundred left over,**" Breeze said. "Anything else we need?"

"How about **that bracelet?**" I said. An iron bracelet with **Regeneration I.** "It's only fifty-five."

Breeze pointed at an item frame containing **a stone bracelet. "How about that one?** It gives one point of **armor.**"

"**Hmm . . .** It's a bit cheaper, too. I wonder **what's better?** Regeneration I or another point of armor?"

"I'm not sure. . . ."

"Anyway, what about yourself? Check **that ring with Swiftness I.** It's one hundred fifty, but we have plenty to spare, **right?**"

Breeze looked **deep** in thought. "It's good. I like **that one** better, though." She pointed to a **wooden ring** with **Strength I.** It cost seventy-five. With that equipped, she'd do slightly **more damage.** "Oh, wait. Look at that ring. It has both **Swiftness and** Strength, but it costs one hundred fifty."

"That's fine," I said. "I can get the stone bracelet."

"**No,** I couldn't do that," she said. "My items are already **better** than yours."

"Then we'll spend an **equal** amount," I said. "**One hundred each?**" She smiled. "**Yeah.**"

I **realized** you **can't call yourself** an adventurer until you've had **the full** item-shop experience. Count your emeralds. What's the best way **to spend** them? The best **bang for your buck?** Well, this item is good, but is it worth buying over that? Or how about **this** and **this?**

Well, those are the price of this, which is **better** than this, and you could buy **two of those** for the price of this and this. . . .

"Hmmm . . ."

The choice was **difficult.** The eternal search for **the perfect upgrades.** Maybe it's a sword that offers **a slight** increase in damage output, or maybe it's that one last point of armor you so desperately need. Or maybe it's a few potions to give you **an edge** in the next battle. No matter the price, you want **that little bit** extra. . . .

The shopkeeper kept **grinning** at us while Breeze and I debated several more possible buys, arguing and joking and calculating. He kept smiling as he offered to show us **more of his wares,** and the jukebox continually blaring that **strange music**—a style called **8-bit,** I'd later learn.

These kinds of experiences are what any adventurer **cherishes.** The **innocent little moments** of being a carefree **noob.**

Right then, **I was fine** with being one again.
As long as <u>she was by my side.</u>

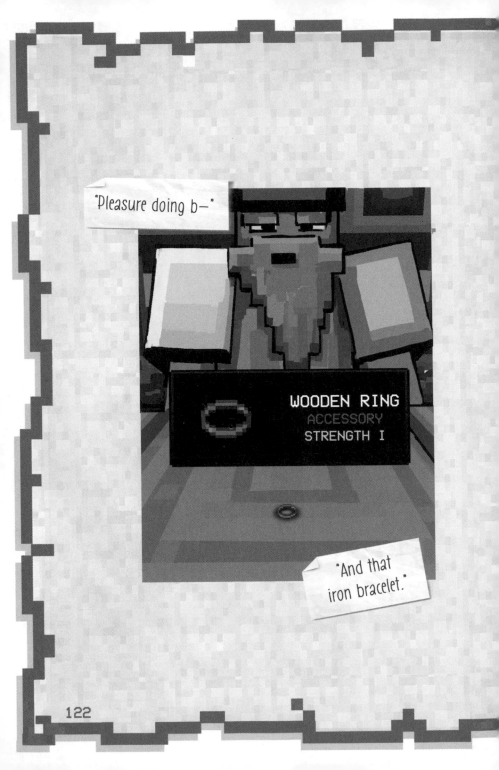

"Pl—"

IRON
BRACELET
ACCESSORY
REGENERATION I

"And don't forget our
brewing ingredients!"

123

". . . Come back anytime."

"And try **that inn I mentioned**," he said. "It has a few rooms with **brewing stands.**"

"Do the rooms have **cauldrons**, too?" Breeze asked. "Buckets? Furnaces? I'd trade anything for a **nice warm bath.**"

"**Of course**," he said, taken aback by this question. "**The Enchanted Dragon** is one of **the best** inns in the entire world. Be sure to try the **mutton.** It's practically enchanted with **Tastiness VII.**"

"Will do," she said.

With **a single sweep** of her arms, she picked up all three piles of ingredients, then **lost her balance** and almost fell into me.

"Um, can you help me out? My inventory's kinda full."

Just after **the sun went down,** we stood before a **massive** building made of oak and dark oak, spruce and cobblestone, and hardened white clay. Panes of **glowstone glass** held the silhouettes of many **jovial** patrons, while **cheery medieval melodies** drifted through the air.

The Enchanted Dragon.

That was the name of this den of noobs, and to its doors **we saunterred** up. **Well,** more like hobbled, really. It had been a long day. Check **the number of updates** today if you don't believe me.

"We'd like a room with a brewing stand."

"That'll be thirty emeralds, m'lady."

"Here."

Ah, yes. An inn. How could **anyone** call themselves an adventurer without ever visiting this most **famous** of traveler hangouts? I'll never forget walking into an inn for the very first time.

Woof: The smoke from the torches **hits you** first, followed by the smell of mutton **sizzling** on a furnace, then the sound of **over two hundred voices,** overpowering now that you're inside. People **everywhere,** heads **thrown back** in laughter, with brightly **colored hair** and **long ears,** or with helmets and wizard's caps, or with **huge** beards hanging over mouths filled with **square yellow teeth.**

In the very back, there were several **mysterious figures** quietly sipping their enchanted drinks, faces concealed by the shadows of their hoods, and **one shady-looking man,** probably a rogue or treasure hunter, carving something into a table with a dagger. And even farther back, a human, **an elf,** and another **human-like** girl—except with **fox ears** and a bushy red tail—danced next to a group of **singing pigmen.** One of them was playing **some kind of** stringed musical **instrument,** while to either side a group of knights in iron armor **cheered them on,** mugs raised, **toasting. . . .**

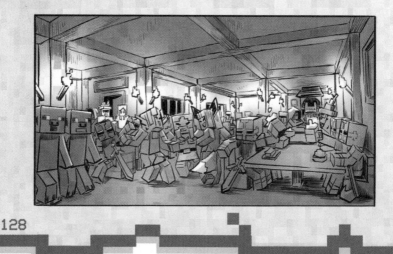

This was what I experienced in **the first few seconds,** and all of it hit me **like a rapidly approaching wall.** Breeze, too. She looked rather **overwhelmed.** We found a table and **sat down** to order some warm food. As if our senses weren't **flooded** enough, our waitress was dressed in **the weirdest-looking outfit** I'd ever seen.

"What'll it be?" she asked.

"**Mutton,**" Breeze said, "and a baked potato. **No.** Two baked potatoes. **And a loaf of bread.**"

The waitress **squeezed** her shoulder. "Wow. Long day, **hun?**" After noticing **our swords,** she continued. "Of course. I know **treasure hunters** when I see them. **Any luck** so far?"

"**Not exactly,**" I said, and nodded at Breeze. "I'll have what she's having and . . ." I looked past her, at two humans in leather. Between bursts of laughter, they were **sipping potions.** "What are **they** having over there?"

"One of the **finest** potions in all the land," the waitress said with a smile. "**The Noob Rager.**"

"Noob Rager?"

"**Best potion** you'll **ever** drink," she said. "Gives a nice burst of **energy,** too. A young man gave us **the recipe.** A treasure hunter, much like yourselves, but **different.** One of those **mysterious** travelers from a faraway land. . . . **Anyway,** he called it **an energy drink,** which is a kind of potion they have in . . . **well,** wherever he came from."

*Ah, she must be talking about . . . **of course**.* I gave the waitress a knowing smile. "I'll take one."

"**As will I**," Breeze said.

"Bread's on the house."

Considering she's like half a block tall, Breeze sure can put away a ton of food. She must have two food bars.

And that potion **really was** amazing. It tasted **better than melon juice**—and **the energy!** It was like a potion of Leaping, Swiftness, and Strength all **rolled into one.** I wanted to order another right after I downed the first.

"I wouldn't advise that," the waitress said. "Drink **too many** and you'll go **right to sleep** after the effects wear off! **Buff overload,** they call it."

"I like to live **dangerously,**" I said.

"As you wish, m'lord." The waitress whispered to Breeze, "**Just so you know,** he's going to crash in **exactly** one hour."

After our meal, **the empty bottles** reminded me of how we needed to trade for **ingredients.** Following the shopkeeper's suggestion, we went from table to table to see if anyone had a few melons and gold nuggets to trade. **As luck would have it,** a blue-haired elf girl and one of those wolf people *(another odd couple)* had exactly what we needed.

"Good luck, guys!"

"We'll trade again!"

Another person had **a handful of blaze powder,** which we needed to **fuel** our brewing stand. At this point, we had a total of fifteen emeralds to our name, so we decided to **call it a night.**

On the way upstairs, that **waitress** from earlier approached us. She **glanced around** before speaking to us in a lowered voice. I could **barely hear her** over the noise coming from the dining hall.

"If you **really are** treasure hunters," she said, "could you **do me a favor?**"

"Define '**favor,**'" I said.

"Well, I've **always wanted** a necklace. **A nice one,** you know? I was hoping to craft one myself, but I need **a frost opal.** That's my favorite **gemstone.** If you two happen to find one, could you **bring it to me?** I don't have much in the way of emeralds, but I do have **these.**" In her palm were several **brilliant white coins.** "They're a special type of coin," she said, "crafted **ages ago.** So long ago, in fact, that their original name has been **lost.** Some believe they were once the official currency of the **ancient people.** Now many simply refer to them as **quest tokens,** because this is what **the king** usually gives to someone completing one of his many quests."

"So they're **like money?**" Breeze asked.

"In a way," she said. "**Follow me,** I'll show you."

She took us **downstairs,** into the basement, to a spruce door surrounded by **many signs.**

132

QUEST TOKENS ONLY!!!

QUEST STORE
NO NOOBS!!!

RARE ITEMS
EPIC LOOT

DRAW WEAPONS = BAN
MINE BLOCKS = BAN
TOUCH STUFF = BAN

ONLY ONE PERSON
AT A TIME!
NO EXCEPTIONS!!!

DO ANYTHING
BUT LOOK AT
THINGS AND BUY
THINGS = BAN

NO QUEST TOKENS
= NO ENTRY

As we **approached,** two guards **in obsidian armor** immediately **rushed** in front of the door, **without saying anything.**

"This is called the **Quest Store,**" the waitress said. "Several such stores exist throughout Ardenvell. Here, you can find many **unique items** the king has donated as possible <u>**rewards.**</u>"

I was overwhelmed with a sense of **wonder,** almost as much as when I first set foot in Owl's Reach. I had to get in there—**I just had to!** But those guards wouldn't move. I asked them if I could maybe just **take a peek** inside, but they didn't reply.

The waitress **grabbed** my shoulder. "**I wouldn't advise that.** You could get **banned** from entering the Quest Store. **Permanently.** If you want to shop here, you need to show them you have **quest tokens.**"

"So you've offered us **a quest**," I said.

"**I suppose** you could call it that, but that makes it sound so **serious,** doesn't it? I'm no king, **only** a waitress. . . ."

"**We'll see** what we can do," Breeze said. Finding a quest was definitely **awesome,** but we were both **totally exhausted.** After waving goodbye to the waitress, we went back upstairs and checked out **our room.**

Our room **was nice.** Especially compared to what I'd been sleeping in since I'd left Villagetown.

Before we started **brewing,** we took off to the bathhouse. There, we each found **our own personal** 3x3 cauldron. The block below the cauldrons contained **lava,** so the water was actually **warm.** Since we're farther north, **it's colder**—especially after sunset. **Honestly,** I don't know how the zombies around here **survive.** They must wear clothes enchanted with **Cold Protection.**

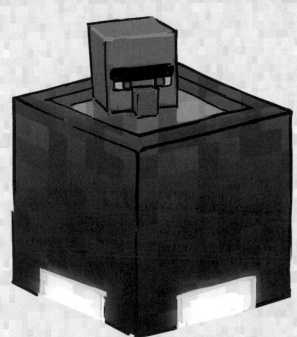

Yes, a bathroom **all to myself.** There was a **public** "bathing pool," but it was full of pigmen and dwarves. So we noped out of there and spent **twenty emeralds** for two **private rooms.** And no, the water wasn't **that** hot. I'm not some brewing ingredient, **okay?!**

135

We **returned** to our room. I asked Breeze a question that had been **on my mind** ever since that battle with the pigmen.

"Breeze? How did you **wield two** swords?"

Silence. That **dark expression** again. She didn't want to let me in on **her little secret.**

"**Your father** must have taught you," I said. "He must have. I saw him do the same thing once. When we were **defending against the wall breach.**"

She turned to the furnace, which was crackling away. "It's . . . **an ability,**" she said.

"**Ability?** What are you talking about?"

"You know how an enderman can **teleport?**" she asked. "How a ghast can **breathe fire** or a spider can **climb walls?** Well, people are capable of **similar feats.** Some are **magical** in nature, like spells, while others, such as duel wield, are **physical.** Their **complexity** varies as well. Some are easy to learn. **Others, nearly impossible.**"

"Does that mean **you can teach me?**"

"I can **train** you," she said. "The same way my father trained me. It would only take **twenty or so** minutes."

"Twenty minutes?! **Seriously?!** Why didn't you tell me about this **before?!**"

She **shrugged.** "Just **slipped my mind.** My father only recently showed me how to do it. And he didn't want me to tell **anyone** about it. He said most of us **aren't ready** yet."

"Well, I'm ready! **Super** ready! I'll be the best student you've ever seen! **Promise!**"

"There's **one thing** you should know," she said. "You can only learn a limited number of abilities over time. If I show you how to duel wield, and you come across **another ability** in the near future, you **may not be able** to learn that one."

"Why not?"

"Because learning an ability **takes experience.**"

"**Got it.** Hmm. But . . . how does that work?"

"If you happened to meet another person who knows a different ability, perhaps something better than duel wield, they could **train you.** According to my father, there are **over a thousand** different abilities. Some are **better** than others. Most are **common** and known by many in the Overworld. The best are **rare, highly sought after,** and can only be learned from some **ancient hermit** living on a mountaintop, **a nymph a faerie** in some secret cove, or **a wizard** in some remote tower. **Like that.** My father said there are even items that can teach abilities. Usually **enchanted tomes.**"

"Interesting. . . . Okay, I've thought about it quite a bit, and now **I've made up my mind. Teacher,** please teach me how to duel wield. **Err,** train, I mean."

"Are you sure?"

"**A hundred percent.**"

And so, Breeze began **training me** in the art of duel wielding. **As a precaution,** we wielded sticks in each hand. Before long, and after much **frustration,** I began to effectively wield two sticks at the same time.

I brandished my two "**weapons**" while shouting with excitement. "**Yeahhh!!**"

She gave me a little clap. "Oh. You should know that any ability **will improve** the more you use it. You'll be much better by the time we've cleared that dungeon."

"Maybe I should **skip the two swords** and just stick with my shield, **right?**"

"Well, there will be times when you need to do **more damage.** With duel wield, you'll always have that **option.**"

"I guess **you're right.** When I need more defense, I can use my shield, and when I don't, I'll swap the shield out for another sword. Sheer versatility. **Kinda like Batman.**"

"Who's **Batman?**"

"**This guy** Kaeleb was telling me about. He can do all sorts of **cool things** to handle any situation, like . . . throw **smoke bombs** to escape, or use this thing called a **grappling hook** . . . or **deflect** arrows **with his cloak** . . . or **fly** with his cloak, and . . . and . . . why am I still talking when you don't seem interested in this at all?"

"**Um . . .**" Breeze gave me a blank look. "I know we've been avoiding it, but we really do **need to work** on those healing potions."

138

"Of course," I said. "**Let's do this thing.** I still feel kinda **energetic** after chugging those potions, so I'm probably going to craft **one million** potions. **At least** one million."

"You mean brew?"

"Yeah. Also, how do we craft those **golden melon things** again?"

Needless to say, **I didn't** brew one million potions. I didn't even brew one. Okay, **I almost** brewed one. I put a base potion on the stand and threw in one of those golden melon things that Breeze had crafted.

But it had been such a long day, you know?

Yes, **I fell asleep.** No, I'm not proud of it. And yes, Breeze made a total of fifteen healing potions. In her nightgown.

*So the waitress **was right** about those energy drinks! Exactly one hour after I drank that second potion, the potion's buffs wore off, and **thunk,** I dropped like an anvil. . . . Anyway, **sorry, Breeze!***

SATURDAY

It was **still dark** when we set out. A **beautiful** sunrise crept behind us as we rode southwest. We had to stop to **admire it.**

Only then did I notice just how many **flowers** there were. A countless number, as far as you could see.

"Pink roses," Breeze said, swinging off her horse. "They're quite **uncommon** this far north. This must be a flower field. It's one of the **rarest** biome types, I think. It has to mean something. A good omen?" She turned to me. "Do you **believe** in that kind of thing?"

"Considering where we're going," I said, **"I'll believe in anything,** so long as it means a better chance of **not getting clobbered** by ten zombies at once."

We walked through the field **together,** then stopped as the sun came into view. **We said nothing.** I think we stayed like that for **a very long time.** I didn't know what was on her mind and couldn't have **guessed,** but she was clearly **thinking** about something.

"Kolb told me **so many things** before I left," she said at last.

"Like what?"

"He said our world used to be something called a **'server.'** A **Minecraft** server named Aetheria. And the players of that game **dreamt up everything** we see now, their countless ideas added, **over time,** through a series of updates, modifications, with every structure built, by their hands, through **some interface.** Then, one day, that world became this world. A world that's **more** than just a video game. . . ."

"You believe that?"

"I prefer not to, **of course.** It's much more **comforting** to believe they were **summoned** to **our** world."

"Breeze, you and I both know **we're more** than **game** characters. And even if we once were, we aren't any longer. **We exist.** That's all that matters, **right?**"

She said nothing, but I knew from her expression that my words had had **some effect.** I wanted to **believe myself,** too. I felt **lighter,** uplifted, and once more I gazed at the beautiful expanse before us: **the way the light scattered** across what had to be **millions** of petals . . . a game couldn't have created this. Although I didn't understand the **technology** of Earth, I knew no machine was capable of producing a world like this. Even if it was **a thousand times more complicated** than our redstone.

Breeze **held out** a bottle filled with water, which **sparkled** in the sunlight. The bottle's unique design indicated that it was **a splash potion.** A splash **water bottle.**

"**Here,**" she said. "I had some leftover gunpowder, so I made several of these."

"**What are they for?**"

"When thrown, they'll create a **burst of water.** This can put out **fires** or harm creatures with a **vulnerability** to water or affinity to fire. Another thing I learned from Lola."

"I wasn't even going to ask," I said. "**I just assumed.**"

And I thought: *Thanks again, you creative little redstone engineer.*

We stood at the edge of a **wide cliff** overlooking the plains below. You could see **forever:** perhaps a thousand blocks away, **the emerald greens** of the plains met the clay browns of **savanna.** That's called **a boundary,** where two biomes merge in a perfectly straight line. Far beyond that, the brown grass turned green again, although a different shade than the plains. Almost **cyan.** That biome was **mountainous,** with the grass turning to foothills rising gradually in steps, leading to **vast gray peaks** capped with snow. All this under a cloudless, **sapphire sky**—a blue so deep I felt lost within it whenever I looked straight up.

But this scene had a flaw. Someone had left **a dark spot** on this painting of sheer perfection. . . . There it was, far away, nestled in the middle of a million grass blocks. **The Tomb** of the Forgotten King.

If that place had once been built by the hands of some human, through some advanced **computer interface,** on some world known as Earth, **you couldn't tell.** Even from here it seemed **ominous,** a dreary slab at odds with the **vibrant** greens surrounding it, all black obsidian and storm-gray bedrock, red torches burning low.

"We're finally here," Breeze said.

I nodded **absently** and stared ahead, feeling a sudden chill run down my back. We were running into **the unknown.** We had no idea what kind of **traps** that tomb contained, how many monsters there were inside, or **how far down** it went. **Truth be told,** I didn't even know what a **puzzle** was. I was **terrified** at the thought of fighting another boss.

But Breeze didn't share my sudden lack of confidence. She turned toward me **with a smile. Nodded.**

"Let's go!"

SATURDAY—UPDATE II

I learned some things **about dungeons** today. Before, I'd always thought they were **single rooms** with a handful of monsters and **one or two treasure chests.** After all, that's what our teachers said. And every book I'd ever read on the subject had said the same exact thing. So **imagine my surprise** upon actually standing before one.

Go ahead—imagine it.

A simple underground room, **they said.** No larger than a 7x7 chamber, **they said.**

Yeah, well, **they were wrong. Just a tad.** Like the ocean has **a tad of water. . . .** *(Seriously—I know I'm supposed to be a brave warrior and all, but can I* **hurgg** *now?)*

I'll be honest:
<u>I was terrified.</u>

The little skull next to the doors was a nice touch. It had glowing red eyes. I turned to Breeze.

"Judging by the looks of this place, this must be **the home of a giant wither skeleton. . . .** Neat." A pause. "How about we just **forget about it?** We'll just tell the blacksmith we couldn't find his glowmoss. . . ."

"And maybe he'll send us on **another quest,**" Breeze said. "A **pumpkin pie—eating contest,** perhaps?"

I smiled. "What's **this?** Breeze **joking around?**"

She smiled, too, although it **quickly faded. All business.**

"You said this place is protected somehow?" she asked.

"That's what that one guy told me. Think of it as a biome-wide **enchantment** that **prevents the mining of blocks and the placement of activators.** Actually, the placement of everything."

"If you don't mind, I'd like to see this **for myself.**" Within moments, Breeze crafted **a wooden button.** When she tried placing it against the bedrock to the left of the door, **it fell to the ground,** as if it had been dropped. It failed to cling to the wall the way buttons always do. **This was, of course—**

"**Impossible,**" Breeze said. With a look of **utter disbelief,** she tried placing the button against the dirt with the **same result. "What in the Overworld . . . ?"**

I was wielding my stone pickax at this point and swung at those doors with everything I had. One swing, two. **On the tenth,** my pick flashed red . . . and shattered, **crumbling into little gray cubes before my very eyes.** *(There was also a sad little sizzling sound: "p'tweeeeeuu . . .")*

What's interesting here is that my pickax had almost **full durability.** It had gone from approximately **95%** to **zero in an instant.** I glanced at the single brown cube in my hand *(which had once been part of the handle).* "**The Nether?!**"

When Breeze tried **digging** with her iron shovel, she accomplished the very same thing. That is to say, **she accomplished nothing.** After her shovel flashed red and crumbled, she stared down at the iron cubes at her feet, **thoroughly unimpressed. "Hurmmph!"** It was the first time I'd ever heard her make that sound, a sound villagers often make when **annoyed.** Indeed, what we were currently experiencing . . . it was simply **unbelievable.** No matter what, a button **always** stuck to whatever surface you placed it against, and a shovel **always** mined dirt in a very short time, but here . . . well, let's just say we didn't go chopping at some grass with our swords to see what might happen. **We knew what would happen.**

"So how far does this extend?" Breeze asked. "The enchantment, I mean. Is it really **biome-wide?**"

"**I think so,**" I said. "Any biome that **contains a dungeon** can't be modified at all. Otherwise, **trolls** and **griefers** could put up **obsidian walls,** TNT traps, monster spawners, **lava moats** . . . apparently the Builders didn't want anyone **messing** with their creations."

"Got it."

A huge problem, then—**the enderman in the room,** or more appropriately, the iron golem in the room—immediately confronted us. If we really **couldn't place or mine anything** within this biome, that meant:

1.) Without beds, **sleeping would be difficult.**

2.) Old tricks involving the terrain—such as emergency shelters, dirt pillars—were **not an option.**

3.) The **most pressing** issue was something I hadn't yet thought of *(but Breeze had, obviously)*: She tried placing some **fence.** As expected, the single fence post, instead of securing itself to the ground, **fell over.**

"So what are we going to do about Shybiss?" she asked.

Ah, yes. Without any fence, she couldn't **tie up** her horse. If we left Shybiss out here, she could pull a **Meadow** on us and **take off.** I was so close to **hurgging.** So close. **Eto** had mentioned this in the armor shop, but I never really thought about what kind of **problems** it would cause. I almost suggested we **bring Shybiss into the dungeon** with us, but I knew how Breeze would have responded to that. Luckily, she's **way smarter** than I am. She decided to walk around the dungeon and check things out. Guess what was back there? Is your answer "**some fence posts**"? Well, **you're correct!** Congrats, you've won **one million emeralds** and **a stuffed Urg the Barbarian doll!**

Whoever those Builders were, they were very considerate of us adventurers. They left behind some fence posts for people to tie horses to. They forgot the beds, though, and the cauldron full of rabbit stew. . . .

"Well, that's **one problem solved**," she said. "But whose horses are **those?**"

"**Other adventurers,** I guess? Who knows, maybe we'll run into them and we can group up." I showed Breeze **the obsidian key. "Ready?"**

Regarding Breeze's response, I could write something **mundane** here, like:

She nodded. "I'm ready," she said.

But even though I'm barely an adult, I'm trying to be a **better writer.** She **nodded?!** How **boring** is that? Let's cross that one out!

~~She nodded. "I'm ready," she said.~~

Boom! Away with you, **boring** description of Breeze! And now for something **a little more interesting,** such as . . .

***

I didn't have to ask if she was ready. Her expression **said** that she was ready to go in there and **drop zombies** until her résumé no longer read **"warrior"** but **"zombie farmer,"** until so many **dropped items** littered the ground that the items actually **spilled out** like water,

150

until that place was no longer known as the **Tomb of the Forgotten King** but **Item Mountain. Not only that,** but until **so many experience orbs** were swirling through the sky above that explorers **five biomes away** actually got lost because they mistook those orbs for the sun. *(Assuming they don't have a compass . . .)*

To open a locked door, one only needs to touch it with the proper key.
Who knew?

The doors led to a single room **lined with redstone torches.** An **obsidian** staircase led downward, and there was **a large sign** near the doors.

THE TOMB OF THE FORGOTTEN KING
HEAD BUILDER: IONE
APPROVED BY: ENTITY303

We turned back to the staircase and began our descent into the depths of the dungeon.

What's that? You're scared?
So imagine how <u>I</u> felt!

The hall below was **three blocks wide** and mostly the same as the surface room: **obsidian under bedrock.** The walls had these . . . **alcoves,** I guess. They held what looked like flowerpots, but they weren't flowerpots at all. They contained a **gray gunpowder-like material.**

"Are those **ashes?**" Breeze asked.

"**Looks like it.** As if this place isn't **creepy enough.**"

We had no idea what to expect, so **I went in front,** my shield raised, sword readied. Breeze trailed behind several blocks with her enchanted bow **ready to fire.**

That was when **I heard a scraping sound** coming from the hallway to the right. Moments later, **a zombie** shambled around the corner. **There's no point** in describing this battle in any detail. You know how it played out. **Two arrows** and **a diamond sword** later, the zombie went down. Smoke. Experience orbs. A stone sword, five or so swings from breaking. Leather armor in worse condition. But **here's the thing.** It also dropped <u>**six emeralds**</u>.

I glanced at Breeze. She glanced at me. Silence. The squeak of a bat.

"**So . . .**" she said, "every time we kill something in here, **it drops emeralds?**"

I looked down at the pile of items.

153

"I'm not sure. **Eto** said the monsters didn't drop too many. But maybe six **isn't too many** to him."

We heard more scraping around the corner. **Another zombie,** with a sword, shield, and full suit of armor, **all crafted of gold.** We took that one down like the last, **without too much effort.** And like the last, this one dropped every item it carried, the golden breastplate being **enchanted with Protection II** . . . along with **five emeralds.** We exchanged glances again, looked at the pile. More sounds came from around the corner. Three zombies, maybe, **maybe four,** five, six possibly, **no, at least seven.** Well, no, that's way too much noise. Definitely **eight or nine.** We glanced at each other again. It was our first time in a dungeon. What we knew about such places came from outdated books written **hundreds of years ago,** books written by villager librarians who had never even set foot in the Overworld. Even so, after seeing the **gemstones scattered across the floor** . . .

we knew **exactly** what to do.

Trash!

The!!

Dungeon!!!

After that **small battle,** the only direction left to go was forward. The problem was, there was another **iron door** standing in our way. The key didn't work on this one. We had to find a way to open it.

We couldn't find anything, though. We **searched everywhere,** but we couldn't see any buttons, levers, or pressure plates. Before long, I was pressing on **random blocks,** thinking there could be a secret button somewhere. Breeze tried pulling on all the torches, hoping one of them was **a lever in disguise,** to no avail.

Nothing budged, and I was about to **hurgg.** I didn't, though. I managed to **stay calm.** My mind was like a diamond, **clear and sharp, unbreakable** and . . . anyway, I noticed **something different** about the alcove to the right of the door.

It had a small 1x1 shaft
leading down to the floor below.

Two possibilities: either this is how dungeon monsters deal with garbage, or I had found a secret passage.

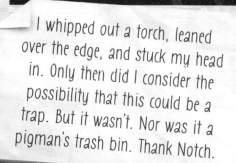

I whipped out a torch, leaned over the edge, and stuck my head in. Only then did I consider the possibility that this could be a trap. But it wasn't. Nor was it a pigman's trash bin. Thank Notch.

"You've gotta be kidding me. Breeze, come look at this!"

At the bottom of the shaft was **a golden pressure plate;** a line of redstone was **connected** to this **activator,** and it most likely linked to the door. All we had to do was **drop an item on it** and the door would open.

So Breeze tossed in a **beat-up leather helmet.** Nothing happened.

"**That's weird,**" she said. "I thought you could activate pressure plates with items."

"**I thought so, too.** Huh . . ."

I kept staring at the golden tile, thinking back to what little we'd learned in school regarding them. "**Wait,** aren't golden pressure plates **special somehow?**"

Breeze shrugged. "I don't know anything about redstone, remember? If only **Lola** were here. . . ."

At the mention of Lola, I **suddenly recalled** a time when she had been talking about pressure plates with **Max.**

"I remember her saying something about iron pressure plates," I said. "Something about how **they're heavier?** Or heavy?"

"Okay, **iron is heavy,** but so is gold."

"Right, I don't know what she meant by that. Wait." I was starting to remember something. . . . **Wait . . . Wait . . .**

"**Weight!**"

The weight of the items on top of it **directly affects** the signal strength of these types of plates! A single item would only send out redstone power for maybe a block. I explained this to Breeze, then tossed in a pair of leather leggings. **Still nothing.** An iron breastplate with Protection I and Breaking III. A wooden sword, a stone sword, a pair of leather boots. An egg. A tulip. A stack of seeds *(we were short on ideas)*.

The door **stayed closed.**

"Well, the redstone line could extend for **quite a ways** under the floor," I said. "Maybe we just need to throw more stuff in?"

So we did, throwing **pretty much everything** we'd looted from those zombies earlier. And an egg. And a tulip. And a stack of seeds *(yes, I know . . .)*.

That was when I heard **a click** to my left. **The door had finally opened.**

"So I guess this is what Eto meant by **puzzles.**"

"Huh?"

"Never mind."

We took down **another group** of zombies, along with some skeletons. We fought **perfectly.** We timed our swings so **nothing** could get close. And when the last skeleton fired at Breeze, I dashed in front of her **with my shield raised. . . .** Beyond **emeralds** and **the usual trash-tier items,** one dropped **an obsidian sword.** I'd **never seen** an obsidian sword and was shocked to learn that its damage is actually **one less** than diamond. And with **half the durability.** Still, it's way better than anything else we've found so far.

Whenever the situation calls for it, I'll swap my shield out and begin **dual wielding.** According to Breeze, the **Defender enchantment** increases the wielder's armor by its power level. Kind of like **a mini-shield.** So I'll still have better-than-normal defense wielding it in my off hand. As for the pink handguard, or whatever it's called, I'm not sure what that's about. Breeze thinks it could be a type of material known as **"coral,"** but that's just a guess. *(Can more advanced swords be made with three or more different materials?)*

We encountered **another puzzle.** Another pressure plate. It was situated at the end of a horizontal shaft, or tunnel, so there was **no way** we could drop any items onto it.

Do you know how we managed to activate it? **Think about it for a second.** I'll **count to five,** and by the time I'm done counting, you need to come up with the answer.

Ready? One. Two. Three. Four. Five. And?

Is your answer "Runt drank a potion of Shrinking II to become one block tall so he could walk down the tunnel?"

Wrong! First of all, what kind of noob do you take me for?! There is no such thing as a Shrinking potion! *(Item scholars, you're free to correct me if I'm wrong.)*

In truth, the answer was **far simpler.**

Are you ready? Let's test your **knowledge.** You can still think some more, if you'd like. If you didn't come up with an answer and are still thinking, stop reading immediately. Unless you give up, I mean. **And no cheating, eh!** Don't go reading further and then pretend you came up with the answer!

Okay. Anyway. **The answer is: arrows.**

On a golden pressure plate, a single arrow has enough weight to send **a redstone signal** out one block. Since a repeater was placed next to the plate, **boom,** the door was opened. **Of course,** Breeze is the one who handled this. She said **she** should be the one, so we wouldn't **waste resources,** whatever that means. . . .

 Wait. Was she suggesting that **I'm a bad shot?!** She was, wasn't she?! **That's it!** Now **I have a bow,** too, you know! One of those skeletons dropped one. Okay, so it might be two or three shots away from breaking, but **that's enough** for me to hit that pressure plate myself and show her who's boss. **She'll see.** Hold on, I'll update in a second. I'll take my time with this, hold my breath, aim carefully and . . .

Okay, clearly that bow had problems. I say "had" because the bowstring snapped on the eighth shot. My aim is normally dead-on.

The next room was . . . um . . . **interesting.** It was a long hall with **a spruce door** on the end. Oh. And the **obsidian** floor was covered with more of those golden pressure plates.

Hmm . . .
I'm no dungeon expert,
but something isn't
right here. . . .

It's the **color scheme!** Those gold tiles simply do not go with this dungeon's **gloomy aesthetic!** I might even go so far as to say it **clashes,** if I dared to use such a strong word! Just kidding. **I know it's a trap,** okay?

"I know what this is," I said to Breeze. "It's one of those arrow rooms. You **step in the wrong spot,** and **arrows fly everywhere.**" I announced this **proudly.** "Yeah, that's what this is. Urg the Barbarian had to get around one of these things in the last book. It looked similar to this."

"Well, **if this is an arrow trap,**" she said, "shouldn't there be **some of those face things** in the wall?"

"Face things? You mean **dispensers?**"

"**Yeah,** I think so?"

I'm pretty sure that's what she was talking about. A dispenser is a block that can hold other items, and it **releases them** upon activation. Anyway, she was right. If this room was some kind of arrow trap, it would have had dispensers **in the walls.** But the walls here were **just bedrock.** Could it be?! Was it possible that the Builders used some **ancient, mystical** technique to create dispensers that **looked** like bedrock?! No. Not really. It was just **normal bedrock.**

Standing in the doorway, Breeze moved up to the **very edge.**

"I think **it's the ceiling,**" she said. "It's **much lower** than the other rooms and it's made of **cobblestone.** Until now, we've never seen any cobblestone. . . ."

I retrieved **a handful of seeds** from my inventory. "**Let's find out,** shall we?"

I tossed the seeds onto the pressure plate directly in front of the doorway, like I was feeding chickens or something. Nothing happened. The pressure plate sank down, sure, and the seeds clearly activated it, yes, **but that's it.**

"**Try farther out,**" she said.

So I gathered the seeds and tossed them **two blocks** from the door.

Again, this pressure plate **sank in . . .** and **the entire ceiling** flew down with a **deafening** crash—the sound of **over fifty sticky pistons** firing all at once.

Breeze said something, but I couldn't hear her over the noise. She **dashed** in just as the ceiling went up, **grabbed the seeds** and dashed back. I don't know how she moved so fast. It reminded me of the time we first met. *(Was it another ability?)*

The ceiling crashed down **a fraction of a second** after she returned, then went up again and stopped.

We didn't say anything for a moment, just **stared** ahead in silence, our ears ringing. At least, **mine were.** I'd read about trapped rooms, of course, but never in my **wildest** dreams had I imagined **one like this.** I pictured it now: the ceiling of sticky pistons covered in a grid of redstone, the complex trails leading to the floor. Or subfloor. What is that called? You know. A floor under a floor.

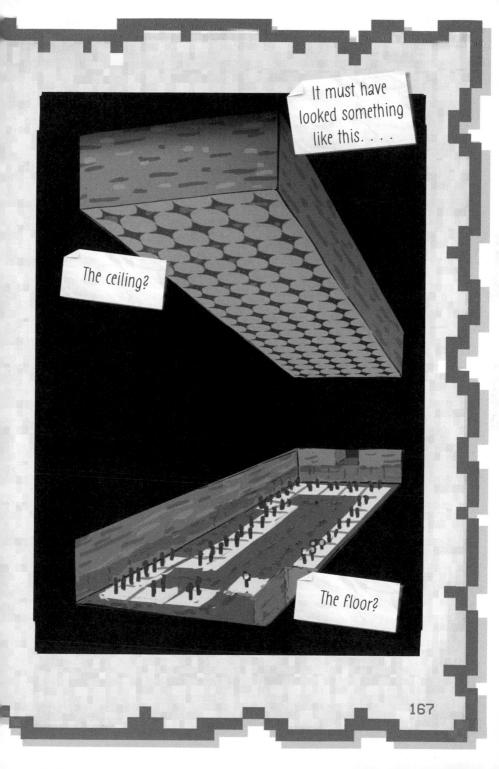

167

"So this is what the Builders are capable of. . . . Just **what kind of lunatics** are we dealing with here . . . ?"

I didn't **dare** imagine how much damage **a ceiling** would inflict.

In short, we had to figure out **the correct path.** One wrong step, and we'd become **villager pizza.**

Since **the entire ceiling** came down, throwing items in front of us like a reverse trail of bread crumbs wasn't an option.

The answer was right **in Breeze's hands. A fishing pole.** The lure was **heavy enough** to trigger the plates. We could use it to **safely test** which areas were safe and which areas . . . um . . . weren't safe. This was a **time-consuming** process (and deafening). If any nearby monsters weren't **already aware** of our presence, well, they surely were now.

Thirty minutes later, we mapped the safe route. I'm going to include **a drawing of the safe path** here, in case anyone ever visits this dungeon in the future.

By the way, even though we figured out which pressure plates were safe to step on, that didn't make walking through that room **any less terrifying.** After today, setting foot into any building with a low ceiling is going to give me a **serious** panic attack.

STICKY TRAP MAZE

The humans said there's this thing called a wiki that's like a huge book of information on various subjects. If we ever make a wiki about dungeons, this drawing needs to be added.

Another trap. This one was **pretty obvious,** yet there was **no way** to tell what kind of trap it could have been. It was **a long corridor, three blocks wide.** The floor, made from **soul sand,** was completely **covered** in pressure plates. **Cobwebs** filled the remaining space.

We were going to have a **hard time** advancing with all that. Not cool!

Yes, **soul sand** can slow you down, even underneath a pressure plate. **Ask me how I know. Go on.**

Cobwebs **obscured** whatever sat beyond. I turned to Breeze, who was still holding **her fishing pole.**

"Probably **dispensers** on the other end," I said.

"Arrows, you think? Can arrows fly through cobwebs?"

"I guess we'll find out. **Pole it!**"

Breeze sent out her lure, which hit a stone plate. **It didn't activate.**

"**Right.**" I sighed. "These plates aren't weighted."

"What do you mean?"

"I'm not really sure, but . . . I think that kind of pressure plate only works when **a living creature** steps on it. Guess we'll have to test this the hard way, huh?"

170

I held my shield in front of me. Breeze followed directly behind me. Sure enough, after I stepped onto the first row of pressure plates, **arrows went flying everywhere,** accompanied by blue-gray swirls. **"They're enchanted?** Please tell me those aren't Wither arrows."

"Slowness," Breeze said.

"Wonderful."

While we slowly advanced, and I do mean slowly, **another volley** was unleashed. An arrow struck my shield with a **clang** and bounced off. I was quite happy to have a shield equipped— next to the soul sand and spider webs, the enchanted arrows would have slowed us to a complete stop. We would **never** have gotten out of there.

Approximately nine million arrows later, we reached the end. **All I could taste** at that point were cobwebs. That's not even the worst part. We couldn't loot the dispensers: they were, like everything else, protected. And we couldn't **collect** the arrows themselves. They **crumbled into nothingness** seconds after striking something. *(And yes, I tried grabbing one super fast, but the arrow crumbled as soon as I touched it.)* **No free arrows** for us. Those Builders, man . . . they really thought of everything, didn't they?

As soon as we were in the clear, Breeze headed for the door, then **stopped.**

"That's **odd**," she said.

"What?"

"The door's **open**."

"**Hurmm.** Maybe it's the **same people** who left those horses? C'mon, they might be close."

We stood before **a vast chamber** with, thankfully, an extremely high ceiling. The style of construction was noticeably different here. Although **still gloomy,** all obsidian and bedrock, it was **beautiful** in a way. I'm no expert, but I had **the impression** that it was the work of a **different Builder.**

They'd somehow engraved portraits into the obsidian. I didn't recognize any of them.

Well, no—I recognized one.

Entity.

Can you believe that this guy was **the nicest wizard who ever lived? Me neither.** With a look like this, you'd never expect him to offer you some cookies and tea. I'd be waiting to be **polymorphed** into a baby rabbit and/or teleported to the **Void.**

"What's the point of this area?" I said. "**Where's the challenge** in walking around giant, empty halls?"

"Looks like someone has already **taken care of it.**" She pointed down a hall. **Countless items** were scattered across the floor. Sword. Axes. Pieces of armor. More common were the **remains of monsters—** bones, spider eyes. . . .

So someone else had **cleared** this area. They must have been in a hurry, because they **didn't bother taking anything.** One of our nicer finds was **a gold ring.** It had a fancy name: **Ancient Band.** That ring was totally mine, because dude, just **look** at that armor bonus.

There was also **a bracelet made of redstone. Critical Strike** means it increases damage dealt through critical hits by **one per power level**—that is to say, **one heart.** Needless to say, **Breeze took that one.**

**REDSTONE
BRACELET**
ACCESSORY
CRITICAL
STRIKE I

The rest of the stuff was inferior to what we had on. Gold axes, iron swords. Some with **low-level enchantments.** We took everything anyway. We could trade this stuff for **a few hundred emeralds** back in Owl's Reach. A question **popped into my head.**

"Y'know, if someone already cleared this area," I said, "how come the zombies from earlier **were untouched?**"

"I think they'd only **recently spawned,**" Breeze said. "That's one of the things Kolb mentioned, before I came looking for you. Monsters **spawn continually** in dungeons."

"Through **monster spawners?**"

"Yes. Well, something like that. Except **they're invisible.**"

"Then the other people **must be close,** if the monsters here haven't respawned yet."

"Probably."

She said this **absently,** as she was now staring at a nearby wall where there was **a section of iron blocks** instead of bedrock. **Above this** was a massive stone sign. I'd **never seen** a sign like that before.

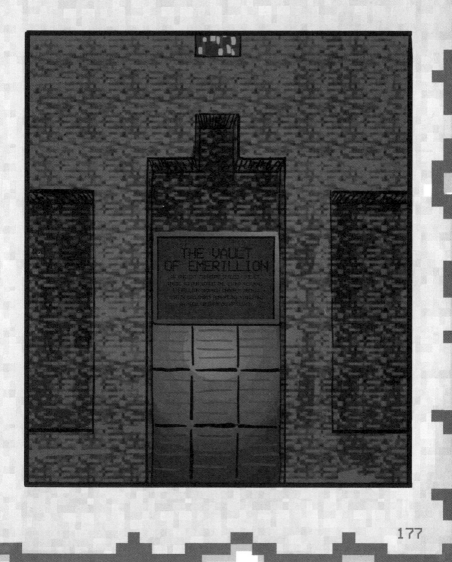

I could draw **another picture** of this sign, closer up so the words could easily be read, but I'm currently pressed for time. **I'll just write the words down here:**

The Vault of Emerillion
An ancient treasure sealed forever.
Until to our world the light returns.
Emerillion Grayson CharBot Aeonia
Martin Declan335 Robert303 XiangFang
Rainbow_Creeper Creepyguy101

"**Ancient treasure**," I said. "What's that about? And **who are all those people?**"

"**Builders**," Breeze said, approaching the vault. "This dungeon **isn't really a tomb** but one of the many **mazes** created, thousands of years ago, **to store things** that pose **a threat** to our world." She paused. "I think."

She had that **dark expression** again, **troubled.** She definitely knew something, and that wall had **made her think about it again.**

She had to know **something,** because she had **never** really talked about this kind of stuff before. Breeze, a history buff?! **That'd be a shocker.** The two go together **like me with bows.** Like Emerald with mud. Like Stump with anything that isn't a cookie or a cake.

178

"And how do you know all that?" I asked coolly.

"My father made me read so many books." Breeze forced a smile. "Let's continue, shall we?"

Oh, nice excuse there, I thought. *She's definitely hiding something. Now is the time to confront her.*

Another thought hit me. *(Yep. I totally forgot about confronting her.)*

"Wait. Here's a question for you, Ms. I-Not-Only-Know-How-to-Destroy-Monsters-in-the-Most-Efficient-Way-Possible-but-Am-Also-Secretly-a-Farmer-and-a-Librarian. If this dungeon contains **dangerous** stuff, things sealed away from the rest of the world in order to protect it . . . well, what things are we talking about, exactly? Like, **giant boss monsters,** or maybe **redstone war machines,** or cursed **legendary-tier** weapons—or possibly a giant boss monster wielding a legendary weapon, or possibly duel wielding two such weapons or riding an aforementioned war machine . . . ?"

My **silly** question failed to elicit any emotional response, only an answer:

"I believe this dungeon holds one of **the Eyeless One's creations,**" she said, "which fought in the final battle of **the Second Great War.** It can never be completely destroyed, only **subdued** for a time. And yes, I suppose that's what the humans might call **a boss monster.**"

179

"And what about this vault? How do we open it? And what does it contain?"

"I . . . well, um, I'm not really sure. I have a guess as to what might be in there, but it would take a long time to explain, and . . . anyway, I don't how it can be opened."

"Hurmm . . ."

*Why is she being like this? She really is **hiding** something from me! **Why?!** What does she know? Can I trust her? Man . . . what am I thinking? Of course I can trust her. **Anyway**, it's not a good time. The village is counting on us. Every second matters. **Twenty-five hundred emeralds. Let's go!***

I **studied** the vault again, looking around for some kind of activator. **Sadly,** the only thing being activated around here was **my curiosity.**

Interestingly, there was a horizontal shaft in the wall, **six blocks above the stone sign.** If you look at the previous drawing, you'll see it. It was obviously **the key to this puzzle:** bright flickering **blue light** emanated from within. *(What could that be?!)*

Of course, if this dungeon worked like the rest of the Overworld, it would have been easy to get up there. Just place **a dirt pillar** and you're done. But again, in a place like this, you have to **play by its rules.** So maybe that tunnel contained a button and we needed **a** Flying potion. Who knows . . .

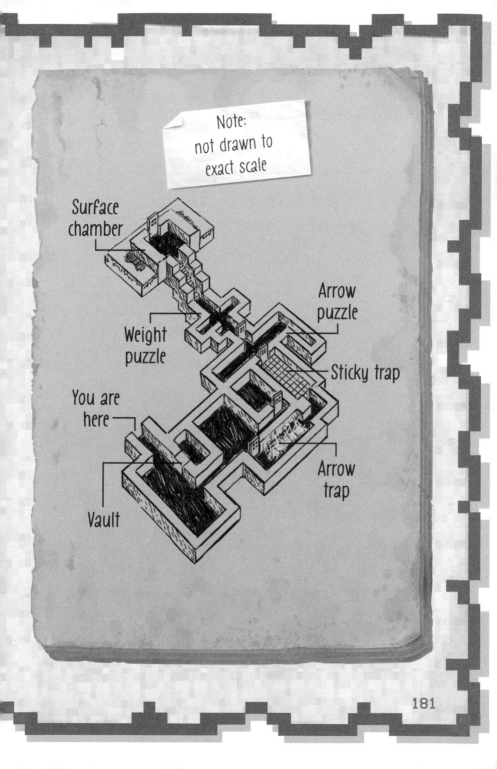

Note:
not drawn to
exact scale

Surface
chamber

Arrow
puzzle

Weight
puzzle

Sticky trap

You are
here

Arrow
trap

Vault

"Whatever," I said. "It doesn't matter, anyway. We're here to save Villagetown, right? So let's find more zombies, take down as many as we can, collect all the emeralds, find that moss, receive the blacksmith's quest reward, and trade for an advanced crafting table. Sound good?"

At this,
Breeze gave me the biggest hug.

Why? I'll never know. I asked her, but she just shrugged. Then she mentioned how hugging me was like hugging an iron golem because of my armor. And with that, we continued onward down the silent, empty halls.

The next hall had **nothing** but wooden doors. Each door led to a small room five blocks wide, five blocks deep, and three blocks high. Most of these rooms held **little of interest: bookshelves,** mostly, and every last book was in **some weird language** neither of us had ever seen. However, in one room we found **not only** bookshelves but also **one of those wolf people** browsing them.

Faolan
the Wizard

Note the potion on his belt, for quick access. The humans—or players—call that a "hotbar." Whatever that means.

He claimed to be not only **a wizard** but also **a scholar** of ancient history and connoisseur of fine potions. More important—far more important—he offered to **teach us a new ability,** magical in nature: **Analyze Monster.** With this, we could see not only **the names of creatures** but also:

1.) A green bar representing **their life force.**
2.) Any and **all status effects,** buffs, and debuffs currently affecting them.
3.) A visual indication of exactly **how much damage they receive** equal to the number of hearts lost.

Interesting, yeah? I consulted with Breeze, who thought it would be **a good idea** for both of us to learn this. **So we did.** It took all of **five minutes.**

Faolan mumbled the words of **some magic spell** and summoned **a transparent blue cube** with eyes. **An ice slime.** I knew it was an ice slime because that was the name **floating over it.**

ICE SLIME

"A golden icon is a **buff**," the wizard said. "A light-blue icon, a **debuff**. As you can see, this slime possesses **one of each**. That is because of the ice slime's cold affinity. It will take **increased damage** from any fire-based attack and less damage from cold. Indeed, with this knowledge at your disposal, you can easily exploit the weaknesses of monsters."

"Why are there **infinity symbols** underneath the icons?" Breeze asked.

"That's the **duration**," Faolan said. "Normally you would see numbers there, **counting down** by the second. But status effects provided by an affinity are **permanent.**"

As I listened, I noticed that the text floating over the ice slime **had disappeared.** "Huh? What happened? Why did it vanish?"

"This ability only works **when you're actively** looking at a monster. For your convenience. Otherwise, larger battles would become quite . . . **busy.**"

"**Oh.**" I stared at the slime again. Sure enough, **the overlay reappeared.** "Cool."

I turned to Breeze. "It's **almost like magic,** huh?! Just wait until we're back home! I'll start teaching everyone how to do this stuff! And we can **trade abilities** with the Legionnaires!"

"**Yeah.**" She was staring at the slime, seemingly lost in thought. She suddenly turned to the wizard. "**What happens if we train** this ability up more? What benefits will it provide?"

"**Additional information,**" the wizard said, "such as a monster's armor, stats, abilities, worn items, and, finally, at the highest level of skill, **their inventory.**"

"**Wow!** That could **really** come in handy," Breeze said. "**Thanks a lot.**"

"Glad I could be of help." **He paused.** It seemed like he wanted to ask something but was too shy to do so. "**Err,** what village do you two hail from, anyway?"

"**Villagetown,**" I said. "You know it?"

"I've heard of it. It has **a wall,** right? **Smart move.**" He looked **a little sad.** "I wish mine had had **the same. . . .**"

He told us he came not from a village but **a city.**

186

Diamondhome. The largest port city in the world. It was attacked two months ago—completely destroyed. Many people made it to the ships, though, and set sail. Where they headed, he didn't know. He had stayed behind, freezing zombies with blasts of ice until his magic was depleted. Forced to flee from his hometown, he returned a day later . . . to ruins.

"I'm sorry to hear that," Breeze said. "The same happened to my home village. Shadowbrook."

The wizard nodded gravely. "So I've heard. And not everyone managed to escape, correct? Some were even captured. . . . I'm so sorry. I can't imagine. . . ."

The two lowered their heads.

"Maybe you could come stay at Villagetown." Breeze finally said.

(I was going to suggest that, actually, but didn't want to interrupt their moment of silence. Gentleswordsman, remember?)

At her suggestion, the wizard's cheeks turned a little red. "Oh, I don't know," he said. "Are you sure they wouldn't mind taking in someone like me? My magic isn't even all that strong yet. I'm still just a neophyte, really. . . ."

"Hey, I'm sure the people of Villagetown would be more than happy to have an actual wizard around," I said. "Isn't that right, Breeze?"

"Definitely."

Faolan nodded. "Hmm. Very well. I shall go there soon."

"Well, you're more than welcome to come along with us," Breeze said.

"That's right," I said. "We're heading back as soon as we finish up with this quest we're on."

He shook his head. "I'm afraid I must decline. I still have much research to do. The libraries here hold a vast wealth of knowledge lost through the ages. But I shall make my way there as soon as I'm finished."

"Great. Hope to see you around. Oh, sorry. I'm Breeze, and this is—"

"Runt."

So yeah, long story short, we picked up a new ability and recruited Villagetown's first wizard. Neophyte or not, he'll be a welcome addition. (In other news, I learned that "neophyte" is basically the polite version of "noob.")

Oh! Breeze wants me to include one more thing. Players talk about buffs and debuffs to describe the effects of spells. Buffs are temporary magical effects with a certain duration. For example, a golden apple provides two buffs upon being eaten: Absorption I for two minutes and Regeneration II for five seconds. A debuff is the opposite. It's a negative effect that you want to avoid at all costs, like those slowness arrows from earlier. Pretty simple, right?

And that concludes our lesson for the day. Please make sure to leave an enchanted apple on my desk before you leave. Class dismissed!

The twelfth update for today. And **what an update** it is! You're **not going to believe** what happened. In fact, I'm so pumped up after what just happened, **I'm shaking,** bouncing around, like a slime wearing boots **enchanted with Leaping II.**

Well, no, that doesn't make a lot of sense, really, because boots would look ridiculous on a slime—especially a baby one. **Here's the real problem:**

Slimes can't wear boots bro

Yes they can this is my diary and slimes can wear boots if they want to

*Note: The above should have had punctuation like commas and exclamation points. That isn't a mistake, however—oh no. I purposefully left them out to achieve a kind of **rushed feeling,** like a little villager kid writing about his first time eating a slice of enchanted cake: DUDE WOW THAT CAKE = AMAZING EPIC LEGENDARY TIER 10/10 WOULD EAT AGAIN #1 FOOD ITEM IN THE OVERWORLD!!!*

Okay, so slimes can't wear boots. **Very well.** So what about a spider, **then?** But spiders have **eight legs** . . . so it would need to enchant like **four different pairs** just to get the effect of one enchantment—and honestly, spiders might climb cacti and do a lot of other silly things, but not even the **noobiest** spider would enchant multiple pairs of boots like that!

Yeah well at least spiders can wear boots, okay???

They can, okay???

Okay???

OKAY NEVER MIND
PLEASE FORGIVE ME I'M SORRY!!!

Sorry. I got a little carried away there.

Okay, so anyway, **here's what happened** just now. We were wandering the halls again and heard **a shout,** followed by **an eerie howl** and **another shout.**

"Sounds like they're not too far away," Breeze said, meaning **whoever had left those horses tied up** outside earlier. "**C'mon!**" She began sprinting down the hall.

"Hey! **Wait up!** This armor reduces my movement speed, remember?!"

Bedrock walls **blurred past,** along with torches and pillars and the occasional item, **the remains of some monster.** The **shouting** and **howling** grew **louder.** And, upon turning one last corner, we **stopped completely** in our tracks. The hall merged with another **massive room,** and in the center were **two people locked in combat with three wolves.** One person was wielding a large emerald sword and wearing a near-complete suit of leather armor. He was missing the helmet, and we could see **a wave of spiked yellow hair.** The other person was in **a suit of obsidian** and wielded a bright red ax in each hand.

As for the wolves, well, I'd never really seen **wolves like that** before.

Now was a good time to test Analyze Monster. I almost felt like a wizard.

FELHOUND

25:37   25:37

I'd read about **felhounds** before. They're nothing more than **a scarier version** of wolves. Strangely, I thought I'd read that they didn't exist in the Overworld. **At any rate,** each felhound was affected by **two different buffs.** The gray shield was **Stoneskin,** which provides an armor bonus of five per power level. The little **II** in the bottom right-hand corner meant **its power level was two.** The golden rabbit's foot was **Haste I,** which increased movement speed and attack speed **by 25%.** After Breeze fired a weakness arrow at the wolf I was focusing on, a third icon appeared. **A broken sword.** That was the Weakness I debuff, which reduces attack damage by four.

The young man with yellow *(almost orange)* hair glanced over his shoulder. "**Nice!** We could **really use some** help right about now!"

Without a word, **I charged in** between the two strangers. All three felhounds **immediately focused** on me. I'm not sure if it was **the giant owl** on my shield or what, but they just wouldn't stop **attacking me.** The giant owl often thwarted their efforts with a **clang.** How **humiliating** for them, right?

Meanwhile, Breeze **unleashed more arrows,** and the other two swung their weapons **frantically,** like they were mining the Overworld's **last diamond vein.** I'll skip all the details, but basically

felhounds fell one by one in a flurry of arrows and ax swings. *(Along with some really graceful sword work from yours truly, I might add. Oh, and that guy with yellow hair.)*

After the battle, the **obsidian-clad** warrior bent down, collecting the **emeralds** the wolves had dropped. His swordsman friend turned toward Breeze:

"**Thanks,**" he said. "That would've taken **a lot** longer without you two."

"It took long enough as it is," I said. "So, **um,** are dungeon monsters normally this tough?"

He shook his head. "**Not really.** At least not around here. Actually, I'm not sure what those felhounds were doing here. You usually won't find them in **low-level** dungeons like this. And **those buffs!** Why did they have Stoneskin and Haste? **So weird . . .**"

Breeze moved up to **join us,** slinging her bow across her shoulder. "They could have been **summoned.**"

The swordsman shrugged. "**It's possible.** Not sure why someone would do that, though. . . . I mean, **griefing** used to be a thing back when this was just a game, but now . . ."

At this point, I noticed that the other person, the one in obsidian armor, **was standing still.** Many emeralds were still scattered before him. He hadn't picked them up and wasn't attempting to. In fact, he wasn't moving at all. It was as if he'd been **frozen.**

Well, that's odd, I thought. *What's his problem? He's been like that ever since Breeze and I started talking. . . .*

As **I stared** at this person's back, the usual information appeared above him. **The name. The life bar.** It seemed Analyze Monster worked on people as well. **It took a second** for my mind to process this person's name. **My mind just couldn't accept what I was seeing.**

No. **No, no.**
N-n-nnnnnoooooh!

But the name was there, **real,** and it was spelled correctly.

And it was a weird enough name to possibly be **unique** in all of the Overworld. And it was the name of someone I'd known, someone **I'd** hated, someone **I'd never** expected to see again. . . .

SATURDAY—UPDATE XIV

Pebble. *Pebble!*
It was really Pebble!

When he **turned around,** I couldn't believe my eyes. Not only was he **alive** but also he was **in a dungeon** with some human and equipped with **some pretty amazing stuff.** *(Are those redsteel axes I see?!)*

PEBBLE

"**Wow!**" he said. "What are you two doing here?"

I approached him, **desperately** searching for words.

"I, **uh** . . . well, we, **um** . . ."

The human, whose name was simply **S**, flashed **a wry grin.**

"I take it you three **know** one another."

"We do," Breeze said, eyeing Pebble **coldly.** "Unfortunately."

I glared at him as well. "Looks like the Overworld has been **treating you well.** Let me guess. You're no longer the Pebble you used to be. You're a **changed** villager now."

"As a matter of fact, **I am.**"

S was still **grinning** when he turned to our former **bully.** "Don't tell me **he's** the one you . . ."

"**He is,**" Pebble said.

"So you told him?" I asked, still glaring.

"**Of course** I told him," Pebble said. "I tried blowing up the wall, **tried blowing you up,** and I don't even know why. I could apologize **a million times.** It still wouldn't make me feel any better about it. I . . ."

"**Yeah?!** Well, maybe you should have—"

Breeze **shouted over me.** "You have **a lot of explaining** to do! You nearly—"

I shouted **over her,** and we both began shouting even louder and at the same time.

"People don't just randomly go **crazy** like—"

"Enough!!!"

That shout came from **S,** and it sounded louder than a TNT blast. **We fell silent** and continued to **glare** at Pebble while S continued.

"**Listen.** He told me the full story, every little detail, and I personally believe he was under the effect of **Confusion III.** It's **a strong debuff** that clouds your judgment. It can even make you believe friends are enemies. The third-level variant can last for **entire days.** Instead of being angry, you should take it up with **the Eyeless One.**"

"Last I heard," Breeze said, "he's been **rather busy** for the past several months."

"**That's right,**" I said. "You're telling us **the Eyeless One** cast a Confusion spell from **a million blocks** away?"

S shook his head. "**It's not like that.** As far as I know, there is no spell that can inflict Confusion III—only **a potion.** It's typically used for crafting **a really powerful arrow.**"

When S said this, I recalled **the battles** that took place in our village. Pebble was always pretty reckless; that was **his style.** He wasn't afraid to take damage, and as a result, he often **chugged healing potions** in the middle of combat. Had someone really **swapped** one of his healing potions for a potion of **Confusion III?**

As if reading my mind, S suggested **this theory** as well. But I **didn't believe it.** Didn't want to. **I wanted to be angry** at Pebble.

I know that's **immature**. If he really had been **brainwashed**, it meant Pebble **wasn't such a bad guy** after all. As much as I didn't like it, this possibility had to be considered. . . .

"Why would someone do that?" I asked.

"More important," Breeze said, "**who** did it?"

"I think these are questions we should deal with later," Pebble said **glumly.**

S nodded. "**He's right.** The monsters around here are going to **respawn** any minute now. Let's move, people."

Pebble was now but a single block away.

"**I'm really sorry,**" he said. "**Really.** I'll do anything to make it up. **A million** emeralds. Anything. Can we just leave all that behind?"

Psh!
As if!

So he tries blowing me up with TNT
then thinks all it takes to make it right is a few apologies?!

I wanted to **shout at him** some more, tell him everything I'd been **bottling up** inside like **a potion of Rage XI,** then leave with Breeze right then and there. But **I had to be better than that,** didn't I? I was bitter about what had happened, but my feelings weren't the most important thing in the world. If **working with** Pebble increased the odds of **Villagetown's survival** by even the slightest bit, how could I refuse?

The past is the past. What was it that Kolb once said? Face the problems you've not yet had? **I extended a hand.**

"**Thank you,**" Pebble said, while giving me the strongest handshake of all time. "You won't regret this. And . . . do you mind telling me **what you guys are doing** here?"

"**Um,** basically . . ."

I told him everything regarding our mission, **summarized:** how Kolb wanted me to retrieve **an aeon forge,** how I needed **twenty-five hundred emeralds,** and how some random blacksmith had sent me on a quest for a handful of so-called *glowmoss.*

"Glowmoss? **The boss drops that,**" S said. "You won't find it anywhere else. C'mon. He's **just past those doors.**"

As S took the lead, Pebble spoke to me **in a low tone:** "Don't worry; this guy really knows what he's doing. I think he might know **everything.** He's already taught me so much. . . ."

And suddenly, after exchanging **uneasy glances** with Breeze, I found myself walking down another corridor with *(I can't believe I'm writing this)* **Pebble the Exile** to my left. Ahead of us, the human named S walked in a casual way, as **confident** as he was **mysterious.**

He stopped before
a pair of **massive** doors
and turned around.

"He's wrong, you know.
I don't know everything. I
suppose that's what drives
me to keep exploring this
insane world. . . ."

"That, and a
promise. . . . Where are
you, Emerillion . . . ?"

If you look at the **previous drawing,** you'll notice that the doors behind S were **five blocks tall.** That was **no embellishment.** I go for **accuracy,** remember. No, those doors actually were five blocks tall, and they led to an **enormous** chamber. With **an enormous giant zombie.** He was sitting on a golden throne on the other side of the room.

"That's the boss," S said. "Obviously."

"Why is he just sitting there like that?" Breeze asked.

"That's normal," Pebble said. "Most of the bosses wait for you to engage. At least the lower-level ones."

"How many bosses have you fought already?" I asked, somewhat surprised and more than a little curious.

"Three. No, wait." He turned to S. "Does that Skull Lord count?"

"Nah. Their scripting is pretty complex, but I'd classify them as minibosses. Quest monsters, really."

Scripting? Quest monster? Hurgg . . .
I was totally lost. And it sounded like Pebble
had been on quite the adventure.
Yeah, I was jealous.

S stepped forward. "Looks like he's also got Stoneskin II and Haste I. Hmmmmm. You know, there's an item that gives those two buffs. And with a duration of thirty minutes, no less. What's it called again? Diamond wafer? Yeah. First the felhounds, and now this . . . very strange."

It was extremely strange. If what S said was true, someone was trying to hinder us. Pebble said it best:

"I don't like this, guys. Just have a funny feeling. . . . Maybe we should leave."

"We **really need** that crystal," S said, and glanced at Breeze and myself. "We're on a quest to **light a beacon** in the mountains to the southwest. We need the enchanted **voidcrystal** this guy drops."

"**Ohh,**" I said, pretending to understand.

Breeze drew her bow. "So **what's the plan,** then?"

S smiled again. "**Simple.** We just wait here until his buffs wear off."

What a great idea, I thought, and peered at the boss from afar to see **how long** we had to wait.

A chill hit me as I did, a horrible realization.

23:53—I hadn't really made the connection until seeing this number.

"If the duration was originally **thirty minutes,**" I said, "**then the person behind all this was in this room** just six minutes ago, right?"

S shrugged. "**I guess so.** But there's no one else here."

The four of us **scanned** the room. Especially Pebble. He looked positively **spooked.** But then, he'd looked like that **ever since I first saw him** today. He was like a **completely** different person. Before he was **all bravado,** all the time. Now he gave off **a kind of doubt.** What had made him this way? His time in the Overworld must have been **quite different** from mine.

"Guess we'll just **have to wait** and find out what this is all about," he said.

And so, after **slowly approaching** the center of the room— *still twenty blocks from the giant zombie*—we waited. For the **looooongest** several minutes, we waited. Silent. **Glancing around. Idle chatter.** I rearranged my inventory. Well, that potion would go better there. . . .

Until finally . . .
precisely five minutes and thirty-seven seconds later . . .

an exact time calculated by observing the duration of the boss monster's buffs . . . Breeze gave **a slight gasp.** She was looking up and far away, near one corner of the ceiling. **I followed her gaze** to a most unbelievable sight. **A potion.**

Mysteriously, it was **floating** fifteen or so blocks above the obsidian floor, **slowly sailing** toward the boss—turning slightly, bobbing up and down—**as though dancing** in the air. . . .

It was **so enchanted** that it had a faint glow, like violet torchlight. **Its destination** was, of course, the zombie's right hand. The potion looked so tiny in that **block-sized fist,** and **the zombie didn't chug,** oh no. It was more like **a little sip.** To the gasps of three villagers and a human, **a third icon** appeared next to the first two. **A golden heart.** That was **Regeneration V,** an **extremely strong** healing buff. Its duration: **three minutes.**

"This is **too weird,**" S said.

Again, Pebble said it best: "S? **Let's get outta here.**"

Suddenly, I heard a faint **crackling** sound from behind me. I glanced over my shoulder. The hallway leading out was now **sealed with a wall of ice,** ice that shimmered almost like it was enchanted.

Shrill laughter resounded from overhead. Familiar laughter. A laugh I hadn't heard in quite some time. We slowly turned around.

Now, perched on top of the throne, was an old man in a deep red robe. Red hat. Black sunglasses. Bushy white beard. It was the same person I'd bumped into earlier in Owl's Reach who had matched Stump's description of a suspicious character named Cocoa Witherbean.

But now, upon hearing that laugh, I knew that this person was none other than . . .

It was the same villager who had **betrayed** us so long ago. Even with his name hovering over his head, **it was hard to accept.** This was a person known for being totally clueless—**incapable of basic combat,** let alone **magic.** But the person now standing before us could apparently **fly, turn invisible,** and **conjure walls of ice. . . .**

"You **seem so surprised,**" he called out. His shrill voice was unnaturally loud. "**So was I,** upon seeing **you three** show up here **together.**" He hopped up and down **like a giddy child.** "Oh, isn't it **wonderful?!** Here you are, **Villagetown's very best,** and I'm going to **erase all of you** in one go!"

"I take it **you know this guy,**" S muttered to Pebble.

"Yeah."

"Might've been good to let me know **you were being hunted** by a crazy old wizard."

"He wasn't a wizard then. **Just some fool.**"

"**Fool?!**" That was Urf. "If anyone's a fool," he shouted, "it's her! She—"

Breeze **fired an arrow with unequaled** speed. I'd never seen an arrow fly so fast or with such **perfect** aim. **A critical hit.** An arrow sticking out of Urf's **forehead.** At least, that's what would have happened, had he not instantly **blinked away**—*zip!*—like **an enderman.** The arrow struck obsidian instead.

Now Urf was roughly ten blocks away from his original location, **hovering in the air.** "Care to try that ag—"

Breeze **didn't hesitate.** Her second arrow flew **as true** as the first. But Urf was **faster still.** Again he blinked away. Urf appeared on top of **the giant zombie's head.**

"**Are you done?** I can do this all day, m'lady."

I've seen Breeze get **angry** before, but nothing matched her expression right then as she lowered her bow. It was **pointless** to continue. She knew that. She was only wasting arrows.

"Why are you doing this?" Pebble shouted. "**We never did anything to you!**"

"**Wrong!**" Ghostly flames erupted around Urf. "You **humiliated** me! You **laughed** behind my back! And then you **replaced** me! Me . . . replaced by a human!"

The flames crackled and **grew brighter.** "Of course, I was going to use my magic on you while you were dealing with **Nethy** here, but I've come up with a much better idea. It's the best way to **end this little story.**" He smiled. "It's true, I didn't know anything before. However, **my master** taught me well. . . ."

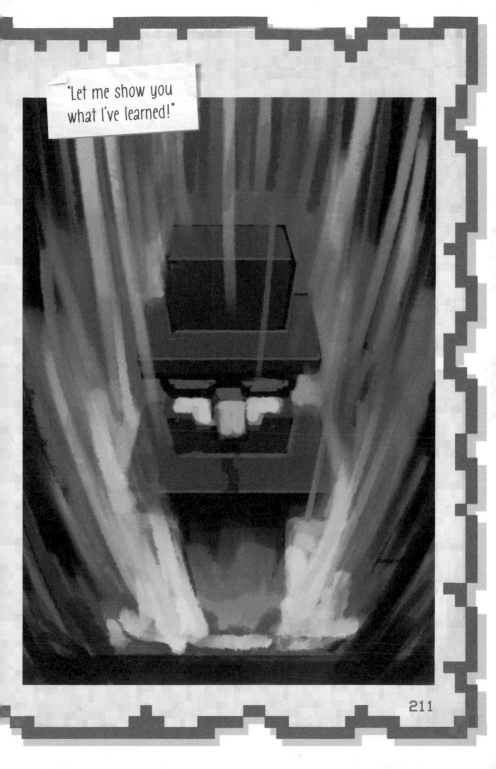

211

Shrouded in flame, Urf **closed his eyes** and began mumbling, like Faolan had when **summoning** the ice slime. Then he vanished in a flash of **brilliant orange light. No,** not quite. He sank downward, **into the zombie,** in a fraction of a second.

Still seated upon the massive throne, the zombie **jerked violently,** then **closed his eyes** and fell **completely still.** Thankfully, **S the All-Knowing** explained what had just happened: "I think he just cast **Soulshift.** It lets you **control a monster** by occupying its body. It isn't **supposed** to work on bosses, though. . . ."

I sighed.

So Urf was now **in control of a boss monster,** one that could **easily** beat an iron golem at arm wrestling. You know, it's just **not** my lucky day.

The huge zombie **opened his eyes.** Then he **slowly** rose, glanced down at himself and laughed: *hurhh, hurhh, hurhh.* . . . And when he spoke—even though his voice was **deep** and sounded nothing like Urf's voice—there was no doubt in my mind that it really was the old man.

"You might be wondering **how** I'm capable of this," he said. "My powers were increased by **the master** . . . the **kind** master. So kind is he, in fact, that he asked me to **spare your lives** if you would only **kneel before me.** But no, I won't give you that chance. I may have failed to get rid of you **before,** but **I won't fail now.** . . ."

212

As he spoke, I recalled how Stump had seen Urf in Villagetown. He'd been there the whole time, **spying** on us. Doing who knows what. Disguised as **Cocoa Witherbean.**

If S was **right** about that potion, Urf was probably the one behind it. It's a simple task, **renaming a potion.** All you really need is an anvil. I could picture it so clearly now. Urf changed the potion's name, turned **invisible,** crept into Pebble's house while he was sleeping, and slipped the potion into Pebble's inventory. And Pebble, pushed so hard during training, had been too tired to notice the potion's different color. . . .

Thinking about this, **I flew into a rage.** I shouldn't have charged in, **I know.** I should have **waited** for S to give us some command. To be honest, I barely even remember this moment. It was just a blur. I **shouted** something, and before I knew it, I was standing **before the giant zombie** possessed by a **completely** deranged old man.

I swung my diamond sword at ~~Nethersoul~~ **Boss Urf.** The blade left a crescent in its wake, and **hearts appeared**, indicating the damage dealt—one. A single point. **That is to say, practically nothing.**

Since **Stoneskin II** increased Urf's armor **by ten,** on top of whatever protection the boss monster had naturally, attacking him was like trying to mine obsidian with **a beetroot.**

And he had **Regeneration V . . .** so what little life I'd taken was **immediately** restored. There was, of course, one more problem. **Laughing** at my pitiful display, he struck me with one of his **furnace-sized** fists. Despite the **Surefooted enchantment** on my cloak, I **flew back ten blocks** and landed on my back near the others. I lost three hearts. I'd forgotten to raise my shield. **I was shocked, okay?** It isn't every day you see a **former noob** directly controlling a giant.

Boss Urf once again **laughed** creepily.

"I suppose we shall see who's **the nooblord** now." And he began lumbering forward.

"He can't cast spells right now," S said. "When **Soulshifting,** you only have access to **the monster's abilities,** and **Nethersoul** has none. Only **high** melee damage." As Breeze **helped me up,** S turned to me. "We need someone to **mitigate that damage.**"

I looked at him suspiciously. "**Mitigate . . .**"

"We need you **to tank,**" Pebble said. "We didn't bring **shields.** Didn't think we'd need any."

"**Oh.**"

I glanced at the approaching boss. **Again:** furnace-sized fists. Then I shrugged.

"Yeah. Sure. No problem."

Breeze handed me two potions: Stoneskin I and Regeneration II. The latter had an extended duration. Eight minutes. She gave me a hug and said, "Come back with your life bar intact, okay?"

Then she ~~kis~~

No, I can't write about that in here! I'm a warrior, got it?! I have no time for mushy stuff! Okay, fine! She kissed me on the cheek! That's not so weird, though, right? I mean, I heard about this one village where kissing another person on the cheek is totally normal, like a handshake! So it must have been like that in her old village! Yeah! That must be it!

Well, for some reason, I felt more courageous. Could it be that she's secretly a wizard whose kisses give some kind of buff? Whatever it was, it worked. I charged back in. Pebble and S were right there behind me.

"We'll be on either side of you," S said. "If he goes for one of us, make sure to move over and intercept his attack."

With Boss Urf now towering before us, I raised my shield. *Intercept. Mitigate.* S made tanking sound so fancy, you know? But there's absolutely nothing fancy about being pummeled by a zombie who most likely wrestles ender dragons in his spare time. Oh well. At least with my shield I was only knocked back half a block.

As my shield **absorbed** blow after blow, the amount of damage Pebble, S, and Breeze put out was **simply incredible.** Pebble's axes were **redsteel.** Although their individual attack speed was slow, an ax has **higher damage** than a sword. Duel wielding them almost seemed **unfair.** Breeze cycled between normal arrows and the Weakness variety, using Weakness only when **the debuff** was about to **wear off.** On top of that, she threw a **splash healing potion** at my feet the few times I took damage.

S used a sword ability called **Overblade.** It was **the coolest** thing I'd ever seen. With a loud battle cry, he jumped into the air—**sword raised over his head**—and slammed down into Urf with **such force** that Urf **bent over backward in pain.**

He looked **so ridiculous.**
<u>Urf, I mean.</u>

Twenty-five damage—or **twelve and a half** hearts—with **a single strike!** It was **shocking.** To give you an idea, my maximum health is **twenty-two**, or **eleven hearts.** Even so, Urf's life

218

bar only **shrank slightly**—maybe **10%.** I wasn't sure if that was the monster's life or Urf's, or **a combination of the two.** Either way, he was **nearly indestructible.**

And even though S took away a **significant chunk** of Urf's life, without his Overblade ability, Urf's **regeneration** equaled our damage output. With every one of our attacks, his health bar went down ever so slightly, only to **bounce right back up again.** At some point, Urf actually **stopped attacking** and **laughed.**

"You call that **damage?** You won't even get me to half! This is **so much fun.** I—"

The zombie/wizard/noob **cried out in pain** and bent backward again as S landed another **Overblade**—then he did it **again** before he even landed.

Having lost roughly **30% of his health,** the sound Urf made could only be described as **pitiful.** Naturally, I expected S to follow up with **a fourth** Overblade, because why wouldn't he?! But he went back to **standard-issue** sword swings, the kind we practiced in class. I looked at him **in despair.**

"What are you doing?! **Keep using that jump move!**"

"I can't," he said. "It's on **cooldown.**"

"**Cooldown?**"

"**Time limitation,**" Pebble said. "He can only use it **three times** per day."

S grinned. "I would be **overpowered** if I could just **spam** it over and over like that, right?"

". . ."

It gets **worse. My shield broke** upon blocking Urf's next attack. With my left hand, I **drew my obsidian sword** and joined Pebble and S in swinging away **frantically.**

"**Keep at it,**" S said. "Once that Regeneration buff **wears off,** he'll stop out-healing us, and **it's over** for him! **We're almost there! Fifty-five seconds!**"

Urf offered no response.

*Hhmm. What's this? He's not **playing around** anymore? Seems like he's a little **worried.***

Now forced to **block** Urf's attacks **with my swords,** I wasn't knocked back very far but still took considerable damage. Breeze threw **splash healing potions** to keep our health up. Our life bars were all somewhere around **50%.** Sometimes, I just couldn't move **fast enough.** We were never going to make it until his Regeneration **ran out.**

53, 52, 51 . . .

Each second felt **so** long. Then, all of a sudden, the arrows stopped. **Breeze was out.** Drawing her swords, she joined us in **the heat of combat,** a blur of emerald and diamond. Then I remembered something—the arrow with the **obsidian point** and the **creepy face**. I had **no idea** what it did. Normally you can see an item's **stats,** but that arrow's properties had been **masked somehow.** Still, by the looks of it, that arrow did **something bad.** And hitting Urf with something bad seemed to be our only shot, seeing as **he was going berserk.**

Blocking another fist with my swords, I turned to Breeze and **handed her** the projectile.

"I'm not sure what this does, **but . . ."**

The look on her face indicated that this arrow did a lot. *(Her face then indicated that I was an elite noob for not telling her about it earlier.)*

"Hurgggggaaaaaaaa!!"

Pebble flew past us. He'd glanced over—to see what I was talking about—allowing Urf to catch him off guard.

"Uwwwaaaaaaaaaaaaaaaaaaaa!!"

And there went S.

SATURDAY— UPDATE XVIII

There was no **long and detailed discussion** about what the arrow did. Breeze took it and **fired**. Striking Urf **square in the chest**, the arrow didn't do all that much damage *(only three)*, but the **debuff** it *inflicted* . . . it was **such a joyous sight**.

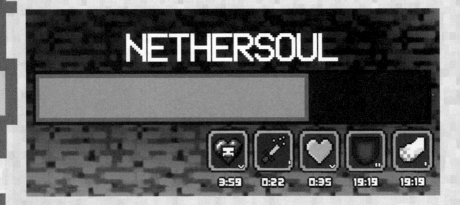

The skull with the gray heart was **Wither**—a **damage-over-time**, or DoT, debuff—**Wither V,** in fact. In this case, Wither V was strong enough to **counteract** Urf's regeneration, and in thirty-five seconds, when his Regeneration wore off . . .

"**Where'd you get that?!**" Urf howled. "I can't . . . **I won't** . . ." Like an enormous **baby throwing a tantrum,** he swung wildly and randomly at all of us. "**I'll take all of you with me!**"

222

"Stay together!" Breeze shouted over the roars. "The splash doesn't reach very far!"

We drew closer to one another, and she threw a potion at the ground. The splash hit everyone, healing us somewhat. Then we immediately split up again so he couldn't strike all of us at once.

"You ruined everything!" Urf shrieked.

He began focusing on Pebble, who couldn't do anything but hold up his axes in defense.

"You were supposed to deal with him! You were supposed to join us! You drank that potion! I saw you!"

Urf's left arm swung through the air like a tree trunk, and a fist slammed into Pebble.

"Why—"

The right arm this time.

"Didn't—"

The left again.

"It—"

Finally, both fists came crashing down, and sparks flew from Pebble's axes as Urf sputtered in rage.

"Work?!"

At the end of this furious assault, above Pebble was a mostly red life bar with just a sliver of green. . . .

"Get back!" I shouted. When he didn't, I pushed him aside and stared up into the wizard's glowing red eyes.

"So it was you! You made him crazy!"

"I did! And I'll do much worse! Your little village will come to an end! If—"

From somewhere not too close, I heard a scream. Breeze. She was now behind Urf, tearing into him, her swords, like her hair, a flash of brilliant green and blue. Urf whirled around in a total frenzy. She never even blocked, trying to match his damage output. But there was no way she could. Even without his regeneration, he was still at 35% with an ample boost to his armor and attack speed. Looking back, we should have kept our distance and let the Wither debuff wear him down further. But everything's so clear in hindsight.

Breeze! No!

I sprinted around Urf, toward her, each second an eternity, and each millisecond accompanied by a beat of my heart, the swing of a weapon, the right-to-left movement of green bars, a shout, or the ring of sharpened emerald through hard, withered flesh.

I was only five blocks away, and saw that her health was less than Pebble's. A thin green line. Three blocks. She looked up. So slow. Time had stopped. She was looking up. *What's she looking at? Move.*

Get to her. And it seemed like forever until I saw **the shadow,** like that of a cobblestone pillar, quickly moving toward her.

A fist
slammed down.

When the smoke finally **cleared**, all that remained were **scattered items** on the ground, including **two swords** and a pair of black leather boots. All thought **left me. All feeling.** I took a single step forward, **silent.** All four of us stared at **the pile** on the ground without saying a word. **Even Urf.** His expression was almost one of **regret**, if a zombie **could** display such an emotion. But soon, **a deep laugh was welling**

up inside him, which he let escape—at first **slowly** but then **stronger and stronger.** All I can remember here was **three loud battle cries,** swords flashing before me, another sword to my right, axes to my left, and Urf staggering back **again and again.** Only later did I realize **that I was wielding her swords.** I must have picked them up. . . . Breeze had taken him **to 25%,** and we took him **to 7%,** but it **wasn't enough.** He fought back just as crazily, and **we struggled even more** without Breeze and her potions. In the end, he **cornered** us. Backs pressed against the wall, each of us was one hit away from **going out just like—**

Why didn't she dodge . . . ?

I failed her. Didn't make it to her in time.

No, she can't be gone! It's some kind of trick! It has to be!

"This is **so crazy,**" S muttered. "What's happening? Why is an **NPC** doing this?!"

"**Runt,**" Pebble said, "I . . . **I'm sorry** for being such a jerk to you before. I don't know what was wrong with me."

"Will you guys **stop that?!**" S hissed. "**Focus!** We need a plan!"

"We can **charge** in," Pebble whispered. "**Flank him.** He'll probably take us out, but . . . **we should do it for Breeze.**"

"**For Breeze!**" I said.

I still **refused** to believe she was gone. There had to be **some other** explanation. She couldn't . . .

"It's a pity, what happened to her," Urf called out.

He was some distance from us, where **he'd been waiting. The Wither** had worn off by now.

"But you should feel **relieved** to know that you will be joining her very soon." A **hideous** smile appeared across his equally hideous face.

"I'm afraid this is the end."

"It is the end . . . **for you!**"

Startled by the voice, the three of us looked around. **It was her voice.** I saw a slight figure appear behind him. **It was her.** As if she could have been **beaten** by a noob like Urf!

Barefoot and **wielding a greatsword,** she was already in the air before he began to turn around. She used **Quietus**—an ability that only works a monster on **who isn't facing you.** The damage it deals is **proportional** to how injured the monster is. With a zombified Urf already **in the red zone,** this ultimate ability **finished him in one go.**

NETHERSOUL

The red flashes of his life bar gave way to **nothing but an empty border.** He **staggered** forward, looking at Breeze, who'd landed a safe distance from him. Then, **trembling with rage,** he bent his head upward and howled.

'Immmmmmmmmmmmmmmm— p—p—posssssssssible!!!'

His scream **ended** abruptly; his body **pulsed** bright red, then **flashed,** a slow strobe that illuminated the entire room. With each strobe was a crackling sound like static. At last, **the monster** Urf had possessed crumbled into countless **bright red cubes,** which quickly disintegrated, until all that remained was a **pile of items**—including **a small gray item chest.**

From nowhere and everywhere came **a woman's voice,** as **cold** and **emotionless** as an iron golem's:

The dungeon Tomb of the Forgotten King has been cleared. All traps and monster spawners have been deactivated. Additionally, any remaining hostile monsters have been purged. Please note, this dungeon will reset in exactly one week. . . .

She said some other stuff, but I can't remember the rest.

"That's **the announcer,**" S said. "It's part of a **mod.** Never mind. It'd take too long to . . ."

I can't recall what else he said, either, because **I wasn't paying attention** anymore. Not to him, anyway, and not even to the treasure pile. The **real treasure** was right in front of me.

Well, maybe a
little to my left.

Putting away her **massive sword,** Breeze ran up and gave **me the biggest hug.** Then **Pebble** gave me **a hug,** followed by S giving Pebble a hug. Breeze and Pebble **almost** hugged but there was **awkwardness** there because of the whole **he-used-to-be-a-bad-guy** thing. Finally, we **broke out laughing** and had a group hug. I just used the word "**hug**" a lot, but what do you expect—we were just **happy to still be alive,** okay?!

"Will you **please** use a healing potion?" I said to Breeze, glancing at her life bar again. "With your health **that low,** I'm afraid to even breathe!"

So you want to know **how Breeze survived.** You also want to know **why** she was **barefoot** and wielding **a greatsword.** Well, dear diary, **don't you worry.** I asked for you. Right after she used up the rest of the splash healing potions on everyone. (We practically bathed in the stuff.)

She explained how she'd **sidestepped** Urf's attack at the very last moment and used an ability called **Smoke Bomb.** It creates **a large smoke cloud** around you, and you **turn invisible** for a short time. To make the illusion of her demise more convincing, she **threw down** her **swords** and the **emeralds** she'd collected, then unequipped her **boots** and **accessories.**

"**Honestly,** I'm surprised I didn't realize that," S said. "That was way too much smoke, and there should have been some **experience orbs.**" He gave her an **approving** nod. "**Nice move,** I have to say. A rather unconventional use of **Smoke Bomb** but **effective** nonetheless."

"Yet **another** ability," I said. "So you have been holding out on me! **Why all the secrecy, huh?!**"

"**You'll learn more,**" she said. "As soon as we get back."

"And what about **that sword?**" I asked. "Where'd you get that?"

"My father **gave it to me** just before I left. Said I should always carry a backup."

Again, the tone of her voice indicated she was **hiding something.** I narrowed my eyes. Something was definitely **going on** here. Some kind of **secret.** I was almost certain. What was it?!

Luckily for her, Pebble—after glancing around **superstitiously** again—totally changed the subject.

"Hey. Guys. **What happened to Urf?**"

"Good question," S said. "If the monster you've Soulshifted into is **defeated,** you'll **reappear** nearby. But it seems like he really is gone. Those are **his items. Besides that chest, I mean.**"

"We'd better not **take any chances,**" Pebble said. He still had that fearful look. "Let's **grab the loot** and **bounce.**"

Everyone turned to **the pile.** Normally, the boss would have **only dropped that chest.** The items lying around it had **belonged to Urf.** There were books on **ancient history.** Books on **magic, monsters,** and **dungeons.** That's what S said, anyway. Like those books we'd seen earlier, they were all written in **unknown languages.** *(By the way, knowing a language is an ability. There are many: Common Tongue, Ancient Tongue, Enderscript, etc.)*

We sifted through countless **stacks of blank paper, low-level potions,** and monster parts used in brewing like **spider eyes** and **bat wings.**

Of course, his worn items were also there. While his hat, sunglasses, and shoes had no **enchantments,** his robe—excuse me, **his gown**—had **two.**

234

NETHERFORGED GOWN

CLOTHING
CONTROLLER I
FLAMEWEAVER I

"I should have known," S said. "All Nethermancers, upon first starting out, are given such a gown. Those enchantments boost fire and summoning magic, which a Nethermancer specializes in."

So Urf was a type of wizard known as a Nethermancer. Wielding magical fire. Inflicting hideous plagues. Summoning undead minions and controlling them like slaves.

Urf had decided to enter Nethersoul's body, and that was a major error on his part. Had he simply held back and summoned an army of skeletons, we definitely would have lost. His anger had gotten the best of him.

Anyway, there's no way I'd wear that gown. Especially considering the fact that Urf used to sleep in it.

"Maybe he was the one behind those zombified animals," Pebble said.

"You've seen them, too?"

"Everywhere. Especially in the forest to the south. Still give me nightmares."

"Only **Nether Rot** could be capable of doing such a thing," S said. "It's a spell—that is, an ability of a magical nature—that inflicts a **horrible debuff** similar to **Wither.** Except when your health hits zero, you don't die. **You turn into a zombie.** Of course, being a **disease,** the debuff will also spread to any nearby life-forms. Works on animals, too. "

"It must have been him, then." I sighed. "Guess that's **one mystery solved.**"

Back to the items.

Urf had also been carrying a **most curious weapon.**

FEY CUDGEL
WEAPON (STICK)
ATTACK SPEED 1.5
AVERAGE DAMAGE 2
STUN II

A stick.
An enchanted stick.

I wish I were **joking** here, but alas, I'm as serious as Urf was when he wrote that one handbook. It's not totally **worthless,** though.

I guess. According to Breeze, **Stun II** has a 20% chance of inflicting **paralysis.** According to S, the duration of said paralysis is . . . **one second.** For some strange reason, Breeze seemed **very interested** in this weapon. **Why?** Honestly, I can't see how the **small chance** of stunning a monster for one second makes up for such **pathetic damage.** Not only that, but the item reminds me of Urf's tales of bonking a zombie on the head **with a stick.** Plus, I believe the word "fey" has something to do with **faeries.** That means I will **most definitely** pass. Regarding Urf's former inventory, it seemed there was only one item left, which happened to be none other than . . .

KOLB'S SADDLE
MISCELLANEOUS
RIDING I
ENDURANCE II

"THE COOLEST SADDLE FOR THE COOLEST
HORSE IN ALL THE OVERWORLD"

When I saw this, my mind became **a slimeball.**

No.

Nono.

Nononono.

Nuh–ooohh.

NONOPINEAPPLE . . . ?!

*Why is this here?! **Why?!** What does it mean?! What does it meannnnnnnnnnnnnnnn?!*

*Think. **Think.** Logic. **Logic.** Don't panic. Stop breathing like that! Explanation! Need! Explanation! Why is everyone looking at me?! Look innocent! **Act casual!** Oh, I don't know how to whistle! Not my fault! **Not!*** My! Faultttttt!!!

"That's strange," Pebble said. "**Kolb's** still in **Villagetown**, right?"

"He is," Breeze said. Then she gave me **the sternest look,** probably the way Stump's parents look whenever he burns the cupcakes.

So what this means is . . . thinking logically here . . . Urf stole Meadow. . . . He took Kolb's horse and . . . Well, maybe Kolb had two enchanted saddles? That's possible, right???

"**I'm not sure why** Urf was carrying that," I said at last.

"So you guys know Kolb?" S asked. "**Small world.** We've been friends since the server launch." He picked up the saddle. "Maybe I should **return this to him.** I'd like to ask him what—"

238

"No, **that's fine!**" I said, **snatching** the saddle out of his hands. "I'll be meeting up with him soon anyway."

Lucky, this whole thing was **quickly** forgotten when S opened **the small gray chest.** It was time for the real loot. **The boss loot.** According to S, most of the items found in a boss chest are **randomly generated.** After opening it, he added, "**Let us pray to the gods of RNG.**"

I'd heard a few **Legionnaires** say this exact phrase several times before. **RNG** has something to do with **random events**—I think it stands for Random Number Generator. So praying to the gods of RNG means hoping you **get lucky?** Is that right? Well, let's just say **his prayers failed. Take the following item,** for instance:

GOLDEN COW
DECORATION
AURA:
PROSPERITY III

A golden cow. The size of a child's toy. Seriously. I couldn't make this stuff up. Apparently, when placed in a room, this little cow gives off **an aura** called **Prosperity.** At level III, it gives anyone crafting nearby a **3% chance** of crafting **double** the amount of whatever they're trying to craft.

I suppose I can see the uses there, but still, it's **weird.** If the gods above really are the ones who determined this loot, well, they must be laughing right now. I'm not, however. **Next.**

BED OF ROSES
FURNITURE
GOODNIGHT I

It's official: **the gods really are** laughing.

So it goes like this—there are **several different types** of bed enchantments, and they're all appropriately named: **Goodnight, Sleepwell, Sweetdreams,** and so on. The Goodnight enchantment gives you two extra temporary health, per level, upon waking up the next day. You'll see it in the form of **golden hearts** added to your life bar. This **buff** will last the whole day, only vanishing when you take the appropriate amount of **damage.** Not bad, I guess, but you won't see me sleeping in it. **I do have dignity,** you know. **Next!**

ENDERPOUCH
ACCESSORY
POCKET III

Oooooh, now **this** I like. What is it, you ask? Only **a miniature ender chest** that you wear on your belt. The **Pocket** enchantment is like a small **extradimensional space.** Any item with this enchantment functions as a container. Not only is the size of your inventory effectively **increased** but also you can retrieve items from the container **in record time. Pocket III** means three additional squares, meaning I could put **three different potions** in it. **So Batman.**

I don't yet have a **belt,** but I totally grabbed this. As soon as Breeze explained what it did . . .

DRAGONSKULL HELM
ARMOR
RESILIENCE VI

Hmm. Classic **tank gear** that greatly reduces damage from critical hits. What's not to like?

First of all, it's **kinda cool,** but I dunno. **It's a dragon** skull. Something **Urg the Barbarian** would wear. Or a Nethermancer. Just **not my style.**

But more than that, I'm not so sure about my future as **a tank.** I've tried it out, and I like **protecting** my friends, but dude—**taking damage gets old. Really old.** In fact, if you happen to be an aspiring adventurer, I advise doing anything to not be the tank. Like, **make up a story** about how a zombie in iron armor attacked your village when you were a little kid and **you've had nightmares** about it ever since. Then wipe away **imaginary tears** and say something about how you can't even **look** at a shield without wanting to cry.

Next!

THE SAPPHIRE FLAME
QUEST ITEM

"THE FLAME MUST SHINE ONCE MORE, ELSE ALL OF AETHERIA SHALL PERISH."

"And **there it is**," S said, holding the crystal before us.

Breeze traced her fingers across its surface. "I've heard of **a temple with the same name**. Does this crystal belong there?"

S nodded. "**It does**. It's **required** to **light the beacon** located on the temple's roof."

"**What happens** when you do?" I asked.

"At night, its light will be seen **from anywhere** on the main continent, and even the outlying isles, like **the brightest blue star**."

"It's an ancient **warning system**," Breeze said. "Those living in remote areas will know to **prepare for war**. Every village should have at least **one librarian** who knows what the blue light means."

"You sure know your **lore**," S said, giving her a **quizzical** glance.

"**I do**. And I know that completing your quest will be **far from easy**. Surely the Eyeless One has already sent a considerable number of **his minions** to that temple."

S clutched his chest. "Wow. I think I'm **in love**." When Breeze gave him **a cold look** *(me too)*, he raised his hands defensively.

"Joking, **joking**. Wait a sec. Are you two *an item?!*"

Breeze **blinked**. "Item?"

I have **no idea** what he meant by that, either. How can a person **also be an item**, let alone two people?

"**Never mind**," he said. "Anyway, **yeah**. You're probably right. I'm sure monsters are **guarding** that temple now. The last thing **Herobrine** wants is someone **lighting that beacon.** Good thing I've got **my dark apprentice** here. He won't let me down."

He slapped **Pebble** across the back.

"How about we hit **Owl's Reach** again? I saw a few guys hanging around there who **owe me a favor.** I'm sure they wouldn't mind **coming along.** After seeing what that **Urf** guy was capable of . . ."

"He was such **a noob** before," Pebble said. "I don't get how he became **so powerful.**"

S grinned. "That's **power leveling** for you. **Old Eyeless** probably just kept summoning a bunch of monsters and weakening them for him. It's a **cheap tactic** and one the **Boss Wizards** used to employ a lot back in the day, even though it's **against server rules.** Or **was,** I should say. The rules don't exactly matter now. . . ."

"**The Boss Wizards,**" I said. "I think I met some of them. Who are they?"

"**A clan. One of the foulest.** The complete opposite of the Lost Legion, really. They had no interest in proper player etiquette **before the crash** and infinitely less interest now."

"But the ones I talked to **didn't seem so bad** to me."

S shrugged. "They might **act okay** in the cities, where it's **safe.** But when you're at **the end of the line,** in places like this and in situations like the one we just faced, well, they'd leave you without a second thought. **Don't trust 'em.**"

244

"We ended up **grouping with some** of them a few days ago," Pebble said gravely. "Didn't . . . **go so well.**"

S made an **annoyed sound** and scratched the side of his face but said nothing.

"Anyway." Pebble looked at me like he'd been **holding in** the most important question of all time. "So, **uh** . . . how's Villagetown doing?"

"Surviving. Barely."

"Kolb seems to think **an advanced crafting table** will help turn the tides," Breeze added.

"**It'll definitely help,**" S said. "With that, you'll be able to **craft obsidian weapons and armor.** About the same as iron, really, but once you make **an obsidian farm,** you'll have **an infinite supply.**"

Obsidian farm?
Sure, I slept **a little** in farming class,
but I don't have a clue what they're talking about.

"Listen, all we really came here for was **the crystal,**" S said. "You guys **take the rest.** Sell whatever you don't want. **Or sell it all.** The boss dropped some **pretty lame** stuff this time around."

"**Appreciate it,**" Breeze said.

"What about **the glowmoss?**" I asked.

"Oh. Sorry. It's in **one of those chests**," S said. "**Minor quest items** load in those."

Yes, you may have been wondering about the **eight ender chests** in the back of this room. **I checked five** of those chests; **all** were empty. However, after I slammed down the fifth lid, Breeze was right there beside me, sticking out her tongue. And also dangling **a soggy green item** in front of my face.

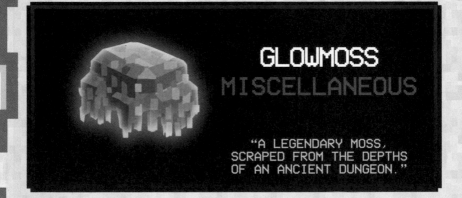

Legendary moss, huh?

How moss can be used to **craft armor,** I don't know, and **I don't really care.** When I looked at this item, which seemed to be little more than phosphorescent slime, I saw not moss but a **pile of emeralds—750,** to be exact. Shortly after I **stuffed** that thing into my inventory, there was **a faint crackling** from behind us. The blocks of magical ice Urf had created were **vanishing.**

(I'm guessing Nethermancers don't use ice spells too often. How can ice exist in the Nether?!)

S returned his **emerald greatsword** to the scabbard on his back. *A bit jumpy.*

"**All right,**" he said. "Since we're both headed to Owl's Reach, I guess we might as well **head there together,** yeah?"

"**Yeah, if Shybiss** can keep up," I said. "That's **her horse.** Not sure what happened to . . . **mine.**" *Quick! Change the subject!* I turned to Pebble. "**So um,** after you've lit that beacon, are you gonna **come back?** Considering how what happened before wasn't your fault, I'm sure the mayor would **pardon you.**"

"**I'm not sure,**" he said. "I already **promised** S that I'd go traveling with him. He's been working on **a ship.** You should see it. We still need to **find several items** to get it up and running, though. One of the items was in this cave. **You wouldn't believe—**"

"Like he said," S **interrupted** with a smile, "it still needs **a lot** of work. But maybe **someday.**"

(There was something strange about the way he cut Pebble off like that. Why all these secrets?!)

The **former bully** looked at me and shrugged. "I'm sure **I'll visit** at some point, Runt. Until then, tell everyone **that I'm . . . sorry.**" He **looked around** again. "**Can we leave now?**"

With that, we left the dungeon. Just as that **mysterious voice** had claimed, the halls were now **devoid** of monsters, and the golden pressure plates only clicked lightly when we stepped on them. Of course, I stared at that vault again as we walked past, wondering **what it could possibly contain. . . .**

Diary of an 8-Bit Warrior

Diary of an 8-Bit Warrior: From Seeds to Swords

Diary of an 8-Bit Warrior: Crafting Alliances

Diary of an 8-Bit Warrior: Path of the Diamond

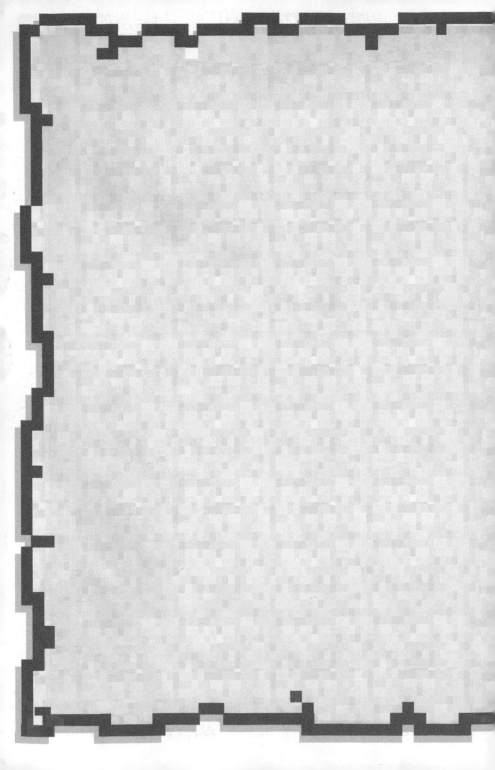

Cube Kid is the pen name of Erik Gunnar Taylor, a writer who has lived in Alaska his whole life. A big fan of video games—especially Minecraft—he discovered early that he also had a passion for writing fan fiction. Cube Kid's unofficial Minecraft fan-fiction series, *Diary of a Wimpy Villager*, came out as e-books in 2015 and immediately met with great success in the Minecraft community. They were published in France by 404 éditions in paperback, with illustrations by Saboten, and now return in this same format to Cube Kid's native country under the series title *Diary of an 8-Bit Warrior*. When not writing, Cube Kid likes to travel, putter with his car, devour fan fiction, and play his favorite video game.